Also by Guy Haley

Champion of Mars

Reality 36
Omega Point

CRASH
Guy Haley

SOLARIS

First published 2013 by Solaris
an imprint of Rebellion Publishing Ltd,
Riverside House, Osney Mead,
Oxford, OX2 0ES, UK

www.solarisbooks.com

ISBN: 978 1 78108 120 4

10 9 8 7 6 5 4 3 2 1

A CIP catalogue record for this book is available from the
British Library.

Designed & typeset by Rebellion Publishing

Printed in Denmark

It is in the interest of mankind, not simply of those of us fortunate to be burdened with the task of wealth creation and prosperity maintenance, to step outside the bounds of our solar cage, and commence the great adventure that has awaited our kind since the first time a man raised his eyes to the stars.

The Earth is not room enough. Mankind requires space to grow, the Market requires space to grow. Only in the great, limitless spaces of the cosmos will our species find what it requires to spread the noble cause of human persistence into the deep time of the future. We are in the process of conquering the Solar System, but only beyond the great gulfs of interstellar space are gentler worlds found, places where mankind may not merely survive, not just harvest materials to be sent to the motherworld, but truly prosper and spread in glorious diaspora.

We live in a time where the majority of the wealth is held by a minority of the people. I admit that this number includes myself. I have striven all my life to use my wealth to improve the quality of life of my fellow citizens, but some time ago I came to the realisation that we must head out and onwards, as the first true men did when they left Africa and walked in triumph across the globe. As the pioneering men and women who crossed to Australia and America in the forgotten past did, as the great explorers in the age of mercantilism sailed the oceans in search of new markets, so will we sail the stars and found new outposts of mankind. With space to multiply and create new worlds rich with opportunity for all, the people of Earth will be granted the chance to exercise their capabilities to the full. This is an age of new pioneers, of new opportunities. Our success here on Earth has been our downfall, we are too many for all to be free, we have used too much for everyone to be wealthy. The inequality we see every day is the product not of human selfishness, but of the natural constraints of our environment. Through the Gateway Project, we will fling open the doors of the prison, and humankind will stand astride the stars of the galaxy as a new-minted colossus. From this day forth, wealth will no longer be restricted to the few; all humanity might share in the universe's bounty.

– Part of the speech delivered by
John Karlton, CEO of Lodestone Inc.,
at the official launch of the Gateway Project.
Tokyo, Japan, June 25th, 2153

In the wake of the financial collapses of the early 21st century, living standards dropped across what was then termed the 'developed world,' in essence those states of Europe and their former colonies where the original inhabitants had been extirpated and a European society established... As we have seen, the consequences of the Third Industrial Revolution were far-reaching, overturning much of contemporary economic thought. In a grand twist of irony those who could still find employment reverted to a semi-artisanal state not dissimilar to that experienced by their ancestors, before the First Industrial Revolution concentrated the new worker class in the new towns and cities of that time.

Despite the optimistic predictions of various commentators, chief among them Eisenstein, Korolev and Kang, there could be no return to a pre-industrial state. Over-population became the issue that it still is today, and although we evade the doom of Malthus, another, more insidious lack than the shortage of food became pressing – employment. Successive technological advances throughout the 20th and 21st centuries led to a vast over-provision of able bodied workers... Not for them the leisured lifestyle predicted by the futurists of the 1950s, but one of poverty and marginalisation. In an economy driven by the accumulation of wealth, the absence of the means to accumulate money effectively excluded an increasingly large proportion of the world population from both the benefits of advanced science, and from an engagement with any form of power structure.

One class did, however, prosper in these times. That exclusive echelon of the social order known now as 'The Pointers' was drawn from the more financially robust members of Western Europe's ancient aristocracies, scions of industrial families enriched in the first two industrial revolutions, clans of oligarchs enriched by the collapse of communism, and those catapulted into the realms of megawealth by the financialisation of business in the 1990s and early 2000s and the growth of celebrity-worship. This concentration of wealth in the hands of the few is sadly not unique to our time or situation. What is different about the Pointers is their longevity; much like the aristocracies of Medieval Europe and Asia, they have lasted. During the centuries of industrialisation, society became fluid; to lesser or greater degrees dependent on the precise era, with the great wealth generated by any one family as often as not lost within the space of a century… and now in this consequent period, this social mobility has ceased…

In the Medieval Period, agriculturally productive land was the source of all wealth. Control of it and those who worked it became ever more entrenched within the class of the nobility. Revolution and rebellion did little to unseat this; it was only when new means of creating large fortunes came into being that this *ancien régime* was truly challenged, and eventually toppled.

As is the way with all human activity, the accumulation of virtually all wealth by one small class of people has proved cyclical. Over the course of the last 250 years, the Pointers have arisen from the industrialists, merchants and financiers who toppled the prior land-based hierarchy…

…in the case of the Pointers, prominence is due to their domination of a finite resource; not actual, physical resources as in prior aristocracies, although many of these families attained their wealth through the monopolisation of the production of raw materials. The resource the Pointers so jealously guard is wealth itself.

So abstract a source of power it is at once ridiculous and unassailable. Ridiculous, because their superiority is effectively built on the compliance of those they oppress – money, unlike land, is a fiction. Unassailable, as its illusory nature makes it extremely easy to totally control. The Pointers have become adept at protecting this wealth, for we live in a time where only wealth generates wealth. Virtually all avenues to the creation of wealth have been shut off or are entirely in the hands of the Pointers. Only the Pointers have the money to invest in the creation of more money, and as the protection of their finances has been removed from their direct control and placed in the phantom hands of virtually infallible, multi-generational algorithms, it seems their grip on power is even more tenacious than that of the medieval robber barons. Furthermore, the assets the Pointers command are so vast, that their fortunes make the worst excesses of ancient emperors seem restrained by comparison.

– Excerpt from one of Professor Todeo Hiyazaki's series of banned lectures on the Pointer families

PROLOGUE

AT FIRST, DARIUSZ Szczeciński was dead, then he was not.

Machines hurried him to life more quickly than they should. Preservative fluids were sucked from his circulatory system with haste, warmed blood pumped into their place. Mechanisms whose own time was shortly to come ran cursory checks, the provenance of emergency. High percentiles were lowered, risks were taken that would not ordinarily have been taken. For long seconds, the essence of Dariusz hung upon the fences that separate the living from the dead.

Bursts of electricity massaged his heart to activity. Neurons long dormant sparkled, chains of lightning arced through ganglia. Briefly raging, the storm of activity housed by his skull flickered out once more.

The machines noted. The machines adjusted. The machines applied the correct voltage just so, recalibrated their potions of amino acids and adrenaline. They ministered to their charge diligently and with grace as death rode down upon them.

Dariusz stirred in his coffin. The miracle of consciousness prepared itself to manifest. The machines felt no satisfaction. Their power supply dwindled. The machines felt no fear.

The not-quite-mind of the deck segment allowed the revivification process to run its course, and turned from Dariusz to save as many others as it could before its own feeble unlife was extinguished.

Pseudo-amniotic liquid drained. Dariusz awoke slowly. He felt nothing, at first; nothing but the cold and a hazy contentment, denying him awareness of the peril of his situation. That was a mercy.

A pleasant chime announced his reanimation.

His wellbeing, chemically donated by the sarcophagus, was fleeting. He blinked eyes sticky with amniotics, and coughed violently, bringing up a sheeting flood of the same. He was on his side, rather than half-reclined. Gravity greater than Earth normal pulled at him uncomfortably. His face was pressed into the front of the sarcophagus. Fear penetrated his post-hibernation fug. He could not get out! The lid – the lid was stuck. It made feeble clicking noises, reached a point at which it jammed, then arthritically shut again, jarring his face. Repeat.

Dariusz braced himself against the back of the sarcophagus and kicked against the lid. He was weak; his feet, numb with cold and slick with the fluids of the deathsleep, skidded on the plastic. His body shook. He wriggled feebly, until he gained himself a better situation. He arched his back against the moulded hibernation couch, doubled over into a foetal position, feet braced on the lid. He waited for the lid to cycle back to the start of its failed opening, and pushed with his legs. He grunted with effort as the door attempted to close again. The lid was ignorant of his desire to escape, and its mechanisms pushed cruelly against him. Panic lent him strength, he made animal noises as he fought his weakened muscles, something tore in his back. His constricted neck made it difficult to breathe. His existence contracted to a point of pressure, flesh against machine. And then, release. The lid ceased pushing and began to open once more. He followed its motion with a hard shove. The lid opened a fraction further, he heard a scraping as the mechanism caught, there was wild hissing as pneumatics burst. Resistance abruptly ceased, and the door flew open.

Dariusz tumbled with it. His slippery body skidded from the pod, falling sideways. The topography of the deck was all to hell: the floor was a canted wall, and the corridor had become a gaping pit.

Dariusz bounced from the smooth surfaces of other sarcophagi, banged painfully into an open lid. The air in his lungs, so recently replenished, was knocked from him. He tore his arm on jagged carbon, skidded as the curve levelled, and plunged into a thick pond of spilled amniotics gathered at the bottom. Stunned, he sank into the morass, and it had him. The hibernation deck had become a pitcher trap.

The amniotics made a milky nowhere, featureless as the womb; not dark, but a dirty whiteness in all directions. Its density lent him buoyancy; up from down became an impossible guess. He thrashed. His newly woken lungs burned, the need to open his mouth and suck in the fluid he knew would kill him passed from urge to necessity.

His feet found smooth, hard plastic. He pushed off hard, only to slip. The fluid was slicker than oil. He fought his body's demands to breathe as hard as he fought the amniotic's grip.

Without warning, he was free. His head broke the surface. At first he could not tell, so viscously the fluid clung, until it ran from him in reluctant streams and he took a roaring breath of the ship's stale air, pulling the sharp reek of the pseudo-amniotics, the tang of burnt plastics, charred metal, and putrescence into his lungs.

Thus was Dariusz reborn on a new world.

Fluid sprayed from him as he flailed to and fro, still wild from his struggle. He locked eyes with a startled woman. Naked like he, her hair as closely cropped as his, as weak as he was, gaunt as a ghost. Her breasts were flat against her chest. In her thin arms she cradled the head and shoulders of an unconscious man.

A muffled banging came from overhead. Dariusz looked up. Through the viewport of a sarcophagus, he caught the outline of a face. It vanished into greyness and fluid filled the pod.

"We've landed end on, and at an angle," said the woman. Her voice was a surprise; Dariusz had forgotten speech. "The fluid is not draining away. They're going to drown." She said this matter-of-factly, eyes on the pod. She was observing, as one might observe the death of an animal in the wild – dispassionately, scientifically almost. Her lips were compressed into thin lines. She shook hard from the chill of the amniotics pool, but made no attempt to escape from it. Her skin was grey.

Dariusz looked around for something, anything, to push the window in and release the trapped fluid. The thumping on the lid grew more frantic. Dariusz bent down and searched the pool's floor, but his fingers encountered only smooth edges. There was one final thump, and then nothing.

They watched as the pod completed the revivification cycle and opened. A young man tumbled out, limp and lifeless. He landed in the pool face down. It took four attempts for Dariusz to hook his hands under the body and roll it over. He pressed his fingers to the man's neck. There was no pulse.

The woman looked on, face blank, as Dariusz pulled the man to the edge of the pool. He rested him as well as he could on the curving wall of sarcophagi. CPR proved nigh on impossible. Dariusz was weak. The liquid had lost none of its chill, and he shivered in great, quaking spasms. His hands slipped as he worked the man's arms to pump his lungs free of the amniotics. When he had done this, he struggled to roll him over, nearly losing him to the pool twice. He pounded with feeble linked fists on his chest, pausing to put his own freezing lips onto the man's. They were both as cold as corpses.

"I don't know why you bother," said the woman. "We're all dead anyway."

Dariusz glared back at her, although he feared the truth of what she said. He persisted in his efforts for fifteen, twenty minutes, but he was not so skilled as the machines at bringing back the dead.

Exhausted, he stopped, and the man's corpse slid into the pool. He did not, could not, stop it. It sank face down, until only ridge of his shoulders and the nub of his skull showed. Dariusz stared, his eyes drawn to a marbling of red in the white liquid. He had forgotten he had cut himself. He felt no pain. He was too tired to check how badly he was hurt.

He turned to the woman. She returned his stare unblinkingly.

"You are wrong," said Dariusz. His voice croaked. It was not this bad last time he woke.

Last time? There had been a last time. Fragmentary memories flitted through him, elusive and unwilling to give up their secrets. Dread clutched at him, bringing with it a feeling of profound responsibility.

He remembered something else, a vivid flash of a briefing. He was no longer in the freezing pool, but elsewhere, a hundred years away. The man in the suit, with eyes in bruised sockets, said: *hibernation sickness worsens, the longer one is under.*

The flash went, bright and painful light in his eyes. He tried his inChip; there was no response. Other memories burst into being, brief as fireworks. His sense of self cracked. He was close to dissolution. Weakness, organ damage, brain damage, psychosis. Death. Hibernation was a generous gift-giver.

"The sickness should be not be so pronounced. How long have we been asleep?" he said. He pinched the bridge of his nose, pressed fingertips against closed eyes until coloured sparks rained. He shook the storm of memories out, concentrating on the moment; on escape, and survival. "We are not all dead. I am not going to die. Not today," he said.

Action helped him, pushing thoughts of what might have happened to the ship, and the sense of responsibility...

Responsibility? Another flash, a tube. A prick of blood on his thumb...

...to the back of his mind.

He pulled himself from the sucking fluid, pressing down with flat palms. He squatted on the lip of the pod, panting with the effort. Out of the freezing pseudo-amniotics, he felt better. The air was chilly, but not freezing as it had been the last time he woke. Their voyage was over. They were no longer in space, of that he was sure.

He reined in his aggression. He was behaving like an animal, his brain falling back on atavistic patterns. The operations of his neocortex were scrambled, his human mind was racing to piece itself back together. He could not trust himself until it did. He was working on instinct alone.

Speak, he had to continue speaking. Speech is the fount of reason.

"If we don't get out of here," he said, "we are finished."

Assuming no one came for them. No one had yet.

Talking forced his thoughts to coalesce, cognition forming around language. He marshalled his logic, tried to push past the pain that pulsed in his arm and the deep shivers wracking his body.

He squinted in the gloom at the pods, looking for their numbers – there was something important about the numbers, something that meant a great deal to him. Which number? He craned his neck to peer around the curve of the corridor-turned-shaft. Only on three of the sarcophagi could he see status panels glowing blue. Medical details scrolled over them. The rest were either red or blank, their power gone. In either case, their occupants would be dead. An awful fear filled him.

He thought out to the machines of the deck. His inChip was offline still. Voice, then.

"Activate emergency revivification procedure in all remaining pods," he called out, as loudly as his neglected vocal cords could manage. There was no response. He tried again, appending his colonist's rank and identification code to the command.

The woman laughed, a dry, desperate sound. She still made no attempt to move herself or her companion from the fluid. "What are you doing? We're on emergency lighting. There is nothing to command."

"The Systems core should function," said Dariusz.

"Not if we've been ejected, it won't. And we have."

Dariusz looked at her, his face demanding more. "How can you be sure?"

"I'm a junior ship's engineer. That's the only explanation. Each deck has been ejected. We're not on the ship any more. Don't you see? We've failed." Her face lost some of its impassivity. A deep tremor ran over her body, interrupting her shivering, and she began to cry.

He attempted to orient himself. There were two exits from each hibernation deck segment, one onto each of the spinal corridors that ran the length of the *ESS Adam Mickiewicz*. If they had landed so that one door was directly upwards and the other against the ground, they were finished. Was she right? Ejection? If so, why were they not horizontal? A crash, then? Had the whole vessel plunged from the sky? Impossible. The chances of surviving that were minimal. He tried to bring to mind the details of deck ejection, where the doors might be, how it was all supposed to work, but his mind was a shattered mosaic. Frustrated, he banged on a sarcophagus hard with his fist, staring at the woman as if she were to blame.

"We're dead, we're all dead," she moaned.

She put her hands to her face. The man she was holding slipped under the fluid.

"Don't!" said Dariusz. He pushed off his perch and back into the pool. He fought through it, reaching the other side as the man's face was going under. He hauled the man up, and pushed him at her. He grabbed at her hands; she fought him with small fists, but he was stronger. When he had her wrists, he moved her arms firmly, wrapping them around the unconscious man's neck.

He took her face, his fingers distorting her cheeks as she sought to turn away. He looked deep into her eyes.

"Don't let go. Whatever you do, don't let go of him." He looked around. "You have to get out of the fluid or you will get hypothermia. The air is warmer. You will feel better."

She nodded. She wiped her tears from her eyes with her forearm, leaving a slick of fluid across her cheeks.

They struggled together to get the unconscious man to where Dariusz had been sitting, where they wedged him into place. The deck canted some fifteen degrees off the vertical, and leaned twenty-five degrees off horizontal, further disorienting them. Once the woman was secure also, Dariusz checked the man. He had a pulse, a weak one, but he was alive.

"What is your name?" The words felt odd in his mouth, familiar, but not of his first tongue. There was another language there, a more comfortable one. He did not seek it out.

The woman looked startled to be asked. "Mar... Marina."

She was not from where he was from; nearly, but not quite. Nations. Different nations.

"You are... Czech?" he guessed. The majority of passengers on the *Mickiewicz* were central European. They spoke Lingua Anglica to each other, yes. The language he spoke now. He remembered.

"Yes." In the dark, her eyes appeared unnaturally large.

"Well, Marina, we need to work together, if we are to get out of here alive, okay?"

"There could be anything out there," she said.

"Maybe," said Dariusz. "We will not know until we try to get out. Let us worry about one thing at a time. Can we do that?"

He searched his memory. Gaps as wide as the gulfs of space remained. The niggling feeling of responsibility troubled him. He ignored it, searching his scrambled mind for information relevant to survival. "The decks," he said. "When ejected, they halve, yes?"

The woman nodded. "They split along the join with the spinal corridors, into semicircles. Like half a pineapple ring."

Dariusz smiled encouragingly. He had not eaten pineapple for years, it was too expensive – *had* been too expensive, he corrected himself.

"That means," he said, "that our deck half has come down on one end."

"It shouldn't have." The woman was defensive of the ship.

"It has. One door must be above us." He spoke aloud, but he was addressing himself more than the woman. "Too risky to try and climb up. The other door?" He looked across the pool to where the woman had been standing. "One of the doors will be under the pool? Right there?" He took one of his hands from her shoulders and pointed.

She nodded again. The liquid was drying to a crust on her skin. She shivered less violently, and her colour was returning in uneven blotches. Her lips, however, remained white. "Maybe we should wait," she said. "Perhaps someone will come along. We don't know if we reached our target or not. The air might be poisonous outside, if there's any air at all." A deep shudder passed over her.

"We can't wait. How much air have we got? Do you know?"

"Not much," she said. "We'll suffocate. What about the *Goethe*? When will they come for us?"

"How long have you been awake?"

She shrugged. "Half an hour. Less."

"And how long do you think we have been down?"

She looked at the emergency light panels. They were growing dim.

"You're going to try to get out no matter what I say," she said. Her tears had stopped now. Her eyes were sharper.

"I'd prefer it if you agreed to escape with me."

She considered a moment, looked around at the dead pods and at the unconscious man. They gave no advice. She bit her lip. "Okay," she said. "Okay. Under the pool. I'll tell you what to do."

Dariusz waded back into the liquid, knocking the corpse of the drowned man. He crouched down, arm extended, searching for the door activation mechanism. After a few moments, he found it. The door control wasn't working.

"It's broken."

"There's not enough power," she explained. "We're on batteries. The lights will go out soon. There is a manual override in a panel underneath. You have to push the top two corners. It should unlock itself."

Dariusz fumbled about in the muck until he found what he was looking for. He depressed the panel. His fingers were growing numb again. He helped the panel hinge outward and felt inside, where his hand closed around a smooth bar.

"There is a handle," he said.

"Grab it, twist it ninety degrees clockwise. It is a pump. You have to prime the door pneumatics manually. Five sets of fifteen. There's a button on the end of the handle." Marina's voice was becoming steadier as her role overtook her fear.

"I have it."

"Whatever you do, don't press that until you are finished, or you'll have to start again. It vents the gas," she explained.

Dariusz did as asked. Priming the door was arduous under the liquid, and became harder as he reached the end of the first set. The fifteenth depression rewarded him with a small *click*.

"The handle has gone slack, have I broken it?"

"No. You've primed the first cylinder. The fifteenth depression rotates a new one into place."

Dariusz continued pumping. Each time, the work grew harder as the pneumatics pressurised, then there was a click and the tension abruptly slackened.

There was a groan behind him.

"How's he doing?" he said, without looking back.

"He's warming up and waking. Do you think he is going to be okay?"

"I don't know, I'm not a medic."

"Do you think we will be okay?"

Dariusz did not answer, but carried on pumping.

"He looks okay," said Marina. "At least on the outside."

"Do you know him?"

"No. Not really," she said. "I know his face, I think I saw him when we were put under. He wasn't in any of my training groups."

By the time Dariusz had the fifth cylinder primed, he was freezing again. On the surfaces around him, the slime was drying to scurf, but the deep puddle would take a long time to warm.

"I've done it. Now do I depress the button?"

"Yes."

"Okay." Dariusz did so. There was a hiss from the wall, the rough sound of something shifting reluctantly. A ripple appeared in the liquid, then lazily-forming bubbles: first one, then two, then many, blistering the surface with a spawn-like mass. The amniotics began to drain away. Dariusz put his head close to the bubbles and sniffed the air as they burst. There was a scent like cinnamon to it that the smell of the amniotics could not overpower. "I have no idea if this is going to be breathable."

"What will you do?" said Marina.

No dizziness. No sickness. Nothing. But it was too soon to tell. He felt far from normal, and had nothing reliable to measure the effects of the air against. "I am not dead yet, at least," he said.

The door stopped opening. Dariusz felt about with his foot.

"It's about fifteen centimetres open," he said.

"Well done," said Marina. "Now, you have to do it all again." The lights flickered. "We'll be out of power very soon, each segment has limited battery life. These hibernation units are energy hungry. I better see if there are other survivors. If the machines don't wake them, they'll die when the power goes."

"There are three up there." Dariusz looked over his shoulder and gestured with his chin. "I couldn't see if anyone else made it. A lot are smashed or dark."

Marina nodded quickly. The man moaned softly, and his arm flopped as she wedged him more firmly in place. She stood a moment, figuring out how to ascend to the functioning pods.

The liquid drained away as Dariusz worked, revealing the side and top of the door. By the time he had completed three full priming sequences, the pool had gone.

"Marina!" he called.

"Yes?" Her voice was faint, echoing down to him.

"There's another sarcophagus here, under the fluid, with a blue status panel."

"It will have to wait. I'm trying to short the first one into opening. Carry on with the door. Don't worry, I should be able to get to them all," she shouted.

Dariusz went back to his work. Loud mechanical sounds came from behind him, then human noises: shouts, a scream. Marina's voice off in the depths of the segment, more shouts, cries, calming noises from her. A second voice joined her. Conversation. He remained bent to his task.

He performed ten cycles before he realised the door would not open any further. He'd got it about halfway open, wide enough for him to squeeze under. He peered at the gap. He saw coarse sand under a thick coat of the amniotic fluid, a line of sunlight at the top. What the hell had happened? Memories of his prior waking flashed in his mind.

Marina interrupted his train of thought. The remaining puddles of the pseudo-amniotics slurped around her feet as she approached. He turned. The deck's shadows were thicker, now he had seen the light. The unconscious man was no longer so; he sat upright, cradling his head. Two others stood behind Marina, a man and a woman, leaning on each other for support. Marina held out a jumpsuit and a bottle of isotonic drink to Dariusz in one hand. In the other, she held a tablet, screenglow fuzzy blue.

"You need this," she said. "You will be dehydrated, and your chemical balance will be off."

He took the drink without a word and drained it. It tasted disgusting. The other two survivors peered around themselves, wide-eyed and shaking.

"What happened?" the man asked. "Where are we?"

Dariusz ignored them. He brushed the dry amniotics from his body, then struggled into the jumpsuit. The smartcloth adjusted itself to fit, the feet hardened into boots, the cloth cleaned his skin. He felt better for it. "I am going to go outside," he said.

Marina passed him the tablet. "Use that to gauge the atmosphere. We'll concentrate on getting the last two pods open. It should not take long."

Dariusz knelt to scoop sand away from the door, widening the space, and the band of light broadened. He narrowed his eyes against it. A soft wind blew, and the scent of cinnamon grew stronger. He breathed it for a minute. No immediate ill-effects.

"Breathable," he said with a smile. He judged the hole wide enough, and bent further.

"Don't go far," called Marina. "We should stick together."

He stopped. "I won't," he said. He drew in a deep breath. "Okay," he said. "Okay." He put his head into the gap under the door and pushed himself through.

It was not so tight a squeeze as he expected. He squirmed up and under the door and out into the sunlight.

He was at the bottom of a trench; banks of loose material, ploughed up by the deck segment, stood two metres over his head. It was hot. The shock of the heat after the chill of the deck made him feel unwell, and he bent and vomited salty drink threaded with amniotic mucus. He had to sit for a moment in the shadow of the sand banks.

It was very quiet. The light breeze carried with it the cinnamon scent. The sky was dazzling blue, slightly different from Earth's, and the air was thick in his lungs.

The ejected deck segment loomed over him, half a ring thirty metres across, leaning drunkenly into the wind. It had come to rest on one end, the bulk of it arching like the tail of a metal scorpion out of the ground. Feeling a little better, he moved to check the condition of the deck. As far as he could see, it seemed to be intact, so he went around the other side, to where the rockets were, to see if he could discern why it had landed so badly. The sand slipped under his feet as he walked, and he was glad it could not get into his boots. He stepped into the full sunlight, and winced at its strength; the sun was larger than Sol. There was an orange, brassy tint to its light.

He knew then, without any doubt, that this was not Heracles V, the target of their mission.

On the underside of the deck crescent, the funnel mouths of seven rockets protruded. He squinted up at them. Only four of the seven showed signs of firing. They had been lucky to get down in one piece at all.

If this had happened to them, what about the others? There had been seventy-eight hibernation decks on the *ESS Adam Mickiewicz*, making one hundred and fifty-six segments, if all had ejected. There were thirty-seven ships in the fleet in total, although assuming nothing had gone wrong with them, each would have gone on to its respective target world. But where was the *Mickiewicz*'s sister ship? The paired craft were not to part for any reason. Evidently they had.

He had to get out of the trench.

Climbing the sand was harder than he expected. The combined effects of hibernation sickness and the heavier gravity left him gasping. The sand cascaded under his hands and feet; he glanced back, worried that he would bring the whole lot down on the door. He lacked the energy to excavate the route anew. He moved himself along the deck's flank to where the sandbanks were lower, and used the buried hull to aid his climb, pushing himself up the berm and rolling down the other side. He had to stop once more, but he did not vomit, and the nausea passed quickly. He hauled himself up.

A line of debris stretched all the way to the horizon. Fragments of the *ESS Adam Mickiewicz* were scattered liberally across the desert. Smaller pieces lay everywhere on the sand as if carefully placed, larger chunks were buried in the ground, and around these the sand was scorched. Half a kilometre away, another deck segment, perhaps the other half of Dariusz's own, burned ferociously. Over the horizon, pillars of black smoke marred the perfect sky.

Dariusz's mind convulsed. The world tilted with it, and he fell slowly sideways, demolished by guilt. He had done this.

Something had gone wrong, very wrong, with Browning's plan.

"What have I done?" he whispered. "What have I done?"

"Anyone who believes in indefinite growth on a physically finite planet is either mad, or an economist."

– Kenneth Boulding

PART I

Earth
22nd Century

Let's take a closer look at one of the star systems. This world, orbiting the orange sun Heracles, is typical of the kind of planets the colonists might expect. [A blue world, marbled with cloud, springs to the fore. It is labelled 'Artist's Impression' in text so small it is almost impossible to see.] Orange stars are cooler than our yellow sun, and the Habitable or 'Goldilocks' zone – that part of the system where conditions are neither too cold or too hot but just right for life [Reassuring smile in voice.] – is closer to the star than here. Heracles V orbits closer to its star than Earth does, but its position in the area [The planet shrinks, we are tilted on our sides. A top down view of a planetary system spins dizzyingly into place. Twelve worlds orbit it, Heracles V highlighted in green; text boxes scrolling by too fast to read pop in and out of existence around it. The Goldilocks zone blinks in light blue.] is perfect for life to have developed. In fact, scientists have detected possible oxygen traces on three of the moons and worlds in this system also. Long-term studies seem to indicate pretty conclusively that our star system is actually *inhospitable* when compared to many others.

Every system has been assigned a pair of starships to investigate and settle favourable worlds they might find there – in Heracles' case it is the *ESS Adam Mickiewicz* and *ESS Goethe*, both carrying colonists from central Europe. The vessels' survey teams carry sophisticated equipment that will enable them to best use the resources they find upon each planet, or, in the case of their being little or no life, how to introduce adapted Earth lifeforms to create a biosphere where people can comfortably live. By the time the stargate opens, in seventy years' time, multiple, comfortable worlds will await Earth's teeming multitudes. Let's go and talk to some of our bold pioneers now... [No mention is made of the difficulties, the chances of failure, the vast cost, or the fact that most of the audience this propaganda is intended for could not possibly pass the entrance tests to join the effort.]

– Public holograph film,
part of the popular weekly series To The Stars!
broadcast worldwide, 2155-2165

CHAPTER ONE
The Market

WITHIN HIS PLAIN virtspace at Consolidated Holdings, Karl Njálsson watched the Market's numbers play. He was a *quant* – a quantitative analyst. An old title, and somewhat quaint, given how far its meaning had shifted, but one that carried with it still a certain weight and freedom. One such freedom was of expression. Other quants decorated their workspaces with whimsical imagery. They made them palaces of ice, or of impossible neo-modern architecture, or of pornography. Not Karl. Karl favoured a minimal display, a flow of primary coloured numbers in streams around him. What stocks were up, which were down, a space here for non-tracked stock that was nevertheless of interest, a larger space for the simulations that mirrored the Market's own trades. He had gone through a phase of sensory experimentation, adding sound effects or odour and flavour markers to his investors' portfolios, and he had experimented with his avatar, vainly reducing his large nose, strengthening his chin, adding gloss to his hair. It had made him feel a fake. On a whim, he had crafted a cartoon world of anthropomorphic creatures to shout out important deals, a caricature of the trading floors of old. Bears and bulls and dancing numbers featured heavily, all trite. They'd distracted him, and he'd torn it down after a day. It surprised him to learn it, but it turned out Karl liked the world as it was, unpleasant though it may be.

It was possible, Karl thought, that he was deliberately suppressing the artistic side of his nature in order to limit distraction. Whatever meaning the word once had, securities now meant exactly that: security. Karl wanted to know himself, was prone to introspection. How could he second guess the Market if he could not second guess himself? Vulgar virtspaces were nothing but sightseeing tours of one's own id; how foolish to be diverted by such things. Karl did not like to use his imagination for anything but market possibility. He often thought he had conjured up his half-assed imaginariums as a demonstration of how inappropriate they were.

Imagination was a facility that hindered his work. Daydreaming was beneficial, true, but playing with that imagination, making it real... People with imaginations hoped too much, or feared too much. Imagination and anxiety were close friends, and no one wanted an anxious quant. Quants invented scenarios to run against the Market's own, and that required a small degree of creativity, but *analysis* was the bedrock of such scenarios, not imagination. Consolidated Holdings had some appreciation of this theory, and the neural interface shunts that connected his flesh carcass to the wonderlands of the net where the Market worked carried imagination dampers, should the quants wish to use them. Were he in charge, and he intended to be one day, Karl would make their activation compulsory. Facts were king in speculation, imagination was the killer of fortunes. If that made him bland, so be it. Better to be bland and rich than colourful and poor.

Karl's sense of time was subjectively slowed by the shunt's mechanisms so that he could comprehend the Market's activity. Without slow-time, monitoring the Market's billion trades per second was impossible; even with it, Karl could do little but follow the broader trends. That was enough. Karl was only a balance, a human overseer to an industrious quantum slave. Once upon a time, quants drove the markets, but now they watched, vigilant for cascade effects. One erroneous outcome plot could demolish the values of healthy companies in seconds. In event of a rare error, the Market could crash or force a bubble, and then a bigger crash would ensue. It wasn't likely, it didn't happen often, but such errors as there were in the system had a tendency to multiply themselves. The Market was not infallible, but it was far less volatile than when people were directly involved. Provided the quants remained vigilant, boom and bust was a historical horror.

The shunt brought many benefits, and another was to enhance Karl's prodigious mathematical talents. He spent some time on his scenarios, gaming against the system, assigning rankings to holdings he thought the Market might or should push. The stock tickers glowed brighter as he touched them with his mind. He insisted on seeing these actions as physical, extending his avatar's phantom arm to the numbers and pressing them, although it all took place in the ghostworld of the net. Disincarnate interaction with the Market was uncomfortably vertiginous.

He selected his stocks desultorily. Once, it had amused him to pit his own predictions against the Market; now, he was bored by his own clumsiness. Statistical arbitrage was a dying art for humans. There were firms where quants still took a greater hand in driving trades, but they were outperformed by those firms where the Market was left to its own devices, and Darwinian economics won out. In an earlier age, Karl would have been an exemplary trader. His accuracy ratings were a solid sixty per cent – more, if you isolated his knack for shorting. The Market averaged eighty. But every year, the Market became more accurate; the quants would ultimately follow the hundreds of other professions rendered irrelevant by technology into history.

Karl watched the numbers twist around each other, streaming off into the uncertain distances of virtspace. The Market worked silently.

Karl traced the Market's own dealings with itself for eight hours of subjective time. The famine in South Asia had pushed up food prices across the board; the ripples in their elevated values, once anomalous, had become part of Karl's daily world. Coltan was scarce, copper down, General Carbon struggled still. The establishment of a new Lagrange processing point hiked shares in Kosten...

Karl narrowed his eyes. That was interesting. He brought up a detailed report on Kosten Enterprises. Too high, surely. He went further, dragging up ancillaries and associated industries, suppliers and competitors. What he saw made him dig deeper. It wasn't just Kosten, all the major corporations involved in off-world construction were up. He frowned. He cut and pasted the stocks of a few thousand related companies into his own simulation, and watched the stocks climb. So far so good, but something seemed a little off. His fingers danced on virtual air, bringing up fifteen parallel traces on simulated portfolios. He set a variety of scenarios, each with differing opening parameters, backdated the start to two years ago. He watched. In the main, his scenarios followed the Market. A couple of individual stocks fell away here and there where they had not in reality, but that was not unusual. Only in two were there severe drop-offs across the board, but as these were the more extreme scenarios he'd plotted, Karl was not concerned. Seven of his scenarios ran close enough to the Market to be worth continuing into the future.

The scenarios overtook the current day's trading. Three months out, six months out, twelve. His simulations pulled in hard data: past performance, anticipated tech breakthrough, the resources crisis, historical trending and soft data (most human-behavioural in nature: emergent memes, aggregate social approval, cultural morale ratings, and a variety of minor factors). There were billions of potentials he could have included, but he did not; in that, he was crude and obvious where the Market was subtle and opaque. The Market could and did explore all options to an individual level, a new invisible hand, guiding Adam Smith's original. To do the same was impossible for Karl. To human minds the financial markets were stochastic, to the Market they were not. Karl's job was to make sure the hands behaved themselves, that was all.

Karl let the simulations run, and turned his attention to the Market's continued trading. He became engrossed in the interplay in the prices of conservation semicharities, their financial ecosystems more complex than those of the natural world they sought to protect.

An urgent chiming.

One of his simulations was collapsing. Then another, then a third, a fourth, the soft light of their graphics turning angry red. Karl frowned as stocks tumbled, all around seven years or so out from the present. Alarms ran into and over one another in shocking cacophony. He silenced them with a gesture.

He checked the Market's actual investments in the field again, going through them one by one rather than cutting and pasting them as he had for the simulations. The Market was playing the long game, there was no doubt about that, and with most of the major Pointer clans' money. There was very little of the to-and-fro lending between Market sub-units indicative of the network anticipating a collapse. Of course, the various portfolios it ran for the Pointer families were all in competition with each other, according to instructions from their human holders, but these... They looked unusually homogenous. That was strange. Surely the Market had not missed the bubble?

He followed a few lines of inquiry, but could find no identifiable reasons for the Market pushing space corporations so heavily. He stared at the numbers, tapping his steepled forefingers against his lips.

Something wasn't right. As long as the Market made money for the Pointers – the 0.01 per cent of the population who held 80 per cent of the world's wealth – no one cared what it did. He cared now. The Market was not behaving rationally. The thought he was witnessing one of its rare mistakes thrilled him as much as frightened him. There had been no major errors during his time as a quant. He tried to think dispassionately. He was a soldier in peacetime, yearning for war. He had been trained to act, spent all day waiting to act, but had never been called on to act. Was action needed, or did he need action? That was the question. His heart quickened.

There was a twinge of pain behind his eyes. His shift was coming to an end.

Annoyance bit him. No doubt there were multiple, obscure factors at play here, whose roots extended far into the world; the kind of chains of cause and effect that humans never caught. It was one thing to track the Market, another to see what it saw. The scope of its power was awesome.

The Market was held by some to be prescient; its inscrutable activities fuelled conjecture by all manner of flesh and blood charlatans. Numerological horoscoping, monetary divination, modern day soothsayers. They were about as accurate as reading the entrails of pigeons. It was ironic to Karl that something designed to eliminate irrationality had fostered it.

He checked his clock. Four minutes remained of his shift, subjective time. He resisted the temptation to up his slow-time arrest to the maximum and investigate further. His headache was building. Pain would compromise his judgment. He had to do this properly – the bubble would not manifest for years in real time, he had centuries of subjective time to track the causes down and eliminate it. He could tell Hwang, but he would not. This would be his find, his glory, promotion maybe. He would go to it on his next shift. He should sleep on it, yes.

The Market worked in mysterious ways, but not so mysteriously that he couldn't work it out, given time.

The shift clock beeped shrilly. Time was up. He felt the presence of Hwang as an itch at the back of his mind. His shift was over. He withdrew as Hwang entered. Consolidated Holdings promised unbroken vigilance to its customers, and unbroken vigilance was what they got.

Karl opened his eyes, his real, flesh-and-blood eyes. He was in darkness. Muffled voices, the movement of hands on his body, the support technician about the messy procedure of disconnecting him.

The helmet came off first, blank and sinister. The chair rose to an upright position, and Karl felt his muscles cramp. He had not been away long, but his body took exception to being ignored.

Karl grimaced at the metallic drag of the shunt needle. The withdrawal always seemed to take far longer than was possible, as if the shunt were reluctant to let go of his brain. The sensation was unbearable, as if the organ were being gently unfolded and drawn from his skull along with the interface. Primitive, this direct connection, but the microseconds lost in wireless transmission from Market to quant were unconscionable. Karl gritted his teeth.

The sensation ceased. He heard the tech behind him wipe the needle down, unscrew it from the shunt cable and push it into its sterile case. He put the locking plug in and closed the case with a click.

Karl sat forward. The tech handed him a tissue to wipe off the fluid dribbling down his neck, then set to work on the saline drip. A nurse handed him his supplements and a glass of water; Karl took them, then nodded gratefully as he was handed a slack handful of painkillers. She applied drug impregnated patches to his skin and withdrew.

He went through his medical check silently. None of the staff ever spoke to him. At shift change, he left one world of loneliness for another.

An hour later, Karl was showered and dressed in his uniform of cold grey smartshirt and formal blue jeans. He dialled up his gondola, went down to the lobby and headed out into the close night. He had a booking at Portis, and a good date with a high-rated playmate. He'd been at work for a total of three hours, only twenty-five minutes of that inside the Market. He had earned fifty-six times the national monthly salary in that period.

He ignored the pain in his head. The boat pulled up at the Wall Street canal wharf, and his inChip informed him that he had time to change, if he wished. He ordered the boat to head for home.

Not prepared for the outside world, he set his inChip to an entertainments channel and blocked out the city.

"AND THEN, I mean, we went to Tihuana, and my, my, ain't it hot there!"

Karl nodded disinterestedly at the playmate. He'd requested beautiful and was not disappointed. The man was a living sculpture of Apollo: gym-built muscles, strong face, tall, good teeth, oiled black curly hair, a good tan – a real one, not out of a bottle or from pills, gene-tweaked maybe, but that was a species of real. Good faces cost good money, and that suggested the playmate was gifted in his work.

Karl's interest in finding out whether that was the case or not was waning as the man prattled on and on about himself. He had one of those high voices some gay men cultivate, one that slid up and down the octaves as he melodramatically recounted yet another tedious, shallow anecdote about his tedious, shallow friends. To be at the beating heart of the world and then come to this... Karl's eyes were cold as he nodded and smiled and sipped at his drink. He didn't like it when they talked so much. He made a note in his inChip to specify that next time he ordered.

"And he was all like, yeah, well the tequila here is strong!" The man let out a giddy, squealing laugh and held his hand up to his mouth. Perhaps catching Karl's disapproval, he apologised. "Oh, I'm sorry, I'm not much of a wine drinker, this has really gone to my head."

Karl smiled a little harder. He didn't doubt the man was unused to wine. He'd have to fuck for a week solid to pay for one glass.

The residue of his headache bothered him, but if he were honest with himself – and he tried to be – it was the anomalous stocks that stopped him from relaxing. A feeling of foreboding he couldn't shake had stolen up on him.

He glanced away from the man – Eduardo or Ricardo or something. Never a good sign when he couldn't remember their names. The sex was no good for him if he didn't make some kind of connection. That's why he'd brought him here to Portis, or so he told himself, to get to know him. Not that he was doing a spectacular job of that.

The restaurant interior was faced in marble. Water flowed in streams along the partitions between the tables, tinkling down artfully sculpted waterfalls into small pools where fat koi swam, thence into channels cut into the floor. Bonsai were displayed on priceless lacquered tables along one wall. The colours of the trees and water were reflected by the restaurant's subdued greens and blues. All was designed to calm. The room was generously sized, with wide gaps between the tables. In an overcrowded world, space was the principal definition of wealth. Only the very wealthy ate at Portis.

Water cascaded down the windows, making a fluid sculpture of the cramped city outside. Karl figured they were going for oriental mystique. Naturally, it just came off as yet more New York fakery. *Plus ça change.*

Karl pushed his glass around the spotless tablecloth. He enjoyed the texture of the cotton under his fingers after the falseness of the virtspace; cool and crisp.

Karl liked Portis. The restaurant was an island of calm in an ocean of humanity. He found the crowds of the city archipelago unbearable, and needed somewhere quiet to unwind. Karl came here often.

Manhattan drew people in by the thousand. Everyone these days was poor, unless they were exceedingly rich. Service of the rich was one of the only ways to end up in the thin middle class band in between. Eduardo or Ricardo or whatever was another leech swimming the canals of NYC, ready to suck on the wealthy; only he was going about it more literally than others.

Karl snorted.

Eduardo or Ricardo halted mid-flow, which was a pleasant surprise. Karl reckoned he'd said about fifty words himself all evening. Had he had the inclination to say more, he doubted he would have had the chance.

The playmate made an uncertain smile, unsure if he was being laughed at. He reached out a well-manicured hand to touch Karl's, and raised his other hand to his throat. He'd painted his nails green, matching his shift, and the décor. The guy had done his research on the restaurant. Karl's smile tightened. That the Playmate had tailored his outfit to Portis but seemed to have done little to find out about Karl was unprofessional. Eduardo, or Ricardo, or whatever the fuck his name was, was probably so excited to be taken to Portis that professionalism had gone out of the window. Karl could just picture him bouncing around his tiny curtained space in a public dorm, squealing and clapping his hands and chattering excitedly about his date. Or maybe Eduardo or Ricardo was going for the big score, abandoning discretion in a bid to win over Karl into a relationship? Displaying himself, warts and all. Another, more permanent way to the money, marrying it. Yeah, there was that touch of desperation to his manner. Brave, to let the truth show, but a crass play if so. If this self-centredness carried over to the bedroom, Karl'd be making a complaint, and that'd get him fired. Let him see how cocky he felt when he was reduced to servicing reefers for pennies.

Karl was well within his rights to order the guy out of the restaurant right now, take him home and enjoy what he'd paid for, but that wasn't his style.

He allowed the playmate to touch him. Let's see where this goes. Karl only wanted sex and company. *As soon as this guy realises that,* he thought, *he'll give up the gabble and maybe he'll get his game back on.*

"You seem a little distracted." Eduardo/Ricardo's smile was polished, seductive, but vacant.

"It's nothing," said Karl. "Busy day at work. Got a lot on my mind. Please, carry on. Forgive me if I don't speak much, I'm happy just to listen. It calms me," he said drily. Eduardo/Ricardo did not see the lie.

The playmate's smile grew warmer. Karl imagined kissing his lips. Unlike the man's calculating eyes, they were full and generous. He felt a twinge in his groin. Not a total washout, then.

Karl smiled at the playmate, and it was only partly forced.

Eduardo/Ricardo opened his mouth to resume his endless prattle, but a female voice, soft Southern States accent, cut him off.

"Karl? Karl Njálsson?"

A woman in a clinging, shiny mood dress that covered very little of her body stood behind him.

"Karl! It is you!" she said. She bent forward, revealing a pretty, coffee-coloured face framed by tightly curled, dichromatic hair.

"Cassandra?"

She pouted. "Hey now, when did you ever call me that? Long time no see, Karl."

Karl's heart rose for the first time in the evening. "What, two years?" He turned to his date. "This is Cassandra De Mona, we studied advanced math together."

Ricardo/Eduardo gave a pained smile.

"Sure did," she said, her pale green eyes glittering with mischief. She nodded at the playmate. "Call me Sand. Pretty thing you got there," she said to Karl. She smiled in a predatory way, exposing her very white teeth. "You still paying for them? I might take him for a spin myself."

The playmate, threatened, gave her a sour look. "I'm off fish, dear," he said.

"Charming," said Sand. Her smile grew wider, although her dress belied it by turning an angry crimson. She had a broad mouth, upper lip slicked icy white, the lower graphite black, matching her hair. "I suppose I'd be an idiot to expect manners from a hired cocksucker."

Karl winced. "Please forgive Sandy, she's a little brusque."

"I'm not brusque," said Sand. "Don't get me wrong, some of my best friends are gay" – she winked at Karl – "but I don't like to be mouthed off at by those who should know their place." Her face went hard. "If you're too prejudiced to take my money, fine, but I bet you're just scared I'd make a proper man out of you."

Eduardo/Ricardo's mouth gaped. He looked imploringly to Karl. Evidently he was used to being the one handing out the insults.

"Don't listen to her. She's goading you," said Karl. A note of pleading entered his voice, making him angry. He gave Sand a warning glance. "She can't help herself. She's really about as judgmental as Buddha." This was not entirely true, but Karl was keen to defuse the situation. It was difficult enough to get a table at Portis as it was.

"Except when it comes to judging who I don't like, then I'm a little more Old Testament," said Sand sweetly.

"She's a pilot, a rockhopper spacer, you know what they're like."

"Oh, I bet he has a real good idea," said Sand evilly.

"I had no idea you associated with people like –" said Eduardo/Ricardo.

"As if that'd bother you," said Sand. "So long as you get paid, right? But you don't want my money, so are you after something else? Gold digging? Marriage to Mr Billion-Dollar-Right? You're shit out of luck here, you aren't Karl's type. You should think about getting a proper job, rather than selling your ass and hoping for a big princess wedding to come out of it. Ain't never gonna happen."

Karl could hear forks hitting plates, and angry mutters from the tables closest to them. The playmate was preparing to leave, packing his things into his clutch bag.

"Look, Ricardo..."

Ricardo's face went hard. Karl inwardly cursed.

"Eduardo?" he guessed.

"My name is Donnie," Donnie said frostily.

Karl drummed his fingers on the table. He gave Sand the kind of stare he used to give her; the one he saved for when she started bar fights. "Look, I don't think this is going to work out, why don't –" he said. He was interrupted by the playmate.

"You're right there!" he said. *How the hell could I forget Donnie?* Karl thought. "You might look down on me, but I'm still a person, and I won't sleep with just anyone."

"Is that a fact?" said Sand.

"Fuck you," said Donnie. He stood quickly, knocking into the table. Karl caught the wine bottle as it wobbled; he wasn't so wealthy as to let it spill. People were staring. Karl saw a diner complaining to the maitre d'.

"Donnie, wait," he called.

"Is it just me, or was that just a little half-hearted?" said Sand.

"You're not helping, Sandy."

She smiled. "Aren't I, now? Is that a Chelon piece you're wearing?" She nodded at his outfit, her corkscrew hair bobbing madly. Karl's white jumpsuit flared out from the middle, cinched with a belt. A wide triple collar circled his neck. 'Doesn't seem like you. Way too fashionable.'

In truth, Karl felt ridiculous. He was conscious of his age and his spreading waist. He regretted the choice.

"Look who's talking? You look like a Christmas tree, Cassand*ra*."

She punched him playfully on the shoulder, scowling in mock outrage. Her dress faded to blue.

"Shut it, you ridiculous man! I'm going all chic, aren't I? Big day." She did a little shimmy, and then her face changed, a flicker of insecurity under the bluster, mirrored in the shifting colours of the dress. "Tell me, honestly, what do you think? Do I look okay?"

Karl sipped his wine. Typical Sand: not seen her for two years, scares off his date, then acts like nothing happened. He looked her up and down. The top of her dress was a T-shape that covered her breasts and navel and not much else, and the skirt was a hobbling fishtail, with wide vents cut out of it down the outside of each leg. She was showing more flesh than cloth. "Honestly?"

"Yeah, come on, I blew three week's pay renting this gear. Do I look okay?"

He smirked. "You look terrible." He burst out laughing.

She deflated momentarily, then caught his expression and smiled. "Terrible? Check out *your* shock frock in the mirror, fashion boy, then call me terrible again."

He stood up. It was good to see her. Karl did not have many real friends. "Give me a hug, Sand."

They embraced, eyes closed, happy.

"Long time, no see," she whispered in his ear. "Too long." She kissed his cheek, and gave him a hard squeeze.

"I think we're causing a scene," said Karl sardonically.

"You here for a drink?"

"A meal, only I think my date's going, and I don't like eating alone. So yeah, a drink."

"Mine's not here for another hour and a half."

Karl raised his eyebrows. "Early, aren't you?"

"It's kind of a work thing," said Sandy evasively, flapping his question away with her hand. "Unlike you, I don't get to joints like this very often, so I figured I'd run up a bit of a tab first, because I'm sure as hell not paying. Want to join me?" She watched as Donnie was shown out. "Sorry about that, but I can't have that anti-girly thing that he had going on there."

Karl shrugged. "I prefer the strong silent type, personally, and he was a real talker. You know, the 'OMG Girlfriend!' type." He put his hands up to either side of his face by way of demonstration, and smiled ruefully. "A real goof with the agency. I've got a lot on my mind."

"Their goof, or yours? I mean, you're paying, right? Why are you taking him out to a place like this? You're not still looking for love, are you, Karl? Why not use the datesites like everyone else? You live in a damn computer all day, surely you can trust one to find you a lay that's not going to piss you off."

And that was kind of the point. He thought about explaining, but she knew it all already. He said, "I guess I'm an incurable romantic." Pat, cliché, and untrue. He'd been cured of romance long ago.

"That's you through and through, Karl." She looked him up and down. "You haven't changed a bit."

"Maybe on the outside. A lot has happened in the last two years." He kept his eye on the maitre d'. Most of the diners had gone back to their own conversations, casting looks at them ranging from the scandalised to the amused, but the complaining couple were still angry, and the maitre d' was struggling to calm them. Karl sighed inwardly.

Sand smiled warmly. "Come and tell me about it, then. Company's paying."

Karl took a moment to make up his mind. He hadn't seen Sand in over two years; sure, he'd kept tabs on her via the usual social networks, and they'd flashed a few messages back and forth, but she'd been busy with her life, and he'd been busy with his. The odd message was no substitute for a body meeting. She was volatile, she was unpredictable. Hell, someone like her was dangerous to him, now.

She was a lot of fun.

"Sure," he said. "Looks like my date's not coming back. I just have to deal with this."

Karl took the arm of the maitre d' and apologised directly and quietly into his ear. A little something pushed into his personal account smoothed away his frown.

Sand and Karl retired to Portis' bar, a darker space lit by glowing water. Within an hour, they were getting drunk.

"What's it like?" said Sand. "Being so close to it?" She giggled, and stuck her tongue out slightly, touching her top lip. Her lipstick rippled graphics in response. She had become languid in her gestures. Flirtatious, Karl thought. Not that it had any effect on him. Why did she always try? "Is it true what they say?"

Karl took another slug of wine. He'd stopped sipping it some time ago. They'd drunk three bottles, a small fortune's worth. "What do they say, Sandy?"

She rolled her eyes mockingly. "That the Market's *alive*! Wooo! Spooky!" She rotated her glass in one hand, causing the wine to slide up the bulb.

"It's not alive, Sand. It's just a machine."

"That's not what they say," she said. Her eyes sparkled. "All those brains in all those bottles, thinking, thinking, thinking. They say it's alive. It *is* alive."

"You just said that."

"Yeah! But, you know, it knows... *Is* it alive?" She gestured vaguely. "All that stuff!"

"Are all pilots so articulate?"

"You should meet my colleagues. Some of them just grunt."

"The Market doesn't know anything, Sandy. How can it know anything? Okay, so some of its components are alive, but it's not *aware*, it's not sentient."

"The brains are." She pulled a face.

"No, they're not. They're not people. The architecture's organic, but it doesn't think, it's a tool. It's all just math and behavioural economics, you know that. You studied the principles in class with me."

She laughed. "That doesn't mean I understood it, now." She sloshed her wine from side to side. Hiding embarrassment? Well, well.

Karl sighed. "All it does is what people used to do, only it does it better. It stops things getting out of hand. It eliminates negative human heuristics, irrational behaviour, bandwagons, that sort of thing."

"Then it dictates what is successful," said Sand.

"No, it only anticipates human action, and eliminates inconsistent variables."

"Then what are you for?" she said.

"I'm just a check, Sand."

She smiled lazily at him. "A fine way to use your education; a financial doorstop."

"I could trade – some people do – but there's no point, the Market outperforms us all."

"Right, and only the rich can afford to use it, so they get richer. The delicate balance, the old and the new hands, the protection of the self interest of the hierarchy, the furthering of greed... Blah, blah, blah." She hunched lower and stared into the wine glass. "That's why we're all so damn poor."

Karl shook his head. "No, it's not. We're so damn poor because there's isn't enough to go around. Not for everyone. There are twelve billion people on the Earth, Sandy. There have to be checks and balances. Without the Pointers, who'd provide jobs? They're as stuck as we are, we struggle, they have their..." He waved his hand around and smiled, a feral smirk, tinged with bitterness. There was a lot of bitterness in the NYC archipelago in those days. "*Noblesse oblige.*"

"You and your damn French. You sure are a romantic at heart."

"Ah, gay Paris!"

They both tittered. Karl became serious again. "It's a kind of evil, Sandy, but a necessary evil. Wealth doesn't create itself. And wherever there is wealth, there is inequity. It's a sad corollary, but I can deal with that."

Sand made a point of looking around Portis. "You are sure on the breadline, aren't you? Poor little Icelander. Accessing the Market through middlemen like you *costs*, Karl. The people who pay your wages are the only ones with the money to do so. They've locked the rest of us out."

"Please. Anyone can be rich. You just have to work at it. And everyone can work hard, if they choose. Okay, I'm comfortable, but I worked hard, you worked hard. Look at us now. You're an astronaut, I'm a quant. We didn't get that by sitting around whining."

"We had opportunity, Karl. Not many do," countered Sand. "And we'll neither of us ever be rich as the Pointers, no matter what we do, and they don't work for it, they're born to it." She met his eyes. "That's not fair. Or does that count as whining?"

Karl sighed. They'd had this argument many times before. Their opinions would diverge further the more they drank. "Yes, yes," he said irritably. "No one but the Pointers will ever be super-rich, but it's a consequence of wealth creation, Sandy. Some people are always going to have more. Now can we please talk about something else?"

"They don't have more, they have *everything*, Karl."

"Who ever said life was fair?" said Karl. "It never has been, and trying to give everyone lifestyles we simply can't sustain has exhausted the Earth," he said. "The Pointers can be massively wealthy, keep millions of us in jobs, and spend money on forest reserves and social projects when they feel guilty. Enough of them do philanthropic work to make them all worthwhile."

"Ah, a megayacht and a fleet of matching airplanes... Philanthropy at its finest!"

"Sand, it's that, or every man woman and child can be ten dollars richer each. How long would ten dollars last you, Sandy? Where's the sense in that?"

Sand pushed herself up off the table and lounged back in her chair. "Tell that to the no-jobbers I passed on the way here, Karl. Tell that to the shantymen and the reefers in their shacks out on the Jersey bars. They'll be lucky to see ten dollars in a year."

"You know it's not so simple." He leaned forward. "You're richer than most; you need to deal with that, or envy and guilt will hollow you out from the inside."

She shrugged. "No I don't. It doesn't matter. I'm getting away from it all. I'm blasting off, baby, for good."

"Oh, yeah?" he said. "How? You going to live on the Moon? It's no different up there, Sand."

She smiled knowingly and shook her head.

"Mars?" he ventured. "The belt?"

She looked about cautiously. Her voice lowered to a whisper. "Not even close. You ever hear of the Gateway Project?"

"No," he said. "Should I have?"

"It'll be announced soon. I think I can talk about it without getting assassinated." She pushed a well-manicured finger down onto the rim of her glass. Like her hair and lips, her fingernails were tinted alternately black and white with active paint. "Not a word to anyone else, though, okay?"

Karl nodded.

Her voice dropped further. "It's a colony effort. Interstellar."

Karl nearly spilled his wine. "What?" The idea was preposterous.

"Shush! Keep your voice down."

He leaned forward. "You can't be serious."

"Deadly. I've signed on as a pilot. Got the contract, the works. It's a big play, Karl."

Karl began to speak, then stopped. Sand teased all the time, she was infuriating in as many ways as she was charming, but when it came to it she didn't like to lie, not outright. "Really?" he said hesitantly. He felt suddenly sad.

"Really."

"How the hell has this not been made public?"

"It's the Pointers behind it, why do you think?"

Karl pursed his lips. His mind strayed to the anomalous equities he'd witnessed. "Space is just space, there's no money in it. It's a vanity investment, made by people brought up on too much science fiction with too much money and not enough to do. Like – tell me, what's the cost of bringing back a ton of ore from the belt?"

"How should I know? I just fly it back."

"I thought they had computers for that," he said.

"I'm a check, like you," she said mockingly. "I make sure the tugs don't go nutso and crash into the sun. It's real exciting sitting there with my feet on the flight desk for three months at a stretch."

"Come on, think, how much?"

"I'm just not interested in all that," she said.

That annoyed Karl. There were plenty of people like Cassandra, ready to bellyache about the status quo without understanding how it got to be that way. How the hell did they expect to change it, when they just had a bunch of half-assed opinions? "Be interested!" he said, a little too hard. She looked affronted. "Please, humour me. Think about it."

"Well, it's nowhere near as much as it was. We don't lug the ore all the way in. The Lagrange point processing facs mean it's only pure metal that comes to the orbital factories, and then processed material is ferried down the elevators. That's where I've been for the last six months: shuttle runs between LG12 and the belt."

Karl tapped his forefinger on the table. "That's only good for things in space, not if you want to bring it back down. Even with the elevators, volcanic mining and pelagic stripping are both much cheaper methods of getting hold of minerals. I wonder..."

Sand raised her eyebrows, urging him on.

Karl didn't answer straight away. "Why this? What possible advantage can there be to the Pointers in funding a colony effort outside the Solar System? They'll never see a return on it, not if they land on a planet made of diamond, tiger bones and caviar. Who's behind it?"

Now it was Sandy's turn to get annoyed. "Don't you believe me, Karl? I've the contract right here." She tapped her temple. "Why's it so hard to believe? Mankind's always spread out. It's what we do. You blamed science fiction; maybe that's it. Some of these guys have trillions. If they want a shiny vanity project, why not play cosmic explorer? It's not the first time some hooray's dashed his cash on space. It's gotten me a job, and it's getting me the fuck out of this dump."

Karl's eyes shifted to the other patrons in the bar. No one reacted to her lack of decorum.

"You should be happy. It's a brave new world, Karl." She saluted him with her glass. Her smile turned to a frown when he did not return the gesture. "Why the concern?"

Now it was his turn to drop his voice. "I noticed today a bunch of stocks on the up and up."

"So?"

"They were all space stocks."

"There you are, then," she said. "The Market thinks it's profitable. You said yourself it's pretty smart, it's way ahead of you on this one."

He waved a hand. "The Market does not think. The Market is not smart. The Market is a packet of algorithms at the Pointers' beck and call."

"But?" she said.

"Two things," he said. "Let's say, hypothetically, that the Pointers are planning an effort. The stock of all the companies indirectly involved in the venture should see an immediate pick-up, perhaps sustained over the medium term, at least while whatever spaceship they're building is constructed."

"*Star*ship, Karl. And not one; a fleet."

He stared at her blankly. That made it seem even more unlikely. "Are you sure this is real? Have you joined some kind of cult? There are some real whackjobs out there."

"Karl!"

"Okay, okay! Let's assume it's happening, then. Hypothetically" – he stressed the word – "those companies that provide services, parts, craft, whatever, they make money, but those that fund the expedition will take big hits right off, because there is no financial return, none whatsoever; anyone can see that. It'll be a one-way trip, it's lunacy, and the Market does not tolerate lunacy, that's the whole point of it."

"So?"

Karl's disquiet redoubled. "So the Market should have picked that up by now. I see no signs that it has. Sure, the stocks are rising, and that's fine, but where are the safeguards? Where are the alternate portfolio spreads? Where's the betting against? I see none of it, Sand. The Market plays against itself."

"And?"

"And it's not."

"So it *does* think," she said, giggling a little. She squeezed his hand on the table. "I'm sorry, you look so serious."

"It doesn't think," he said, with some exasperation.

"Then what, conspiracy?"

He shrugged and took a drink. "When aren't there conspiracies? The rich plot to keep the poor down, the poor plot against them."

"The Market is the one thing they all agree on, Karl. It's tamper proof."

"Ah, so you do remember something. *Supposedly* tamper proof."

"You've always had too much of an imagination," she said.

"No, I haven't," he said. "Imagination in my line of work is a weakness."

"Yes, you have! You've half-convinced yourself that you don't, but you do. You always did. You've spent so long pretending that you can't pretend, that it's become second nature." She gave a sly grin. "And that's a massive act of imagination, isn't it?" Her dress played a series of gentle chords, a politeness to Karl to let him know she was about to be distracted by her inChip. She squinted at him drunkenly. "Uh-oh, my date's here. Gotta go."

"I've been meaning to ask about that. This is kind of an odd place for a work date."

"Says the man who takes his rentboy out to the poshest joint in town."

"Humour me. What gives?"

This time Sand's embarrassment was plain. "Well, it kind of is a work date, and it kind of isn't."

Karl made a quizzical expression.

"Well, uh – dammit, Karl!" she looked sheepish. "They've kind of paired us off."

"Paired you off? Like…" He raised his eyebrows. "What, like eugenically? A breeding programme?"

She nodded, biting her lip.

"That's outrageous!"

"Says the gay man with the gay parents who wanted a little gay baby," she snapped. "It's the chance of a lifetime. Dating's not worked for me, I might as well let the corporate science boys match me up. Where's the harm? I can always ditch him later. They say they want their pair bonding permanent so there'll be stability in the new colonies, but I can't see them enforcing that fifteen light years from nowhere if we get sick of each other."

"You're going that far?"

"Much further, Karl. Watch the news, you'll see soon." She looked over to the entrance of the bar, where a tall man was framed in the brighter light. A waiter gestured in Sand's direction. "Look, let's meet up and have one last drink before I go. I'll be able to talk more about it then, okay?"

He nodded and gave her a tired smile. "Okay, Sandy. Nice seeing you."

She ruffled his hair. "Keep it real, Karly."

He batted her hands away. "You too, Sandy."

They never saw each other again.

KARL ARRIVED AT the office early the next morning. Sand's revelation had fuelled his curiosity. He had not slept. He was short with the techs as they wired him for Market interface and pushed the shunt into his neck.

As soon as he was in, he called up his simulations of the previous day, and collated overnight market trends on the space sector. He extended the scope of his investigation to cover any corporate entity at all that might have something to do with the venture – health, medical, heavy equipment, anything that might provide equipment or supplies to aid a far-flung colony effort.

He still did not believe it.

Today, he left the imagination damper in the shunt off. "Music," he said. "Something heavy and complex... Beethoven, symphony number seven."

He commenced the dissection of two dozen portfolios as the symphony began. The instruments involved in the trades were unfeasibly complex, equities and bonds interleaved with one another, some real junk mixed in with super-class AAA-plus companies – lots of R&D outfits, peddling barely tested technologies, some of it feasible but not off the drawing board, some of it firmly in cloud cuckoo land. With all these portfolios buying into these products at the Market's behest, the price of the fringe institutions would climb sky high, and that could bring it all crashing down as soon as the promises they made proved to be hollow.

"And that," finished Karl aloud, "will be pretty damn soon." His concerns deepened as he searched out the project's financiers. Sandy had given no indication who was fronting the capital to build a fleet of starships, but he had his suspicions. He had a list of eighty-four likely candidates soon enough, all with portfolios with a heavy space slant, all in synchronous upswing. Worryingly, there was no sign the Market was concerned about their prospects; as far as he could see, it was pushing money in from every trade account that had greenlit space and/or high-risk investment strategies – enough, certainly, to fund the construction of a fleet of starships. "This can't just be insider knowledge, the curve's too steep," he said under his breath. If it were, then he'd expect one or two portfolios to take off as the Market adopted an investment pattern, with others following as the Market responded to itself, and then further patterns of mid-level betting and those predicated on outright failure. This had not happened. All of them had started going up at the same time. Either the Market knew something he did not, or there was widespread manipulation going on. "That's impossible, isn't it?" he said. "What the hell are you playing at?"

The pendulous march of the Seventh Symphony's second movement was in full voice when pain skewered his mind, pinning his thoughts in place like so many butterflies.

His virtspace shivered. Numbers crackled and were replaced by nonsense symbols, the streams of data winked out. Requests for trade deletions and simulation wipes were logged and confirmed by a mind not his own. He screamed, feeling his avatar disassociate as the virtual environment collapsed around him. The music played on as his mind was vivisected.

Karl screamed louder and clutched at his avatar's head, and it came apart like stale cake under his hands.

The lights on his couch in the real world flashed frantic red. Alarms wailed. The shoes of emergency medics squeaked across the floor. Karl heard none of it.

They checked his heart, which beat still. His body was warm, passing its chemicals to and fro, processing its proteins and energising its cells, doggedly pursuing the complex dance steps of life. When they passed their machines over his skull, there was not the slightest indication of brain activity.

To all intents and purposes, Karl Njálsson was dead.

CHAPTER TWO
Captain Anderson

ANDERSON SAT, LEGS out, head against the cream leather, knees bent slightly, hands resting limply just before his crotch – the posture of a yogi, or a doll carefully placed on a shelf. He had been told to wait, and so he waited. He did not pick up any of the active flimsies from the coffee tables at the end of the sofas. He did not stare at the receptionist as the other man waiting did, beautiful as she was. He did not look around the white room at the expensive, bespoke furniture or the faddish surroundings – different every time he had been to visit his employer in person.

Anderson waited.

Anderson was an Alt. The Pointers had needed slaves; servants could be faithless, androids were too simple, actual slaves were illegal. Hence the Alts: altered humans, genes recoded in such a way that legally, they did not count as human. Or so the Pointers' scientists had argued. By the time the endless court hearings had been exhausted, the Alts already were. They were freed, but as they had been created to utterly obey the Pointers, they as good as denied their own emancipation.

Anderson had been gengineered to Petrovitch specification. Raised in Petrovitch schools, personality-sculpted to intensify and focus his natural tractability. He had been told to wait, and therefore he would wait until he was told otherwise. He did not care about his status. He had no musings on servitude, he had no care for the opinions of others on whether Alts like him were human or something less, he did not care whether his intense loyalty counted as a form of slavery, he did not care about anything. He cared that his assignments were fulfilled. That was all that mattered. Call it pride, call it compulsion. The distinction was meaningless to him. Fulfilling his orders was all that mattered.

Anderson thought. He was not bereft of free will, he was capable of applying his mind creatively, but only rarely did

55

he use these gifts to scrutinise the human condition. When he indulged, he felt sorry for others not like himself; those who had no purpose or direction, those who spent their time striving for something they could never have, or lived half-lives choked with despair at their station. He felt sorry, too, for the Pointers, his masters, ridden to desperation as they were by the tyranny of choice. In his servitude he was free.

His mind wandered.

He was at school, receiving his education. Programming, the equalists called it. He did not care.

He was in the Congo, gunning down a man who ran at him with an ancient assault rifle. The man was fierce, a warrior. Fear was in his yellowed eyes nonetheless. Anderson did not fear anything. He cut the man in half with a half-magazine of high velocity bullets. Simple security work, five hundred deaths like this one on his tab. Murder, the equalists called it. He did not care.

He was in a laboratory, being gene-matched and tested. *In vitro* gestation had its uses, but the old ways were best. He was shown to a room with low lighting, a woman of perfect form upon the bed. An Alt like himself. Selective breeding, the equalists called it. He did not care.

There were not many like Anderson. The Alts were few in number. They aged, and did not breed true. Anderson was a special creature. He was a rare breed. All Alts were servants, servants of the rich, servants of the Pointers. A legal loophole. Not quite androids, not quite human. Their creation was now illegal. Slavery, the equalists had said. Anderson did not care.

Anderson waited.

Presently, the woman with the perfect teeth and perfect breasts and perfect face and ass and arms and hands and legs that registered on him only as shapes, looked over at him from her place behind the reception desk.

"Captain Anderson? Chairman Petrovitch will see you now."

Anderson stood immediately. He was tall and well muscled. The receptionist blinked at him as he brought eyes so grey they appeared silver, the mark of an Alt, to bear on her.

"If you would go –"

"I know the way," he said.

*   *   *

ANDERSON'S MASTER WAS the fourth most powerful man in the world – Ilya Petrovitch, American Faux-Russian. Small, jowly, old; *how* old was impossible to say. The rich buy years as poor men buy potatoes. Dissolute in his distant youth, ruthless now. His face sagged, pulling at the corners of his eyes. His lips were full, his bone structure narrow. Not a Slavic face, not at all.

Ilya made a show of reading Anderson's file, projected as a hologram that stayed exactly forty-five centimetres in front of the Pointer patriarch's face as he walked around the room. "You have been a loyal servant of ours for a long time," said Ilya. He peered at Anderson, searching for something. When he did not see it, he smiled. "Of course, you could be nothing but loyal. I mean only that you are prodigiously talented. And by that, I am sure you are aware, I mean that you have survived as long as you have. Congo, Surinam, Argentina, the Lunar Eurowar... Everywhere you have been, you have returned from; alive, and in one piece. And you have accomplished nearly every mission we have set you. Even for one of your kind, that makes you extraordinary."

Anderson did not react, he stared into the distance. He had no role here but to take his orders. He waited for his orders to be delivered.

"Not that any of this preamble matters to you, does it, Anderson?"

"No, sir."

"I find you fascinating, did you know that?"

"No, sir."

"No, sir?" said Ilya. "Aren't you interested to know why?"

"No, sir."

Ilya walked up to him, examining him closely, so close the old man's perfumed breath chilled his neck. Ilya often did this. Anderson had thought the old man might be attracted to him. The thought was framed abstractly, in terms of how Anderson should service that attraction, should it exist. So far, Ilya had not pressed the matter. "You really aren't. A shame, and an asset to me, of course."

Ilya dismissed the hologram with a thought, and sat down. "I am old, Anderson; very old. I feel it now. I do not look my age. I would have lived far longer than you, were I not to order you to do what I am about to order you to do. Curious yet?"

"No, sir."

"Of course not." Ilya rubbed at his elbow and lifted it with a grimace, stretching out some pain of age. "Fascinating. You know, when my brother, God rest his soul, proposed the development of the Alts, I was dead against it. I thought the future lay in drone warriors, or androids, or perhaps cyborgised soldiers." He shook his head. "I did not think that the human body was capable of withstanding the rigours of modern warfare, no matter how altered. How wrong I was. I overlooked one thing, you know what that is?"

This time Anderson answered. "Sense of purpose, strength of will."

Ilya jabbed a finger at him and smiled. "Yes, yes! Exactly. You cannot programme purpose into a machine. You cannot increase the will of a man through cyborgisation. Machines, bio-mechanical interfacing... Expensive, difficult to maintain, crude. Tailored lovers, designed accountants, born warriors? Very valuable. But limitless loyalty? Beyond price!"

He sat back. "You would stand there all day, were I to continue to ramble on, but I will not waste your time. I will tell you what I want you to do." He sighed. "You are to accompany my sons Leonid and Yuri as a member of the Project Gateway Interstellar Colony effort, head of security for the *ESS Adam Mickiewicz* and the Heracles V colony." A pair of flimsies on the coffee table by Ilya activated, bearing animate files detailing the lives of his sons.

"Sir?"

"You will not have heard of Gateway. It is not wide knowledge, yet. The Pointers' great vanity project, or the venture that will save mankind. The Earth is dying. Some of the others don't believe this; they see an expansion beyond the Solar System as a way of spreading their genetic heritage, or increasing the wealth of their family. Others think it will re-energise the Market. They all have their reasons. Not me, no. For me, it is a matter of survival. I feel it in my bones, we have taken too much. It is time to move on and take from somewhere else. I am sending my offspring because I want something of the Petrovitch family to persist. Leonid is a good boy – confused, yes, but there is the potential for greatness in him that is lacking in my other feckless children."

Anderson slid his eyes sideways. "And Yuri, sir?"

Ilya nodded approvingly. "You are not mindless, not mindless at all. A wastrel, yes, like too many of the others, but there is a core of steel in him that is easy to miss. It is there nevertheless. You are to protect them, to aid them in their efforts in founding a new world. God alone knows what they'll find out there – rocks, most likely, but I will not rule out spear-waving savages or octopods with muskets. I would be a fool to do so, and I am not a fool." He paused. "Do you think me a fool, Anderson?"

"I have no opinion, sir." He looked at the man who owned him for the first time since he'd come into the office. "But no, you are not a fool."

"So I am sending you. I cannot send an army. They'll need soldiers of your rare quality."

Anderson nodded. "They will, sir. I am the logical choice." He said this without conceit.

"You are to leave your current posting immediately, and begin preparation. Choose ninety of your best operatives, a mix of Alt and human, not all of one or the other, you understand?"

"Yes, sir."

"Good. Here are my preliminary plans." Ilya blinked over a large file into Anderson's inChip. "The restrictions on the total mass you may carry can be revised upwards for you and your men, and there will be space set aside for military equipment, but this is limited. We're not sending an army, just insurance. However, the fabrication units and auto-factories being sent with the mission will possess a full complement of military patterning. We will build what we cannot take with us."

"Yes, sir."

"At this stage, you are not to share this information, nor make any announcement of the venture to anyone, do you understand? Early days, yet. Early days."

"Yes, sir."

"I called you here to give you one additional order. I am the head of this family, am I not?"

"Yes, sir."

"And so your loyalty is to me and, ultimately, me alone."

"Yes, sir. Of course, sir."

"Confirm loyalty code: Alpha. Geronimo. House of Cards. Ambivalence. Quadrilateral."

Anderson stiffened imperceptibly. His mind shifted in a way that was designed to be pleasant to him.

"Loyalty code confirmed."

"Then listen very carefully to this. I will not have my family reduced in circumstance. You are to protect them, but you are also to protect the station of the Petrovitch family. Do you understand? If my sons propose anything that will diminish the Petrovitches' position, you are to prevent it, even if it goes against their orders. Understood?"

"Understood, sir."

"Be subtle. Leonid will doubtless try to abdicate responsibility. Guide him to see his errors, do not force it or you will lose him. Yuri is a back-up. He might surprise us both, in the right circumstances."

"Yes, sir."

"There's a good dog." Ilya may have wanted to provoke him, but Anderson did not care.

"Yes, sir."

Ilya ran his fingers over the flimsies of his sons. "Yes. There's a good dog," he said absently.

"Yes, sir."

THE SHIPS

THE FLEET WAS begun long before the initial announcement. Rumours got out, as rumours do, spacers' tales of shipments heading to nowhere, of personnel and equipment that went someplace that was no-place. Who listens to spacers? Best not to. The rumours stuck, did the rounds, tall tales took root in the fertile grounds of the popular imagination and grew into myths, took their place next to secret alien labs and asteroids made of iridium, next to space whales and ghostships, and phantoms in spacesuits – skull faces grinning through dirty visors – tap-tap-tapping on the windows in the long dark of interplanetary transit. Folktales, foaftales, nonsense. The truth is far more astounding. The Pointers have the money to fund the leap beyond, and the Pointers have the money to have it kept quiet.

Now the truth is revealed to the world. Shuttles carry cameras, shuttles carry newsmen and dignitaries who knew all along, flying them between berths of gossamer threads that glint in starlight. Encased by the webs are long needles of composites – the spines of ships yet to be. Each is five kilometres long, naked yet and ugly with it. Limbed machines, as angular as any nightmare, clamber over the spires, mechanical spiders weaving carbon compounds into hull plates, bulkheads, drive housings, and airlocks. Seven cradles for seven ships. Seven hulls are complete, away, undergoing main drive tests that loop them out in majestic arcs towards Saturn and back. Once done, final fitting awaits: hibernation decks, cargo grapples, life support. All those things that frail humanity needs to survive. For now the ships are the sole province of machines.

A further seven spines are being born, forged in automatic factories 0.1 AU distant from the cradles. Specks in the night betray their location, further specks – the catch of sunlight on a hull, the flare of an ion drive – reveal the streams of tugs and haulers bringing materials in from all over the system: ice from Europa, iron from the belt, carbon dioxide from Venus, hydrocarbons from Titan, people from Earth. In a fortnight, tugs will ease the spines from the factories and shepherd them to the webs, and another seven ships will be begun.

This is Sand's job, this hauling of parts. Eighteen months of it now, and the wonder has worn off. She is bored and lonely. She heard of Karl's death only four months after the fact. She is mostly saddened by it, but she remembers what he said, and what she said, and in the dark watches before sleep she suffers the attentions of paranoia.

In the distance (how far is impossible to say; space is not easily confined by the measurements of the human eye), albedo smudges show the edge of the belt. Past that the bright lights of the giants. Past that, the edge of the system, the place no living human has yet been. Here, halfway out, are the arks that will bear men and women away and change that fact forever.

Stocks rise, the Market trades. Rich men grow richer.

CHAPTER THREE
Dariusz in Szczecin

DARIUSZ SZCZECIŃSKI ROLLED his coffee cup in his hand, watching the grains swirl. The coffee was bad: weak, brown rather than black. Rain battered relentlessly against the glass walls that stoppered the ends of the Brama Portowa and made of it the Bramkowa Bar. He was tired, groggy with it. Worry can do that to a man.

It was hot outside. The passive air con panels set in the roof whispered urgently. The thick brick of the old city gateway kept out the worst of the heat, and the coffee was cheap, the two reasons Dariusz was there.

The bar's holo was mute, the images it projected in the air eerie. A news piece on food riots in Mesopotamia gave way to yet another Gateway press conference. The billionaires, the corporate heads, the scientists behind the scheme, they'd all become as familiar as his family. At first, everyone assumed they were insane, or that it was a stunt of some kind, and that the story would disappear from the news.

Apparently not.

The press conference faded out. The *Zheng He* swung around in the air, the largest of the ships, the gateway ship itself. Dariusz read the subtitles spinning around the base of the picture: English, Mandarin, Hindi and Spanish. No Polish. Colonise the stars, they said; take mankind from his failing home. Dariusz had heard it many times before. His interview for the effort was the day after tomorrow.

And, of course, they would reject him.

He wanted another coffee, but couldn't afford it. His balance blinked nothing but red numbers when he called it up on his inChip. It would be another three days before his social security payment came in. He had at least one hungry day ahead of him. The city owed him nothing, and he depended on it for everything.

There was no work, nowhere to go for handouts but the city, and it was parsimony personified. There was no pleading with a city, no matter that he carried its name.

He watched the subtitles scroll round and round the base of the cone of ghosts. He stopped reading them and stared through them, until they became abstract and meaningless, until his eyes hurt. That small act of nihilism satisfied him.

"These televisions have translation settings for Polish too. All of them. What does it tell you when even the Poles do not turn it on? The world is becoming homogenised, my friend, more and more every year."

Dariusz started. A man sat at the table uninvited, putting his coffee cup carelessly onto the wood. The watery brown liquid sloshed over the rim.

"Good day, Pan Szczeciński," the man said. He was well dressed; late fifties, maybe. It was nearly impossible to tell how old anyone was anymore. The poor aged quickly, the rich not at all. The man wore a long light raincoat, ankle boots, formal jeans. His eyes were large, curious, and searching. He was balding, which made him out to be poor, or possessed of the intellectual vanity of the deliberately badly groomed. He spoke Polish with an accent Dariusz didn't recognise – he wasn't using translation software. "There's no one sitting here, so I'm sure you don't mind."

Dariusz looked around incredulously. The bar was completely empty apart from himself, the barman and this man.

"Look, I'm having a bad day. I'm not in the mood for..."

The man cut him short. "I am sorry. This will take only five minutes of your time. I am aware of the kind of day you are having, and why. Don't ask if you know me. You don't. I know you, let's leave it at that. And I know you're looking to join them." He inclined his head toward the holo. "I know also that they will reject you, as no doubt do you. Perhaps I can help." The man smiled. There was something hidden behind it, but it was otherwise sincere, not like the smiles he'd had at the Office of Employment in the morning. Get a job, they'd said. He'd told them about his interview for the Gateway Project and it had made no difference. He had two months of basic security payments left. Then...

Dariusz checked his surroundings. No one was listening, no one that he could see. He was feeling reckless, angry at the morning's disappointments. Why not?

"You have five minutes. Pan...?"

The man gave a flurry of smiles in succession, each one different to the one before, as if he would rather communicate this way, without words. "I'd rather leave my name out of it for now, if it's all the same to you.'

"Sure," Dariusz said. He dropped his gaze from the stranger's face, back to his coffee.

"Your interview is tomorrow."

Dariusz nodded. "What of it?"

"You have no hope."

Dariusz stared into his drink and shrugged. "Maybe, maybe not."

"It is how it will be. They will not take you because you do not conform."

Dariusz looked up sharply. "You know a lot about me."

The man smiled again, fleetingly, slightly sorry. "Dariusz Szczeciński, 37, one child, wife Lydia, geoengineer, or should I say ex-geoengineer. Born Kraków, September 14th, 2120."

"All public; I am supposed to be impressed?"

"Very well. You are afraid of wasps and other stinging insects, you insist it is a rational fear, yet it is listed on your medical file as a true phobia. You are not talkative, a private man, you are classed as a INTJO3 on the revised Myers-Briggs scale."

"Also impressive, if it weren't all on my company records," said Dariusz.

"How about this, then?" continued the man. "Your first girlfriend was Barbara Kosinska. When you kissed her, the very first time you kissed anyone, you were twelve, she eleven. She cried, and you ran and hid in the forest for hours, terrified you had hurt her. Your parents called the police. You never told them where you had been or why. For some, this might be an amusing anecdote, but for you it has been a source of shame. Hardly the crime of the century, my friend. I don't know why you let it bother you so much."

Dariusz studied the man unguardedly. Had he told anyone? A friend? An old lover? He could not recall. He doubted it; he was a fundamentally private man. "What the – ?"

"You see, I know everything about you. I apologise if it feels as if I am intruding... But..." He smiled again. "How can I apologise? I *am* intruding, in every way." He took a sip from his cup and sucked air through his teeth. "Bad coffee." He placed the cup down, became businesslike. "You will be rejected because those in power do not like to be defied."

"I've worked hard all my life," said Dariusz. "I have done nothing wrong. I am qualified for the job. I have a chance."

"General environmental macro-engineer? A skilled role, and one that will be much in demand on a new world," said the man. "You have experience, too."

Dariusz made another noncommittal movement with his arms, and hunched lower to the table. "The Western Union, USA, New Jericho, North African Federation, and Russia. A few other places, on and off world. I'm *over*-qualified. I should get it."

"But you do not sound confident."

Dariusz shrugged.

"In your eyes, maybe you are over-qualified, and definitely in mine. But not in theirs. You know what I say to be true." The man sighed and looked around the clean brick arch of the bar. The building was in essence a tunnel, where carts in earlier centuries had rumbled through walls long ago demolished. It was twenty five metres long and six high at the apex of the arch. A long bar ran down the left, and glass and brushed steel partitioned it. "This gate was built by Frederick Wilhelm I after he bought the city from the Swedes in 1720," he said, with another brief smile. "It is a grand statement, a flash of Prussian power. Where you sit was once a thoroughfare, a way into the city. Now what?" The man shrugged. "The walls it pierced have gone, and Poles, not Germans, come here to drink coffee. It has been a backdrop for a statue, a guard post, bar, a shop, an art studio, a house and now it is a bar again. Were it not for the name of this bar and the plaque on the outside, you would never guess what this place once was. The name of Frederick Wilhelm adorns the exterior, as do sculptures of Mars and Hercules. This place was a statement; artistic, yes, but undeniably a statement of wealth and military might. The question is, what does it say now?" The man sat back and smiled again.

"Your point is?"

"My point is, Pan Dariusz…"

"Oh, please," said Dariusz drily. "You know more about me than my own mother does. Call me Darek."

The man exhaled hard through his nose. "Very well, Darek," said the man, switching without embarrassment to the familiar form of his name. "My point is, where is the kingdom of the man that commissioned this gate? Absorbed by Germany, which was smashed in two world wars, then absorbed in its turn into the old European Union. The language that adorns the Brama Portowa – its fourth name, by the by – the Latin, it was once a mark of permanence, of continuance of knowledge. And now…? This edifice, once a marker of power, is a historical footnote, where Poles drink coffee."

"What of it?"

The man drummed the fingers of both hands on the table abruptly. His smile evaporated. "You are not a fool, Pan Szczeciński, do not play at one. Let me spell it out for you; no matter what the rulers of one age might believe, their rule is fleeting. Things change, no matter how concrete they may seem." He laughed. "Why, only the concrete remains, and even that will crumble, given time."

"This bar is made of brick and stone, not concrete. Both are more durable." Dariusz placed his cup down and made to go. "Now, if you will excuse me…"

The man grabbed his wrist, and yet his friendly, curious expression did not change. "You have no job, no prospects. Your son is seven." He jerked his head toward the window. Rain was pouring, steam hovering over the hot pavements. "It is autumn now; one hundred years ago, snow would be coming in a month or so. Not now. Tell me, when did you last see snow? The world is changing too fast. Do you know what kind of world Daniel will live in? Don't you want something better for yourself? For him? You fear it will all come undone. That is why you have applied for the Gateway Project."

Dariusz paused. "Go to hell. How do I know you're not a corp agent, tricking me into sedition?"

"You don't, you don't. Although you will soon know I am not." The man released his grip and held out his hands. "I come with an offer. One that will appeal to you. Frederick Wilhelm, Darek, he didn't see change coming. Our rulers do not either. The nought-point-nought-one per cent don't see it, because although they know that their actions can change the world, they forget that the actions of the likes of us can too."

Dariusz glanced about, suddenly concerned.

"This is dangerous talk."

"No one can hear us, I assure you." He picked up his cup, and looked at it as if it confused him. "Five years ago, you were fired for refusing to take mood enhancers while working for Dai-tan in the Congo."

"I was within my rights. Who needs a happy engineer anyway? Do you know what that stuff can do to you?"

"If you're unlucky," said the man. "They assumed you would not be unlucky, or rather they did not care if you were. There are other engineers."

"Why should I take the chance on their say? Refusing the enhancers did not affect my ability to work."

"That's not the way they think, Darek! For them, it is better that you *fit in*. That you are *obedient*. That you *feel* how they want you to feel. They want obedience on the Gateway Project too, they need it. The brightest and the best are going, yes, because the Pointers will need all man's cunning to tame their new kingdoms, but also only the most loyal. Your refusal is a black mark against you. What would you say if I could make that mark go away, scrub it clean, get you a berth on the voyage? You're more than qualified. You'd be going, were it not for that."

"How are you going to achieve that?" said Dariusz. He did not sit down again, but he wanted to hear what the man had to say. He needed hope, he needed a way out.

"You're being careful, saying nothing to incriminate yourself, but I'm sorry to say simply associating with me is a crime." He held up his palms. "Don't worry! They check the surveillance for this place, they'll see nothing, because there won't be anything to see. Don't you think it funny that there's no one else in here, Darek? You come here often. Usually full at this time of day, isn't it?"

Dariusz looked around the bar. "What have you done to me?"

"Nothing permanent. Let's just say neither of us is really here. If you walk away now, you'll leave by that door and find yourself sitting at this table and staring at the TV display, not out in the rain."

"You've virt-jacked me?" said Dariusz incredulously. "How? Most of my inChip's functions aren't operational; I can't afford to unlock them."

"You're an engineer. You know these things aren't foolproof." The man shrugged. "It is safe."

Dariusz grunted. "Nothing's safe."

"This is. I'm going to give you an address. You won't forget it. If you are interested in learning more, come. Trust me, this is a genuine offer. Think about the gate, Dariusz, think about the transience of power. Ask yourself, what would you do to change the world for the better? Or would you rather let the inequality of the Earth be transplanted to flourish in alien soil, and oppress mankind forever?"

"You said yourself, nothing is forever." Dariusz pulled up the collar of his coat and strode through the deserted bar to the door. His hand hit the thick glass. November warmth seeped through its invisible lattices of carbon insulation.

"Pan Szczeciński!" shouted the man. "What if I were to say you could take your boy with you? Get out of this dying world forever? I'm talking about a new world, Darek! A new world!"

The door swung open, letting in a blast of damp heat. Dariusz stepped out into the blood-warm rain.

He blinked. He was back in the bar. Several of the tables were occupied, and a low buzz of conversation filled the place. The lenses in his eyes palpitated, like they'd been open and staring for minutes. The in-mind overlays of his chip fizzed and jumped, before resuming their usual hopeless displays of debt and locked functions.

He looked around himself cautiously. No one was paying him any attention.

An address blinked on his inner-eye display. 'The Dąbie Sailing Club.' The road was out in the suburbs to the southeast, by the lake.

His hand tightened on the coffee cup. It had gone cold.

"Falling asleep, hey?" said a waiter as he approached the table and wiped it down. "Tough times. Makes me feel like going sailing, yes, sir. Water's still free, isn't it?"

Dariusz looked at him as if stung. The waiter bent down and gently extricated the cup from Dariusz's hand. "Let me take that, get you a fresh one, compliments of Bar Bramkowa. You look like you need it. Or would you rather have a beer?"

Dariusz scrabbled to his feet, knocking his chair back noisily. A couple two tables over stopped talking, looked up at him disinterestedly for a moment and returned to their conversation.

"Are you okay, friend?" said the waiter.

"I'm fine." Dariusz swallowed. "I need some air." He shunted some of his last remaining credit from his inChip to the bar. The waiter's pad chimed. He glanced down at it, and when he looked up again, Dariusz was on his way out.

"Are you sure you're okay?" the waiter called after him.

Dariusz pulled up his collar, the sense of déjà vu overwhelming. He hit the glass door and was out onto the plaza and into the warm November rain. A bicyclist rang his bell angrily as Dariusz stepped in front of him.

The square was full of bikes, crisscrossing the pavement between its lawns. Advertising drones whisked overhead, shells hidden within their projections, soundtracks blaring.

"Apply today!" one shouted. "Skilled citizens needed. Freedom, prosperity, self-determination!" The accompanying holographs showed the men from the television in the bar, then shots of the dockyards where the Gateway fleet was being assembled.

The projector detected Dariusz's interest and swooped closer to him, dazzling him with light-woven models of spaceships in dock, gridded superstructures being extruded by dozens of insectile machines. It looked artificially slowed. The more

Dariusz watched, the more the construction resembled the feeding activity of a swarm of ants played backward, creating an animal in a slow frenzy of regurgitation.

The association made his skin crawl.

The advertisement's tailored pseudo-personality engaged Dariusz, its too-perfect face rippling as the rain passed through it. The rain intensified, and the pedestrians and cyclists hurried as they crossed the square. A few cars shushed through standing water along the plaza's edge, following their prescribed tracks. Dariusz stood stock still, as unconcerned by the rain as the machine.

Images of finished vessels – although their real counterparts were years away from completion – appeared in the air. The vessels resembled delicate mushrooms laid on their sides – thin stalks, five kilometres long, leading to a dome-shaped cap of ice – the ship's particle shielding. Beneath the cap were the rings of the hibernation decks, where thousands of men and women would spend the voyage asleep. Containers clustered all the way down the spine below the rings, ahead of the three space-to-surface shuttlecraft clamped onto it like remoras on a shark behind the boxes holding the starship's solar sails. Toward the stern, the secondary cap, much smaller than the first, shielding tanks holding the fuels necessary to initiate the antimatter reaction, and finally the drive units, twenty-eight of them, each as big as a tower block.

"Pan! Are you a man of skill? Do you crave a new start?" the face of light said. It smiled. There was a chirrup from Dariusz's inChip and an icon blink in his mind, informing him of authorised data access. The machine found what it sought. It logged his pending application and abruptly turned away from him, seeking someone else. Had he already been tested and found wanting?

Dariusz stood in the rain. The address for the Dąbie Sailing Club blinked in his mind's eye.

He would like to say he had nothing to lose, but he had: Lydia, and Daniel. They would be punished for his transgressions; not openly, that was not the way of the plutocracy, but they would be punished. Like he had been disbarred from the future because he had exercised the rights he supposedly enjoyed. He had fallen for society's propaganda. Nobody had rights, nobody but the 0.01 per cent. His father had hauled himself from the bottom by sheer effort, and Dariusz had tried hard all his life to climb the money ladder a little further. He did not complain as he did so, submitting his skills and considerable talent to the yokes of the Pointers. As he saw it, you could either get your head down and work hard, hoping for some scraps off the high tables of the rich, or you could complain and get dead. He'd always told himself that it wasn't a difficult choice to make.

And now he was heading back down, back into the sump of the starving and the hopeless, the teeming masses with nothing to do. That little bit of latitude the Pointers gave was an illusion. He should have taken his pills like a good boy.

Indecision rooted him, as rain ran into his collar. Should he go to Dąbie? He flipped the question around in his head. What had he to gain, what had he to lose?

Thunder rumbled. The weather became more extreme with every passing year. He thought of what he'd seen, those sights that woke him in the night, that made him fret: the crumbling megacities that could barely feed themselves, the crowds, the failed landscapes, the grinding poverty. Europeans thought they had it bad; they had no idea. He'd seen what few of them saw, and what had he done? He'd applied sticking plasters to fatal wounds, helped build fences for the rich to hide behind.

His own city was threadbare, its people worn out. There'd been talk of a population crash for a long time now. As he looked around the world he lived in, Darisuz could hear the clashing steel jaws of the Malthusian trap. The Pointers said the Market and mankind must expand together or fail. He had always suspected it might be simpler than that, a matter only of survival. Earth was all used up.

He made his way across the plaza, away from the former gate. He used some of his last little money to release a paybike from its stand. He turned left onto the Trasa Zamkowa, the wide road that ran to the bridge over the river Odra, undecided where he would go.

He waited for a gap in the flow of cyclists, and pushed off.

The city's heart fell away behind him. Szczecin wore its history lightly. Most of it was less than one hundred and ninety years old, and those parts that appeared older were not always so. It had been a fulcrum of nations for centuries. It was the battlefront of cultures, a stage set for dynastic ambition, a cruel ethnocentricity always beneath the surface, and had been levelled for it. Reconstructed Renaissance buildings stood side by side with Prussian-era apartment blocks, broad 19th-century boulevards led to communist-built parks. For a brief time of hope, this city had been the face of a brave new world. That dream had long died, and the new worlds of today were light years distant.

He went over the bridge, weaving his way through the flocks of bikes. The bridge was a 20th-century relic, constructed for automobiles. Of its eight original lanes, two car tracks remained for those few who could afford personal vehicles, and the rest had been set aside for cyclists and horse traffic. The bridge arced high over the Odra, then came down again in the city's port lands. It was overgrown and dangerous now, most of the docks overflowed with water even with the Swine Mouth barrage shut. On the far side of the river, the road had been raised up on a levee.

Polluted marsh stretched either side of him, the boundaries of the river blurring into the land. Dariusz passed through the landscape of decayed buildings and collapsed warehouses. Trees grew freely in the streets, vigorous away from the water, blanched and skeletal where they had been overwhelmed by it. The ancients had sited Szczecin well; the old city was unchallenged up on its hill. Down here was another matter.

Dariusz passed the turn for Nowa Metalowa, the road that would take him home to the woods and sandy hills of Podjuchy.

He headed southeast, toward Dąbie.

THE SHIPS

TWENTY-ONE SHIPS HAVE completed or are near to completing their secondary construction phase. Their decks are in place, their basic systems active and undergoing tests. A further thirteen keel-spines have been laid. Three of those nearest completion are side by side, tethered by high tension cables to the construction site hub. The number of installations has grown, the construction site rivalling the largest of the Lagrange manufactory clusters.

For the last fourteen days, the spider-machines have been weaving a lattice to the fore of each vessel. Before, the ships somewhat resembled artless candlesticks – blocky drive units at the tip of a long, bare scaffold. A kilometre from the drives come the cargo section and auxiliary craft sections, the clamps still empty. Next, a prickly array of comms gear behind the boxes housing the sails, then a gentle flaring, where the ships take on a measure of elegance. Round hibernation decks, segmented one from each other, fill out the top third of the vessel, growing in diameter until the prow, where they stop. Ugliness reasserts itself in a round plateau studded with boxes, catches and spikes.

The spider-machines work around this rough end, puffing out clouds of high tensile carbon wires, a framework for what will come next. When they are done, a hazy cap, shaped like a mushroom, blurs the stars. A smaller, second framework is just discernible forward of the antimatter flasks. Next comes the water; the ships are moved to a new berth for this procedure.

In a space thick with stolen comets, machines bearing heated tanks crawl along the lattice. Nozzles swivel, spray water in minute amounts, which freezes instantly. So they build, a half millimetre at a time, the great shielding caps of the spacecraft.

It takes months to lay down the water. Many methods were debated for their construction, as all aspects of the ship's construction were debated. A single, seamless block, reinforced by a carbon lattice, was the final decision.

When these three are ready, they move away, pulled by tugs. In their final form the long mushrooms have square roots and round shields, long, warted stems, flaring gills and wide, brimming caps, four hundred metres thick. Enough to snag the highest energy particle, and stop it from wounding crew and machine. Essential; the ships will travel fast.

The first completed are laden with dummy cargo, their hibernation pods filled with dummy passengers and dummy fluids. Each gathers three shuttles to it, which are real, as are their pilots; Sand among them, tasked with evacuating her ship's skeleton crew should the space trials go amiss. The engines were tested some time ago, but the sails must now be calibrated. The ship's tertiary drives emit excited ions to push them slowly to a point some seven thousand kilometres distant from the facility, where the sails are deployed with puffs of gas, circles of monomolecular super-fabrics unfurling against the black. They deploy as gracefully and unhurriedly as flower petals. Within a day the three mushroom-ships have sprouted wings, so thin as to be barely visible. They confuse the eye, refracting the ships' images.

Three clusters of boosting laser stations have been laid out along the ships' route; one outside the asteroid belt, the next past icy Neptune, the last at the very edge of the system, the most distant outpost of mankind. One station for every four ships, three lasers per station. There have been problems here: cost overruns, breakdowns, a major disaster, hushed up but fatal nonetheless for the men and women engulfed by it. Stocks drop, then recover. One Pointer family is reduced to penury. Unheard of, but these are unprecedented times.

The ships edge out past the belt, gathering the solar wind. Their acceleration is minimal, and Sand chafes under the long days aboard the empty, echoing vessel. She wanders the ship but is disturbed by the faceless mannequins in the hibernation pods and crew facilities. She is tense, as all the crew are tense.

Past the belt, the first laser array is activated, and their speed climbs as the ships' wings catch beams of focused light. Sand is put in mind of surfers waiting an age for a wave, then the heady rush of speed and power when it comes... but there is no exhilaration. A slight change in redshift, barely discernible; an uncomfortable push that interferes miserably with the ships' centrifuged illusion of gravity. Otherwise, nothing aboard the vessels alters. Sand is bored.

They coast to Neptune, a journey of many weeks, accelerating all the while. The timing of the second relay is tested, adding its power to the first, and then all the lasers are cut dead. The ships reel in their sails and flip laboriously end over end. Precious antimatter is annihilated in their main drive units to bring them to a halt, a deceleration measured in fortunes burned per second. The ships stop short of the edge of the orbit of Pluto. Sand looks back. The sun is a big star. She has never been this far out. Further on, armies of robotic drones patrol their passage through the Kuiper belt, clearing away the few objects that might pose a threat to the fleet. A kindness, here; the fleet will have to brave the Oort cloud alone.

Twice as far from the sun again as the outer belt is the frontier, the place where Sol's heliosheath tails to nothing, and interstellar space begins.

For the first time in her career as a spacer, Sand feels uneasy. She will not be returning, the next time she comes this way. Her comrades notice the change in her demeanour, but none comment upon it. They feel the same.

Under ponderous ion drive, the ships head back toward the light.

CHAPTER FOUR
The Dąbie Sailing Club

THE SIGN WAS a battered, rotting piece of wood. In a crazed mess of paint flakes, the corpses of words read 'Klub Zeglarski Dąbia' – The Dąbie Sailing Club.

Dariusz stood astride his bike, feet planted on the muddy track leading through the reeds to the lake.

The lakeside was silent. The rain had stopped and fog rose from the warm earth, clinging to the bulrushes and leaching the scene of colour. Dariusz was a soul lost on the shores of Elysium.

A tram rattled by on the levee behind him, a clatter of mechanical noise swallowed by the mist.

Dariusz was nervous. He was not a coward, although he believed himself to be. He was precisely the opposite: he feared a great deal, and it was a trait that he despised, so he would often take risks that others would not. His loathing of his fear imbued him with a reckless bravery.

It was this that placed his foot on the pedal of his bicycle and pushed him off, even as his misgivings beset him.

His bike squelched down the muddy track. Everything here was permanently waterlogged. The skeletal arms of drowned trees loomed abruptly out of the mist and disappeared as quickly, growing sparser as he drew closer to the lake.

He heard the boats before he saw them: the slap of water on hull, the jingle of metal fittings against mast and board. A copse of rod-straight lines describing precise, metronomic arcs suddenly resolved themselves, the masts of the boats rocking in time to the ripples of the Lesser Lake Dąbie.

A spur of the track led under a scaffold gateway in the yacht club's fence. He stopped, his foot sinking in the mud. Seven sailing boats of varying sizes, only one big enough to merit a cabin, were tied to two short piers among the reeds.

A shabby hut stood close to the head of the piers. No smoke came from its iron chimney, and the blinds over its windows were drawn.

Dariusz leaned his bike against the hut, and walked to the bank where the piers extended into the water.

"Hello?" he said. His misgivings prevented him shouting. "Hello?" he tried again.

"Pan Szczeciński?" A man appeared from the cabin of the largest boat. He was big as a bear, but his expression was warm. "You came, then?"

Dariusz was instantly on his guard. "Where is the man I spoke to in the bar?"

"Browning?" The man shrugged. "Who knows? None of us have ever met him. That is for the best, in this venture. I am Arkadiusz Żadernowski. Please" – he gestured to the boat – "if you would come aboard for your lesson. You may ask what you like and speak what you will as we sail; *Juliana* will not reveal your secrets." He reached down and tossed a bright orange life-jacket at Dariusz. "For your safety."

Arkadiusz offered his hand, but Dariusz declined to take it. He jumped from the pier and landed easily.

"You are comfortable on boats? You will make a good sailor."

"I have spent a great deal of time on boats while working, but know little of any of this..." He gestured helplessly to the profusion of lines and winches that cocooned the furled sail.

"Then I will teach you. Let us commence. As you have good balance, perhaps you would help me untie *Juliana*."

Together they untied the boat. Arkadiusz activated a noiseless electric engine, and guided *Juliana* out through the channel of clear water onto the Lesser Lake.

"We will head out into the main lake," he explained.

He had Dariusz help him to deploy the sail. There was only a slight wind blowing, but the canvas filled readily, and pushed them at a pleasing speed over the dark surface of the water. Arkadiusz killed the motor. He steered the boat and told Dariusz what to do, and the engineer was too cautious to question him. He relaxed into the task; he enjoyed physical work.

The land drew in slightly to either side at the narrows of the Lesser Lake, and then they were on the expanse of the Greater Lake. Only then did Arkadiusz stop his sailing instruction.

"We should be safe out here. Sorry for all the subterfuge, but you understand, I'm sure. Best keep your voice low and face turned down. If anyone is watching us there's still a risk they can grab our conversation via direct acoustics or have someone lip read us."

"Sure."

"I've been told to keep this brief. Please don't ask anything about our organisation; we work in cells, and I don't know anything to tell." Arkadiusz smiled, but there was little humour there. Anyone defying the Pointers could expect little mercy. "As Browning should have said, we can make sure that you and your son get onto the colony fleet. That mood drug thing? Forget about it. Gone. We will do this in exchange for a small service."

"That's what concerns me," said Dariusz.

"And so it should. I'll get right to the point, Pan Szczeciński. We are opposed to the promulgation of the current system. If we let this poisonous inequality out into the stars, then large portions of humanity will spend *centuries* working for a lot of undeserving pigs. The current crises have forced this on us, making us a hard, uncaring society mindlessly supporting the elite, but it doesn't have to stay that way. We are not opposed to the colony effort; we just want to level the field a little."

"How?" said Dariusz.

"Knowledge is power, my friend. At the heart of every one of the colony ships is a central computer – the Systems core, they call them. An organic, android unit. We're proposing a little – ah – reprogramming."

"You want me to interfere with the central units controlling the colony ships?"

"Not those – well, not entirely. It's the central data cores, the colonies' libraries, we're interested in; the sum of human knowledge in a bottle. A very useful thing, but controlled by the Pointers completely. We want to reengineer the Systems core to make this information free, let it out and about so anyone can access it; and we want to keep it that way. It's simple, really. All the colonists will be implanted with top of the range inChips. All that stops them interfacing freely with the cores is the Pointers. We want to introduce a virus that will disable their security protocols on your ship, then broadcast it to the rest. Call it an attitudinal adjustment for the colony brains."

"That's all?"

Arkadiusz huffed out his cheeks. "Well, no. Not quite. There'll also be another dataset encoded into the virus, one targeting the *Zheng He*, the wormhole ship. It would be better for us all if that wormhole is never opened. We'll be in for a hard time of it here, but it's for the best. I'm sure you're well aware, Pan Szczeciński, that we are approaching a point of ecological crisis, but I don't need to tell you that, do I? You're a geoengineer. If we can disrupt the colony effort, the Pointers'll have nothing to prop up their rule back here. Revolution, my friend. And if we're unsuccessful here, we hope you'll be able to export yours back to Earth, in time. The Pointers' rule won't survive in both places."

"Two acts of sabotage, then, one bigger than the other."

"Yes. I understand it is a large thing to ask of a man. Feel free to decline."

Dariusz's strength drained from him. "If I do, there's no way you'll leave me alive. My God."

Arkadiusz cleared his throat in embarrassment. "Do not invoke God, Pan. He can do little, and is in the pay of the elite. When the people have money, they have confidence; when they have no confidence, they hope; when they have no hope, they pray. This is why our time is one of religion. The Pointers control that too."

The boat continued its progress over the lake. The mist was dissipating.

"How do I deliver this virus?" said Dariusz.

"That's actually the least complicated part. You carry it inside you as a retrovirus. The big weakness of an organic system is that it's susceptible to infection. We'll set it up so that you get woken nice and long into the voyage. You get up, infect the computer with a drop of blood, then go back to sleep as if nothing happened. I know what you're thinking – they'll check – but we'll hide it well, and we'll try and fix it so they don't find out you did it. No point offering you a new life if they execute you when you get there. By the time they realise their security has been compromised, it'll be too late, especially once the Pointer's more, ah, stringent colony government protocols become common knowledge. So, you can have your revolutions on your new homes, and when it becomes clear that the wormhole will never open and there'll be no paradise for folks to flee to, we can live through hell and finally get ours. I think you get the better deal, personally."

Weak sunlight broke through the mist. They were heading back.

"You have until we get back to the marina to decide."

Ten minutes? Less? thought Dariusz. "What will you do with my body?"

"Nothing. You'll leave, you just won't get far. InChip malfunction leading to aneurysm. I am sorry, it has to be this way."

Dariusz fixed his eyes on the approaching headlands that nipped the neck of the Lesser Lake.

"I'll do it," he said eventually.

Arkadiusz grinned broadly. "That's fantastic," he said, relaxing visibly. Dariusz wondered how many other candidates they had for the role. Not that many, he thought.

"On one condition," he added. "I want my wife as well as my son to come with me."

Arkadiusz frowned. "We thought you would ask this question. In truth, I am not sure that can be done. Your son is no problem, a bright kid, stable, good physical scores, healthy genome. The wife? No, you know she's unstable, got a higher than fifteen on her basic psychs. We can fix a misdemeanour, but fake medical documents, especially when they'll be testing and retesting the training programme? No way."

"You knew I'd ask that, and you still asked me before you'd looked into it."

"I did not say that. We *are* looking into it, but we are running out of time. You must consider leaving her behind. For what it's worth, I'll make sure she's okay."

"No. Absolutely no way. No deal. Get in touch when you have a definitive answer. If you can't arrange passage for my family, you can pull the plug on me any time, can't you?"

Arkadiusz became emphatic. "I have to have a firm yes or no from you before you leave."

"Contact your superiors, then."

"I can't. Cells. One way communication."

"Then no deal."

"It's a break in protocol."

"Find someone else, then."

Arkadiusz was quiet for a moment. He spun the wheel one way then another, lining the prow of the *Juliana* up with the pier. "I'll see what I can do," he said eventually. "I make no promises."

They reached the marina in silence. They tied up *Juliana* with minimal words. Arkadiusz leaped over the side of the boat without looking back, unlocked the hut and went inside. The sound of muffled conversation came from within. He came back out a few minutes later, his mouth set.

"Okay," he said. "We can try. It'll be hard, but not impossible. You go whether or not we can manage it. I promise we will try our hardest. Do we have a deal?" he held out his hand.

Dariusz hesitated.

He thought of Daniel.

"We have a deal," he said, and clasped the other man's outstretched hand.

CHAPTER FIVE
Atlantic City

LEONID WALKED ALONG the New Jersey shore, cool winds tangling his hair. His nose ran, and he let it, snorting back the snot like a commoner. His tutors would be outraged. Fuck them, he thought. Fuck them all, and all their pointless etiquette. His hands were buried deep in the pockets of a coat that, should his mother see him wearing it, would have had her retreating to her room for a month. It was a coat of the kind real people wore, bought for durability, suitability, and cost. He had been pleased with the purchase when he'd made it. It was authentic. Now it pissed him off, clinging to his conscience as the fraud it was. He could buy a million coats like this, or the company that made them. For all he knew, he owned it already. There was nothing he could do to distance himself from the fact that he was a Pointer. He would never want for anything. That made his rage worse, and flavoured it with guilt – every person he passed on the street would sell their children to have what he had, what he hated.

He made his way slowly along the Pleasantville seawall, a broad, sloped revetment of earth and caged pebbles. Care had been taken to landscape it, but could not overcome the ugliness of its components. A herringbone walk of bricks covered the top. Out to his right were the Lakes and Absecon Bays, although they had ceased to be bays sometime in the last century. The salt marsh they once contained was deep under the water, the two bodies of water joined into one through all but the lowest tides. He supposed the old names stuck because of the human need for continuity, pretending like nothing ever changes, like his grandfather swapping Peters back to Petrovitch.

On the other side of the water were the Jersey Bars, the remnants of old Atlantic City. Windowless buildings stuck up from rubble, streaked with birdshit and rust. Lights twinkled in the scrofulous little settlements built on the larger islands. The wind carried the taint of refuse and sewage from them.

There were many people out on the revetment, despite the unpredictable weather, and for this reason Sunday night on the walk was his favourite time; crowds brought him anonymity. So often isolated in his rarefied existence, he was never left alone. He found a richer isolation in the crowds. Among the teeming poor, he was free.

He leaned on the sea-facing railings of the walk and closed his eyes. All up and down the bars, the bells of buoys rang, warning of the reefs of yesterday's streets. The bells merged with the waves and the babble of the crowds, and the clashing discord of music from the broadwalk's streetstalls and the tech of people aggressive enough not to employ acoustic dampers. They brashly let their music leak out into the world, a blend of come-ons and fuck-yous. The trick was telling them apart.

Leonid breathed in the scents of processed food and body odour, the chemical tang of the sea. He let his mind roar with it all, disengaging his inChip's functions so that his brain could wrestle with the raw, unprocessed data.

Leonid loved it, the chaos and sheer exuberance of the world beyond the fences of the rich. The hairs on his arms stood up.

The approach of the limousine quashed his spirits. He pretended not to see it, the blunt-nosed shark prowling through the masses. The crowd recoiled from it, recognising it for what it was. They had nothing to fear. It had only one prey.

Leonid pushed himself from the railings and walked faster than before, hunched low.

He could not hide, not in a crowd, nor in a desert, not anywhere. He was hunted, he'd been hunted all his life.

The car pulled level with him. A window opened.

"Get in," his father said.

Leonid did not look at him. He kept his eyes fixed ahead, taking in the pale evening sky, the lights, the people.

"I'm thinking, father."

"Get in, Leonid."

"No."

The car kept pace with him. The poor, the real people, got out of its way as it trundled along the walk.

"I have no idea why you come here to wallow in filth, when you have the world at your feet."

"I said, I'm thinking. I came here to think."

"Leonid, you are twenty-nine years old, but you behave like a boy. You have responsibilities. You are late for our meeting and you are embarrassing me. You are embarrassing our family. Get in."

Leonid rounded on his father suddenly, and the car came to a gentle stop. His father's driver was an expert. His presence was one of the many, many things he could not stand about his father. Only Pointers had the money to pay for a human driver.

"Why can't you leave me be for half an hour, dad? I'm just taking some air."

His father stared at him dolefully. He was in his early hundreds, but looked sixty years younger; the ageless rich.

"You're late for the meeting. Get in now. I will not ask again."

A door at the front of the car opened and a man the size of a small hill got out.

"Good evening, Mr Leonid, sir," said the man. He had the hint of an apology in his smile. He folded arms the thickness of Leonid's waist.

"Evening, Sullivan," said Leonid.

Leonid considered fleeing into the crowd. There was nowhere to hide – his inChip gave out his location constantly, the one function he could not turn off – but the thought of flight for the sake of it...

He could not. Leonid was terrified of his father.

The limousine's middle door slid open.

Leonid got in.

LEONID SAT WITH his father, uncomfortable in stuffy jeans and shirt in a comfortable briefing room at the company headquarters in the Manhattan AP. Soft lights, expensive drinks, furnishings worth more than human lives. A company scientist tried his damnedest not to look out of place as he delivered his lecture.

"Acceleration at that magnitude exerts an unforgivable amount of stress on the human body. For both acceleration and deceleration, a human body needs to be cushioned against the effect, and if you're under for that, you might as well be asleep for the entire journey. It's far more cost effective in terms of resources to keep all expedition members asleep for the whole of the voyage, it's easier to shield them from cosmic particles, they eat less, and they won't go insane. At relativistic speeds you're still looking at seventeen to twenty-one years subjective time to get to the Du Bois cluster, and that's a significant chunk off anybody's life. Of course, there is an additional cost in terms of the doubling up of certain members, tripling in the case of key personnel, but the defrayments there are far outmatched by the savings in having them sleep the whole way. The mass of the additional expedition members is less than the mass of supplies – or the means of generating supplies – for an animate crew. And mass, in this situation, is everything." The scientist gave a nervous smile. He held a baton that contained his devices for presentation and explication. He played with it constantly, shifting his grip on it, passing it from hand to hand. He was as discomfited as Leonid. Ilya had that effect on everyone.

Ilya nodded approvingly, and the scientist inclined his head gratefully. Ilya had a solidity to him, a charisma that made him appear more real than everyone else in the room. He was used to being obeyed, and people obeyed him unquestioningly. They grovelled for his approval. Leonid was a shade in his presence, an inferior copy. The old man raised his eyebrows, urging Leonid to actively engage in the briefing.

"Why the redundancy?" asked Leonid. "Why the extra people?"

Ilya sneered. "Excuse me, Doctor Kernow," he said to the scientist. He turned on his son. "All the best schools I have sent you to. And why?"

"Why don't you tell me?" said Leonid testily. "I doubt it was for my benefit."

"Then whose benefit was it for?" said his father levelly. "Three generations, my son – that is how long, to a historical average, that a family's fortune will last. Five, if they are lucky to be blessed with prudent sons and daughters. Our fortune has lasted six generations. Your schooling is intended to ensure our fortune survives for another six generations, and if you are clever, which I pray you are, you will give your children the same treatment I have given you; not for my sake, not for your sake, but for the sake of our *family*." Ilya leaned forward, jabbing at Leonid with a thick finger. He pronounced 'family' with great emphasis, turning it halfway to a growl. "There is no other responsibility than this. Do you understand me?" At first glance Ilya looked fat, but he was not. Squat and powerfully muscled, he was in the prime of his life despite his great age, a silverback of a man.

Kernow looked from one to the other, face pale and fixed. Leonid caught the look of fear in his eyes and let the matter drop. He did not care if he argued with his father, but it could go badly for their servants to witness it.

"Yes. Sorry, father."

"Might I answer your question?" Kernow was addressing Leonid, but looking to his father. The old man gave a curt nod.

A holograph appeared in the air, a detailed schematic of a hibernation pod. Kernow gestured to it with his baton. "This is the Mark IV hibernation system. We've run extensive tests on it, but there is still, unfortunately, a failure rate of eight per cent."

"Failure rate?" said Leonid.

Kernow smiled sadly. "The occupants don't wake up."

"Natural wastage, a consequence of any venture," said Ilya casually. "Easily got around. This, my boy, is why we include additional expedition members. The deployment of extra resources is necessary when taking a risk. Is that not right, Doctor Kernow?"

"Indeed it is, sir. I am sure we will, given time, bring the risks down, but a failure rate of eight per cent has been judged acceptable for this first effort."

"Leonid, do you have any other questions for the doctor?"

"Thank you, doctor. Most illuminating," he said limply.

"Now you remember your manners," grumbled his father.

Doctor Kernow bobbed his head and left the father and son alone. Ilya pushed himself up out of his chair with a sigh. It was a weary noise, ripe with disappointment.

"You mean to send me," said Leonid.

Ilya went to the room's drinks cabinet and selected himself an 18-year-old Scotch. He held the bottle up toward Leonid, who shook his head. Ilya got two glasses out anyway. "I would have thought that obvious, Leonid. You have been included in this process since near the start. Only you have sat in every key meeting with me, although you disdain to show an interest. I did not think it necessary to spell it out to you. Was I wrong?"

"You were going to formally tell me at some point; announce it."

Ilya finished pouring his drink, and recorked the bottle carefully.

"I did not think it necessary," he repeated. He was holding his annoyance at bay. This was always the way their conversations began. Ilya tried to teach him something that he regarded as of great importance, Leonid's anger made him unreceptive. They progressed from there to fighting. Tonight was different. The old man looked up from under his brows. He wasn't pleading with his son, exactly – the likes of Ilya Petrovich did not plead – but there was the promise of conciliation. Leonid debated whether or not to take his father up on it.

"Leonid, Leonid, Leonid, my son." He walked back to the nest of sofas and handed Leonid the drink he did not want, as he had handed him so many other things he did not want. "Times are changing. You are growing. You are young by the standards of this age. When I was a boy, you would have been a man already. It is time to take the responsibilities of a man."

"What are the responsibilities of a man? How to spend your money, father?"

Ilya laughed a little at that, much to his son's surprise. "No, I have plenty of other sons who can do that perfectly well for me. I absolve you of that duty."

Leonid's eyebrows rose. He took a sip of the drink, for want of something to say. It was warm and mellow, redolent of peat and heather.

His father held up his glass and nodded appreciatively at it. "It is good, this, yes? One of the best, of this age at least. A lot of time and expertise goes into making a drink such as this."

He sucked a residue of it from his top lip and nodded. "This is a drink of the land that made it. It is poison, of course, but delightful poison." He sat back, never taking his eyes from his son's face. "If we could be savoured, what would our chemical signature tell us, Leonid? We are of no land. Are we Russian? No. Our names are a nonsense, a product of a period when it was fashionable for Americans to reclaim their ancestry. From the moment our forebears set foot on these shores until a century back, we were simply Peters. Suddenly, it was not enough for citizens of this nation to say they were Irish or Italian. They tried to become so, laying claim to something their ancestors had tried so hard to shed. Ironic, don't you think?"

Ilya's eyes had a strange light to them. Leonid found it hard to breathe.

"We are not American, either; not really. We Pointers are citizens of the world, countrymen of no man. We rich are stateless, refugees adrift on rafts of money."

Leonid struggled to talk. He managed a modicum of defiance. "I am sure the world's many real refugees would appreciate that sentiment."

His father tutted. "Leonid, my boy, allow me a little drama. No one would deny me a small metaphor now. This is important."

Ilya sat forward again, cradling his glass in his massive hands. It was unusual to see him move so much; ordinarily he was an implacable colossus, as much of stone as flesh. Leonid realised that for once, just for once, his father was uncomfortable about something.

"We rich, we are not apart from the world, no matter how hard some of our kind try to make it appear so. It has always been a source of great sorrow to me, Leonid, that you and I do not see eye to eye. I, like you, think that our wealth comes with a great deal of responsibility, that we cannot leave the poor to wallow in poverty, that –"

A flush of anger coloured Leonid's cheeks. "You know that is not what I feel. We have no *right* to our wealth –"

"Please!" His father held up his muscular hand. "Let me finish. You think it different, I understand that. One day, you will not. I know you disagree with me, but tonight I do

91

not wish to argue. May we acknowledge that and continue without argument?"

Leonid took another drink. He gulped too much and it burned his throat. His father took his silence for assent.

"Thank you. We have every right to be rich, Leonid, because our ancestors fought for it; they nurtured their wealth, they grew it. But that does not mean we have the right to squander it, or hoard it, or abuse the privilege it grants us." He pursed his lips. He looked tired. "If I had been less adamant on pressing home this point while you were a boy, then perhaps we would not so often reach this impasse. If so, your despair at your heritage is my error. Being rich is a privilege, Leonid. It brings with it responsibility to those around us."

"Noblesse oblige?" said Leonid drily.

Ilya slapped the arm of his sofa with his palm and pointed. "Yes, yes. You goad me with the term, but yes, if that makes you happy. That is exactly what it is. We have the responsibility to use our wealth wisely, and if we do, then we have every right to remain rich. Your rejection of wealth, this is where you are wrong, son. The natural order of human affairs is a hierarchy, as has been proven time and again. Even in the smallest unit of human civilisation, a hierarchy prevails. Set up a society without hierarchy? Hierarchy asserts itself. Of course, decisions, wealth, resources, all might be held collectively, but there are always, always" – he wagged his finger – "those whose opinion carries more weight, those whose votes break ties. Make the society more complex, and then the hierarchy becomes accordingly complex. Men were made to be ruled, they cry out for it. We are fortunate to be rich, fortunate to have the right to be rich, but we are rulers if we like it or not. It is the worst kind of dishonour not to live up to one's responsibilities."

"Very well, father, so we do not argue tonight. Tell me, what are these responsibilities in relation to the Gateway project? You would have me go and plant the flag of the Pointers on some virgin world? Really, father, I thought –"

His father cut him dead. "I did not say that, did I, Leonid? What concerns me is the survival of our family. This idea of supplying our world with goods and elevating everyone to luxury is a nonsense; even should the *Zheng He* open its ridiculous, improbable star gate and the Market throw wide its arms to encompass all the heavens, I do not believe it will work."

Leonid smiled unpleasantly. His father had always had a penchant for plodding theatrics.

"Our responsibilities are this: we must guide mankind out of the Solar System, before it is too late. People look up to us. We have to do it. If the Pointers will not do it, who will?" said Ilya.

Ironically, it was Leonid who hated the word *Pointer*, the word Ilya used freely and without embarrassment. It had been given to them by the lower orders, it intentionally made them sound like dogs. The Pointers had claimed it as their own, as they had claimed everything else on the planet for themselves.

"I have chosen you to go to represent our family. You, and Yuri. He is older than you, but he will be left in no doubt that it is you who are in charge."

"Should I not succumb to the eight per cent peril," said Leonid.

Ilya acknowledged this with another mild shrug. "Redundancy needs to be built into the system."

"So I am to be your bold ambassador."

"You are to be the governor of the first extra-solar outpost of our family. It is a great role, the breaking of new territory, one not filled by any man for four generations. This is not some dusty Martian station, but a whole new galaxy of possibility. You should be proud! I am."

"And me, father? What is my risk?"

"It is eight per cent. You run the same risk as those you will lead. I would have thought that you, of all people, would have appreciated that. In this, the Pointer and the rest stand equal. It can be no other way."

Leonid felt that this was as it should be, but that his father had acknowledged it so freely poisoned his own conviction.

"You will be accompanied by loyal servants of our house."

The word 'house' made Leonid's skin crawl.

"I have put together a team of experts, but they will all defer to you," his father continued. "Scientists of various types, their leader will report to you, and I expect you to be sensible and not interfere with their work overly much. Engineers, agricultural specialists, and some military. No!" The hand went up again. "I will not hear any objection. You will be a long way from home. Our next round of discussions will include introductions to your key advisors. They will be your wisdom, Leonid. You must listen to them. A king is only as good as his advisors." Ilya drained his glass. "I have other matters to attend to. You must excuse me." He stood, and a servant appeared with his overcoat.

"Father, I do not want to be a king, not of any kind."

His father favoured him with a weary smile. For a moment his true age shone through his expensive health treatments and clothing.

"Do you not understand anything I have tried to tell you? Your reluctance is why I am sending you. I will not set up a tyrant."

You accept and promulgate the tyranny of money, thought Leonid.

"Good bye, Leonid."

His father left the room. Leonid sat where he was, waving away the servant that came to ask if he required anything. On impulse, he stalked over to the window, and stared down at the pavement and the limousine on the road, and the canal beyond it.

The chauffeur snapped to attention, and opened the rear door.

Perhaps his father was setting him free. Or it might simply have been that he was disposable; there were other heirs to the Petrovitch fortune more like-minded to Ilya. He was his father's youngest son, after all.

As he watched his father walk out from the front of the building, stiff with age yet still as unstoppable as the march of time, he thought both were probably true.

CHAPTER SIX
Yuri

YURI STOOD UPON the balcony and howled into the warm gale. Rain splashed into his Martini. Far below his feet, waves crashed into the roots of the tower. Light, music and laughter were at his back, the raging forces of nature in his face, and Yuri felt alive.

Yuri was a creature of the night, of parties that ceased two dawns after their beginning, of ladies whose imperfections were smoothed away by clever lighting, of flashing lights and lurid holos. The day held few charms for him; sunlight shone hard on a hard world. He could not bear to look at it.

Yuri had all the benefits of his brothers. Antenatal genetic tweaking made him superior to other men. Not a creature, not a freak or an Alt; he was a Petrovitch through and through, his genes his father's and his mother's, but they were the best his father and his mother had to offer. His mind was quick, his body perfect, his senses sharp. He would live two hundred years or more.

But Yuri drank. His father sent him to rehabilitation centres and to hospitals of the mind, the places where the rich adjusted themselves to better enjoy being rich. Yuri escaped. His father infested him with medical technology to scrub his blood. Yuri had them driven from his system by electromagnetic pulse. His father fed him drugs to counteract the narcotics Yuri took. Yuri found stronger drugs. Yuri gambled, and womanised, and shouted venom at his father while consuming his wealth.

If Yuri was not paralysed by fear of what others might think of him, he would have wept. But Yuri wanted to be strong. Yuri wanted to be admired.

Yuri wanted to be loved.

He vented his sorrow into the storm, hiding it in wild laughter. Excess was his armour, profligacy his weapon.

"Sir."

Yuri ignored his minder. He ignored most of what his father told him, and of what those his father sent to watch over him said.

"Sir!"

Corrigan, the man's name was. An uncouth British thug, tasked with harrying him at every turn. Yuri pretended not to remember his name. Yuri was not granted an Alt as a guard, for fear of what his authority over it might engender.

"Sir, I must insist you come inside. You'll be blown off the balcony. Come inside!"

Yuri felt the wind. He leaned into it. The noise of the crashing waves grew as his head cleared the balcony. Let it take him. Let it throw him away as he had been thrown away by his family. Yuri the dissolute. Yuri the failure.

A hand. Pressure on his bicep. Yuri whipped round, outraged, his self-pity flipping instantaneously to anger.

"You are coming inside now, whether you like it or not," said Corrigan. His clothes ran with moisture, wicking the rain away, but his hair was wet.

"Release me!"

"No."

The hand pulled at him, dragging him away from the thrilling precipice.

"Get off me now! I will have your head for this."

"No you won't." Corrigan's grip strengthened. His hand was so huge it encircled Yuri's arm entirely. Yuri, his perfect body wasted by drugs and inattention to eating, was rock-star skinny. "Listen to me, you little prick; your dad has told me to do whatever I must to keep you safe, and I will. I don't give a fuck what you threaten me with or what you say. I've got carte blanche from daddy, and I will kick your feeble little arse through those doors right in front of your friends if you don't get in out of this bloody storm, alright?"

"You wouldn't dare!" hissed Yuri.

"Try me."

Corrigan's grip tightened, and Yuri stifled a whimper.

"That hurts."

"Get inside."

Corrigan half-guided, half-dragged the faux-Russian to the open doors. Once inside, they slid shut, two quarter spheres of glass that joined into a seamless hemisphere covering half the balcony. Rain drummed against the glass.

Yuri's costume was soaked, his feathers bedraggled, his makeup ran. He sagged in Corrigan's grip and let out a shrill laugh. Corrigan let go of him.

"You're a fucking mess," the thug said disdainfully. "Go enjoy your party. Not too much, mind; I'll be watching."

Yuri rubbed at his arm as Corrigan strode off into the crowd, rudely pushing Yuri's friends out of the way. Servants hurried over to him with towels and fresh paint. They fussed over him, soothing him, clucking over his wounded pride.

He hated them all. Curiously, he thought, he did not hate Corrigan.

"DO YOU THINK the new order will be strange? Food and luxury for everyone, they say." Oswald stared into his drink. "Makes one feel rather less special, don't you think?"

"Ozzie, Ozzie, Ozzie." Yuri draped a waif-thin arm over his friend's shoulder. "The plebs aren't coming!"

"I rather thought they were. I rather thought that was the whole point," said Oswald. He was prim, fat, someone who could have come from anywhere. Like many of the Pointers, he was white. A citizen of the world. A citizen of nowhere.

"Then you *rather* better do some thinking, eh?" Yuri mocked. "A wormhole!"

"But it's what they say on the holo. It's what my tutors say." Mika, a timid little mouse of a girl.

"Oh, Mika," said Yuri. He caught her chin in his hand and lifted it up. "You are so beautiful, and so very fuckable, and so very stupid." Her smile vanished, and she pushed at him. He squeezed tight before he let go.

"Who will pay for its upkeep? Who will pay for the ships to take people to this wormhole, and for the ships to take them from the other end to wherever it is they'll end up? How much do you think a ticket will cost, dear Mika? A year's wages?

97

Ten years? A lifetime? No, there is no more opportunity in the stars than there is here on Earth. The poor might slave their lives away to buy a ticket, to find nothing for them to do there but slave some more. Build a world with robots, not with men. There are too many people here. Why let them infest the stars? Let the unwashed masses have the dying Earth. The stars belong to the rich." Yuri gave a dazzling smile. "As is only right." There was a bitter, underlying irony to what he said, that he hid from his friends. He wanted to provoke them into disagreeing – it was expected that Pointers make some pretence at caring – but none of them did. Yuri grew angrier.

"The Earth is not dying," said Mika quietly. "It's a leftist lie."

"They've been saying so for years," agreed Hesperon, a tall youth whose athletic prowess was only outdone by his cruelty. "It's nonsense."

"The world ends incrementally," said Yuri. He put his other arm around Hesperon's shoulders and hung between his friends. "What is normal for us grows but slightly worse in our lifetime, and that slight worsening is normal for the next generation, who know nothing else. By little steps we walk the long road to Armageddon." Through a gap in the crowd, he could see the rain streaming down the balcony door. In his womb of luxury, the sea's wrath was distant. How long would it remain so? His friends did not notice the shift in his focus. He hung from them, their costumes' accessories clamouring for his attention. All he saw was the storm. "There are neither enough circuses nor bread to keep the masses happy in the face of that hard little reality, so we feed them hope instead."

"You're a cheery bastard, Yuri," said Oswald. "I need another drink."

Yuri laughed. His attention left the tempest, and returned to the circle of glitter and perfect bodies. He removed his arms from his friends and clapped his thin hands together. "I try my best. Now, excuse me, I must mingle." He swirled his cloak of feathers and disappeared into the crowd.

The party was in full swing. The third of the bands had begun to play. Holographic art writhed in the air in time to the music. The finest delicacies in food and intoxicants made their way around on platinum trays borne by naked girls. The uppers and lovebombs were taking effect, and many of Yuri's friends were naked, or playing kink games on the dungeon stage for all to see. Playmates and bodies-for-hire stalked among them. There were few parties as notorious as Yuri's. He owned the Crystal Tower. He owned the people that serviced his companions. He owned the companies that provisioned them. Yuri was surrounded by the cream of the world's jaded youth, all Pointers, all fabulously wealthy, all fawning over him to ensure they'd make the next guest list. They had everything they could ever possibly want, and it was not enough. Yuri gave them distraction from their lack of fulfilment. He was among his own kind. They loved him; they loved him for his parties, but even bought love counted.

The event should have been perfect. But this was to be his penultimate extravaganza. He'd make the announcement later, following it with details of his final frolic, one that would shock the world with its debauch. That made him happy, on a certain level. Underneath his purchased joy, he despaired.

His father was sending him away.

The band played on.

THE SHIPS

In the sole luxurious room of the staging posts, Yuri watches shuttles ply back and forth to the fleet and awaits his turn. Around him are his brother and his servants. He feels empty inside. Is this how Anderson feels?

Sand, flying a crew transfer pod out to the *Mickiewicz*, feels the fear of departure keenly. She is wondering: why did I sign up for this?

Anderson does not care.

Dariusz is in the crew transfer module held by Sand's shuttle, strapped in. The transfer module is cramped. He is surrounded by people, all of whom look the same – grey jumpsuits, shaved heads, taut faces. They are elbow to elbow. It is uncomfortable. There is an unpleasant tension to the air, like animals trapped too close together. The smell of human bodies, even washed and deodorised, is somehow offensive.

Some of the faces he knows, some of them have trained alongside him in the long, long programme. None of them he would call friends. Dariusz developed a reputation for being aloof, and he was. He could not forget the thing that nestled in his blood. He feels it now, although there is nothing to feel: a presence inside him, filling him up with a purpose that is not his own. He could not and cannot stop thinking of what he has been asked to do. More pertinently, what he has *agreed* to do.

Seven years. It has been seven years since Dariusz agreed to Browning's plan in the bar. They never met. An injection from a man on a dark night, then he heard nothing from the movement again. For all he knows, it is a joke, of a particularly elaborate kind. He turns the facts over in his mind like they are pebbles, smooth and cold to the touch. He was accepted into the programme. He remained in the programme, as his wife was rejected, and rejected again. The movement must be real. He has decided that many times. Doubtless he will do so again.

He remembers police, grim-faced, standing framed in the porch as rain hammered from their caps and capes. He knew why they had come before they opened their mouths. He did not think to ask them in out of the rain. He stood numbly, staring at the square carp pond behind them in the garden.

Lydia was overjoyed that he and Daniel were to go, even though she was not. He should have seen that as a sign.

They had found her in the Jezioro Szmaragdowe, the emerald lake, they said. The name was poetic, the place was not; an old gravel pit whose depth was its only notable characteristic. She had been dead for a few hours, they said.

Lydia was pleased he had found a way out for their son. His eyes fixed on the corner of the pond in the garden. They kept the carp they would eat on Christmas Eve in there. Not any more. He thought, incongruously, of sawing the fishes' heads off with a knife. The quickest way to kill them. It seemed barbaric. The policeman's gun took up the lower part of his vision, covered over by his transparent plastic cape.

Did he know why she did it? Did he have any ideas? The policeman assures Dariusz he was not under any suspicion.

No, he says. Yes, he says. We are leaving, my son and I, she had to stay behind. Too unstable. He involuntarily casts his eyes skyward. One of the policemen follows his gaze. Dariusz has never felt so blank. He is a skin stretched on a frame of bones, scraped of flesh and feeling.

Unstable? The older policeman says it in a way that suggests he knows it already.

You will have to come with us, to identify the body, says the younger.

And to answer a few questions, says the other. You are not under any suspicion at this time, he repeats.

Dariusz feels guilt. He knew this would happen. Arkadiusz said they would try, but he knew it would not be enough. He rebuked himself, feeling part of him recoiling from his mind. To save a son, lose a wife. Cold. He knew it would happen. He cannot deny it.

Danieł.

Dariusz goes with them. What is he going to tell Danieł?

On the shuttle, years later, his eyes swell again from his loss. He is not alone. Many people are crying. Conversation is subdued. A few of the colonists are excited, most are not. There are no windows in the crew transfer pods. One hundred people sit ignorant of their place in the cosmos. The trip over to the *ESS Adam Mickiewicz*, so short in principle, drags on.

A clang of metal on metal announces their arrival.

After an interminable time, the doors hiss open, and Dariusz steps onto the deck of the *Mickiewicz*. The craft is utilitarian, but glorious in its boldness. He feels sick at what he is to do.

They are sent off to their decks in groups. Each deck is filled piecemeal, they are too cramped to take all their passengers at once. Dariusz does not see his deckmates as he is put under. Like a fish, he thinks, dying alone in an alien environment. It is the last thing he thinks before, temporarily, death overtakes him.

457236803 805 857303 8008 692 845 825
654 5972940 882 65 1002592 834 37 4368 304
445 683 931 80 684 897 947 8620 00 124 803599
945 862 9762820 895 847562 6324 881 805 803 778
882 846 822 82 845 780
835 825 725 7603 72 793
7845 7321 782 785 782 82 88 7865 78 1 7821
799 7305 708 796 7885 7879
7321 7447 853 740 759 716
759 7623 784 851 732 7 70
783 734 788 720 7243 788 7349 7607 58 740 7836 733 7324 9876666 8304
79717 6142 4846 52 6632
6000 66 8 6800 874 8865 875 6431 6734 068
653 852 64 8 6023 6008 68 6830 60
83 6840 60 806 7 803 82 827
658 656 562 6680 847 8200 602 6685
624 6654
883 6000
34 6988
321 5720
854 855
833

CHAPTER SEVEN
Sabotage

REALITY STARTED WITH a chime.

Dariusz came awake precipitously and painfully. His lungs were full of chill. He opened his mouth in panic. He gaped until he coughed, a rush of cold liquid spilling down his chest. He coughed again, his stomach muscles wrenching. He was pinned in place and could not bend forward, could not clear his airways easily or comfortably. He panicked, soundlessly, until he managed to inhale properly, frozen air rushed into his lungs, and when he breathed out his panic came with it. He struggled against the restraints as he screamed. Pain stabbed his arms and legs. He had been buried alive, trapped in the cold Earth to die a second time.

"Hibernation sequence emergency termination underway," said a dispassionate machine voice. "Stages one through three complete. Stand by for ejection. Emergency decompression in five, four, three…"

Memory rushed back. Not dead. Aboard the *Mickiewicz*.

"No!" croaked Dariusz. "C-c-countermand that. Continue with standard waking cycle."

"State identification."

"Szczeciński, 501-36, geoengineer first rank."

Dariusz's inChip sounded its note in his mind, telling him that the machine had accessed his personal records, checking his authority.

"Emergency decompression halted. Proceeding with standard waking programme. Remain still."

Dariusz shivered. He was freezing. Thick, icy pseudo-amniotic fluids filled the sarcophagus to his waist. A drain gurgled hungrily by his feet, and the level dropped quickly. Soft blue illuminated the interior. A few centimetres from his face the square window showed the dark outside. Another stab of pain in his arm as needles withdrew.

"Resanguination complete. Stabilisation under way. Remain still."

The hibernator hummed and hissed around him as it adjusted his body chemistry. He shivered violently.

"Biochemical cycle complete. Remain still."

The sarcophagus lid opened to the report of a klaxon. Yellow light came and went in the window as the beacon flashed on top, granting brief, jaundiced glimpses of the corridor. There was a hiss as the pressure equalised. The sharp smell of refrigerant gases diminished, replaced by stagnant air.

The lid opened, spilling light and Dariusz Szczeciński out into the corridor.

He gasped as his hands hit the deck. It was thick with frost. He stood, wobbly as a faun.

"Lights!" he said. A spasm of coughing wracked him. Gratefully he bent double, and spat up gobbets of fluid.

Reactive panels in the ceiling glowed.

Dariusz shook. The metal floor burned his skin.

"You are in shock. You must remain here to await the arrival of emergency drones," said the voice.

Dariusz ignored the voice. The hibernation deck computers were electronic, not organic, and could only sustain low-level personality facsimiles. They were ill-equipped to adjust themselves to novel circumstances where a simple solution already existed, in this case summoning the medical drones. That simple solution had been deactivated. No team of drones would be coming to his aid. The computer would realise, eventually, and call for aid from elsewhere, but he should be done by then. He was fortunate only machines looked over the sleeping expedition. If Browning's plan had worked, he should be free to move around – if he did not succumb to hypothermia. Shivers marched convulsively over his skin.

The deck, being circular, sloped upward in either direction. The ship spun as it sailed onwards, centrifugal forces granting the deck an apparent gravity of a quarter g – here, at least. As he got closer to the ice shield cap, the decks would increase in size, their 'floors' falling further away from the ship's axis, so the feeling of gravity would increase. 'Down' was away from the axis – his feet were pointing out into deep space, his head towards the ship's spine. The shield cap was two kilometres to the left of him, the drive and secondary cap some three kilometres to the right. Sarcophagi lined both sides of the corridor.

Using the wall to steady himself, he walked slowly up the curved floor to a locker set between two hibernation units. The names of their occupants were displayed on panels above each sarcophagus in blue, their vital signs dormant. The interiors were dark. Dariusz's face reflected in the plastic windows, obscuring the sleepers. He passed one whose status panel had turned to red – a hibernation failure – and was glad he could not see inside.

Dariusz's fingers were clumsy with the cold and years of disuse. He keyed open the locker on the third attempt.

Inside the locker were jumpsuits of smartcloth, and shrink-wrapped packs of a dozen litre-bottles each. The bottles held post-hibernation recovery fluids, a cocktail of minerals, tailored vitamins and proteins. He pulled the suit out, dragging bottles onto the floor with it. He looked at them dumbly for a second, forgetting what he was doing, where he was; his limbs were weak and unnervingly elastic. More shivers. He was going to die if he did not hurry. With hands that refused to bend, he wrestled his unwilling body into the suit. It took an age. When he had himself in the garment, it zipped itself up. He gulped down two bottles of the drink as the jumpsuit adjusted to his body, forming shoes around his feet and altering its fit. They were flimsy-thin, but warm, warmer once the heating unit activated. The drink tasted vile, salty and sweet, with an unpleasantly synthetic strawberry flavour. He vomited twice. He had been told that this might happen. He had been told a lot about the after-effects of hibernation, but being told never matches experience. This was akin to a combination of severe flu and the worst vodka hangover he had ever had. He hoped the signs of his early waking would be lost in the general chaos of the scheduled revivification, or he'd be dead.

He drank some more.

He sat panting from the effort. The simple movements exhausted him. After a time he felt a little better. His inChip said ten minutes. It seemed longer.

He walked around the circular deck until he reached the orange door leading into the access corridor that ran the length of the ship. There were two of these, on opposite sides. It did not matter which Dariusz took. The door bore the number '14A,' and a coating of frost as fine as fur. He shivered violently once as he keyed open the door, and then the chill fled his limbs.

The door opened silently into the accessway, a tube five metres across, its bottom floored with textured carbon panels. Another orange door, leading into the other half-segment of his hibernation deck, stood opposite him.

Pipes ran along the ceiling of the corridor. Along its length, every so often, were lockers and panels. His task would be easier, he thought, if he could open one of those to deliver his cargo. Every twenty metres, the corridor was framed to either side by paired, numbered doors, leading onto other decks.

To Dariusz, the corridor appeared to slope downwards, as it followed the outside of the vessel's widening bulk. Down at the end, directly behind the massive ice cap, was the Systems core and the nutrient feed he must access. Frost glinted off every surface. The air was sharp. His breath plumed on the way out and caught uncomfortably on the way in. His hands tingled as feeling returned. He was grateful of the smartsuit's facilities.

He walked on shaky legs, gulped from the nutrient drink. He had two thousand metres to go; it might as well be two thousand kilometres.

He passed along the corridor, slowly at first, then with increasing speed as he regained something of his strength. He supposed he could thank the drinks for that. His heart ran fast, a combination of waking from hibernation and nerves at what he was about to do. He did not trust his body: hibernation was dangerous, and an emergency awakening made it more so. Every unaccustomed twitch or twinge in his organs made him stop and bring up the medical data from his implant.

He broke his journey at deck 46, Danieł's deck. Families were kept apart in case of major deck system failure. Parents are afflicted with fears only other parents can understand; out here in deep space, Dariusz's fears were redoubled.

He went into the B half of the deck and called for the lights. Thirty-two decks nearer the cap than his own, it was six times the size, with three concentric levels. He called for the lights, and began to search. The names of those within stared at him in cold blue, a few an unfortunate red.

Eight per cent. Eight per cent. Eight per cent. The figure went around and around his mind, spinning like the ship and generating its own frightening gravities. He counted down the numbers, seeking the pod that held his son.

He found it. The panel above the sarcophagus glowed blue.

Dariusz let out a sigh of relief and pressed his face against the transparent panel. It numbed his face. "My son, my son," he whispered. Danieł was safe.

He spent a time peering into the viewport, searching for a face, but as before he saw nothing but the grey of unlit amniotics. He kissed the panel, then left. There was no guarantee he would see his son again, but for now, at least, he lived.

At the prow of the ship, the decks became very large. The last deck was over two kilometres in diameter, its outer corridor close to six and half kilometres long.

The entryways to the last five decks were sealed with large double doors, big enough to admit maintenance and loading vehicles. Whereas the lesser decks seemed to be pierced by the access corridor, with the last five it was the other way round, the access corridor bulging high as the deck passed through it. The illusion of gravity here, further from the rotation's axis, was stronger, but still weak.

Dariusz made it to end of the corridor and opened the leftmost door of the primary deck. Inside the entrance was a rack, containing a dozen white bicycles. He took one and headed for the second radial shaft, one of four lifts that climbed to the inner ring. He pedalled like an old man, his joints aching. It was a relief from walking. The action was soothing, and his mind wandered back to the time he chose not to turn for home, and instead rode to the Dąbie Sailing Club.

His thoughts lost in the whisper of the tyres, he did not hear the security drone until it was upon him.

Dariusz glanced over his shoulder. Flashes from the drone's warning lights bounced off the corridor walls, picking out details in red and yellow.

He pedalled faster, flicking through the gears of the bike. He wobbled, then picked up speed, his stiff legs aching. He glanced back repeatedly. He still could not see the drone directly. The drone let out two whoops.

"Warning. Warning. Unauthorised access. Halt. I am authorised to use force. Halt and await processing." Its mechanical voice echoed up the corridor. The noise of its fans rose as it accelerated.

Dariusz whipped past the first radial lift shaft to the inner ring. The drone was coming closer; there was no way he could outpace it on the bike, and it was another fifteen hundred metres to the lift he needed. He pedalled frantically, seeking to gain as much ground as he could, making it most of the way to the next shaft. When the drone was close, he squeezed the brakes hard and jumped off, dropping the bike to the floor beneath him. He cleared the handlebars, but caught his shin a painful blow on the pedal as he leapt. He fell to his knees beside the bike, flicked the quick release mechanism on the front wheel and drew it out, then scrambled to his feet and stood with the wheel in his hands. He'd have only one chance. Adrenaline washed away his fatigue.

The drone came round the corner quickly. It was a metre long, nearly two across, the fuselage shallow, similar in appearance to a manta ray. Two ducted fans provided lift and direction. A sensor cluster was set in the middle of its forward facing, a bubbling of glass eyes and obscure metal probes. A small ion-stream stunner was mounted below that.

Dariusz flung the wheel at the drone, forcing it to dodge, and he dropped as it opened fire. A debilitating charge of electricity carried on a stream of ionised air cracked into the wall above his head. The drone was going fast, and could not correct its flight in time. Dariusz spun on his heels and leapt at its rear as it passed over him. He scrambled half onto it, grabbing the top of one fan housing. The machine was light, and struggled to bear the weight of a man, even under the low gravity. The drone pitched to the side.

Fans chopped at the air half a centimetre from Dariusz's fingertips. He jumped up, pushing himself further on top, grabbing the drone with both hands either side of its sensor cluster. He wrestled hard with the machine as it bucked underneath him. "Halt! Halt! Halt!" the drone shouted, its siren wailing. It fired again and again, the air cracking and filling with the stink of ozone.

Dariusz gritted his teeth as he pushed the drone toward the bike. He forced it down, bringing one of the fans close to the upright handlebar. With a final effort, he speared the fan on the handgrip. The fan shattered, its remains tangling with the brake lever, cabling and handlebars. Dariusz sprawled backwards as the entire machine spun round, dragging the bike all over the floor. He kicked at it manically, his teeth gritted, driving it toward the side of the corridor. Sparks flew from the drone as it smashed repeatedly into the wall, breaking its remaining fan housing. Dariusz flung his arm up as shards of rotor blade whistled at him.

The drone was immobile, one fan jammed solid, the second whining pathetically, bereft of its rotor blades. Dariusz climbed to his feet, approached the robot cautiously, and kicked downward with his heel. The first blow smashed in its primary sensor cluster. The second destroyed its weapon. The main body was too tough for him to breach without a weapon or tool of some kind. Undaunted by its crippling, it continued to bellow warnings, the lights embedded in the fuselage still blinking. The drones were networked. There'd be more on the way. He had to hurry.

His heel hurt from where he'd kicked the drone, and he limped as he ran. His lungs burned. It was a hundred metres to the next radial shaft, an insurmountable distance in his condition. Only thoughts of his son drove him onward. The sounds of sirens and turbofans came from everywhere, hard to place in the curving corridor.

As he ran toward the second lift, two more drones banked around the slope of the corridor toward him.

"Halt! Halt! Halt!" they cried.

Dariusz quickened his pace and raised his hands, instinctively protecting his face. They shouted three warnings before firing. By the time they had finished, he was skidding underneath them. Their fans thrummed loudly as they swung around in the air, bringing their guns to bear again, but he was already through the door. Ion streams criss-crossed the corridor, as he slapped the door touch panel and dived in. The doors closed.

The lift was an open platform, the shaft walls exposed. The controls were simple – a big red button for *stop*, a big green button for *go*. Simplicity was a virtue on a ship traversing a dozen light years. He slammed the green button with his hand without getting up, and leaned against the control podium as the lift jerked into life. He panted, his muscles in agony.

The lift proceeded slowly. Below him, he heard the door open and the drones come through, but they could not get to him through the floor of the lift. He looked upwards. Orange doors lined the shaft, leading off to maintenance shafts and servicing bays. No drones came from above. He was nearly at his target. He watched the door to the nutrient monitoring room slide closer.

The lift stopped without warning; emergency override. He jumped to his feet. The bottom of the door was level with his chest. He jumped for its control panel, overshooting on his first try, propelling himself well past it in the low-g. On the second attempt, his fingers brushed the panel and the doors opened. The lift mechanism *thunked* underneath him, and he jumped again, grabbing at the open door. He hit his arm on the lintel, but managed somehow to clumsily scramble inside as the lift platform descended.

He activated the door's closing mechanism and locked it, although it wouldn't stop the drones. He folded his arm and drew back his elbow, then drove it hard into the glass touch panel that operated the door. The glass starred, but did not break; the pain was considerable. The lift had reached the bottom of the shaft. He swapped arms and tried again, and the cracks in the glass spread. The sounds of drone fans approached. The door chimed, unlocked, and began to open. He gritted his teeth against the pain and smashed the glass with two more swift blows. An alarm began a persistent complaint. He had the smartsuit lengthen its sleeve, covered his hand with it, then reached into the door mechanism and ripped out all the optics his fingers could find.

So much for leaving minimal evidence.

The door stopped, a quarter open. The wind from the turbofans of the drones stirred his clothes as they jockeyed for a clear firing position. He removed himself from the doorway, pressing his back flat against the wall.

He searched the room. It was small, a three-by-three-by-three-metre cube. His target was behind the panels lining its rear. He checked the line of fire from the half open door. The drones shouted their repetitive warnings and bumped like drunks into the door. If he stayed to the left of the panel, he should remain out of their line of fire.

He rushed over to the far wall, dropping to his knees and sliding as he did so.

The panels were attached by simple flip-up butterfly latches. One half-twist undid each clasp, and he had the access panel off quickly. Behind it, bathed in sterilising ultraviolet light, was the nutrient tube, passing through the small box on its way to the *Mickiewicz*'s biological brain, itself asleep and dreaming. A sampling junction, sealed with a plastic cap, projected from the tube. All he had to do was contaminate the computer's nutrients with one drop of his own blood; the virus hidden in his body would do the rest.

He tried biting his thumb to release the blood, but could not force his teeth into his skin. He considered trying his arm, then remembered the door panel.

He went back to the door, keeping clear of the drones, leaned back on the wall, and darted out a hand to snag a piece of black glass from the floor. It was safety material, and had shattered into squares, but the edges were sharp enough for his purposes. He discounted his thumbs and fingers as too sensitive, instead scoring the skin of his left forearm with the glass. After three attempts, a single, ruby drop welled up.

He rushed over to the open panel again, ignoring the drones' stunners as they fired unsuccessfully through the gap. He unscrewed the cap on the nutrient feed; another siren sounded in discord with the first. He dabbed his right forefinger into his blood, then dipped it into the nutrient gel. He resealed the cap, and the flow started once again. The alarm did not stop, but became shriller.

The blood was a brief dark tendril in the light blue.

He waited for a long time

For an hour, there was no noticeable difference, and he was afraid that it had not been enough. He decided to unscrew the cap again and introduce more of his blood into the system, but as he reached for it, the lights flickered. He glanced up at the ceiling. They did not blink again.

There was a clatter from outside, and the noise of the drones ceased. A rumble built, deep within the ship. Dariusz felt a push, different from the force generated by the ship's spin.

The main drive.

The feeling did not last. The rumble faded again, and the *Adam Mickiewicz* continued on its long journey as if nothing had occurred.

Dariusz, feeling more anxious after his sabotage rather than less, headed back. He stopped at a random deck, scrubbed the contents of his outfit's memory and slipped out of it. He took another smartcloth jumpsuit from a locker on the deck, along with a bottle to replace the one he had taken from his own deck. He tried to arrange the contents of the locker to look undisturbed, then did the same on his own deck. He took the empty bottle into his pod with him, and wedged it by his feet. He'd have to be quick to get it out before anyone noticed.

There was nothing he could do about his vomit. He hoped it would be overlooked in the confusion of the landing.

He lay back in the moulded pod. "Erase datalog, last three hours, Szczeciński, Dariusz M.," he said.

"Comply," said the deck's voice.

He double checked the files. All record of his excursion had been expunged. He should not have the clearance for this. Perhaps Browning's scheme had worked.

Uneasily, he activated the sarcophagus' mechanism and returned to the realms of death.

PART II

The Crash
Time unknown

I say to you, my children, I say to you that it is the sacred duty of mankind to spread across the stars. Rejoice, for that sacred duty will soon be fulfilled! Have I not taught you, that the purpose of life is to create life? That that is God's ultimate purpose for His creation? How better to spread it than establish a nursery of change and evolution, one that cannot fail to create clever beings who yearn to leave their cradle and go beyond? That is God's will.

Since the dawn of time, man has pushed ever onward. We have been tested. We have been shown our darker sides. We have killed, and we have despoiled. There has been a heavy price for man and the Earth to pay. The great animals that once shared this world with us are no more, eliminated one by one as man passed into their territory. Now, the very systems that govern the Earth itself are in turmoil.

But do not mourn! Do not mourn, I say. This is the plan of the Lord God! These follies of ours have been sent to test us! These are the birth pangs of a great outpouring of life! As labour leaves a mother exhausted, so does our own elevation to an interstellar species tire our world unto death. This is the price we must pay to fulfil our holy duty, for leaving paradise is the task that God Himself has set us! This is the way it has to be! The Earth has suffered. Earth may die, but how many more worlds will now feel the touch of life? How many dead planets will we seed with the lifestuff of our home? How many more worlds will now give rise to intelligent beings, who may start the process anew? We are alone in the cosmos, we are unique. But it does not always have to be so. There are no others? So be it! God made us to make them. Let our children stand proud amid an extended family, let our children's children straddle the stars where there will be room and plenty for all!

Do babies mourn the loss of their placenta? No! They are ignorant of its services, they are indifferent to the sacrifices that their parents make. Parents die, and so worlds die. All that matters to God is that life does not end, that the children go forth and beget more children, and thus the chain remains unbroken. We kill one world to seed an infinity; this is the holy purpose of man. Rejoice! You live, each and every one of you, in the time of the apotheosis of humankind.

– Sesele Maka, prophet of the
Church of the Revealed Cosmic Truth

6487828903280378970631608920284552350...
386287750562126416054100228345217486024141616
148681909100006430678478463019196946039367
402262187676266868647592638224294064517009
8622849581386617660170418
6456920672817603782135D
7697217567057074765139974766
73857788709873678967476
12574447864748738617822
766752878476561782272738
37578227763720724376887349786578921481786570272418762269869604
765422565942684640268225
6680564760098644486564864414673466804
8832886874806003600868268682069476027
8884662866600447888820289963
8741665418
0886802017
621889781
015230-1
0590

Sand blinked eyes gummed with sticky fluid. The window in the front of her sarcophagus was a grey blur. Sounds made little sense; her skin crawled in some places, and was numb in others. Her proprioception was confused. She did not recognise her limbs for what they were, finding them horrifying, inhuman attachments.

She screamed, and it turned into a racking cough. Fluid spilled over her chin.

She remembered where she was, she remembered who she was. Her sense of self returned. Anaesthetised and bewildered, she said, "Sand. I am Sand." It hurt to do so. She spoke again, and her voice grew in strength. "I am Cassandra De Mona. Sand. I am Sand."

Fluid flowed out of the drains at the bottom of her pod. There was a painful tugging at her arms as needles were withdrawn.

Through the fugue, she realised something was wrong. The hibernation pod was frantically going through its revivification process. This was supposed to be done slowly. Sharp tingles ran all through her limbs. She grimaced at the pain. Her muscles were heavy as wood.

"Pilot De Mona. Emergency waking protocols engaged. Remain still. Crisis activation. Report for duty," a machine voice said.

Sound became clearer as fluid in her ears broke its surface tension and drained out. Shadows moved across the tiny window. She blinked, her vision sharpening as the machine pumped drugs into her body to reactivate long-dormant physiological processes.

Klaxons blared outside. There was a rumble. The ship juddered.

"What's…" She coughed. "What's happening?"

"Pilot De Mona. Emergency waking protocols engaged. Remain still. Crisis activation. Report for duty," the machine said.

A loud *bang* rocked the vessel.

The restraints holding her in place retracted, and Sand pounded feebly on the sarcophagus lid. "Let me out! Let me out!"

"Prepare for emergency ejection in five, four, three…"

A shadow went past. It returned. A blurred face peered in, then moved away.

There was a loud clunk, and the lid of the sarcophagus flew up, spilling its remaining pseudo-amniotic fluids onto the floor. Sand slipped as she got out, and fell onto the floor. She lay groaning, curled in a foetal ball.

"De Mona! Pilot De Mona! Give me your arm. Damn it, Sand, give me your arm!"

A hand grabbed at her upper arm, and Sand batted at it. It seized her hard. The gentle, million-pinpricks sensation of a hypospray followed.

"De Mona! De Mona! Get up! Get up, damn it!" The woman shouting at her had some kind of accent. The ship's personnel were Central Europeans; the fact flitted unbidden across Sand's mind, along with a jumble of disassociated memories and urgent compulsions. She remembered: *ESS Adam Mickiewicz*, pan-national corporate group, engineered middle-Euro culture, Russian refugee contingent, faux-Russian American owners. The information crowding her confused mind was relentless. She fell out of herself, into a black tunnel. Her body went into spasm. A hand pulled at her. Another hypospray.

The convulsions abated, leaving Sandy's senses reeling. The vortex retreated from her mind. She rolled over and vomited again, emptying lungs as well as stomach. Cold gripped her every muscle fibre, hard. Movement brought her arms and legs stabbing pain.

"Get up *now*, pilot! Now!"

Sand dragged her head upwards, blinking until the blurred figure standing over her resolved itself into the captain,

Danuta Posth. Her shaved skull glistened wetly, her jumpsuit was smeared with amniotics. She was shaking with post-hibernation shock, her breath hanging in clouds on the chill air of the vessel, and worry hid in the creases of her face. Her air of authority, however, was undiminished.

Sand didn't like Captain Posth. She thought her cold and overly officious.

"C-Captain?" She wiped her mouth. "What's going on? Are we there yet?" She caught sight of her hand. Her fingertips were ugly with deep wrinkles, and her skin had lost its coffee brown colouring, become grey and blotched.

"Get up." Posth was shouting to be heard over the alarms. She went unsteadily to a locker, pulled out a micropore towel and a uniform and threw them at Sandy. "We have an emergency."

The *Mickiewicz* growled underneath them. The feeling of gravity intensified and slackened.

"Is the spin out?"

Posth was furious, fear lurking behind the anger. "Everything's out. Something's wrong." She leaned in close before she spoke again. "Everything's wrong. I can't explain here."

Sandy pulled herself to her feet. She dressed as quickly as her quivering limbs would allow.

She followed the captain along the curved floor of the hibernation deck. The crew were scattered throughout the decks in case of localised systems failure, and there were back-ups for each one. They pushed past opening hibernation pods. Gasping civilians were huddled all over the place. Some of the sarcophagi gaped open, sickly sweet stinks emanating from them. Still more were dark, their status panels red.

"What the hell happened?" Sandy said.

"I have no idea," said the captain grimly.

"How can you not know, ma'am?"

Posth gave her a cold look over her shoulder. "Keep it quiet, pilot; we're awake and we have a situation. I'll brief you fully on the bridge." Her eyes slid to a pair of shaking colonists being tended to by a woman in marginally better shape. "You," Posth said to her. "Get everyone you can into the post-revivification lounges. The nearest is deck seventeen. Keep the decks clear."

The woman wiped at her mouth, as if trying to massage her lips into operation. She nodded dumbly.

They reached the intersection of the deck with the lower spinal corridor. A stocky man was waiting for them there. Ludwig Brno, the ship's senior operations officer. He frowned as a pair of colonists, one with his arm over the shoulders of the other, bumped into him. He said nothing until they were out of earshot.

"I've got a two-thirds complement for the crew, ma'am," he said, falling in with the captain. The three of them headed for the bridge. His eyes were wide with disbelief, making him boy-like. "Hibernation failure's well over thirty per cent."

"De Mona is the only officer I could find alive. Who else is with us?" said Posth.

"Danovitz, Kruger, Mori, Oldberg, Gomez, Hankinson, Johnson, Mdele, J Schmitt, R Schmitt, Kaczynska and... I think that's it, ma'am," Brno frowned. "I've got Oldberg, Mdele and Hankinson scouring the other decks, but all the other officers' pods they've found so far have failed."

"Ship?"

"Hankinson's wrestled us back under control. We're out of the woods for now, a decaying orbit, but a slow one. We've got a few days."

Posth's face was grim. "Call them back in, everyone to the bridge. We can't afford to waste any more time. We'll make do with who we've got. Anyone else who wakes up is on their own."

Brno gave a curt nod, and spoke into a device at his wrist. "All officers, report to the bridge, report to the bridge." His words echoed out around the *Mickiewicz* on every system: the tannoy, data nets and the personal inChips of the crew.

"And get any security personnel you can organised. Not the Pointers' men! Post a detail on the primary diameter intersection. Set the rest to patrolling the corridors of the hibernation decks. The last thing I want is a mass panic."

"What about the passengers?" said Sand.

"Give a ship-wide order to get all those awake into the post-revivification lounges," said Posth. "They've had their training. They'll have to fend for themselves for the time being, we've got bigger problems. We'll get the emergency protocols shut off for all except crew and crucial colony personnel, if the Syscore remains discriminate enough to pick them out. We'll keep whoever else is not awake under until we land."

"The Pointers, ma'am?" said Brno.

Posth swore harshly in German. "We have no choice but to wake them all. Some of their representatives have already found their way onto the bridge."

Brno relayed the captain's instructions, while Posth radioed the bridge and ordered the emergency waking sequence shut down.

Sand's head reeled. Her mind was sluggish, her skull so chilled it felt gripped by a vice. A mass emergency revivification like this would only take place under the worst imaginable circumstances.

Her legs steadied as they made their way to the head of the ship. Several times, they were forced to push their way through groups of confused colonists. A couple of hundred were awake, and some of the more self-possessed harried the captain with questions. Posth pointedly ignored them as Brno shouted at them to get to their assigned PRV lounges. A security team, as ill-looking as everyone else, joined them and formed moving cordons front and aft of the small group of officers. The corridor became claustrophobically full, and Sand was glad when they reached the intersection that led into the cap deck corridor. A team of seven ship's security men, all armed with pistols, kept the gathering crowd back as Brno, Sand and the captain turned left into the broad corridor running around the inner circumference of the main shield cap.

The cap corridor was quiet by comparison. There were no hibernation sarcophagi, everything immediately behind the cap was dedicated to running the ship: command deck, main systems controls, EVA pods and the like, and extensive systems of the Syscore itself. As they marched toward the bridge, they passed a wrecked bike and a smashed security drone.

"What the hell...?" asked Sand.

"Sabotage," said Posth, not stopping. "There were two more security drones deactivated on the lift platform of Radial Two. Someone, somehow, got to the Syscore during the voyage. We don't know who, the datalog's been wiped."

They reached the doors to Radial Two. The second and third downed drones had been placed to one side and been cordoned off with tape and poles. "Evidence. We'll get to the bottom of this if we survive our current predicament," said Posth. "I'll hang the bastard myself."

There were more people by the Radial Two lift, ship's personnel rushing up and down, although how many of the ninety-four crew had survived, Sand could not tell. Three more joined them as they summoned the lift. They all stepped onto the platform, and the lift rose. They went past a door that was jammed half-open. "The scene of the crime," said Brno.

"Nutrient feed check room," said Posth. "They introduced something into the Syscore's nutrient mix."

"Is it dead?" asked Sand incredulously.

"Alive, but non-functional. We can't get much sense out of it, and we have little control. Could be the hibernation sickness, but we reckon not. It doesn't affect bottled brains the same way."

Radial Two ended in a blank ceiling. The lift came to a halt in front of a large door leading onto the bridge. It beeped welcomingly as it recognised the officers.

The doors opened.

"Let's get to work," said Posth.

THE BRIDGE WAS a toroid deck. Stations were placed all around the circumference, their chairs tilted so that all bridge officers faced into the centre. A large holographic display in the round took up the central void, divided into numerous sub-displays showing the ship, various status graphics for parts of the vessel – the hibernation decks prominent among them – and a local stellar map showing a bunch of star configurations Sand did not recognise.

As the bridge was right at the centre of the vessel, behind the thickest part of the ice cap, the sensation of gravity provided by the ship's spin was minimal here; grab rails were provided for ease of movement. Posth moved off, pulling herself to her command chair, a large station surrounded by clear glass screens. Sand followed to stand beside her. Hankinson and Kruger, two of the other pilots, were in the helmsman's chairs.

A group of four men dressed in black combat fatigues and armed with assault carbines were close by the command station. They eyed the deck crew suspiciously. Three men stood in their midst, dressed in fine clothes. They appeared fresh and calm.

"The Pointers," growled Posth quietly.

The face of one brightened as he caught sight of Posth. Sand knew him, but could not recall his name. Everything was still foggy. "Ah! Captain Posth, you have returned. Your second in command here told us you might be able to tell us what exactly is going on." He had a charming manner, but brittle. She couldn't judge him for it, no one was themselves right then.

Sand's chaotic memory pulled up the man's identity: Yuri Petrovitch, one of the colony governors. The other was Leonid. They were faux-Russians, their family were the owners of the vessel, the colony, and everyone on board. Yuri gestured at First Officer Maalouf, a bald, rangy man with deep black skin, standing over Pilot Hankinson's shoulder.

"Your officer here would not disclose what he knows."

Maalouf's expression was guarded. "It is better coming from you, captain."

"That simply is not good enough," said the third man. Plump, smooth, American voice – speaking proper English, not Lingua Anglica – Middle-Eastern colouring, exhibiting the signs of advanced yet indeterminate age of the super-rich and their key servants. Administrator Jonathan Amir. "Need I remind you that the Petrovitches are the patrons of this venture? *Nothing* is to be kept from them." The other Pointer, Leonid, looked uncomfortable at this implicit threat.

Posth pulled herself into her chair. "And might I remind you that this is my bridge, and while we are in flight, my authority is absolute? Is that clear?"

Yuri's smile froze, and his brother pulled him back.

"Forgive us, captain. My brother and I are anxious, that is all," said Leonid

Posth gave a curt nod. "Very well. Operations, put up the planet on the main display."

A vast, real-colour depiction of a planet blinked into existence in the centre of the room. One side was shrouded in night, the other a bright desert encompassing half the globe. A star with an orange cast blazed beyond it. A tall, nearly circular mountain range straddled the equator nearest the sun, a whorl of sparse cloud clinging to its peaks. A broad, shining sea curled over the planet's northernmost point, fringed nearer the terminator with green. Elsewhere on the dayside, all was desert. The nightside was black and grey, swirling with weather fronts. A lighter patch on the point furthest from the sun hinted at an extensive ice cap. Clouds boiled where day and night met, and shot the dark through with sparks of blue and white lightning.

Sand's forehead wrinkled.

"Is that Heracles V? It doesn't look like the briefing images."

"It's not Heracles V," said the captain. "Our current position is uncertain. Astronavigation are working on pinpointing our exact position, but we're way off course."

Sand looked at the display again. A marker showed the position of the ship. Only the *Mickiewicz* was visible. Her stomach flipped.

"Where's the rest of the fleet? Where's our sister ship?" said Yuri.

"There *is* no rest of the fleet, sir; no sign of the *ESS Goethe*," said Brno. "We're on our own."

The Pointers and their servants looked at each other.

"We need to talk," said Leonid. "In private."

Posth nodded. "We do. Brno, you have the bridge. Maalouf, Kaczynska, Mori, you're with me." She pushed herself out of her chair. "This way. My ready room."

*   *   *

"A MOMENT PLEASE, captain. I must speak with my brother," said Leonid. Posth nodded and turned away to examine the screens around her chair. She called one of her crew over.

Leonid snagged his brother's arm. Anderson looked away. "You wait here," he whispered in his ear.

"What?" Yuri hissed. "I am mission deputy, I must be included."

Leonid tightened his grip on Yuri's bicep. "Yuri, you're scared out of your wits. I know what you can be like. You must remain calm."

"Oh, and you are not frightened, shot across the galaxy to god knows where? Cool Leonid, is that it? You're pissing yourself. I can practically smell it. I promise you I am not going to make a scene." Yuri glared at Leonid's hand.

Leonid relaxed it. "Okay, okay. Just follow my lead. Stay calm, and don't say anything stupid."

Yuri smoothed down his sleeve. "I love it when you're patronising."

"Keep your voice down."

"I am coming with you."

"Keep it together."

They followed the captain to a round door in the floor/wall of the bridge, which opened to reveal a ladder leading to a medium sized room.

There was a conference table with seating for twelve. Leonid held his brother back and let the crew descend first, to take their places. He did not want to undermine Posth. She stared, openly unfriendly, as he, his brother and the Administrator descended. He had their security team wait outside; only Anderson came with them. Leonid knew he would insist, and was keen to avoid open dissent in front of the bridge crew at this critical time. He had to look like he was in charge, terrified or not.

As was Anderson's way, he did not sit. Leonid resented his presence. His father's motives for sending him and his brother on the voyage were still opaque; he doubted he'd ever be able to figure it out to his satisfaction. The inclusion of an attack dog like Anderson in his retinue was the kind of thing he expected from his father, and undermined his more charitable interpretations of Ilya's motives.

"So," said Yuri brightly. He was keeping up his brave face. Good, thought Leonid. "What's the problem?"

Leonid stayed silent, observing the reactions of the crew.

Posth looked into the face of each of them before she spoke. She was pale. They were all scared, and this scared Yuri more.

"At some point in the voyage here, the ship's Syscore was sabotaged. We've lost contact with the rest of the fleet, and there is no sign of our sister ship, the *ESS Goethe*. As is obvious from the display outside, that is not Heracles V, our target planet. First Officer Maalouf."

Maalouf's irises were so dark as to appear as one with his pupils. Hard eyes to read, but Leonid could see the fear in them. "As far as we can tell, we've overshot our destination system by seven hundred light years."

No one spoke for a good few seconds, as the news sank in. Leonid's heart raced.

"How long?" he said.

"Five hundred years subjective," said Posth. "Give or take."

"The voyage was supposed to last one hundred, Earth time. Us, we were supposed to be under for fifty years," said Yuri. His smile had gone. "And you're telling me we've been asleep for five centuries?"

"Mori's working on exactly where we are," said Maalouf.

"We have not been able to determine our precise location," said Mori, a tall Japanese woman. "Many of the ship's systems are malfunctional or non-responsive." She tapped on the table, and a display sprang up. She tapped again, sliding her fingers over the surface, and a holographic representation of the galaxy popped into being. She zoomed in to an area of space crowded with stars toward the Crab Nebula. "We are supposed to be here, a dozen light years from Earth. As best as I can tell, we are here." The view shifted on for some time, until an icon blinked. "The triangulation tools are not working as they should. I'm getting a different result each time. This estimate is based on my own initial observations."

"Please forgive my questions, Lieutenant Mori," said Yuri. His hands were shaking. "But not working, how?"

"I get different results. Sometimes it locks me out altogether."

"We have similar problems system-wide," added Maalouf.

"A side-effect of this... sabotage?" said Amir.

Posth nodded, and folded her arms tight under her breasts. "Yes. Initial reports suggest someone poisoned the nutrient feed to the Syscore."

"With what?" asked Amir.

"We cannot be sure yet, some kind of synthetic virus, I expect. A gene-rewriter."

"Who did it? Do you have any indication?" said Leonid.

"We should be able to tell, given time," said Kaczynska, the cryonics specialist.

Yuri let out a hysterical noise that might have been laughter. "That part of the system is not operational."

Kaczynska nodded slowly. She was small, brown-haired, solemn. "The datalog was wiped. We've a DNA sample of the saboteur – he cut himself – but we can't sequence it. It's only a matter of time before we can, but even then we have, as yet, no way of checking for a match."

"The colonist database is not working, either, right?" said Yuri bitterly.

"We will find who did this, gentlemen. But it will take time. And we have more pressing problems," said Posth. "It is not a priority matter at this moment."

"How bad is the damage to the Syscore?" said Leonid.

Maalouf spoke. "It is hard to say. An organic virus like that, introduced into the nutrient feed... It's an ingenious way of getting at the ship's brain and reprogramming it –"

"That's impossible!" said Yuri.

"Difficult, not impossible," said Maalouf. "Changing the architecture of the Syscore brain can be accomplished by an engineered retrovirus."

"But that would not affect the programming, would it?" said Amir.

"There is no telling what it is doing," said Posth. "In theory, no, the programs run by the Syscore are only software. But if the underlying hardware is altered, how do we know how it will interpret that software?"

"There's evidence it's somehow leached into our non-organic network. We've been coming up against destructive viruses in many of our electronic sub-systems. We lost a couple, but we've initiated a system purge and clean reboot of each new device as we activate it. That should contain the problem."

"How can a viral infection translate into a digital virus?" said Amir. He was growing suspicious.

"That is unknown at this time. Of course, the Syscore brain is interfaced with all systems, it would not be beyond feasibility to reprogramme it to create a secondary, digital, virus to infect our electronics," said Maalouf.

"Another 'difficult' process," said Amir. "Are you sure there are no other causes?" He looked at the crew calculatingly.

"We are not to blame, Administrator," said Posth.

"Devastating," said Leonid.

"That appears to be the intended result. We could be dealing with the effects forever."

"The Syscore caught a cold?" Yuri gave another disbelieving laugh. Leonid stared at him, silently urging him to pull it together.

"Something like that, yes," Maalouf said.

"We have isolated the Syscore, removed it from contact with all other elements of the ship. Not all systems are down; we have control over the ship's motive systems, although the ride may be bumpier from here."

"Good news, then," said Leonid. "Well done, captain."

"Not good news, sir. I am afraid that is not all," said Posth reluctantly. "We have become caught in the planet's gravity well. We do not have the capability to break free. The *ESS Adam Mickiewicz* will crash."

A stunned silence. Only Anderson was unaffected.

Yuri opened his mouth. Leonid shushed his brother.

"What do you suggest we do?" said Leonid.

"Simple," said Posth. "We're going to have to abandon ship, take our chances on the planet below. We have already selected a number of potential settlement locations, subject to your approval, of course." She nodded. Mori brought up a hologram of the world.

"There's no evidence of rotation," she said. "The world is tidally locked to the star, but it is habitable. There's a large amount of oxygen, most of it is desert but there are signs of life here, here and here around the sea." She zoomed the picture in to a band of fainter light between the night and day side. "In the liminal zone too. Perhaps more, deeper into the nightside. We've not yet had chance to do a full analysis."

"Then we should stand off. We have to assess the world properly," said Amir. "We'll burn, or freeze! Nothing can live on a world that does not turn, with one side permanently presented to the sun, it will be too hot. An inferno, a hellish place!"

"That's not true," said Mori. "On some worlds of this kind, that is probably the case, but not here. The evidence does not support it. It's far out in the habitable zone, and there must be some kind of meteorological temperature exchange going on between the hemispheres, or it would just be a blasted rock, as you say. In fact, we suspect that is occurring now, or is about to occur, as we have observed the formation of several storm systems in the nightside, suggesting the introduction of hot air from the dayside." She pointed out the hologram's miniature weather fronts. "There are small oceans, which, together with this mountainous region on the dayside equator – the 'near pole,' I've called it, and the large icecap on the 'far pole' – are probably the drivers of the temperature exchange. We've identified several potential settlement sites close to the shore of this sea here." Red dots flashed in the band of shadow.

"So we land," said Posth. "Beginning immediately."

"No, no," said Yuri. "All our equipment and supplies are tailored to the expected environment of Heracles V. We're not equipped to land here!"

"Not true," said Maalouf. "We have equipment for all environments. Our information about Heracles V was incomplete. This world is more extreme than expected, but – we believe – survivable. The atmospheric mix is right, there are suggestions of life, and an active magnetosphere. We can live here."

"Fine. If what you say is correct, maybe we can live here, but Amir is correct. We have to stand off. You have halted the emergency revivifications?" said Leonid.

"Yes, sir," said Posth.

Leonid nodded. "There we are, then. Have those already awake form survey teams. We can hold in orbit. We are going to have to stay here, that is clear, but we must take our time before committing to a settlement zone, and be sure."

"And if we are not sure?" said Yuri. "Where else can we go? We have no fuel. We have to land, have to!"

"Quiet, Yuri," said Leonid. "Captain?"

"With all due respect, sir, it will make no difference," said Posth. "We have a limited amount of antimatter remaining. Our ion drives are hopeless in this kind of proximity to a strong well, and although I cannot rule out rerigging the sails, even all together our drives are not enough to free us from the planet's pull."

"We have run multiple simulations," said Maalouf.

"This is a large vessel," continued Posth. "We were awakened too late. We are already being pulled down the gravity well of the planet. This ship was never intended to get this close to a large planetary body. We do not have sufficient power to break free of its grip, and once our fuel is exhausted, our descent will be rapid. We can hold off in a controlled, decreasing orbit for a while, perhaps for four days, maximum, before the ship begins an uncontrolled descent."

Anderson chose to butt in then, much to Leonid's surprise. The man never said anything he did not have to. Leonid was an introvert, he disliked the needless chatter his brother so loved, but Anderson generally made him look like the life and soul. "Someone introduced an unknown agent into our bio-computer, that agent reprogrammed it so that our ship has drifted away from the rest of the fleet, fetching us up at a planet hundreds of light years from where we were supposed to be and five hundred years late?"

"That is an accurate summary, yes," said Posth testily.

Anderson grinned wolfishly and shook his head. Leonid suspected he was enjoying himself.

"I must insist that we begin landing supplies and the construction of a primary settlement immediately," said Posth. "We will keep the remainder of the colonists in hibernation, and wake them in strict rotation, once shuttle space is available for them."

"How many are dead?"

"The support systems were supposed to function for fifty years, not five hundred," said Kaczynska. "We have casualties of over thirty per cent. We are lucky to have as many officers alive as we do."

Yuri looked lost, the last vestiges of his charm sublimating directly to despair. Leonid did not like this turn of events. He asked himself, much to his own disgust, what his father would do in his place. He had to be decisive.

"Very well," he said. "We begin landing immediately. Yuri and I will go down with the first teams to supervise. We'll only be in the way up here." Posth and the others kept stony faces, but Leonid suspected they were relieved.

"I'm afraid I cannot allow that, sir," said Anderson. He stood to attention and looked at a fixed point in the air. "I appreciate your desire to engage with this new property of Petrovitch Holdings, but I insist a basic strongpoint is constructed first, before you set foot on the planet. I will send a detachment down to scout whatever is determined as the most suitable location and set up a broader perimeter. I'm sorry, sir, but I have my orders from your father."

"My father is five hundred years dead, Anderson."

"That might be so, sir, but his orders were clear. I am to intervene should your actions endanger your own life or affect the position of your family."

There it was, baldly stated. Ilya had told Leonid he was being sent as he was a better man. But Ilya's self-reflection only went so far. Anderson was to be Leonid's check. The Pointers' men had the guns. The Pointers' men were utterly loyal. Therefore, the Pointers would remain in charge, no matter how enlightened a ruler – and that was what he had been sent to be, a petty king – Leonid chose to be. Leonid wondered how much of what Anderson said was born of genuine tactical considerations, and how much was to remind the ship's crew of who held power. He wished Anderson would shoot him and remove him from this impossible predicament.

"Then at least have your men watch over the initial survey teams and construction crews. You can do that for me, can't you, Captain Anderson?" said Leonid hotly. "I won't have them stand by for the sake of my safety if anything goes wrong."

"Yes, sir. Of course, sir," said Anderson.

"Then you are dismissed. See to your men now. I will review the landing sites with Captain Posth. You will be briefed in due course."

"Sir…"

"Get out, Anderson," said Leonid wearily. "I'm sure Captain Posth isn't planning on assassinating me."

Anderson looked at Posth like he thought she was, in fact, planning on just that. He left the conference room with ill grace.

Leonid felt more at ease without Anderson breathing down his neck. It felt like his father was right there, and he did not enjoy the sensation.

"My apologies, captain. Can we review the sites you have chosen?"

Posth nodly curtly. "Certainly, sir. If I may call in the ship's pioneer corps?"

Amir agreed. "Please, if possible, let us include any colonist engineers who have awoken? They will need to hear this information at some point. The sooner the better, I say."

Posth considered this a moment. "No word of the ship's position is to leave this room; is that clear?"

"All the men and women aboard have been carefully selected, Captain. They knew the risks, and they are still alive," said Amir.

"Even so, these are risks they were not expecting…" said Posth.

Amir held up his hands, exasperated. Ordinarily he would talk for a week over the smallest detail, he was a filibusterer by nature. That he gave in so quickly was testament to their peril. "Very well."

"Bring up the sites now," said Leonid.

Mori did so. The display zoomed in on a pair of mesas jutting out of the desert. "This is site A," she began. "Defensible, within the liminal zone and of comfortable temperature – note these indications of vegetation." She highlighted a sorry collection of bushes, like sage brush. "We also have strong indications of a water-bearing aquifer all around the mesas…"

Leonid stared at the grainy hologram of his new home.

His new home.

CHAPTER NINE
Sand's Flight

SAND WAS ASSIGNED a security detail – which was overstating it, she thought, as her detail comprised precisely one man. He was to meet her on the shuttle deck. She picked up a bike and made her way to her rendezvous.

The corridor was quieter than before. No more colonists or personnel were waking, and those who had woken were confined to the RVLs. The rest of them would be roused in strict rotation and shuttled down to the planet's surface by Sand and the other pilots, once the initial equipment drop had been accomplished. There had been 14,498 people on board. That number had been slashed to around 10,000. It was still a hell of a lot of folks to get off a starship.

News of their changed destination was being disseminated carefully. The colonists were taking it remarkably well; they were, supposed Sand, all specialists in their own right, the few children aside, and now that a settlement plan had been drawn up, everyone awake was occupied with the evacuation.

Five of seven pilots had made it through the hibernation process. Hankinson and Komorovsky were on the bridge, doing what they could to stabilise the ship's orbit. The other two, Kulicz and Mohandji, had been give shuttle duties with Sand.

The entry to the shuttle decks was an atrium area, intersected by both ventral and dorsal access corridors, and was open all the way around the inner hull. Sand grinned at the sight of people strolling upside down, ninety metres above her head, as she stowed the bike in a rack. The shuttle deck doors were spaced evenly around the hull. From her perspective, there were two in front of her, slightly up the walls, the other directly overhead. She took the leftmost door, went into the suiting room, grabbed her pressure suit from her locker and slipped into it. She activated it and it gripped her body firmly. Flimsy-looking but sturdy,

139

fashioned of dense materials that kept the body's gases from expanding in hard vacuum, by evenly applying force to the skin rather than through the pressurisation of air. It felt constricting to begin with, but was more comfortable and less bulky than older suits. She pulled her helmet collar on, and dangled the helmet from her hand. She was whistling as she strode onto the shuttle deck.

The deck was a long hangar with two points of access to the *Lublin*, her vessel clinging to the outside of the *Mickiewicz*. A large, square hatch, surrounded by hazard striping and a rail, opened onto a ladder that led down to the cockpit's top hatch. A broader opening thirty metres away gave onto a ramp to the rear of the shuttle, and so onto the back of whatever container had been loaded by the ship's automatic stevedore. This was to allow passenger access, when she was carrying passenger pods, or to facilitate loose loading of empty cargo containers. At the moment, the doors were shut. Ordinarily, there would have been a deck crew present, but with things being the way they were, the place was deserted. Sand checked her manifest again.

"Building modules," she said. "Ah well, best get the homestead in place before asking the cowboys in for supper," she said, in a mock Texan drawl. She recommenced whistling, and headed to the pilot hatch.

"You're happy, considering our circumstances."

She started, her hand flying up to her chest. A tall man wearing a spacesuit like hers was leaning in one corner. He could have been a spacer, were it not for the assault carbine he held across his body.

She gathered her wits quickly, shooting him a quick smile to cover her fright. "I like flying, it makes me happy. It's keeping my mind off all this, you know, 'lost in space' shit."

"Fair enough," he said.

"You nearly gave me a heart attack."

"I like to keep people on their toes."

"English?"

"When it suits me," he said.

"Nice not to have to speak Lingua Anglica, annoys the shit out of me," she said.

"Well, you say that, but what you Americans do to our language…" He grinned at her to show he meant no offence.

Sand's smile broadened. She probably looked goofy, but what the hell. The guy was cute. Tall, well-muscled, looking very good in his flight body glove: even, heavy, masculine features, the kind she liked, not one of the foppish girl-boys that periodically came into fashion. A real man. With a gun.

"The name's Corrigan." He reached out his hand. He had a firm grip, but wasn't pulling any macho bullshit and trying to crush her fingers, nor was he giving her the come-on squeeze. A good, decent handshake. "You must be Pilot De Mona. I'm here to protect you from the novelty items in your cockpit, or maybe aliens, if there are any, which there won't be."

She smiled wider. "Cassandra. Or just Sand, that's what they call me."

"Sand? Okay. Wow, you're smiling like we're all going on a trip to the seaside."

"I'm a sucker for an armed man."

"Is that so? In that case, I'm delighted you're so forward, but won't your intended be a little annoyed with you flirting with me?"

"Nah." She flapped her hand. "He's still frozen stiff. He won't mind. Shall we?" She pointed to the hatch in the floor of the hangar bay. "I've got… I mean, man, *we've* got, seventeen runs of supply containers to drop before I can even think about some R&R."

"That so? Doesn't sound so bad. I've been asleep for five centuries; I'm rather glad to be up and about."

Sand laughed. "Right. Yeah, me too. Still. Let's go."

She keyed open the cockpit hatch with a thought through her inChip. Yellow and black hazard striping slid away to reveal a ladder leading down. The top hatch of the ship followed a second later, sliding backwards into its recess. She pointed to it. "Corrigan?"

"Ladies first," he said. He gave a small bow, and shouldered his carbine.

"Suit yourself." Sand clambered down easily. Or was it up? Sand preferred zero-g, even if it did eat your bones. Zero-g was more fun, rotational pseudo-gravity made a nonsense of everything, and the Coriolis effect on smaller units made her want to barf constantly.

There were five seats in the cockpit. Three aft of the pilot's and co-pilot's chairs, for mission specialists or passengers. She settled herself into the pilot's seat as Corrigan came down the ladder. "You can sit there," she said, pointing to the co-pilot's chair next to her. "Just don't touch anything."

"Okay." He sat next to her. Sand was acutely aware of his presence at her elbow. She hadn't been laid for five hundred years, she thought suddenly, and laughed.

"Something funny?"

Sand ran through her preflight, flicking switches and activated systems. The ship shuddered as its reactor woke, the faint thrum of it joining the small electronic noises of the cockpit. Blast shielding on the shuttle's windows screeched open, revealing the interior of a dark segmented shell outside. "Oh, now, private joke." She looked at him and gave her best smile. "Very private."

"I'm not sure if I like the sound of that," said Corrigan. "Or maybe I do?" he ventured.

Sand laughed. "Corrigan, just what is a good looking bastard like you doing on a flight like this? With a gun, no less."

"Just doing a job, ma'am," he said with a mock American accent.

"Man, that's the worst accent I ever heard."

"It's why I'm not in acting." He became serious. "Nothing for me on Earth, fancied a change. You know how it is."

"Yeah," she said. "I guess I do."

"What is that?" said Corrigan.

"Roosevelt?" Corrigan was staring at the mascot hanging from the ceiling, a battered teddy bear, purple and garish as was the fashion when an ex she barely remembered had bought it for her. "You got a problem with my bear? Get out now, if that's how you feel."

"Hey! Steady. No, no problem with the bear."

"Good. He and I have been through a lot of shit together."

"He just doesn't seem very *you*."

"Well, live and learn, gunfighter, live and learn." She keyed the radio on. "This is Pilot De Mona aboard the *SS Lublin*. All systems running a-okay down here. They mothballed this thing real carefully. Requesting permission for take-off."

There was a pause. A voice replied in the cockpit. "Flight control affirmative. You are clear to blow shuttle shielding."

"And there we go. We are good. I've been looking forward to this," she said. "On my mark."

"On your mark, *Lublin*."

She reached out to a toggle switch. "Three, two, one." She flicked the toggle. Explosive bolts detonated with muffled snaps around the shuttle. There was a wash of gas as a short-firing CO_2 thruster pushed the shielding free of the *Mickiewicz*; it spun off into space, so much junk. "Won't be needing that any more," she said. Carbon frost dissipated from the glass as quickly as it had formed, as the *Mickiewicz's* rotation presented the *Lublin* to the system's star. The windows darkened automatically.

"Here we are, shuttles three, just like ticks on a dog," she said, sing-song. She felt a little giddy to be flying down to an extra-solar world. How many people had done that? "Preparing to detach docking clamp."

"You are cleared for launch, *Lublin*."

Sand caught Corrigan staring out of the window as the planet was brought into view by the ship's rotation. It was a glorious, blazing caramel. Her breath caught in her throat. She found it amazing herself, but she was feeling mischievous and put on the airs of a spacer bored past caring by commonplace wonder.

"If you think this is all fun and exciting now, wait until we've done it thirty times," she said. "This is *Lublin*. Initiating launch."

"Countdown initiated. You are good to go."

"Releasing docking clamp in three... two... one. release."

Another switch, a low *clunk* sounded from above.

"Docking clamp detachment confirmed," she said.

They were flung out by the ship's rotation, up and away from the *Mickiewicz*. The four-and-a-half kilometre colony ship dropped away above their heads. Sand gave a light burst on the jets, ridding the ship of the last vestige of centrifugal forcing and bringing them into line with the horizon of the planet below.

The *Mickiewicz* now appeared to rotate. The planet below became steady, their new frame of reference.

"Wooh, that's better. Thanks," said Corrigan. "I was beginning to feel a little queasy."

"Not for your benefit, honey. Drag from the exosphere even this high up'd slow us down real quick, and that makes flying a mite tricky. We need to be belly down for a hot landing, and I like to keep my eye on where I'm going."

Sand depressed one of the pedals by her feet. There was a rushing sound through the floor and another billow of gas vented from the ship's underside, pushing them further away from the *Mickiewicz*. Like much of the equipment on board, many of the *Lublin*'s systems were simple electronic and mechanical devices.

"Easier to get out a wrench than reprogramme," she said.

"What was that?"

"Nothing. Something an engineer once said to me."

Sand briefly pumped the forward thrusters, dropping her ship's speed relative to the *Mickiewicz*, and the colony ship pulled away from them. She gave a couple more outgassings from the ventral thruster as the *Mickiewicz*'s massive engine units came into view; the drives were out, but Sand wasn't chancing getting caught in their backwash should they come online. Once she was a safe distance from the vast ship, she pushed the rear thrusters, pulling level.

"Impressive piece of engineering," said Corrigan. "Five hundred years travelling through the void and it looks almost new."

"Yeah," said Sand, "almost like this was the plan all along."

Periodic bursts of gas puffed from the length of the vessel. Cargo containers were running along the outside of the craft, switching places like puzzle pieces, queuing themselves in preparation for pick-up by the shuttles. The *Kraków* and *Gdańsk* were already out, peeling down toward the planet, the *Kraków*'s bay clutching a hexagonal, rust-red container full of equipment upon its back, the *Gdańsk* a blue pressurised passenger cabin. Within were the first of the colonists, an advance team of engineers, geologists and exobiologists. All suited up, she thought, until the environment proved safe. If it didn't, she wondered, what the hell then?

"Aren't we following them in?"

"What's the rush, honey?"

"What's with all this 'honey' business?"

"I call all men I like 'honey.'" She flashed him a teasing grin. "You object? You aren't going to go all Brit on me, are you?"

Corrigan cleared his throat. He was clearly nervous about the flying. "No, not at all. British reserve is a myth, like London fog."

"There's no fog?"

"Not for a century and a half. Your folk memory of it is an echo of older days."

"My, the gun-toting poet. We're taking a pass around the ship. The sensors are scrambled five ways to next Thursday, along with everything else. I'm to make sure there's no major damage or anything else that might bring our estimated crash time forward."

"That's a hell of a responsibility."

"So's carrying that cannon."

"No, ma'am. I just shoot who I'm told, no thought involved."

"Well, I'm first pilot, baby, and hellish responsibility goes with the territory. Flight control, this is *Lublin*. Commencing inspection."

"Shouldn't you be on the bridge?"

"First pilot, not senior. Hankinson's our lead, and he's at the helm," she said.

Sand started at the drive unit, then maneouvred the shuttle carefully down the length of the *Mickiewicz*, up the mushroom stalk, past the reactor, the secondary shield cap, on by the jostling cargo containers, the shuttle bays, the comms masts, the sail boxes, then to where the hull widened into the segmented hibernation decks, each bigger than the last, until they came to the lip of the mushroom cap of the water shield. She slowed and inspected the colony vessel as it rotated by her. It really had come through its journey unscathed. A little pockmarking here and there, maybe, but nothing serious. "Up front, in the shield, that's where the damage will be. That's what it's there for, after all."

She accelerated, outpacing the ship, speeding up and out around the recurved lip of the shield. She swung around in front, and passed right in front of the prow in a way that made Corrigan inhale sharply. The shield was pitted, riven with crevasses. The rich blue of the oxygen-depleted ice with which they'd started their voyage had become dirty grey. The sight of it reminded her of one of the few times she'd seen snow, years ago, a jagged lump by the side of the road, speckled with grit thrown up by the traffic.

"*Lublin* to flight control. All looks good as far as I can see, the shield has taken a hammering, but it has been out there ten times longer than it should have been. It's in good shape for its age. I'm doing a datadump now, if you can read it."

"Are the shuttles not affected?" asked Corrigan.

"No," said Sand. "They were inactive when the main Syscore was infected. First thing we did when we turned everything back on was make sure the systems that had been isolated stayed that way. It's been scrubbed, recalibrated from file and clean rebooted. I can transmit, but I'm not even to *receive* any non-verbal data."

"Wow."

"Wow indeed."

"Data received," said flight control. Sand couldn't remember the name of the person attached to the voice. "You are to proceed to landing one."

"Will do, see you in two hours." A tight turnaround, but Sand was glad Posth was taking no chances. That Leonid Pointer might have got his way regarding the colonists' slow deployment, but Posth had been firm about getting as many of the cargo containers down as possible.

"You ready for this, gunfighter?" she said.

"Sure."

"Don't sure me, my man, re-entry is no picnic. And I'm doing it all manual."

Corrigan grimaced.

"Don't worry, this is all new to me too," she said with a smile, enjoying the soldier's discomfort.

She aligned the ship, broad tail lowermost, nose up. The shuttle's broad underside was coated in a nanoweave thermal blanket. She'd done space-to-surface runs in the sims and for real on Mars and the Moon, but modern craft back home did not do hot landings on Earth, period. Cargo on Earth came in via elevator.

She wondered how things might have changed back there, five hundred years on; if there were elevators or even people there now. She put the thought away, unwilling to examine it.

"Okay, here we go." The air was thickening, rushing past the hull. The *Lublin* bucked. "I seriously advise you to fasten your seatbelts."

The *Lublin* roared down. The glow of heat from the underside of the vessel coloured the edges of their viewports. Air screamed past the ship as it plummeted, the planet growing beneath them until it filled their view. They rushed over the endless dayside desert, the terminator between night and day approaching quickly.

They were through it in a blink, passing over the liminal zone in seconds, the planet below going black with startling suddeness. Sand could make out little down there, lots of cloud, plenty of lightning, none of the seas or ice cap she'd seen on the bridge. Her ship glowed hot, wrecking her night vision and stopping the ship's sensors from working. They'd have to slow down for that.

They were close to the boundary with the troposphere. The planet's gravity was a quarter of a g higher than Earth's, and the atmosphere correspondingly denser. Good in some ways – the pull might be stronger, but she had more air and so more time to slow down – but worse in others, as there was more atmosphere to fry her through friction.

"Deploying wings," she said. She flicked the wing release safeties, one and two, then reached for the deployment switch. "Three, two, one and out."

The *Lublin* wobbled. There was a metallic noise as its wings reconfigured, shifting from a dart to a delta form. Sand wrestled with the controls, and the quality of descent altered, becoming less violent. "Activating Sabre XIIs."

This was the real test of the day: if any of the micropores on the precooling systems were compromised, they were both dead. She elected not to share any of this with Corrigan.

The engines slid out of their housings, and engaged with a jolt. The shuttle shifted from gliding to powered flight. They were still going at around Mach 5, but Sand had wrested control of her ship back from the planet.

She whooped unashamedly. "Goddamn! This is flying!" She brought the ship round in a steep curve. Corrigan kissed a crucifix he'd plucked from under his shirt. He caught Sand's raised eyebrow and shrugged apologetically.

Sand loved to fly, really loved it. This was the best part of it all. The terminator came into view again, the motion of the craft providing them with a sunrise the planet itself would never experience. She allowed the rush of air to slow the craft further, bringing it down to a manageable three times the speed of sound. Their progress became smoother. Corrigan let out a breath and stopped bracing himself between the floor and seatback. They burst through the strange, linear storm and back into the daylight.

"Nearly there, gunfighter," she said. She flicked a few more switches. A screen came on, giving her a radar-generated map of the terrain below. All useful information for the colony effort, but she was looking for something else. There. The steady pulse of a radio locator beacon, bounced off the stratosphere, not strong and not long range without relay satellites, but strong enough to hear. "Corrigan, this is First Landing."

She brought the shuttle lower, burning through the liminal zone, toward the sunward side of the twilight band encircling the planet.

The mesas they were to build their city on came into view, a pair of them, out of place in the sand and scrub. A dry river bed lined with thorny bushes ran in front of them from the north, turning to the west to where evening sunlight glimmered on the ocean twenty kilometres distant; an evening that would never end. The country of evening. A cluster of dropped containers were scattered around the mesa. Small figures and machines were already at work in the ruddy light, stacking them, unpacking them, clearing the ground to make a landing field to the west of the mesas. A team were already laying down a mesh road from the would-be city.

"High ground," said Corrigan.

"You approve?" said Sand.

"There's no telling what's here. Good to pick a defensible spot, better to be safe than sorry."

"Looks desolate to me."

"We don't have time to be picky. You seen anywhere else that looks more inviting?" Corrigan stared out of the window.

"No, I suppose not," she said. "This is *Lublin*, requesting drop point."

A new voice, weak and crackly, came over the radio. "Welcome, Pilot De Mona. Co-ordinates coming through."

"Co-ordinates received."

She slowed the shuttle, adjusted her course and opened the cargo clamps at the back. "We're not carrying bodies, so we're not stopping," she said to Corrigan. "First Landing control, prepare for delivery."

A klaxon sounded as the shuttle's lower cargo doors gaped wide and the container extruded itself from the vessel's underside. Sand circled once, twice, around the drop point. A container truck and heavy lifting robot waited a safe distance away.

Sand rotated the shuttle's jets downwards, and hovered briefly a few metres above the ground. Dust was blasted into a wide, billowing cloud around the ship. She kept the drop as short as possible to conserve fuel; hovering was a bitch for mileage. She twitched the stick, then hit the cargo release button. The *Lublin* lurched as the container slid from its rails and dropped onto the desert, its own feet taking most of the shock.

"And it's away. I'll be back soon."

"Thanks, Sand."

"That it?" said Corrigan as the *Lublin* turned and rose again. It moved off quickly as its directional jets returned to flight position.

"That's it. Waste of time and fuel setting down, the stuff in those containers is packed just fine, nothing's going to break from a five-metre soft landing. Now we've got to clear out the cooling vents, suck in some gas to replenish the tanks, that'll take a couple of passes through the atmosphere, get some mapping data while we're at it, then we switch to rocket mode, and do it again. And again. And then again a few more times."

They headed back into the night, skimming a few hundred metres over the ground. Under the cloud cover, the dark was less total than it first appeared. There was much fog, but where there was not, Sand caught glimpses of lights on the ground, whole areas that glowed pale green, and flashes of colour, before she pulled up through the cloud layer to get a good radar sweep. She thought of cities, but obviously not. Life, maybe. Weird.

They flew over the nightside at subsonic speeds, crossing the planet's massive equatorial icecap, dragging a wide radar broom across the landscape and puffing out particles from the engine's cooling micropores. The ride was choppy, strong laminar flows in the air bouncing them as they changed altitude, plenty of clear air turbulence too. Fifty minutes later, and they returned to the ship. She flipped the vessel and approached her bay topside on. Docking was awkward, but Posth wasn't willing to release the containers into the void for pick-up so close in to the gravity well. No problem, Sand enjoyed the challenge. The *Lublin* clanged into place, docking clamps biting the upper side of the ship.

She shut off the flight systems and unbuckled herself.

"Two minutes before the next container comes sliding down the rails, ten minutes before we're cleared to launch again. We've got twenty runs to do before we take a break. I need to pee. Do you fancy a coffee? It's five hundred years old, so it'll probably taste like shit."

Corrigan smiled and ran a hand over his shaved head.

"Not used to flying orbital insertion and back? You look kind of poorly."

"Not in forty minutes, no," he said.

"You'll get used to it. Let me get you that coffee."

They were sucking on bitter, rehydrated mess when the container slid down the rails and onto the rear cargo bed. A succession of bangs announced its arrival and lockdown.

Sand sealed her cup and stowed it. "That's it, load secure," she said. "Running preflight checks."

"Roger that, pilot," said flight control. "All running smoothly?"

"Indeed."

"That's the best news we've had in a bad day. Keep it up."

Sand checked the manifest. Hydroponics. Fine.

"Buckle yourself in, Corrigan, we're going back in five minutes." She smiled widely at him. "I love my job."

341746M3KR E01 H833 3000446 H055W71
PCS1 8572846W132 967 9621700024544327469W12155W 9722
9705 1401 8531 83026426456678479820W440 8634947125M5
612187 87828925 455 847682636124651 568257771V
652284582S127 556700M
9456129572570700752 785J
7845732175 706 7074705 5057754 7686
14657336704 736 76867676
7623744479547413 764M5
766 7673 7945561 7972 7783
7237682753765 7243768673407688766 764155677857242487665 654J
7974732504264846452862V
8999045 6289654865655775 6461674685Q 6
6836 6562 6405 6023 6005 6526 8534 675
692 634666264566673586185 58127
765487341546265686447695562026695 6
6241 696466
660606206
543456938
51 62806
6155585J
6M

Leonid stood next to Captain Posth, both of them clutching at the railings to stop the ship's rotation sending them in a slow tumble toward the wall. Or the floor. Was it the floor? The centrifuge effect was so weak at the centre, and so the stations on the bridge were arranged more to deal with high-g acceleration than for the niceties of up and down. Making sense of the bridge's topography would have given Leonid motion sickness, were he not possessed of perfect balance. They stared at the globe hanging luminous and strange in the display void. The display appeared almost solid; Leonid had only the vaguest impression of people moving around on the other side.

"Not a bad spot, I think," said Posth. First Landing was highlighted on the map by a rotating reticule. Leonid felt pleased. The captain was warming to him.

"Yes, it is."

The captain had spent some time explaining the fuel situation. She was right; they needed to get down quickly. He was working on encouraging her original plan without admitting defeat. More his father's style than his, but self-preservation had led him by the nose; the Pointers were loathed as it was, things had gone seriously wrong, this was ripe territory for a revolution. He would bring equality, but in the meantime he was eager to avoid having his head on a pike. Was he getting paranoid? Nothing seemed real after so long asleep, and now this…

"We're going to have to choose a name for the planet, captain," he said.

"Mori has a suggestion," said Posth. "If you would like to hear it, sir."

Yes, thought Leonid, this relationship could work out fine. He needed her more than she needed him. They both knew it.

151

"Of course." He looked about for Mori, finding her sitting, as far as he was concerned, on the ceiling.

"I suggest Nychthemeron," she said.

"Really?" said Yuri, who had yet to recover his shell of poise and charm. "Is that... Greek?"

"Yes, sir. It means a night and day combined. There are cognates in several languages, including in Polish."

"Why not use their word? They're the majority."

"*Doba*?" said Mori. "*Because* the Poles are in a majority. There are no Greeks at all present on board the *Mickiewicz*, and I thought a neutral term would be preferable."

"Do you approve, sir?" asked Posth.

"Sounds suitably mythological, 'Nychthemeron,'" said Yuri. "We were to settle on Heracles, why not on a world with a similarly pompous, Hellenistic name? I like it."

Leonid winced inside. He hoped Mori was not offended. "Amir? Your opinion."

"As you desire, sir."

That annoyed Yuri. "Don't give me that. We asked for your opinion, not ours. What do you think?"

Amir became thoughtful. He showed no sign of awkwardness at his rebuke. Leonid became hopeful that his father had not loaded his court with idiots. And a court, he thought angrily, was exactly what it was. He was thinking in terms dictated by his father. He had to watch that.

"It is a good name. It sums the planet up. A little long, maybe, but it sounds... If you will permit me, it sounds more grandiose than pompous. I think we need a name we can respect."

"Very well," said Leonid. "Nychthemeron it is."

Posth nodded at Mori. "Input the name into all our chart data."

"Yes, ma'am."

They watched as a string of boxes extended out from the graphic representing the ship, depicting the flight path for the latest shuttle launch. The five desks in charge of flight control hummed with quiet chatter, human and computer assisted traffic controllers directing the delivery of supplies and personnel to the surface.

"Fifty-eight per cent of the cargo has been delivered," said Posth. "We have the majority of the wakened colonists on site."

"How many?" asked Amir.

"Seven hundred or so. There are three hundred still awake on board. We will begin sequenced waking of the remainder once they are down," said Posth.

"Good work, captain," said Leonid, because he felt someone should say it. "If I might make a further suggestion?"

"Please do," said Posth.

"Could we consider the…"

There was a wrenching noise. The ship bumped. Under the low gravity, Leonid drifted up, then down. There was a rumble, felt rather than heard. A gentle push shoved them toward the wall.

"What the hell was that?" said Yuri.

"Acceleration?" said Amir.

An alarm whooped.

Posth shouted, "Helm, report."

"I – I…" The man in the primary pilot's station looked over. "I don't know…"

"Hankinson! Pull yourself together."

"The engines, ma'am. They're online!"

"The reactor, too, it's gone through a complete cold cycle, started from nothing. I've got a breach on containment spiral four," said the woman at the reactor station.

"Shut that damn alarm off!" yelled Posth.

The rumbling grew.

"Helm! Shut the engines down."

"I can't, I can't!" Hankinson hammered at the touchscreen in front of him. "It's not responding."

"Ma'am! We've instability in the rotational cycle."

"I've been locked out too, captain," said the woman by the reactor control station.

"Have we got anything?" Posth shouted. "Systems?" Posth hauled herself along the grabrails to a recessed station. The man there did not look up. Cold light bathed his face.

"I'm losing access all across the board," he said. "We're being shut out."

"How long until you can get it back?"

"I don't know!"

"We have seven minutes before we begin uncontrolled re-entry, ma'am," said Maalouf.

"Who still has control over their station? Tell me! Now!"

"Cargo system online, ma'am."

"Hibernation decks online."

"Sensors online."

"Traffic control online, ma'am."

No-one else spoke.

"Is that it?"

Eyes flicked backwards and forwards in worried faces.

"Hankinson, do you have thruster control?"

"I... I..."

"Spit it out! Yes or no!"

"Yes, ma'am. Manoeuvring thrusters are online, ma'am. I'll do what I can."

"Orient this vessel so that it will descend as slowly as possible. Alter heading. Five degrees northwest. I want the descent corridor well away from First Landing."

"Yes, ma'am."

"Traffic control, shuttle status."

"*Kraków* and *Gdańsk* are returning from the surface. *Lublin* is docked, loaded and ready to fly."

"Get Sand out of here. Kaczynska, pull the plugs on all the pods that have not yet woken. Blow them out, all of them, emergency evac. They'll stand more chance off the ship than on it."

"All of them?"

"All of them. There's not enough room on the shuttles for everybody, and we certainly don't have time to wake them up! Get them off the ship!"

"Shall I prioritise the Pointers' men's decks?"

The captain's face went hard, and she did not answer. She stared hard at Leonid, with a look of hatred that took him aback.

"Captain?"

"Yes! Yes! Do it, follow protocol."

Some semblance of order returned to the bridge. Posth spoke, calmly and clearly, cutting through the hubbub.

"Men and women of the *Mickiewicz*. We do not know what has happened. We do not know where we are. We are presented with a stark choice. We have to work as hard as we can to ensure that as much of our cargo manifest and our passengers are deposited on the surface of this world. I cannot order you to stay by your posts. I will not ask you to stay by your posts. Each and every one of you is free to leave and board the evacuation pods, but every one of you that does not do so will buy time that will enable more of our fellow men and women to survive, and with it, perhaps ensure the survival of the human race."

They looked at her, then returned to their posts. Only two left, quickly, and with a haunted air that would cling to them for the remainder of their lives.

Posth gripped the rail.

"Hankinson, I want you to stabilise us for as long as possible. Get as many of our people down as we can."

"De Mona is on the line, sir!" shouted flight control.

"Tell her what she needs to hear. Wait till she's clear before ejecting the first of the decks. The settlement will need that shuttlecraft, and I want her down in one piece."

Posth turned to Leonid's party. "You better get out of here, sir."

"I should stay."

She shook her head. "I've always despised Pointers, and I hope to hell they overthrow you and make you clean toilets for the rest of your life once things are up and running down there, but I've no wish to see you die, and you're no use on the bridge." She pushed something into his hand. A glass capsule, with a piece of broken glass inside it. "The DNA sample of our saboteur. Keep it safe. Find out who he was. Go! All of you!"

"I... Thank you, captain," said Leonid. She turned her back on him. Yuri was pulling at his arm. The ship shook.

"We have to go now," his brother hissed in his ear.

In a moment, Leonid's new-found confidence deserted him. After a lifetime of feeling privileged and useless, Leonid had never felt quite so privileged, nor quite so useless.

* * *

LEONID ALLOWED ANDERSON to hustle him out onto the lift platform, and Amir joined them. The ship rumbled alarmingly, shifting from one side to the other. A ship's junior, sweat on his forehead, met them at the shaft base.

"This way, sirs," he said.

The corridor was a scene of panic. People were running toward the escape pods. They moved too fast for the erratic simulated gravity, banging into each other and tripping.

"There'll be a place for us, sir," said Anderson. "The evacuation pods are code locked. They won't be able to get in."

The junior officer nodded. He swallowed constantly, checking over his shoulder every couple of seconds as if he expected death to ride up behind them. His hands pawed at Leonid and Yuri's backs, urging them on.

Anderson had his gun ready, fixing those who looked like they might cause trouble with a murderous eye. A gesture from the gun cleared their path.

They were nearly at the door leading into an evacuation pod bay when a tearing wrench sounded throughout the vessel. They stumbled with it. People crashed into one another, alarms howled. The lights flickered off for one terrifying moment, red emergency lighting taking their place.

"The ship's rotation!" said the junior. "We're losing gravity."

Colonists and non-essential ship's crew drifted in tight knots, wrestling with one another as they fought for space and stability. The spin cut out completely, the centrifuged gravity going with it..

"This way, sir!" Anderson hung from a strap in what had been the ceiling, his face demonic in the red glow. He reached out his hand. "Take hold!"

Leonid fought his way through the air. The sensation was akin to dreams he had had as a child, where he could fly, but barely, and had been forced to swim inelegantly through the air to escape his enemies. The ship juddered. He slammed into Anderson.

"I've got you, sir, come on," said Anderson. "Grab my belt." Amir and Yuri latched hold of Leonid, dragging the junior along with them. They formed an ungainly train. "The pods are this way. Only another twenty metres to go." The acceleration of the ship pushed at them. Men and women screamed as they were ripped from their straps, but Anderson hung firm, moving hand over hand with unnatural strength, dragging the rest with him.

More people were shaken loose as the ship convulsed, sent into the wall opposite the direction of travel. Alarms sounded. From somewhere came the hiss of escaping air. "Hull breach, hull breach, hull breach," droned a notification. "Hull breach, hull breach..."

The air stirred, a breeze that picked up strength.

Anderson grabbed a man by the evacuation pod bay door and yanked him out of the way. "In! In! In!" he bellowed, deference gone. "Get in!"

Leonid stared as the man Anderson had ripped from his mooring hit a wall.

"Get in now!"

He shoved the Pointers, Amir, and the junior through the door into a short, kidney-shaped corridor with twenty large hatches in it, surrounded by red bands. Leonid flew without control; the ship was accelerating, g-force growing. Seven of the pods had already flown, the rest were becoming out of reach as the geography of the ship shifted. The pods were in line with the ship's spine. The pod hatches were set into the subjective floor, to take advantage of the spin in sending them out into space, but the craft's acceleration had shifted to pull toward the back wall. Colonists were pinned against it, a tangle of bodies, a moaning, multi-limbed horror that shed more and more of its humanity as the g-force increased. Other people lay, gripping pod hatch handles that they lacked the clearance to open. The ship vibrated violently; it would not be long before it broke up.

Anderson grabbed Leonid roughly as he spun toward the clot of bodies. The junior opened an escape hatch door with a thought.

"Open them all!" shouted Leonid. "Deactivate the passcodes! The colonists cannot get in!"

The junior nodded. Lights flashed above each of the doors as they slid open. Grateful colonists clambered in where they could, some fighting to get in, others leaning, stretching arms to grasp the desperate hands of their fellows.

Anderson shoved Leonid into the pod. The planet tugged at them. They were exiting the microgravity environment, deep enough into the gravity well of Nychthemeron for them to feel it.

The pod was small, with four seats. Twenty pods per bay, three bays around the primary deck. Enough to get two hundred and forty people off the vessel, if they were all used. Not enough, there were not enough for everyone, Leonid thought. Yuri came in next, then Anderson. The brothers strapped themselves in. Amir gripped the door aperture. "What about me?"

"Get out," said Anderson. "You are superfluous to my mission objectives." Leonid was chilled. Anderson said it without malice, matter-of-factly.

"What about him?" Amir stared at the crewman, spit flying from his lips.

"He can operate this craft if anything goes wrong. Him we need, you we do not."

Clunks and roars as first one, then two, then three, of the other pods disengaged. The ship lurched.

"Get out!" said Anderson.

"Get in one of the other pods!" Yuri pleaded. His face was white.

"No!" spat Amir.

"Very well." Anderson raised his gun.

"I'll remember this, Anderson," said Amir. "You're a marked man." He shoved himself off from the lip of the pod.

"Now! Go!" Anderson shouted.

The doors slid shut. Escape rockets vented gas, pushing them out of the trailing edge of the shield cap.

The pod lacked all but the most basic guidance systems. It tumbled end over end. Despite his enhanced physiology, Leonid vomited. He was wrenched to and fro, until the pod was caught in the planet's grasp. Somehow, it righted itself, presenting its heatshield to the atmosphere. The passage of air drew dragon's fire from the skin of the lifeboat, and it became unbearably hot.

Leonid was conscious for the entire descent, a tumbling confusion, a blast-furnace roar that ceased with the snap of parachutes deploying, then a minute later, an impact of bone-crunching force.

SAND AND CORRIGAN were returning from a break aboard the *Mickiewicz* when the engines flared into life.

"Shh!" Her hand went onto Corrigan's arm. "What the hell is that?"

"What?"

The ship jerked.

"The engines? Why the hell are they firing the engines?" Sand tapped into the ship's internal comms via her inChip. "Bridge, Bridge, I'm feeling some movement down here. Please advise."

The deck vibrated. Colonists looked alarmed. They looked to Sand; one started to speak, and she waved a hand at him. "Sorry, Bridge, say again?"

The voice in her subdermal was scratchy.

"What are they saying? What the..." The ship lurched suddenly, sending them sprawling. The axial spin accelerated and decelerated without warning.

Sand found herself atop Corrigan. "It's the engines. Looks like whoever pulled the sabotage did a real number on us. Get up. Keep walking. Don't say anything." She grabbed his arm by the elbow. "We have to get off the ship."

"The engines firing is bad?"

"Way bad, my friend. Remember I said to you we had a few days before the ship's orbit decayed and we all had to get the hell out of Dodge?"

"Sure I do."

"Make that about five minutes. We have to get off the ship!"

"What about everyone else?" said Corrigan.

"We let on to what's happening, they're all going to want a ride, and that isn't going to happen. It'll take eight minutes to swap our cargo loadout for pressurised passenger units, longer to get it full of bodies, and we do *not* have that time."

The *ESS Adam Mickiewicz* groaned as Sand and Corrigan made their way toward the shuttle decks. The other two shuttles were off vessel, and holding back. "*SS Lublin*, status," she asked her inChip. Systems were patchy and she had to ask three times before they spat out an answer. The vessel was loaded with its container of heavy autonomous construction robots and ready to fly.

"Okay, we're good to go. Just act as if everything's normal."

Corrigan twisted his arm out of her grip. "We can't leave all these people to die, De Mona. You have to do something."

"Yeah; they can die with us, or without us. Make your choice."

There were too many colonists walking toward the shuttle deck for Sand's liking, all of them scrubbed up and carrying kit bags. *Kraków* and *Gdańsk*'s next batch of passengers. But the other two shuttles were holding off, and weren't coming back in.

A sense of pressure was growing on Sand as the ship accelerated. They staggered as the spin increased. Panic rippled through the knots of colonists in the atrium of the loading bay. Some of them were looking at her and pointing, walking down the walls toward her.

"Shit. Come on. If we hurry, we might be able to get away."

"I'm not happy about this, Sand."

"Fine, stay here and die, then."

The *Lublin*'s docking bay was empty, but it did not stay that way long. A gaggle of colonists followed her, shouting, more coming in to the *Lublin*'s dock.

"What's going on?"

"Pilot, hey, pilot. Goddamn it, talk to me!"

By the time she and Corrigan had made it to the access hatch, a crowd was gathering around them. Corrigan unslung his gun and pointed it at the colonists, keeping them away.

The *Mickiewicz* groaned. The grumble of the main drive unit was now obvious.

"Why are they firing the engines?" shouted someone.

"Will we still be able to get on our shuttles?"

A man close enough for Sand to see his face said it first. "We're going to crash, aren't we?"

Fearful murmurs went through the crowd.

Sand shouted. "Back away! Back away! We do not have capacity for you."

"You're going without us?"

"What about him?" A woman pointed at Corrigan.

"Do as she says, ladies and gentlemen. Stay away from the access hatch." He was stone-faced as he said it.

"Take the children, please, take the children!"

The crowd surged forward. Fights were breaking out.

Corrigan let off a shot. Sand looked nervously to the ceiling where the round had impacted. The crowd backed away, giving them a clear five metres space in the centre.

"Look!" Corrigan shouted. "Yes, the ship is going down! There is no room for anyone aboard this shuttle. Now either you can let Sand here do her job and get this shuttle off the ship so whoever comes through this mess can make use of it, or you can let them die slowly for lack of it, do you hear?"

"What you got in there that's so important, what's in there that's more important than our lives, the lives of our families?" A man with the violence of desperation in his eyes shouted.

"It'll take too long to swap out the modules!" cried Sand. "I'm sorry!"

"What have you got in there?" the man shouted.

"Yeah! Tell us!" Demands went up from various parts of the crowd.

Sand realised that she should keep her mouth shut, but it just slipped out. "Heavy construction units," she said.

"Robots? *Robots* are more important than our lives?"

The crowd seethed, pushing and pulling in at the centre.

"Let us in! Let us in, you bitch!"

A man rushed at the ship access; a small knot of people surged about him like waves around a rock, and then were sucked in his wake. The deck was pandemonium, shouting and screaming and shoving.

Corrigan brought his gun up, drew a bead, and felled the leader with a burst. He went over backwards, feet flipping up in the air, blood spraying over the crowd.

"Rush him! He can't kill us all!"

Corrigan's gun tracked over to point at the new speaker.

"Say another word, and you're next. I said, stay back! Think of the bigger picture!"

"What about the kids?" A woman, her voice trembling. She wore the uniform of a third class social technician, a child huddled into her shoulder. "Can't you take at least a few?"

Sand looked to Corrigan. "You leave on your own without these people's children and I swear to Mary, mother of God, I'll shoot you myself," he said, loud enough for only her to hear.

She bit her lip. Nodded. "I'm sorry, I'm really sorry." She was bent half over, her hands out, placating, every fibre screaming at her to climb down the ladder. She was afraid for herself. The noise of the ship rose to a roar as it drove down through exosphere and clipped the outer edges of the thermosphere. Within minutes, the vessel would be into the lower reaches of wherever the hell they were's atmosphere and shake itself to pieces. She had to get off now. She caught the eyes of the people. They'd stopped fighting. Acceptance was setting in; there was nothing they could do. She had never seen anything like it. Once the fighters gave in, the ones who'd knife you to survive, the will to do anything went from them all.

Except from the parents. The faces of the parents were the worst.

She thought quickly. "Okay! Okay! I can take five children, only five! I'm sorry."

There was a loud crash from outside. The *Mickiewicz* was not designed to withstand atmospheric entry. The crowd started, all of them acting in concert now, their individuality subsumed into the mass. Sheep to the slaughter.

"How many if I stay?" said Corrigan.

"What...?"

"Dammit, listen! How many can you take if I stay?"

"How much do you weigh?"

"What?"

"The robots, the fucking robots push the mass tolerance of the shuttle up to the max."

"Ditch them!"

"I can't get rid of them until I'm clear of the ship and by then it'd be too late!"she shouted, then something came across her face. "How much do you weigh?"

"Eighty kilos."

She did a quick calculation. "I can take two, three more... Two to a seat, maybe, *maybe*."

"Four seats? Then take eight." Corrigan moved away from the lip of the shuttle door. "I'm staying! Eight children can go, eight!"

There was renewed shoving as the urge to protect their offspring overflowed in the parents in the crowd. Sand did a count in the part of her mind not frantically calculating how much longer she had left. There were nine kids there. Nine.

"What are you waiting for?" he shouted. "Get in the cockpit! Get in now!"

Sand stared at him, then slid down the ladder. Corrigan had one of the fathers bundle the children into the access hatch. Sand pulled them roughly down into the cockpit, scared kids who wailed and could barely move. "Get in the chairs," she shouted. "No! Not that one! Little ones on big ones' knees. Buckle yourselves in, and hold on fucking tight."

"That's seven!" shouted Corrigan down the hatch. A pair of children, clutching their parents' hands, stood by him, peering down, moon faces with terror-wide eyes. "Two left."

The cockpit was jammed full. The mass ratio was all off. The cargo she carried was about as much as the *Lublin* could take. The planet down there pulled well over Earth average. She tried to do the sums, but her inChip would not co-operate and the numbers stuck in her head. She was pushing it as she was. She couldn't get three per seat. She couldn't. "I can't take two!" yelled Sand. "There's no room!"

The boy and a girl waited to be chosen. Frantic parental hands smoothed hair and patted clothes, as if presenting them for an award. The children seemed impassive; the parents wept loudly. "Take my son! Take my son!" wailed the boy's mother.

"No! Diana, take Diana!" shouted a father. "She's all I have."

This went on: the crowd, energised by this nucleus of woe, were growing restive again. She heard Corrigan shoot off another burst.

"I have to get the fuck off this ship now, Corrigan, choose!"

He looked down at her, helpless. The ship bucked, no longer rotating. They were coming out of the microgravity environment. Hankinson must have put the *Mickiewicz* belly down to save them from shear.

"Choose!"

The boy made the decision for him. He looked calmly to his mother. "I'm staying here. They have my sister. I'll stay with you, mama. I'll stay with you."

The woman's face crumpled. Diana's father lost no time in pushing his daughter downwards at Sand. Thanks spilled from him as readily as tears. The wailing of the woman whose son had decided to stay was terrifying. Sand grabbed the girl, and shoved her onto the lap of an older boy.

She stepped toward her chair. The people still on deck made fearful, inarticulate noises.

She paused. "Fuck! Bridge, Bridge, come in!"

"This is traffic control, we're a little busy here right now, Sand. Get the hell off."

"I've a hundred passengers crowding the deck. They've backed off. Give me a way out for them."

A pause.

"Goddammit!"

"Tell them to board their passenger pods through cargo service hatches nineteen and twenty seven. We'll eject them. Order the *Kraków* and *Gdańsk* to circle back and pick them up once it's safe to do so."

"There's not enough room!"

"Tell the others to make their way to the shield. There'll be room for some on the escape pods."

"What about the crew? What about you, control?"

"Good flying, Sand."

The voice cut out.

Sand's hand hovered over the docking clamp release; she snatched it back.

"Fuck!" She surprised herself with her vehemence. She hauled herself up the ladder. The ship was shaking. People were screaming. She reached the top, and shoved Corrigan to the side. "Listen!" she shouted. It was hard to make herself heard over the noise. "Goddammit, listen to me!" Her voice broke, tears streaming down her face. She was not sure for whom she cried: them, or herself. They could not hear her. She wiped at the tears with her forearm, and jabbed at the ship's external speaker system through her inChip. Her voice rang out in the docking bay. "Listen! Get into the passenger pods. Go in through service hatches nineteen and twenty seven. Captain Posth is going to jettison the hibernation decks and the remaining cargo. They'll inform the *Gdańsk* and the *Kraków* to pick you up first. It's a small chance, but it's the only one you've got. Any of you feeling fit, get up front, there'll be space for more on the crew evacuation pods."

The ship screamed as its mass shifted. The crowd were unrooted from the floor.

Corrigan gave her a small smile and a nod. "Thank you," he said. "Now get out of here." He turned to the crowd, brandishing his weapon. "Back!" he shouted, "Back!"

She went hand over hand down the ladder, coming off it as the ship lurched, banging painfully into the ladder tube.

"Get back!" The sound of gunfire. "Get b –"

Corrigan's words were cut off as the top hatch popped into place, and the seal hissed closed.

Sand threw herself into her flight chair and strapped herself in, trying to ignore the terrified children in the co-pilot's seat next to her. No time for flight checks.

"Fuck! Fuck! Fuck!" she said as she flicked on the flight systems.

"You're swearing!" came a small voice.

"Yeah?" said Sand. The younger children cried. The older ones tried to calm them. The edges of the outer bay glowed. "If you were flying this fucking joyride you'd be swearing too. Now hold on, this is going to be hairy." She touched Roosevelt for luck.

The docking clamps disengaged. She would not be thrown free this time, with the rotation stilled. She punched the ventral thruster. Full blast, outgassing all her CO_2 stock in one go. She had to get clear of the ship. The *Lublin* leapt from the spine of the *Mickiewicz*, clipping the edge of the bay as it went and tumbling into a spin.

Sand wrestled with the control stick like it was a python. The whole thing was fly by wire, but it had the mother of all feedback built into it, and she was fighting the air of an entire planet.

The shuttle tumbled. The children screamed. She was in a spin. If she couldn't pull them out of it, they'd get into thicker air and burn out. She'd never flown like this. In her idler days trucking back from the belt, supervising the machines that did the real flying from the mine to the Lagrange refineries, she'd fantasised about real piloting, about being faced by a crisis where she could prove herself. Now she had what she'd wished for, and how.

She fired the retros all down the starboard of the ship, desperate to arrest its yaw. The little vessel creaked in protest, the altimeter ticked down in a blur. The gees racked up as they accelerated; Sand's head pounded, her vision retreated to a point at the end of the tunnel. It was just her and the stick. She pulled on it so hard she thought she'd break it. She stopped trying to pull the nose up and pointed it right down, trying to use the drag of the increasingly dense air to stabilise her.

The ship bucked, and she was flying level. She yanked back hard, pulling the *Lublin* out of a steep dive. She had to get its back end to present to the atmosphere, get the nose out of the heat.

She did it, and screamed.

There was the *Mickiewicz*, a great worm of a thing aglow with fire. Debris broke from it, spinning away. Posth was jettisoning the cargo, and containers were shooting off the rear of the cargo rails like bullets. The mass-reactive cap billowed steam. The vessel was going down in a wreath of flames, and she was headed right at it.

Sand yanked the stick sharply left, thrusters sending the *Lublin* slewing. She made it over the top without being struck, more by luck than design.

"Oh, my God."

The hibernation decks blew from the *Mickiewicz*. Starting at the stern and working their way toward the cap, each deck blasted away from the vessel, splitting into two semicircular segments. They were hardened for emergency landing, but a hot touchdown like this had not been planned for. Even in the worst scenarios, there was always time to evacuate. No-one envisaged the ship driving itself into the ground.

The segments tumbled like so many petals from a burning flower. She watched as two of them smashed into each other, spilling their contents into the maelstrom and smearing themselves brightly across the sky.

She jetted away, try to keep clear. A few of the deck segments seemed to be okay, orienting themselves for a safe re-entry profile, but the majority were spinning out of control, fire tailing behind them.

Sand dodged one as it shot from its housing. She put all she had into the Sabres, burning their rocket fuel recklessly, accelerating past the segment. She jerked the ship around as another segment blasted out in front of her. The segment moved with deceptive majesty. She opened up the port Sabres full, let out her remaining manoeuvring gas stocks of the jets on that side, and slammed her foot onto the ventral jet pedal, but the CO_2 in the ventral was all gone. She turned too slowly, inertia sending her in a wide curve right at the hibernation deck.

She reacted fast, slamming on dorsal thrust and ducked down. For a second she thought she'd missed it, just for a second.

The sound of the collision ripped through the ship. Sand was slammed into her restraints, and the few children still conscious cried out. Debris from her ship and the deck tumbled into space behind them. A cacophony of screaming and alarms filled the cockpit. Reality shifted, her blood and breath thundered. She was aware of her body in ways she never had been before. Her sense of self retreated until she became a set of skill-driven responses utterly dedicated to preserving the shell they inhabited.

She did not think; she flew.

The ship hadn't picked up much momentum from the collision – she arrested the spin almost before it started – but so many of her systems were out. She hit the atmosphere barely in control.

Her mind, overclocked by the threat of extinction, seemed to exist without her, observing from outside as her animal body fought madly to save itself. She was aware of instruments registering dangerous hot spots on the hull skin where the shielding had been compromised, aware of the pain of acceleration pressing her back, aware of the strap cutting into her neck. Her body reacted accordingly, reversing thrust, bringing speed down, while the ship's automated systems 'staged their own electronic struggles for survival, cooling and mending as best they could.

The atmosphere thickened, the wings extended, the engines switched mode. The port wing was damaged. Icons glared red and blared harshly at her – one of the four Sabres' micropore intakes was fouled. She shut the engine down before it could explode.

Desert rushed up to meet her, eager to embrace the *Lublin*. Sand's sense of time stretched, slowed further, her brain and body in overdrive. She brought the nose up. Deploy the gear: Yes? No? Options and scenarios fled through her, too quick to catch. She tried to bring landing gear down. In the atmosphere, the *Lublin* was ungainly, energy-hungry. The ground came closer and closer. She vented the Sabres down and back, twisting them halfway to their VTOL position. She extended the flaps, only for half the port wing to vibrate and rip free. The ship yawed.

The undamaged starboard wing clipped the ground first, kissing the top of a sinuous barchan in an explosion of sand. The *Lublin* leapt into the air, swooped down the slipface of the dune. The wing caught again, banging the belly of the craft into the ground and then up again like a stone skipping across a lake. Another impact, and the ship was down for good, slewing across the sand. The port landing wheel tore free, then the nose wheel, and the *Lublin* ploughed the desert prow first. Stone and sand battered the cockpit, and the windows shattered, spraying her and the children with glass and debris. Sand threw up her hands to cover her face as a dune loomed up in front of them. The *Lublin* slammed into it, and she was flung forward, cracking her head on her instruments as the vessel came to a sudden, final halt.

Sand passed out, the screams of dying children pursuing her into the black.

PART III

Desert
1 day after the crash

Barry Loan: ...and now we'd like to introduce our next guest. For generations mankind has been fascinated by the possibility of creating artificially intelligent beings. Mary Shelley started it with her novel *Frankenstein*. How is it, then, that nearly two centuries after the first computers were created, we see no such created minds among us? Are we getting closer to the advent of machine minds, or will they forever remain the domain of fiction? Professor Vikram Patel of the Bangalore Institute for Post-Human Sciences has been studying the formation of intelligence in non-natural systems. We're delighted to have him with us today, in person no less. You've got some rather bad news for us, haven't you Professor Patel?

Professor Vikram Patel: Well, I don't know about bad news...

BL: Your latest study suggests that artificial intelligence is impossible.

VP [looks apologetic]: Impossible for now.

BL [earnest smile]: Why is that?

VP: We've been looking at advanced techniques involving biological brains for robotic units. It's been apparent for a long time that computers cannot simulate intelligent thought. It is possible to create a facsimile of a personality within a digital environment, but it remains convincing only so long as its original parameters are not exceeded...

BL: Like asking something programmed as a receptionist to make a burger?

VP [crosses and uncrosses legs, coughs]: Well, 'programmed' is not the word, and the artificial beings we have currently in society can generalise that much at least... It is more akin to asking a well-trained sheep dog to become a rescue dog, with no additional training. It might try, but its efforts will be clumsy.

BL [taps at a tablet]: And how has your research into grown brains been going? They are grown, right?

VP: Yes, from stem cells collected from volunteers. From my team, actually...

BL [frowns questioningly]: So these grown brains, they also do not exhibit true intelligence?

VP [looks uncomfortable]: This is what we have found. Even when we grow a human brain from scratch, it does not function as one grown in a human body. Naturally, we have not undertaken to create an entire brain, as that would be unethical, but our initial research indicates so.

BL: And this mirrors the work undertaken in China a few years back?

VP: To create a digital copy of an existing human brain. The simulation should have functioned, but it did not.

BL: Why?

VP: Nobody knows, but we are trying to find out. That is the beauty of science, after all.

BL: What do you think?

VP [folds hands on stomach]: Personally? I do not know. Perhaps there is something special about us that infuses the human mind with a higher consciousness. Maybe it is to do with the long maturation process, or – as I suspect – that the brain is more a reflection of its experiences and environment than an expression of its genes. The human brain is developing throughout childhood; we have such a long childhood precisely because we need time for our brains to develop. On the other hand, long-period digital simulations that have attempted to replicate this have led to nothing. Perhaps it is something else.

BL [gestures expansively, his face earnest]: A spiritual angle? The Catholic church is already citing your work as proof of the hand of God; that only an outside force can imbue us with our souls.

VP: I hesitate to call it that – to use the word *soul* – or to defer responsibility for our consciousness to a supernatural force, but some of my colleagues entertain the idea, certainly. Others are examining the idea that the brain is a receiver for consciousness manifest in higher planes of existence, but this is a fringe science and even more unlikely, in my opinion. The brain is incredibly complex, and I am not surprised we have not duplicated it. I doubt we ever will.

BL: You must have some idea if it's possible...

VP: Sentience cannot be forced. It is my contention that it emerges from complex systems. We can't make it; it either happens, or it does not. We could run a million simulations of the human brain that do not result in sentience, but the million and first might develop into a thinking creature. Do you see? We cannot command it to happen. No one can, not God or Prometheus or... I think intelligence's mystery in itself is a cause for wonder enough without appealing to a higher authority. Don't you think?

BL [nervous chuckle]: Well, I don't.... You're the scientist.

VP: The purpose of our work is not to recreate the human brain. As I said, that would be immoral. Rather, we wish to harness the versatility of organic neural networks to deliver better, more flexible machines. The parts that govern balance, vision, environmental feedback, all these things have been accomplished far better by nature than we will ever manage. Why not use them? We cannot replicate consciousness at this time, and that is not our goal.

BL: These machines of yours. You've called them *androids*, a term familiar to most of our viewers. An old term?

VP: I say, why invent a new word when a perfectly serviceable one already exists?

BL: So androids... Why choose that particular word?

VP [firm]: Because they are mimetic, although of the human mind, not necessarily of the human body; you have to allow us a little latitude. Yes, androids.

BL: Machines made with brains derived from human

stem cells. Your androids. This has raised some debate in the Senates of the USA and EFU...

VP: It has, but I'll say to you what I said to them in my depositions. These machines may be derived from human genes, but they are absolutely not human...

BL: But do they think?

VP: In a manner of... Yes, yes they do.

BL: Doesn't that make them human, then?

VP: No, not at all. A cat thinks. Does that make it human? No. It does not. The android units we have made possess far simpler versions of our own minds. They do not think as you or I think, they do not think even as a cat or a pig does, but they do think. They are highly focused on their task – the advantage here is that they are flexible enough to be instructed in all manner of tasks – but their inner lives are a little, well, 'cloudy' is the word I use. They think, but they are not conscious. It is as if they have a dream of sentience, rather than sentience itself. I think much of the controversy comes from our use of human neural tissues; confusion is bound to result. If we had used the cells of an animal, then it would not be anywhere near as controversial. I admit that to some people we might look like Frankensteins, but we are not in the business of creating slaves. That is abhorrent to me.

BL: Then why use human tissues at all? Why not something else; a chimpanzee, or a pig?

VP: Simply because we have a supply, in our own researchers, that we can monitor easily and compare our constructs against. There is no need to keep animals in our laboratory. There is no need...

BL: A matter of cost then?

VP: And of ethics. Animals cannot give their consent for their tissues to be used. And human brain tissue is also far more versatile than that of other animals. But I repeat, we're not making human beings to trap in machinery.

BL: And what applications do you see for your 'dreaming machines'?

VP: Anything and everything. Primarily we've been working on creating a new control system for robotic lifeforms that can live with and around us safely and usefully. But I can see networked android brains being utilised in research institutes, they might be particularly adept at managing large, complex, reactive systems; like financial trading, say. I don't think they'll ever supplant inorganic computers, rather I see them as a supplement, each used for whatever purpose they are best adapted for. You want something to mindlessly analyse protein chains, use an inorganic. You need something to pick the kids up from school, you're going to need something more flexible.

BL: Well, now. We've actually got one of these machines here today, haven't we?

VP: Yes, we have. We call him DOB. Shall we bring him in now...?

— Excerpt from the 2087 interview conducted by
US-Mexican media personality Barry Loan
with synthetic intelligence expert Vikram Patel
(popularly regarded as the moment that
ushered in the modern robotic age)

CHAPTER ELEVEN
Survivors

THERE WERE SIX survivors of segment 14A, out of a total of fifty. How many of them had died on the journey and how many had died in the crash was a moot point. They were all just as dead.

There was Dariusz, close-mouthed and thoughtful, guarding his secret and concerned for his son. Doubtless they were all concerned, for sons and daughters, friends and spouses, but one's own concerns outweigh those of others, and so Dariusz dwelt on the fate of Danieł.

There was Marina, the junior engineer, come back to herself now. Once out of shock, she changed, and set about organising the group. It was to her the others looked to resolve their disputes.

The man whom she had cradled was called Tomasz. Tomek, he preferred, even from people he had just met. A Pole, a construction specialist, he was superficially friendly, but his eyes were haunted, and that he had in common with them all. He said less the longer they were in the desert.

Bernhardt the German systems engineer, jowly, possessed of forceful voice and forceful optimism. Sandra, also of Germany, quiet and withdrawn, who initially took their being marooned worse than the others. Finally Bo, a young Dane, full of the enthusiasm of youth; to him, their predicament was an adventure, or so he displayed. Underneath he almost certainly despaired.

They were shipwrecked in a desert on a world they were not supposed to be upon, the man who had unwittingly brought this fate upon them hiding in their midst. Would they tear him limb from limb if they knew? Perhaps.

The first thing they did was to argue, quite vehemently. The main issue of contention: should they stay at the segment and await rescue, or should they strike out?

Dariusz wished to strike out immediately. To him, it was clear rescue was not going to come. "Look at the wreckage," he said. "Look at it!" He grew animated, angry with their intransigence, angry that he was unable to tell them what he knew. "The ship has crashed. That much is clear." The others, particularly Bernhardt, argued loudly that retrieval parties from the other parts of the fleet would come for them, that his countrymen from the *Goethe* would be on their way.

Dariusz could not voice his own certainty, that the *Goethe* was either not with them or had been destroyed, without revealing his role in the disaster. He could only frame it in terms of opinion, and they all had opinions. "We have supplies only for twenty days, maybe less," he said. "We will need those supplies to make our way out of this desert, because if we wait, and no one comes, we will drink all our water and eat all our rations, and then we will die."

"No!" said Bernhardt, with force. Dariusz had the measure of him. Bernhardt was a man who would say everything with force; firmly at first, expecting to be followed, furiously later if he was not. Such a man might fall prey to violent impulse. "If we depart from this point, how will they find us? The locator beacon is here. The debris trail is easy to follow. If we head north, away from the sun, then what? We will die in the sand as they search for us. Who knows how big this wasteland is?"

"There are devices aboard the deck we can carry, hardened tablets equipped with personal locators –" said Dariusz.

"They are not as powerful as the beacon in the deck segment!" said Bernhardt, growing florid. "Marina tells me the locator in there" – he pointed to the deck, which they never referred to by name; it was a place of death – "will run for decades."

"The range is seven or eight times that of the tablets," said Sandra. She looked to Marina for confirmation, and received a tiny nod.

Bernhardt saw this exchange. Sure that he was winning the argument, his temper retreated. Gently, or gently for Bernhardt, he said, "I am sure they will rescue your son, too. Imagine, how would you feel if they rescue him, and you are a mummy half-buried in the sand?" He gave a hoarse chuckle, a boardroom chuckle, a chuckle favoured by men in a place where there were no women, who justify the obscene salaries they earn by their own obscene sense of self-worth. It was a Pointer's chuckle.

Dariusz thought, but did not say, that he would not feel anything, as he would be dead. "Bernhardt, look." Dariusz pointed at the sun. "The sun has not moved at all in the sky. How long have we been here?"

"Five hours or so," said Marina.

"A place of perpetual noon. This planet is tidally locked. It is the only explanation," Dariusz said.

"Or it revolves very slowly," said Tomek.

"The sun has not moved at all! And even if I am wrong and you are right, Tomek, this is still not Heracles." Dariusz appealed to his fellow Pole, hands out. Tomek's face twitched, and he looked at his feet.

"Then that is all the more reason to wait," said Bernhardt. He walked away, terminating the discussion.

Unable to convince Bernhardt, who was domineering enough to bring the others into line, and caught by Marina's half-pleading, half-commanding looks, Dariusz agreed to stay. He resolved to depart within three days; by then, it should have become clear that they were not going to be rescued. Clear even to Bernhardt. If not, he would leave on his own; they couldn't stop him. If they would not listen to sense, so be it. He'd take his chances. They could die, and they would.

Marina kept everyone busy.

They cannibalised spare smartcloth jumpsuits for headscarves, then knotted the arms and legs of a few more suits together to form an awning, which they stretched from the side of the crashed deck to the sand banks its impact had thrown up. The deck's interior was beginning to smell. Now the emergency power supply was exhausted, the contents warmed quickly, and the astringent smell of the pseudo-amniotics gave way to the round richness of decay. They stripped the deck of useful content the morning they awoke, and did not venture back inside.

They kept time using the clocks on their hardened tablets, bulky, primitive but robust things of limited functionality. Things useful to survival, created in anticipation of inChip network failure and proving their worth in just such a situation. Each had a short-range radio, locator, compass, and a concise native database. Crucially, the tablets also contained environmental sampling capabilities including a compact spectrography unit, toxin detectors, and radiation counter. The counter told the survivors that background radioactivity and cosmic bombardment were well within human tolerance, and this, in conjunction with a clear north/south reading on the compass, told Dariusz the planet at least had a protective magnetic field.

Every eight hours they activated the radio, called out a distress message they had agreed upon, and waited for a reply. Every eight hours they were disappointed, the unit's speakers hissing with empty static. Once, they thought they caught the distant pulse of another beacon, but it faded, and they could not bring it back.

It was hot outside. The smartsuits and the cinnamon breeze kept them more or less comfortable, if they stayed in the shade. They spoke pleasantly enough after their initial arguments, until the heat made them lethargic. They became anxious, and their anxiety was exacerbated by their isolation from the network. Their inChips were useless. Through the tablets, they could send each other brief text messages – that was all. The interconnected nature of life on Earth, and their dependence on it, became horribly apparent. Each became an island. All of them bar Bo eventually retreated into solitude, unfamiliar as it was. Bo tried many times to initiate conversation, to find out more about the people around him, inviting them to speculate on the nature of this world. Tomek and Marina, Sandra too, responded well at first – Tomek in particular, for he found the silence in his mind the most daunting – but one by one they became irritated by interaction. The silence in the camp became leaden.

Bo grew fractious when he spoke, gabbled. He could not sit still.

When Dariusz mentioned he was going to explore the area, Bo pleaded to go along. Dariusz had of course hoped that the Dane would come with him. He was young, and strong, if also headstrong, and if two of them said they would go, the others were less likely to object. "But I'll be looking for other deck sections," he said. "Do you understand?"

"Your son," said Bo. He nodded quickly, as if afraid the offer would be withdrawn. "Of course."

Dariusz took one of the tablets from Marina. It was the tracker, keyed in to the emergency frequencies of the downed colony ship, that interested Dariusz the most. He brought this to the fore of the screen.

"Don't be long, and do not stray too far from us," said Marina.

"What, do you want me to say I'll be back by nightfall?" said Dariusz.

"Don't tease. Please. I don't want anyone else hurt."

"Ten kilometres, no further. We won't stray out of radio range, and we'll call in if we find anything."

Marina nodded. Bernhardt shook his head, smiled as if he had all the answers, but said nothing.

After tying a supply of rehydration drinks and ration packs to makeshift bandoliers across their chests, Dariusz and Bo set out into the desert.

THE NEAREST HIBERNATION segment was silent. Half a kilometre distant, well within sight of the camp, the deck had blazed fiercely for five hours after Dariusz had first emerged. The group had not done anything about it; there was nothing they *could* do. Sandra and Bo had stared at it, horrified and mesmerised in equal measure, and the rest, afflicted with the guilt of survival, had looked away. Dariusz held no hope for what they would find there, and his expectations matched the reality.

A black tangle, barely recognisable. The sand was stained with soot in a wide circle around it. Partially vitrified sand crunched underfoot.

"Poor bastards," said Bo.

"We were never likely to find anyone alive here, or any supplies," said Dariusz.

"Maybe the hull was damaged," said Bo. "Cracked? Re-entry would have blowtorched everything."

181

"Maybe," said Dariusz. Human fat burns hot, he thought. The amniotics were not readily flammable, but once they had caught, they too would have combusted like napalm. There was little left of the deck except its warped, woven-carbon skeleton. Supposedly fireproof, he thought. Nothing is. Anything will burn, given enough heat.

He reached his hand out to the frame and snatched his fingers back; the wreckage was still hot. He checked the tablet. Even up close, there was no signal from the segment's beacon. It had been consumed along with everything else. It was, he told himself – and he admitted that desperation clouded his judgement – too small to be part of deck forty-six.

Bo touched his arm. "Come on," the Dane said. "There's nothing we can do here, and nothing we can take."

Once they were a kilometre out from the burned deck, they picked up other signals. Dariusz looked back. He could see the burned deck segment, but not their own. It seemed that their segment was in a depression, not readily apparent from the camp itself, which might account for their difficulty in receiving transmissions. He mentioned this to Bo, who shrugged. "Maybe," he said. Dariusz radioed back to Marina, to explain his theory and that they might soon be out of contact. She tried to convince him to come back. He refused. Marina said they'd send someone out a little way, so they could stay in touch. Dariusz said it would not be necessary.

There were two segments broadcasting their location within range of the tablet – 19B and 9A – and many cargo containers beeping out their manifests, scattered in a broad sweep. Dariusz was anxious; the trail would likely be wide, perhaps hundreds of kilometres. Who knew if the signal from Daniel's deck would not be picked up just over the next dune? Bo spoke gently of the signals they were receiving. They agreed to head up the debris trail in a straight line and investigate the decks.

They took their time, meandering from their path now and then to inspect pieces of wreckage, their eyes constantly scanning the dun horizon for rescue or other survivors. The debris was nearly all unidentifiable: charred pieces that could have been part of anything. Occasionally they chanced upon a fragment that was recognisable, and as often as not they recoiled from it.

It was hot – hot enough to trouble the smartsuits – the shifting sand was hard to walk upon, and the gravity was taxing. Their bodies had not yet recovered from their rude awakening. Dariusz grew silent and grim. Bo ceased trying to draw him into conversation.

Deck 19B had landed correctly, tipping on its side, deploying its landing gear and firing its brief-burst retros long enough to come down without harm. It was pristine, but empty of people and supplies, suggesting to Dariusz that at least some of the colonists aboard the *Mickiewicz* had woken and perhaps evacuated before the crash. This small hope, welcome though it was, did little to assuage the dragging millstone of guilt that had settled about his neck.

Deck 9A contained nothing but corpses in sarcophagi, their status panels dimly red with residual power. This they ransacked. It was one of the smallest deck halves – decks ten to zero had held only two dozen colonists each – and its supplies were commensurately modest. They took what there was, bundling it up and leaving it within the deck segment doorways to collect on their return to the camp, so they would not have to venture inside again. They rested there, out of the heat of the unmoving sun in the company of the dead, until Bo had an idea and spent some time fashioning a sled from a battered carbon sheet he dragged from the desert. They piled it high with supplies, moving them from the doorway, and left it for later.

There were no more decks singing out in range of their receiver, but they headed a little further anyway. What else was there to do?

The sun beat at them. The sand was dangerously hot; Dariusz supposed it was only of a bearable temperature because of the constant cinnamon wind turning the sand over. Sweat dripped from them. They consumed their isotonic drinks more quickly than they intended.

The Dane stopped, peering into the rippling heat haze that filled the hollows of the land with the lie of water.

"Is that another one?" Bo shaded his eyes with his hands. "I wish we had binoculars, anything." He laughed. "I'd kill for sunglasses. Are you getting a signal?"

Dariusz licked his lips. They were cracked, the skin flaking. He was unbearably thirsty, his head throbbed with dehydration. He dared not waste his drink, mindful of the walk back and his planned trudge away from the camp. Already he had consumed far more than he had expected to. He took only the smallest sip from his bottle. He ran his moistened tongue over his lips, seeking to soothe them.

He pulled up the tablet on its strap. He squinted at the screen, then let it drop. "A faint one. Deck 30A," he said.

"One of the upper medium size range?"

Dariusz nodded. "One hundred and fifty colonists per segment."

Bo sagged, his sense of adventure dwindling as his fatigue grew. "Shall we check it out? How far is it?"

"Three more kilometres, maybe," said Dariusz. "It's hard to be sure."

"That will take us away from the group, well out of radio range," said Bo. "We'll be thirteen, fourteen kilometres away."

"We won't be long."

"Are you going to radio in?"

Dariusz stuck out his bottom lip and shook his head. "There's no need to cause any more argument. It's just outside the radio's effective range. We won't be long." Dariusz checked the radio. It looked like Marina hadn't sent anyone out after all. "They can't hear us anyway."

Bo scratched behind his ear. Where they weren't protected by their smartsuits, their skin was reddening. "Fine by me. Nothing to do but sit around there and wait to die anyway."

They walked onwards. The segment coalesced, hard black lines resolving themselves from the heat haze. 30A had landed well; furthermore, it had been occupied. The ends of the segment pointed at them like truncated horns, open doors black and uninviting, emergency ladders hanging from them. The number emblazoned across its concave centre was discoloured by heat, but the segment's fabric appeared sound.

"No sign of damage," said Bo.

"Not from this distance."

"And there, the doors are open and one of the ladders has been dropped."

"I don't see any movement."

"I think I can see signs of a camp." Bo pointed, bringing Dariusz to a halt. "See? Under the vessel, in the shade..."

Dariusz ran his fingers over the touch screen. "No radio broadcasts except the beacon."

"I can definitely see signs of a camp." Bo was more certain.

"We are too far out to be sure."

"Let's get closer, then." Bo strode on ahead without waiting for agreement..

The Dane had been correct. Scattered under the segment were empty bottles, ration packs and makeshift bedding. The rope ladder hanging from the door swayed listlessly in the hot wind, banging into the hull.

"A camp." Bo spoke without triumph. He simply stated what he saw, in a very Scandinavian way. He was free of the unease that had settled upon Dariusz. "A lot of people... Hello?" he shouted through cupped hands. His shout was too loud, a rebuke to the desert for its silence, and the desert did not take kindly to it.

"Shh," said Dariusz.

"Why?"

"I don't know," he said irritably. "Because." He took a bigger swig than he intended from his bottle. His load had become worrying light. Thank God they had found the supplies at 9A.

Dariusz stepped carefully under the deck. The temperature underneath was little lower than out in the sunlight, but Dariusz welcomed the shade. The ground was disturbed, emergency supplies scattered. Of the colonists, there was no sign.

"Why didn't they use the tablets?"

Dariusz shrugged. "Who knows? I'm going inside. Check around the segment for footprints," he said. "It is possible they walked away, or have gone in search of others. Find their trail, and we can find out which way they went."

Bo nodded, and set off at a slow jog, eyes to the ground.

Dariusz checked over the segment's skin as he walked back to the ladder. The smooth carbons of its surface were heat-scored, but he could see no sign of major damage.

He reached the ladder and grabbed it. His weight stilled it. The silence was welcome; the noise had been too similar to the clacking of bones.

He climbed inside. The interior was dark, and he paused in the bright doorway for his eyes to adjust. Presently, he moved forward.

The same was true of Deck Segment 30A as had been of their own; many failed hibernation pods, some open and stinking to reveal husks of occupants long dead, some closed, holding others no doubt more recently deceased, some open and empty.

Dried splashes of pseudo-amniotics encrusted the surfaces. There, footprints? He looked closely. A lot of footprints. Where were the *people*?

He clambered awkwardly over the sarcophagi. In space and under rotation, the outer circumference of the joined segments formed the floor. The segments landed side on when ejected, if they landed correctly, and so Dariusz's floor was what had once been the forward wall, and the curved walls had been, on the ship, the ceilings and the floor. The segments were not well designed for such an emergency, he thought. They were difficult to move through, there was minimal equipment on them, and their position on the ground was inconvenient to survivors. Jettisoning the colonists' decks was and always had been intended as an action of last resort, an affordable failsafe should the ship's systems malfunction once it reached its destination. Jettisoning presupposed a planet to land upon, and at least one other ship in close enough attendance to perform rescue duty. If these conditions were not met, then the colonists would not survive, so why spend the money? It was callous, but then so much of what the Pointers instigated was callous. He estimated just under half the sarcophagi had successfully opened. Sixty, seventy people, perhaps more.

He heard a sound, a scrabbling that stopped as soon as it had begun, perhaps also a sob. It was hard for him to be sure. He was making a racket clambering over the sarcophagi, his shoes squeaking on the smooth lids where they were not coated in dried fluid. He wished he could move with more stealth, but he could not.

A tunnel led off to the right. All but the smallest decks had subdecks, concentric circles of sleeping colonists; two, in this instance. The subdeck was pitch black, random stripes of red light reflecting from sarcophagus lids. He paused, considering whether the stranger had gone that way. He had little desire to follow.

He caught sight of movement ahead. A hand flashed, a pair of shod feet scrabbled over the curve of a sarcophagus lid. The sobbing returned loudly. Dariusz stumbled and cursed. "Wait! Wait!" he shouted.

He rounded the curve furthest from the doors, where it was darkest, before growing rapidly lighter from the daylight spilling through the second door. He caught up to the fleeing colonist near the exit, framing the stranger in brightness that prevented Dariusz from making anything other than a silhouette.

"Wait! Wait!"

The figure was weeping, backing toward the door. Dariusz came closer, hands outstretched. A woman: a young woman, shaven-haired and jumpsuit-clad, as anonymous as all of them.

"Stop, stop! I'm not going to hurt you!" said Dariusz.

She did not respond. He switched from Lingua Anglica to Polish, then German, resorting to Spanish and finally Mandarin. Still there was no response. She was terrified, the tracks of old tears streaking the dirt and amniotics caked on her face.

Something troubled Dariusz. Why did she not jump out of the door, if she was so scared?

Bo shouted from below. Without taking his eyes off the colonist, Dariusz made his way forward to the door. The girl circled away from him. The ladder for this door had been deployed but then pulled up and so Dariusz tossed it out. Shortly, Bo's head appeared in the doorway, alarmed. Dariusz raised his hand to silence him, too late.

"Dariusz! Dariusz! I... Oh. What's going on?"

"Hibernation damage, some crash trauma maybe."

Bo looked back at the ground nervously. "I don't think so."

The girl screamed, looked frantically from one to the other, then ran at Dariusz. Her nails raked painfully at his sunburned face. The force of her rush bowled him over. He wrestled with her, finally calming her, until she collapsed, weeping, against his chest.

Bo came into the corridor. Dariusz held the young woman. "It's okay, you'll be alright." He waved Bo back. The Dane was agitated; he crouched uncomfortably, anxious to speak.

"Dariusz, listen. They... I think they left. No. I think they tried to *run*. You've got to come and see this. And then we better get the fuck out of here."

Dariusz held the woman tightly, as much for his own comfort as hers. He felt his own tears threaten. How much had they all lost? How much had *he* lost? All of it was his doing. "Okay," he said. "Okay."

"I found them out there," Bo said. They knelt in the doorway, scanning the sand below. The Dane pointed to two messy sets of footprints heading away from the deck in differing directions. Many people. "They go out for about two hundred metres, that one a little further. There's a few dropped items, nothing that says to me that this was an organised march."

"What, they ran away?"

Bo looked back into the dark, where the young woman was curled into herself, near catatonic. "What do you think? Look at her. All the people on the ship, in the fucking fleet, man, they were all chosen for their suitability as colonists." When agitated, Bo spoke proper English. Dariusz struggled to follow it.

"And?"

"Meaning, we're not talking about easily scared people here. What the hell did you think she saw? Do you think the crash alone could do that to her?" He looked Dariusz dead in the eye. "I saw... I saw an arm. In the sand. I thought it was buried, I bent down to pick it up and, shit. It was just an arm. Lean out; if you lean out, you should be able to see it."

Dariusz leaned out, hanging from the door. He had to go a fair way, and the strain on his arms was considerable. "I can't see it."

"Damn, look, I'll hold you." Bo grabbed his wrist.

Dariusz leaned out further. As Bo had said, an arm lay on the sand. It was torn off at the elbow.

"Okay, okay, pull me back in."

Bo did so.

"What do you think did it? It's too early for cannibalism," Bo said, matter-of-factly. "So, what, did they go crazy? Is it some kind of lifeform? There's oxygen here, there has to be life. Is there something out... Out there?" His eyes slid back to the door. "Shit man, you're a geoengineer, some of that must come under your specialisation."

It did. "It's possible. With a tidally locked world, you're normally looking at one side permanently blasted, the other permanently frozen. But there's atmosphere here, there could be heat exchange between the two hemispheres... Obviously there has to be, or we'd have roasted by now. There's oxygen, it's not too hot; I don't see any signs of water, but there could be some. There could be something out there, yes."

"Then what do we do?"

"Your suggestion was sound," said Dariusz. "We get the fuck out of here."

"How can you be sure?" said Bernhardt. "If there were so many of them, why did they not try to contact anyone on their tablets? Maybe there were only one or two of them, not fifty. You said one of the other deck segments had been evacuated –"

"*Looked* like it had been evacuated," corrected Bo. He and Dariusz were testy. The sun had been on them for the better part of a day and a half. They had not dared stop on the way back, and had been forced to drag the terrified girl. They stood in a small group in the shade of their camp, Bernhardt at their front. Already he had elevated himself to the role of village headman.

"The distinction is immaterial, we only have the evidence we have. In point of fact, we only have your interpretation of the evidence." He looked happy with that. Some of the others were nodding.

"EMP, maybe. The crash could have scrambled it all. Maybe they didn't think of it," said Bo.

"We're in some kind of depression here," said Dariusz. "They could have broadcast and we would not have heard them."

"Or maybe alien lifeforms ate them?" said Bernhardt. "Come on! There is no complex life in the galaxy besides that on Earth."

"That we have yet found," corrected Dariusz.

"Plankton and plants, that's all."

"Maybe we just don't fucking know, Bernhardt, so back the fuck off!" said Bo. "Just take a look at her, she's terrified out of her mind!"

Bernhardt folded his arms. "We have crashed. It is not surprising. If one of the others on her deck suffered an episode of psychosis, she would be just as terrified as if an alien monster ate them. You have no evidence."

Bo started toward the older man, stiff-backed and aggressive. Dariusz held out his hand, placing it on the Dane's chest. Bo stopped, but barely. His nostrils flared. "Fuck, man," he said.

"Whatever happened, it only adds to my case that we depart. Bo and I went through our liquids far quicker than we expected. I would expect that it has been the same here."

Sandra took a half-step forward. Her face was angry red, giving way abruptly to white at the edge of her headcloth. "Yes," she said. "The sun is hot, the wind is dessicating. It is very dry here."

Marina stood. She had been comforting the girl; they still had no idea of either her name or nationality. "Dariusz?" said Marina.

"From what I've seen so far, this is a very dry region. I have seen no sign at all of any kind of hydrological activity, which suggests it's either rare or never happens at all. We have to get out of here. I disagree with Bernhardt. With the tablets, they'll find us almost as easily as if we stay here – if they come. If they don't come, then we'll die right where we are, it's as simple as that."

"But what about the creatures –" said Sandra.

"Please," snorted Bernhardt.

Tomek turned to him. "Very well," he said dully. "What about whatever harmed the other colonists?"

"*If* they were harmed," said Bernhardt. "We must stay here, don't you see? I –"

"We're on our own, Bernhardt," said Dariusz. "We have been since the moment we arrived. If there were any hope of rescue, we would have heard of it by now." He lifted the tablet on its strap.

"You say we're in a depression –"

"It makes no difference to signals coming from above, does it? There is nothing: no chatter, no messages, no instructions. The rest of the fleet is elsewhere. The *Goethe* is not with us as planned. We are alone, do you not see that? And we will die alone if we do not act." He looked over his shoulder. "Now we have other factors to take into consideration. We are leaving."

"Let's vote on it," said Sandra.

"Yes," said Marina. "We must stick together. Either we all go, or we all stay."

Dariusz was not happy with that suggestion, but he said nothing. If they voted to stay, then he would just keep arguing with them.

"Agreed?" she said.

There were murmurs of assent from them all; all except Bernhardt, who muttered about the idiocy of democracy.

"All in favour of heading out?" said Marina.

Bo, Dariusz and Sandra put up their hands.

"All in favour of staying?"

Marina and Bernhardt; Tomek too, after some vacillation.

"There we have it," said Bernhardt. "A tie. I say take that as a vote for the status quo."

"Maybe not a tie," said Dariusz. He pushed past Marina and Tomek, to where the young woman sat in the sand by the deck. Dariusz leaned against the carbon hull. Even in the shade, it was uncomfortably hot to touch. "What about you? Do we stay or go?" He said gently.

The woman had calmed since they had found her. She sat listlessly, not shaking or crying, but her face was as devoid of thought as a doll's.

Dariusz persisted. He knelt by her side, and turned her face towards him. "Stay or go? Stay or go?"

A medley of expressions flitted over her face, and her eyes focused. "We can't stay," she whispered. "We can't stay."

A buzz of conversation started up in the group. Dariusz, encouraged, tried to get the girl to speak some more. From her accent, he thought she might be Polish, and so switched from Lingua Anglica to talk to her in that language. It did no good.

He stood and faced the group, who watched him expectantly. "Four against three," he said. "We go."

THEY ATE TOGETHER, slept for a few hours. In the constant light they slept shallowly, dreaming of disaster. They awoke irritable.

They worked steadily, gathering together all they could. When Marina found Sandra tossing away the empty bottles, she made her pick them up, in case they should find water.

"We should save our urine," she said. "It's safer to drink each other's than our own, and only once or twice, or the toxins become too concentrated for our kidneys to filter."

They made comical expressions of disgust, and Bo joked uncouthly about it, but they did not discount the idea. They were constantly thirsty.

Bernhardt set himself to his tasks with good grace, and his occasional grumbles did not detract from his industry. Sandra asked Bo to show Bernhardt how to make a sled for them each, and Bo agreed. Grudgingly they worked together, and became absorbed in the task.

Sandra seemed pleased with the result. "What is it you do?" asked Dariusz as she unobtrusively observed the two men at work. She gave Dariusz the broadest smile he had seen anyone give on the planet: a dazzling white crescent broke across her sunburned face, completely transforming her features. "A sociologist," she said with a degree of mischief. She was, he realised, quite beautiful when she smiled. Noticing this, the beauty of another person, had another effect on him; he realised that he was still alive – and that his son might be dead. The myriad pains the crash and the planet had inflicted on him, thus far pushed to the back of his mind, became oppressive. He felt the enormity of his responsibility, he felt the loss of his wife. He feared for his son.

He struggled to keep his wakened emotions in check, tried to smile back. "I see," he said.

He told Marina he was going to go out from the camp to scan the nearest beacons again, and to see if he could find anything of use in the cargo containers scattered across the landscape. He walked with his head away from the others, hiding his tears. He let the sun burn his neck as he stared at the screen of the tablet, a private penance.

An hour later, composed, he returned from his slow circling. "I've rechecked the manifests of the nearby containers on the tablet. Nothing useful," he said. "Not to us right now. I marked their positions, in case the contents can be retrieved later."

"Are we ready?" said Marina.

"Nearly," said Sandra. She had coaxed the stranger to walk. The girl was dazed, but mobile.

Bernhardt and Bo said yes. Tomek had lashed their supplies to the sleds as best they could.

"Which way do we go?" said Tomek quietly.

"Away from the sun," said Bo.

"Why not follow the trail of debris?" said Bernhardt. "Our chance of rescue will be better that way."

"We can follow the debris trail while it goes northwest, if we assume the sun in is the south," said Dariusz. "It is a longer route, but we are guaranteed more supplies in further decks as we go. We might pick up other survivors also, and it could be some of them have had contact with others." He did not say that they might happen on his son. Everyone knew.

"Sure, sure," said Bo. "But we will have to cut away from the trail eventually. The last thing we need is to be caught in the desert without supplies."

The group voted, and agreed.

They left the deck segment without ado. They checked nervously, at first, for signs of whatever might have harmed the other colonists, but eventually the effort of moving through the desert overcame their fears, and they fell silent one by one.

It was in this state that death found them.

* * *

THEY WERE FOUR days into their trek. The group had settled into a routine of walking for five hours a day, stopping to investigate whenever they came across a beacon signal. They were disappointed in their hope for further survivors, finding three more smashed segments scattered across the landscape. One yielded a locker full of welcome emergency rations. A fourth segment was intact, but empty of people and stores. Arguments broke out over whether or not they should divert from their path and strike directly north. Dariusz, naturally, insisted they stick to their plan. The last deck segment they had passed had been 37B. They were drawing closer to his son.

The arguments receded as each broken deck receded. None were in the mood for talking, and more than one of them were displaying signs of inChip withdrawal. Tomek suffered this the most.

Dariusz caught movement from the corner of his eye: a dark, deltoid shape flowing across the dunes. In the featureless desert, his peripheral vision felt preternaturally sharp, although half the time it found things that were not there. Like his network-starved mind, his eyes were hungry for stimulation, and he did not trust them.

He turned toward the motion and blinked. There was no sign of the shadow. He was about to return his gaze to the sand around his feet when the shadow returned, a stark triangle on the side of a low dune. He swung his head to the south. His spine chilled. He shielded his eyes against the sun and searched the sky.

A black shape sailed on the breeze, wings wide.

The others noticed what he was doing, and turned to look.

"What is that?" asked Sandra.

"I don't know," said Dariusz uneasily.

"It is a rescue craft!" shouted Bernhardt. "Don't you see, it is a rescue craft, they have come for us!" He ran, stumbling from the line, tearing his makeshift headdress from his sunburned scalp and waving it madly. "Hey! Hey!"

"There's no engine noise," said Dariusz. "A glider?"

Marina squinted against the flawless blue. "I don't recall any atmospheric craft like that in the ship's manifest."

"What about aboard the *Goethe*, or the other ships?" said Tomek. He was listless. All of their voices were harsh, roughened by sand and thirst.

Marina shook her head. "I don't think so."

The shape executed a wide, lazy bank, and approached. Dariusz picked up the tablet on his chest; the radio was making a peculiar noise.

"Do you recognise this?" he said to Marina.

She frowned. "No. Not at all."

"You said they would not come, you said they would not come!" Spittle flew from Bernhardt's lips. He jabbed an accusing finger at Dariusz. His voice wavered between joy and fury. "You said! You said no, but oh, they are here now! They are here now! They have seen us! I told you we should have stayed where we were. They're coming to rescue us!"

"I don't think that's an aircraft," said Marina. All of them stirred, instinctively moving apart. The shape grew bigger. The flatness of the sky, the glare of the sun, the reach of the desert made it impossible to judge the thing's size. The strange signal picked up by the tablet increased in volume, a regular, jarring ping.

"Hey! Hey!" shouted Bernhardt. He ran further out into the sand, away from the group.

Bo let his rucksack slip from his back. "Bernhardt..."

The shape drew closer. It let out an unearthly, polyphonic call, a rumbling whale song overlaid by an earsplitting screech that rose higher than human ears could follow.

Bo was sprinting now. "Bernhardt! Bernhardt! Get down!"

The rest of the group scattered, ancient prey responses driving them away from each other. Dariusz ran toward Bo and Bernhardt. Bo launched himself at the German, who had stopped, rooted to the spot, mouth agape. Bo hit him square in the middle, sending them both crashing to the ground, as the thing dipped to the earth.

Dariusz's impressions of the creature were fragmented; a light blue belly, lighter topside, a pair of wings at least twenty metres across. There was the smell, cinnamon like the wind, but far more intense, overpowering in a way cinnamon is not. There was a scream, a human scream, and it was gone.

Dariusz ducked as the thing flew overhead. He followed the creature with his eyes as it passed over them and on, dwindling rapidly. He saw appendages trailing in the wind, and thought he saw, struggling in their grip, a human form. He squinted, and he could not see it any longer.

He turned back to where Bernhardt had been shouting the thing in, drawing it down on them. He lay in the sand, his face contorted in horror as he watched the creature's progress into blue obscurity.

Of Bo there was no sign.

CHAPTER TWELVE
Daniel

THE GROUP MOVED more quickly after Bo was taken, one of them tasked with scanning the skies at all times. They kept, where possible, to shelter: the slipfaces of dunes, the slacks between the hills of sand, staying away from the open unless tempted out by the promise of supplies or other survivors. They pillaged deck segments where they could, but found no others alive. Dariusz went alone as often as not to scout these locations, for with Bo gone, no one else was willing to accompany him. He kept close watch on the nameless girl, to see if she reacted to the flying monster. She did not, leading him to suspect something else may have been responsible for the deaths of her colleagues.

The crescent barchans gave way to endless seifs, the sign of deep, deep desert, although Dariusz did not mention this to his fellows. If they were unaware of the change in the dunes and what it betokened, far better that they remain ignorant. They saw an increasing number of the aerial lifeforms as time went on. At first they were always alone, but five days after the death of Bo they saw their first flock. When the black shapes cut the blue of the sky, the group cast themselves to the ground and waited until the creatures had flown past. No one spoke of rescue any more.

They grew weaker. Tomek became delirious. Their dehydration worsened. Marina reduced their liquid rations. Their solid food ran out.

They began to lose hope.

The wind strengthened, switching round to the north, and became cooler. At first this brought some relief from the lidless glare of the sun, but as it gathered speed the wind threw the desert up into their faces. Eddies of blown sand became sheets. Dust clogged their nostrils, dug into the corners of their eyes, stuck to their chapped lips and scoured their sunburned skin.

They fashioned scarves for their faces from the spare smartsuits they carried, but these helped little: powered, the torn fabric contorted itself, unsure of its role, and unpowered, it was too light to stay in place easily. They plodded in single file, the moan of the wind and the hiss of the sand mocking them. They no longer broke their journey to investigate wreckage. They stopped watching the sky. They slept in huddles, jumpsuits tented over their faces, sleds end-on as feeble windbreaks. When they woke, they had to dig themselves from the sands.

The wind blew harder and the light grew dimmer as dust was thrown up into the atmosphere, bringing a kind of brown twilight on them. They abandoned most of their sleds and formed a chain, hands on each others' shoulders. They took it in turns at the front to lead the way, the others wrapping scarves around their eyes to protect them.

Such was the noise of the gathering storm, Dariusz almost missed the message from the tablet. The signal was preceded by a string of pops and cracks, like water dripping into hot fat.

"This is deck segment 46B. This is a recorded message. We are two hundred and ninety-six in number. If you receive this, please follow our signal origin and lock onto our homing beacon. This is deck segment 46B, awaiting rescue. This is deck segment 46B…"

The signal looped twice, before it was overtaken by the whoop of interference. Dariusz stumbled to a halt, picked up the tablet and stared dumbly at it. Its diamond-hard screen was unscratched, but fat grains of sand crowded the device's every cranny.

"Dariusz!" shouted Marina. Her voice was weak, the wind was loud, and he did not hear. She broke from the line and ripped her scarf from her face. She gestured urgently at Dariusz. "The radio! The radio!"

The group stopped, dropping their loads. They slunk into the shelter of an escarpment half-drowned by a towering dune. Sand streamed around the rock on either side, but in the lee of the outcrop was a measure of respite. Tomek sank to his knees. Bernhardt crouched with his face buried in his arms. Marina dashed to Dariusz and grabbed the unit, tugging his neck painfully with the strap.

"H-h-hello?" She licked her lips. Her throat was so dry her voice died in her throat. "Is anyone there? This is Marina Vodička, junior ship's engineer, survivor of deck segment 14A. Is there anyone there? Hello? Hello!" They all waited, staring at the radio. Nothing came, only the eerie howls of static. Marina glanced nervously at Dariusz. He could not make out her face too well. His head pounded. He did not think it possible to be so thirsty.

"Hello? Hello. This is Artur Kościelniak. Hello?" The voice faded in and out, then strengthened and stayed true. Marina laughed and cried at the same time. The others smiled. Fear retreated, just for a moment.

"Where are you? We are getting no fix on your beacon," she said.

"We boosted our radio, we got a real transmitter up and running. We haven't yet figured out how to crack the beacon unit without destroying it."

"How do we find you?"

"Marina? That's your name?"

"Yes!"

"Don't worry Marina, we've triangulated your position. You're not far. Stay where you are. We'll come to you. We'll be with you in half an hour."

The voice cut out, leaving the group giddy, afraid the voice had been a desert phantom.

Half an hour passed, and then another. They became despondent. Some of them slept. Dariusz watched shrouds of sand rush over the sun, obscuring it in a dance of veils.

There was a high whining that at first he took to be another trick of the wind.

Engines.

Sandra was on her feet, rushing from around the rock to stare up the steep side of the dune. She cupped her hand around her mouth. "They are coming!" she called. "They are coming!"

Dariusz scrambled to her position, and she pointed to the dune's summit.

A large, broad-wheeled ATV rolled toward them. A second crested the ridge like a ship breaching a wave, electric motor shifting pitch with the effort. It skidded sideways on the soft sand, sending up sprays of dust that seemed oddly flat in the heavier gravity.

The lead ATV pulled up level with their shelter. Its six tyres were the height of a tall man, a blocky passenger unit perched atop it. The driver's door opened, and a man got out onto the running boards over the tyres. He leaned over to address them. An environment suit mask covered his face, but his smile radiated from behind it.

"Hi, there," he shouted over the wind. He jerked a thumb over his shoulder back to the ATV's cabin. "The name's Corrigan. Do you guys happen to need a lift?"

"THIS IS WHAT we've managed to salvage so far," Kościelniak waved a hand through the window at the stacks of containers surrounding the base. "First Landing's got a regular shuttle run coming down here, bussing most of it back up to the liminal zone, but it's been decided to maintain this as a forward facility. We don't want too many eggs in one basket, as the English say."

Corrigan nodded. "That we do."

Kościelniak was an Anglophile, and keen to impress upon the others his use of idiomatic British rather than simplified Lingua Anglica. He seemed a decent man, genuinely overjoyed to see more survivors.

"It's a bit premature to call this meagre collection of prefabs a town, yet," Kościelniak said, "but I'd be willing to say it'll be one day. We can't all live in one place."

"Where would the fun be in that?" said Corrigan.

Corrigan was English. He wore the black, paramilitary garb of the Pointers' bodyguard. The group were all wary of him. He was observant, and caught Dariusz appraising him. "Does this bother you?" He glanced down at his uniform.

"Do not worry, Dariusz," said Kościelniak in Polish. "He works for them, but he is a good person, and the only one of theirs here now."

"That's not fair. You know I have no translation facilities anymore." Corrigan tapped the side of his head. Their inChips were still useless, their few native functions aside. No data network existed here either.

"Then I suggest you learn," said Kościelniak with a grin. "Polish is a beautiful language, and there are far more of us than of you."

Corrigan did not look convinced. "Don't do it again. We have to be open with each other. Pull that trick on one of my less enlightened colleagues and you will have a problem on your hands."

"Is that a threat?" said Kościelniak.

Corrigan leaned back. He was heavily muscled. "No, no! Friendly advice."

"One of the good ones, as I said," said Kościelniak.

They sat in a utilitarian prefab cabin of forty square metres, with one wide window. The space was divided into two rooms. From the smaller room, tubular tunnels led across to similar buildings – five in all – that made up the outpost; Desert One, they called it. The five survivors of 14A and the girl of 30A had been issued with fresh smartclothing displaying their mission specialties, but they looked and felt dishevelled compared to Kościelniak and Corrigan. They drank their five-hundred-year-old soup gratefully.

"We're still pulling in cargo containers out of the desert. The location data you've given us is invaluable, and will save us a lot of time. We're fortunate, I think; or rather, we owe Captain Posth a great deal, as she jettisoned much of the cargo and a lot of it came down in one piece. Some of it's been smashed to bits, but…" He shrugged. "In the circumstances, we're doing rather well: many of our prefabs, vehicles, a lot of the hydroponics, basic food supplies… All lying around, waiting to be picked up."

"How many colonists have you saved?" asked Dariusz.

Kościelniak looked uncomfortable, his eyes drawn to the deck segment he'd arrived in. It had come down at an angle on the side of a dune, and was being buried by the storm. "That is a less happy story. There were two hundred and ninety-six of us here, in deck 46B. We had a fatal accident, one death from internal injuries sustained in the crash, and two disappearances

– perhaps one of these raptor things that took your colleague –
so there were four less when First Landing made contact. We're
right on the edge of their transmission range, so it's no surprise
they never found you, that's the primary reason we've kept this
forward base occupied.

"The decks came down in two clusters. The bigger ones,
and therefore the majority of colonists, landed close to First
Landing. But the smaller, sternward decks finished up out in
the desert. We're here for people like you. Most of the original
occupants of 46B have gone on to First Landing. We've had" –
Artur checked his personal unit – "two hundred and forty more
come through here, or picked up by our ATVs. We've been
doing sweeps of the desert as best we can, but the sand plays
havoc with our solar arrays, and there's not much water here,
as you might have seen. There's only so much we can wring out
of the air" – another friendly smile split his black beard – "so
we've not done as much as we want. With this storm, I doubt
we'll find many more. It's building, you know. They say it could
last for days. You were lucky. Twice. It's understood a lot of the
sternward decks got smashed up badly."

"Captain Posth?" asked Marina.

"Dead, it is assumed. Along with most of the *Mickiewicz*'s
crew. They stayed to the end to get as many out as they could.
They were brave."

Dariusz set down his mug, shaking. He hoped the others would
put it down to fatigue. "There were fourteen thousand people
on the *Mickiewicz*," he said. "What are our total numbers of
survivors?"

"You're very interested in population statistics for a
geoengineer," said Corrigan.

"We all should be interested. Aren't you?" said Marina.

Corrigan shrugged. "It's got to be a bit too much. I'm just
glad I'm alive. I try not to think about the dead, just trying to
help the living, ma'am."

"You're not an Alt?" said Marina.

"No," said Corrigan. "But some of my colleagues are," he
added pointedly, for Kościelniak's benefit, Dariusz thought.

"How many are we?" said Dariusz.

Kościelniak's air of bonhomie slipped. He became glum, steepled his fingers, tapping their tips against one another, and looked at them as he spoke. "A goodly portion of our people died in transit. Around a third. Currently, there are six thousand survivors at First Landing. A number of them were on the ground when we lost control of the *Mickiewicz*. Others were fortunate enough to have their decks lock on to the beacon there and land close by. But the decks were scattered, and we've recovered precious few of the escape pods. We do not expect the total to grow much. Over half the colonists and ship's personnel have perished, either during the prolonged voyage or during the crash. How many are dying in the desert as we speak…"

Someone whispered, "My God." Dariusz did not register who; Artur's eyes caught his. The shine had gone from them, and he stared at Dariusz with an intensity that discomfited him. "All as the direct result of sabotage. Someone did this to us on purpose, sent us haring off hundreds of light years from home, then had the ship drive itself into the ground."

Artur kept staring, and Dariusz felt sure he must know something. The floor tipped away under his feet. He sat stock still, terrified he would follow the sway of the world around him and reveal his role in the disaster. He felt sick. He awaited judgment. They all knew it had been him, they must. An overwhelming urge to escape assailed him. He came close to confession.

Kościelniak shifted, breaking the spell. "Still," he said, "we're all here, and for that I thank God. You're all to be taken to First Landing later today. The shuttle is to make one more run before this storm worsens, after which we're battening down the hatches until it's over. Until the shuttle comes back, perhaps you would like to rest? You have suffered a great deal."

The group nodded gratefully. "Administrator," said Dariusz, as the others thanked Kościelniak and filed out. "I have something I need to ask. In private."

Kościelniak, half out of his chair, halted, then sank back down. "Very well," he said.

Dariusz waited as the 14A survivors were led out. Marina cast a glance back at him, her brow furrowed. He answered her frown with a thin smile.

As the door closed. Dariusz clasped his hands together on the table in front of him.

"I must ask that I be allowed to stay. I can't go to First Landing."

"Why?"

"I have to go back out into the desert."

Kościelniak glanced at Corrigan, who shrugged. "I will have to clear it with First Landing, and I am sure they would like to make use of your geoengineering skills, so I can safely say that we will not be allowed to let you leave."

"Please. I have a son. He was on deck 46A. I want you to let me go back into the desert and find it."

"We have not been able to find 46A. Its beacon has not been detected, and most of our efforts have been directed to recovering those elements whose beacons we have found. I am sorry. You must understand, we are conducting a triage of nations here –"

"Then tell me where it isn't, and I'll look elsewhere."

Kościelniak sighed deeply and pursed his lips. He sat in thought for an interminable moment. "I have two children myself; daughters, both safely at First Landing," he said eventually. "Were I in your position, I would consider doing what you are thinking of doing, even if it is almost certainly suicide. I am afraid I cannot allow it.

"I cannot allow you to exit from the rear of this base, nor to make use of the environmental smartgear stored there, and definitely not any of the ATVs we have parked outside. I certainly would not wish you to risk your life checking the area between 220 degrees southwest and 300 degrees northwest, a zone we have been unable to quarter as yet. I have to inform you that I will have a member of personnel passing your door, to make sure you are all right. Only a single man, and he will pass by a couple of times in the night. If I could spare more personnel to ensure your comfort and safety, I would, but we are in a tenuous position. Now, was that all? Do you understand me, Pan Szczeciński?"

"Artur," said Corrigan warningly.

"Do you understand me, Pan Szczeciński?" he repeated in Polish.

Dariusz stood. "Yes. Thank you."

"Corrigan here will escort you to your quarters. Please." He held up his hand.

Corrigan looked at Kościelniak and raised his eyebrows.

"You are one of the good ones, aren't you, Corrigan?" said the base manager.

Corrigan's mouth lifted at one corner. He was unhappy. "Yeah," he said after some deliberation. "I am one of the good ones. Come on."

"You understand," said Kościelniak in Polish to Dariusz. He switched back to English. "Goodnight, and God speed."

DARIUSZ WAS BROUGHT to a room where the others lay sleeping on foam mattresses. Marina waited up for him. The rest were insensible, wrung out by their ordeal; Marina spoke quietly, so as not to disturb them.

"You asked if you could go to find your son?" she whispered.

"Yes, and they could not let me."

"I am not surprised. You are valuable." She was relieved.

"My son is more valuable to me than my skills are to them," he said. "I am leaving."

"You'll die!" she said. Her voice hissed harshly. She looked upward. The wind moaned outside. "The storm is getting worse."

"That's what Kościelniak said," said Dariusz. He opened the door to the corridor a fraction. With the shutters down, the room was dark, the first true darkness he'd experienced for over a fortnight, and part of him wanted more than anything to embrace it. "He also told me that there is a full set of desert-programmed environmental clothing in the lockers by the rear exit to this place."

Marina frowned. "I don't understand."

Darius turned to look at her, one eye in light, the other in dark. "He said he could not let me go, but he allowed me to infer that he wouldn't stop me, so I am going."

"You'll die, Dariusz."

"I might die, but I might find my son. I can't live without knowing, Marina. I will live my life wondering if he perished in the desert."

"Think, Dariusz! He could have come off the ship. He could be at First Landing."

"He could, but I doubt it. This is deck segment 46B, my son is on segment 46A. That Englishman, Corrigan, told me some of the hibernation decks, those with key personnel aboard, underwent emergency revivification processes when the ship approached Nychthemeron. While on the ship, their systems were linked. 46B did not activate its ERP, so nor did 46A. Even if, by some small chance, he did awaken, the state of the segment will tell me that, and I will then know that he stood a good chance of getting out. I have to know, Marina. He is my son, my only son."

"What about your wife? She will lose both of you."

"My wife is dead. She killed herself when we were accepted onto the mission." His voice caught. "She was deemed psychologically unfit to come. I knew it would happen, I knew as soon as she was turned down that she would kill herself."

"Yet you still came."

"She insisted I come, I agreed. I have enough on my conscience." How much, he did not elaborate upon.

"You are not alone. Not everyone is doing this, throwing themselves onto the mercy of this terrible place."

"I am not everyone. Tell me, do you have children of your own?"

She shook her head.

"Then one day, when you do, and I pray that you will, you will understand."

He leaned back and twisted the door handle so he could push it to without the tell-tale click of the bolt. Footsteps padded past outside.

"That's it. He told me there would be one base member patrolling past every so often to make sure we're okay. I suppose so he can say he did his part to keep us all here when I am reported missing."

"Why is he doing this? He'll be disciplined if he loses you. They're going to need your skills."

"They will," he said with certainty.

"Then why is he allowing you to go?"

He looked at her, a darker silhouette in the near-pitch dark, a glint of light reflected in his eyes. "Kościelniak has his own family. Two children, both at First Landing." He opened the door. "Goodbye. Marina. Take care of yourself."

"You too. Thank you, I do not think we would have survived were it not for you."

He paused. Guilt twisted his heart. "Marina... There's something I should say..." He trailed off.

"What?"

"It's nothing," he said, changing his mind. "Nothing at all. Get some sleep. Life is going to be hard for us all now."

He slipped out of the door.

He moved confidently down the corridor; sneaking around would only make him appear suspicious. The complex of prefabs was small, but there was a skeleton crew of twelve on the base, the rest having returned to First Landing as the sandstorm threatened. He was certain he could depart undetected.

The equipment was exactly where Kościelniak said it would be. Dariusz slipped into the heavy smartsuit quickly but with care, knowing that he risked fumbling the activation and delaying his departure. The seals closed themselves. The cloth rearranged itself to suit his body, hardening in response to the conditions outside. The suit held a pocket with a tablet in it, and when he pulled the mask on, the goggles interfaced with the functions of his inChip and tablet, bringing with it his first taste of full virtual interface since he awoke. His networking functions remained offline. It would be some time before the planet – Nychthemeron – had a functioning internet.

He felt better prepared. He pulled out a camel pak, heavy with that damnable all-in-one nutrient drink. He took some dry ration bars, and filled a holdall with more bottles he found stacked in a corner. It was quite a load, but it would lighten all too quickly. He looked around himself constantly as he worked, but he remained undisturbed.

He keyed open the airlock. Air cycling was disabled. They were using the airlock as a porch to keep the sand out, was all, and he did not have to wait. A moment later, he was outside.

The storm enveloped him as tightly as a winding sheet. Dariusz could see nothing but sand on the air. The suit's headpiece came with a variety of functions, including a short-range radar, which projected an outline of the topography into his inChip. It was a ghostly, ephemeral vision of this bellowing world, and the sheer physicality of the sandstorm overwhelmed him. He staggered against its force until he located the ATVs, five of them huddled together like livestock, tubular bodies rocking in the wind.

He chose one at random. The suit provided the access coding. The controls were simple enough to fathom, and with help from his inChip interface, he was driving surely before he'd passed the downed deck segment half-buried in the sand.

He climbed to the ridge of the massive dune to the west of the camp, and headed directly out from there, thinking to transect the area not yet covered by the base personnel until he picked up a signal.

HE DROVE FOR hours. The storm was pushed back one remove by the ATV, but was no less threatening. Between his inChip, the ATV's windscreen heads-up and the suit headpiece, he had a reasonable virtual view of where he was going. The real world remained obscure, and he was forced to trust the machine's interpretation of what was there and what was not.

All the while, the temperature outside was dropping, down to twenty degrees now. The wind direction was coming in from the east-north-east, and he theorised that this was how the planet regulated its temperature; periodic storms exchanging hot dayside air with the colder nightside of the planet. If that was the case, then the liminal, twilight zone between day and night should prove comfortable enough for mankind.

He pondered on this. By most measures, Nychthemeron was a reasonably hospitable world. Had Browning planned for this to occur all along? If so, had the rest of the fleet been infected by his sabotage, and sent out to worlds other than those they had aimed for, or was the *Mickiewicz* alone, and the rest of the fleet gone on to their intended destinations? Or were they all wrecked, and their passengers dead? Żadernowski had said the aim had been simply to wrest control of the colonies from the Pointers by subverting the Syscores. Either he had lied, or had been lied to himself. Dariusz should have been more suspicious, but he had been blinded by concern for his son as much as he was blinded by the sand blasting his vehicle now.

One thing bothered him more than anything else. If they were so far out from Earth, where had the data for this world come from? The change in course, the emergency awakening, the crash, it was all too convenient. Why? Why was that part of Browning's plan? Had Browning been insane? He couldn't rule it out. He mulled it over, but could not concentrate for long. His role in so many deaths gnawed at him.

Something rippled on the screen's topography display, breaking his introspection. Targeting lines in red zoomed in on an object. Biological matter.

He slammed the brakes on and leaned forward, peering through the windscreen. About ten metres forward, picked out in the vehicle's headlights, something dark lay on the sand. He tried to make sense of it through the sandstorm, but could not. He sat a moment, then decided to get out and take a look.

The storm blew into the cabin as he slid back the driver's door. He slammed it shut, then climbed the side ladder in between the first and second wheelsets, jumping the last three rungs.

He walked a few paces, sand rattling against the hardened environment suit. The shape became clear: one of the winged creatures that had taken Bo. Dariusz approached the lifeform cautiously, then relaxed. It was obviously dead, one leathery wing half-furled under its back, the other cast out wide onto the sand. Only the outline of the wing was visible; the rest was shadow under a shroud of sand. Five cruel claws, curled like fingers against a sleeper's palm, edged the wing. Dariusz stopped. He had an impulse to nudge the wing with his boot, but he felt repulsed by it and he did not. He went closer to the body.

It was huge. Dariusz estimated the body measured five metres in length. The wingspan was over twenty.

The beast was finely boned, as one would expect of a flying creature, otherwise it was outlandish to his eyes, a bizarre hybrid of woodlouse and pterosaur. In some respects it reminded him of a manta ray, which in turn reminded him of the security drones. Its camouflaged, light blue belly was presented to the sky. The belly was slightly concave, a cluster of arthropod legs nested in the hollow, curled tightly inward in death. It had a stubby, forked tail at one end, tipped by two bulbous flukes set at forty degrees to one another. He could see no head. He thought it might be incomplete, but it was not. When he walked around to face it end on he saw a mouth set directly into the top of its shoulders, big enough to swallow a man.

A long pair of jointed appendages – palps or rakes, he supposed – tipped with spikes guarded the mouth, one curled, the other flung outwards, mirroring the position of the wings.

It was hard to tell how the creature had died, under its crust of sand, but it showed no overt wounds. He wondered what had killed it; old age, maybe, or disease. Sand skittered over it, covering it grain by grain. Soon it would be buried, the mysteries of its life and death with it. Like the deck at Desert One, and the other wreckage. If they all died here, soon there would be nothing on the surface to show man had set foot on Nychthemeron at all.

Dariusz stared at it a while. He supposed he should take a sample. He returned to the relative comfort of the buggy and climbed into the back, where two rows of three seats faced each other. He and the others had sat in seats like them on his journey to Desert One. He wondered if he would see his companions again.

He found a biology fieldkit in the buggy's supplies, including a sampling kit and a knife, and went back outside.

The creature's hide was remarkably difficult to cut through, and under his gloves it had a rough texture, like sharkskin. He took samples of its skin, a shaving from the tougher, chitinous integument of its legs, and tried to take a blood sample, but either the creature's circulatory system was radically different from an Earth organisms, or it had dried out in the desert. Two samples, then, he thought. He went around it, taking pictures on his inChip and mask visor.

While taking pictures, he noticed fibres in the palps by the mouth. He knelt and pulled off his mask, shielding his eyes from the sand, and took the fibres in his hand. Light grey, with a slight prismatic effect: smartcloth. He peered into the mouth. Rows of horny, recurved teeth lined the gullet. There were more of the fibres, and deeper in, a rag of material.

He looked at the thing's belly, then at its mouth again.

He went back past the grouping of legs, and knelt on the animal's belly, where he stabbed into the hide, and dragged the blade back as hard as he could. The hole he made was rough and ragged, but allowed him to peel the skin and muscle away from the abdominal cavity, making transverse cuts so that he could lay it open. Alien organs presented themselves to him. A bicameral stomach, one side bulging hugely. He slit it open and found the remains of a colonist within. The smartsuit was untouched by the animal's juices, and held together the remains of the unfortunate meal. Only partly digested, skin mushy, bad enough to not be able tell what sex they had been. Their hands were clawed, the distal phalanges gleaming white through the mess of flesh. A moment of horrific realisation put the idea in Dariusz's mind that the colonist was still alive as the creature's digestive acids set to work.

He tried to take a reading of the inChip to ascertain the identity, but could not. He considered removing the head and returning it, but the thought made him retch. He took pictures instead, and logged the position as best he could. Let someone better equipped retrieve the remains.

He returned to the ATV and resumed his drive through the storm. He slavishly followed the buggy's visual cues, and as a result his mind had nothing to do but stew on his guilt and the horror in the sand, and what might have happened to his son.

DARIUSZ SPENT ONE night, and then a second, sleeping stretched out on the seats in the back of the ATV. It was storm-dim outside, and with the buggy's windows darkened, it was dark enough for him to sleep soundly. He was exhausted, mentally and physically. He doubted his own sanity; before Kościelniak had obliquely advised him to take the ATV, he had been going to walk into the desert. What had he been thinking? He would have been dead in hours.

With the temperature at eighteen degrees and him spared the exertions of walking, his supplies were lasting well. The vehicle manufactured its own fuel while he slept, drawing power from the sun where it could and pulling gases into its compact fuelcell from the atmosphere. Humidity was up, markedly so, climbing from nothing to the low teens over the space of a day. By the time Dariusz picked up the beacon emanating from deck 46A, the wind had abated, and the sky had taken on a new gloom, green-tinted, dark as a bottle.

The landscape changed. Rock formations, besieged by the crawling edges of dunes, loomed up suddenly from the murk. For all that they were delineated in lines of light by the ATV's sensors before he saw them with his eyes, their appearance alarmed him, and he drove slowly. The dunes became smaller and smaller, until they were ripples on the floor. Large boulders became common, and his journey became bumpier.

He was close to giving up hope when the soft pinging of 46A's locator impinged on his enclosed world. He quickly diverted it from the headpiece's internal unit, projecting compass arrows onto the windscreen. They blinked red at the edges of the glass, and he swung the vehicle around recklessly until a pulsing target centred itself in the digitally conjured no-place to the front of the vehicle. He resisted the temptation to accelerate, forced himself to calm down. What good would killing himself in a crash do, so close to his goal?

He was not far from the deck segment. Visibility had improved as the sandstorm's fury spent itself, but he still could not see further than one hundred metres. He followed the pinging target on his windscreen, tenacious as a bloodhound, his body tense.

A dark block on the sand, below him as the land dropped. Deck 46 was a large one, and this half had landed well.

He drove faster, the six independent wheels of the ATV bouncing over the rocky ground. The ride suddenly became smooth, there was cracked mud here frosted with salt, a detail he observed but whose importance eluded him, his every thought fixed on the downed deck segment, and Daniel.

He stopped a few metres short of it. The emergency ladders were down, the doors open. Trembling, he flung the door of the ATV open, treading only upon the first two rungs of the ladder before he leapt down to the ground. His imagination alternately tormented him with images of a small corpse, then teased him with joyful reunions.

His relief foundered. He could see no sign of survivors. No, there, a shape on the ground, half-covered in sand blown down from the dunes. He walked over, his legs as water, his heart pounding.

A body, skin already stretched tight with dessication. A few bottles lay around it. A man? A woman, he decided. Not a child, not Daniel. He felt a knot around his heart. Questions clamoured. Had there been other survivors? Was his son among them?

He scrambled for the ladder, and was inside in seconds. There was enough power remaining for the emergency lights, and the sarcophagus panels. Nearly all were red. Their light revealed a nightmarish scene of broken machinery. Sarcophagi had come loose from their moorings, and were piled one on the other, forcing him to wriggle through. He could not see and tore off his mask. He instantly regretted it; the air was ripe with the scent of decaying flesh, thick and cloying. Like strong perfume it filled his senses, threatening to choke him. The sharp, rank smell of spoiling pseudo-amniotics overlaid the odour of death. His gorge rose.

Dariusz struggled his mask back on, breathing short gulps of air. Once it was secure again, he held his breath until the mask's air scrubbers had had time to do their work. He took an experimental breath. Then another. The sweetness had gone. He put his foot down on something yielding. He felt queasy, but forced himself forward, staring resolutely ahead.

He called up a torch beam from his suit's headset. Signs of damage were everywhere. He was amazed the segment had come down so surely. Those sarcophagi not smashed or thrown free from their mounts were silent, their status panels red, their occupants dead.

He found the number he was looking for, as he had the last time, the number stencilled on the side of the sarcophagus. He knelt astride it, his mouth working wordlessly.

Daniel's status panel was red. Daniel had died, perhaps long before the crash. In a moment of insanity he was sure the mask's visual filters were lying to him, and he tore the headpiece from his face, heedless of the charnel stink. He blinked in disbelief, hoping he would see something different, but no; here was the unmediated truth of his son's death. There was the risk, there had always been the risk, but to see it fulfilled, so finally...

He crouched onto the sarcophagus and moaned.

How long he stayed there, he did not know. Blind with grief, he staggered out of the deck segment, half-falling to the ground from the door. He wavered drunkenly on for some time, perhaps as little as ten minutes, perhaps as much as an hour. The cracked pan of the plains became sand again, and he ascended halfway up a low dune before his legs gave out under him and he collapsed.

Dariusz rolled onto his back and lay his head on the sand, uncaring of the granules of sand invading his ears. He stared into the desert sky, a marbled wall of beige sand streamers and racing cloud, the sun a ragged scrap of light. The wind blew sand at him, languid where it had been angry, as if it comforted him. He felt the small impacts of the grains through the smartcloth. It stung his face, but he did not pull the headpiece back on.

I'm in hell, he thought. *I'm in hell for what I have done.*

Dariusz was not religious by the standards of the time – and they were religious days – but in that moment, he genuinely feared for his soul. He was pinned by the weight of his sins.

He closed his eyes. Breathing was a supreme effort. His chest rose and fell. The sound of the air entering and leaving his lungs became a monster's breath. He was a monster, a slayer of men. In, out, in, out, the monster breathes in its cave. The winds of the planet receded, silenced by the thundering drafts of his respiration. The space in his chest had become cavernous, his core hollowed out. There was nothing but air to fill it; all his purpose had gone.

In, out, in, out. He dropped deeper into a fugue of grief. How easy it is, he thought, when one concentrates on the sound of one's breath, to imagine it stopping, the ceaseless ceasing, the warm rush coming no more.

In, out, in, out. In... Out...

Dariusz let out one final breath. He did not inhale. The effort to breathe was too great. He had failed. He had failed Lydia, he had failed Daniel, and he had failed himself, set up and used at the cost of all he held dear, and at his own collusion. He could only blame himself. His anger at the Pointers had made him too eager to believe. He was guilty of the crime of idiocy. Naiveté on such a scale deserved punishment. He had been punished, and now he wanted no more. Sleep, he wanted to sleep forever. He did not deserve to live.

He was no longer conscious when the first droplets of rain pattered onto his face, nor a minute later, when a great metal hand reached down and carefully plucked him from the sand.

CHAPTER THIRTEEN
Sand in the Sand

SAND CAME ROUND to the touch of a small, cool hand. "Pilot? Pilot? Miss?" The voice was distant, distorted at the edges. "Pilot? Please wake up, please." The voice sent vibrations into her skull that made her nauseous. She thought she opened her eyes, but she saw light as rippled as a bull's eye glass, and no images formed. She could smell something pleasant, like cinnamon.

"Pilot?" Shaking, very gentle. A child's voice; a girl. There was an edge to it. "Please!"

Sand experienced a rushing sensation, of reality tautening to its accustomed shape. Her mind filled out her body, and she came to fully. Her head hurt abominably. She lolled in the straps of the pilot's chair in her ruined cockpit. Efforts to move herself upright were inelegant, robotic, not the movements of a person. She managed finally to haul herself back into a proper sitting position, and fought off the waves of nausea that crashed over her. "Okay, I'm okay," she said. She was not.

There was a face. A child. The crash.

She couldn't open her right eye, it hurt. She reached up to her face, to find it sticky with blood. She felt half in and half out of herself. She looked down. The lower half of her body was buried in sand, and the sand rose from her, through the smashed windows, in a slope that went up as far as she could see. Granules trickled onto her and she panicked, fearing an avalanche that would swallow her ship. Her hand flailed, grasped hard at the kid, and she pulled her legs up. They came out easily; the sand was dry and moved fluidly. She smacked the quick release on her harness, swung her legs around, and stood. She winced, and bent double.

"Are you sure you're okay?"

Sand shook her head, and wished she hadn't. The world swung pendulously with the motion.

"No. I feel like I'm going to throw up."

"You should sit down again, you have probably a mild concussion."

"Smart kid," gasped Sand. "And not that mild."

"My mother is... My mother was a nurse." Tears tainted the girl's voice. Sand figured she better pull herself together quick. Sand disliked being in charge of others, she preferred to go and do her own thing, banging up against authority every now and then in a manner that was not much fun for her, nor for the authority. She liked being a pilot, as she was often on her own. She had little idea how to manage other adults, even less of how to manage children. Like most people of her time, she was an only child. There had been no siblings or children of siblings to practise her parenting skills on.

"Okay," she said. She groaned, and her mouth filled with bitter saliva. "I'll sit down. Do you think you could fix me some water or something? There should be some in a locker at the back."

The girl looked confused for a moment before she nodded. She turned to someone and said something in a language Sand did not know. Sand did not turn to see who. Every time she moved her head, she was in danger of falling sideways off the face of the universe.

"What are we going to do?" The girl spoke Lingua Anglica, with a mid-Euro accent. Sand dropped into the international speech.

"Is anybody hurt?"

"Piotr has broken his arm. I've put it in a sling. One of the little ones... One of the little ones..."

Sand looked up. The dead girl had been put in a corner. Broken neck.

Two of the other kids were kneeling by a third, who lay stretched out on the floor.

"Diana's not breathing properly. I have tried to make her comfortable."

"You did the right thing." Sand stood. She had to stop and grip the back of the chair to steady herself. The sense of unreality rushed back at her. She breathed deeply for five breaths, and the void retreated to the edges of her perception. She was going to have to be careful. She hung from the webbing attached to the ceiling, letting her arms take most of her weight. It seemed better than having it all on her feet.

"Let me see her," she said.

The two kids moved aside. There were nine people in the cabin. With the desert spilling through the window, it was cramped.

It was the kid whose father had pleaded at the last to let her aboard, fat lot of good it had done her. Diana was dying; that much was apparent. Her lips were blue and her skin pale. She breathed shallowly, panting. An ugly contusion started at the neck and continued under her shirt. Sand recognised the signs, although she lacked the expertise to treat them; Diana had been thrown against her harness as they hit. It was risky putting two kids into an adult-sized harness. Her ribs had probably shattered, then pushed into her internal organs. From the looks of it, she'd suffered a collapsed lung. Her lungs, holed, were acting as pumps, forcing air out into her chest cavity which was in turn preventing her lungs from inflating properly. Pneumothorax. It was a vicious cycle that would continue until the girl's lungs could not fill at all and she would suffocate. Sand could probably treat that, but the colour of Diana's skin suggested she was also bleeding heavily internally. Without immediate medevac, she was dead. They had no way of treating her here, no autodoc, not even a hibernation pod to stuff her into. And if they did, what then? Drag her out of the desert? Sand had tried to get them down close to the terminator and the liminal zone, but how close? Two hundred, three hundred kilometres?

Sand dithered over what to do. She was frozen in place, her own injury slowing her mind. She just stared at the girl, whose breaths became shorter and shallower as the other kids stared at her. She was unconscious. Not long now.

"She's going to die, isn't she?" said the eldest girl, quietly.

"I don't know what to do to save her. If we had more equipment..." She could not finish. *If* helped nobody. They were all fucked.

"Are we going to die?" asked one of the other kids. Must be Piotr; kid had his arm in a sling.

"Shush," said the girl.

The kids were scared and all looking to Sand for guidance or leadership, or to play mommy or whatever the fuck it was kids needed. Why her? What the hell was she going to do? Two of them were barely six, two more around ten. The boy with the arm, she reckoned about twelve. The girl was the oldest, fifteen maybe. Sand couldn't be sure, she was lousy at telling how old kids were. Kids had always been someone else's problem.

Not any more, she told herself. Not any more.

Diana made a final gasp. Her body quivered once, mouth gaping. A soft, inarticulate noise escaped her throat. Then the two ten-year-olds by her side patted her hands, like they could comfort her back to life. One of the six year olds started to sob, a wet, desolate sound that pricked at Sand more than anything.

Sand took a ragged breath. "No, we are not going to die. I won't let it happen," she said, wondering if that were true, if she had any right to make that kind of promise to them. "We are not going to die. We are going to get out of here. All of us."

The children, teary, dirty, pale with shock. Her responsibility. Fuck.

"You really mean that?" said the girl.

"Yeah. Yeah, I do," she said. Her nausea was retreating to manageable levels.

"What about our parents?" said Piotr.

"I don't know, honey," she said. "With a bit of luck, they got into the passenger pods still on the *Mickey* and got out in time."

"*Mitz-kay-e-veech*," said Piotr.

"I wouldn't bother if I were you," Sand grumbled. "I'm lousy at languages."

The older kids smiled through their sniffles. That made things a bit better. Sand looked carefully around the cabin of the shuttle. The thing was totalled; it'd never fly again, not if a thousand mechanics and their helpful robot buddies spent a lifetime apiece on it. There was no power evident, not the smallest ready light or warning blinker. A blessing, she supposed. She could do without a means of ignition for ruptured fuel cells and tanks.

The nose was buried under the skirts of the dune, but she could see from stress patterns in the glass and buckling in the supports that the airframe had suffered. Her pilot's desk was remarkably whole, but the touch-screens-cum-holo-projectors on the other four stations had shattered. The door leading from the rear of the cabin wouldn't open; she could tell that by looking. As for the engines, well – she sighed and drummed her fingers on the ceiling – Sabres were marvels of engineering, even one hundred and seventy years after the first iterations had first flown, but not when they were stuffed full of sand.

"Write off," she said. "Total write off."

"I'm sorry?" said the girl, who did not understand Sand's American.

"Damaged beyond repair," Sand said in Lingua Anglica. "Broken. We're not flying out of here, that's for certain."

"What are we going to do?" said Piotr.

"We're going to have to walk," she said. Her mouth filled with saliva again. She swallowed with difficulty. "I'm going to need you to help me."

Piotr nodded at her, as did the ten-year-olds. "Yes," said the girl. The six-year-olds looked terrified. They could not understand her. They were too young to have learned the Lingua.

"Chcę mamę," said the crying one. "Chcę iść do domu."

What the fuck was she going to do? The other young one started to cry, followed by the ten-year-olds. They did not bawl or make a noise, but wept quietly, huddling into each other. The quietness of it terrified her. Two hundred kay, walking all the way. They'd all die.

She had an idea. Relief hit her. She almost smiled.

"The robots," she said. "The goddamned robots."

She let go of the webbing and stepped with purpose toward the broken windows, and her leg folded under her. One moment she was moving, the next she was on her back, the girl and the boy – Peter or whatever he was called – staring down at her. She had no memory of the fall.

"I think you are going to have to lie down for a while," said the girl.

"Damn right," said Sand, who promptly passed out.

* * *

SAND WAS ASLEEP for twelve hours, or so her inChip told her. When she came round, the sun had not moved, and she found the fact of that disorienting. The movement of the sun was a fundamental, something a billion years of evolution expected, and it felt deeply wrong to see it so still. Someone had placed a survival blanket on her and put a rolled jacket under her head. Two small bodies lay under more blankets, side by side, at the back of the cabin.

There was no sign of the children, and her heart somersaulted. Then she heard voices outside. Still groggy, she crawled through the smashed windows, emerging into a glaring desert. It was very hot. Sand had experience of deserts on Earth and Mars, but this one seemed particularly dry. A constant, cinnamon-flavoured wind blew from the south, carrying the voices of the children. They were busy under the direction of the girl. They'd done well. Sand was surprised, and grateful.

The kids had dragged out everything they could from the ship and arranged it into neat piles a safe distance away. The girl saw Sand emerge and said something to the others, then came running back to the ship.

"Sit down, sit down! It is not safe for you yet," she scolded.

Sand could only agree. She felt too nauseous to move much, and slid down with her back against the wreck.

"Have we done well?" said the girl.

"Really well," said Sand. Praise did not come naturally to her, but it was hard not to want to make the girl feel good about what she'd done. She'd seen hardened spacers go to pieces in lesser emergencies.

"We wanted to move you, too, but I thought it was not safe. A bang to the head like that..." She let the sentence hang.

"Sure, sure," Sand nodded without thinking, and her head rang like a bell. Her bruised eye was swollen shut and throbbed. She winced. "Have you got anything to drink, kid?"

"Yes, we found it." She called to the others in her language, and one of the little ones ran over, eager as a puppy, lugging a litre bottle of the vile isotonic drink over in his arms.

The girl took it and passed it to Sand. She'd have preferred water – the sickly salt/sweet combination provoked her nausea – but she sipped it determinedly, keeping it down.

"Thank you," she said. "What is your name?"

The girl smiled, and told her all their names. She was Katarzyna – Kasia, she said – and she was fifteen. Piotr, the kid with the broken arm, was twelve. The two ten-year-old boys were Arek and Dominik, although Arek was nine and Dominik nearly eleven. The youngest were five and six, Elenora and Roman. All of them were Poles, but Elenora's mother was Swedish and Arek's father German.

While Sand had been out, they'd pulled together just under ninety litres of the godawful isotonic, thirty kilos of dry rations, five adult-sized survival suits, and an inflatable lifeboat-shelter. There were two tablets. Enough gear to keep five adults alive for a couple of weeks, if they were careful; even cling to life on an airless asteroid if need be. But the suits were too large for the children, and the shelter was designed for zero-g use, and would be too big for them to carry if they could not find and activate one of the robots.

"And these." Kasia glanced back at the other children, playing now in the sand. Sure they were not watching, she pulled out a case from a hiding place behind a piece of shattered hull. "Piotr found them. He did not tell the others."

Sand took the box, flipped it open. Five pistols: the crew's weapons.

Still feeling sick, Sand snapped the box shut and put it to one side. She'd check them later. What did five hundred years do to chemical propellant? The guns looked fine. She hoped the ammunition still worked.

"Now what do we do?" said Kasia.

Sand rested her head on the downed ship and closed her good eye. The sun was too bright.

"We wait until I get my shit back together," she said weakly. "And then we get out of here."

IT TOOK TWO days, by Earth reckoning, until Sand could move around without wanting to throw up. Her black eye went down enough that she could finally see out of it. The light bothered her, but that would pass. She'd retrieved her sunglasses from the cabin, and now felt more or less okay.

"Why do I feel so heavy?" asked Arek.

"Higher-g. I reckon it's pulling 1.25, 1.3. Big ol' planet, this. Bigger than home," said Sand.

She realised she'd slipped again into proper American when she heard Arek asking something of Kasia in that hard, shushing language of theirs. Sand explained herself in Lingua. She was distracted as she spoke, running her hand down the outside of the *Lublin*. The damage looked much worse on the outside. One of the cargo spurs had been torn out of the hull bedding, taking the lower door assembly and its heatshield with it. It was a good job the cargo container had ditched itself when it had. She'd be looking at a pile of crushed robot limbs otherwise. She sighed deeply, feeling profoundly sad. Her ship. A wreck. Sand had nobody else on the *Mickiewicz* to lose, and nobody back home to miss, but for her the destruction of the *Lublin* was a personal loss. The ship was her wings, flight was her life.

"Right, let's find those constructors," she said finally. She caught the container's beacon using the tablet hanging from her shoulder. "Three kilometres, not bad." She asked if Kasia wanted to come with her, which she did.

They left Piotr with the second tablet and the other children; Sand told him that under no circumstances were they to go out of sight of the ship. "Anything happens, call me on the pad and sit tight inside, you got that? We'll be back in a few hours. Do not wander off from here. Hopefully when we get back we'll have a couple of robots to carry all that gear." Piotr explained to the little ones. Roman got excited about the robot. Elenora was too quiet.

She was about to say they'd be back before nightfall, then looked at the unmoving sun. *It's not like it's ever going to get dark*, she thought. It struck her again as wrong.

Sand and Kasia set off. Her inChip functioned, but there was no incoming traffic, no locator dots for her friends, no mail, no messages or silly videos, no announcements or exhortations to be good from the government, no adverts or feeds. The digital

environment on the *Mickey* had been sparse, but out here...
There was nothing. She linked her inChip to the tablet, and
offered to do the same to Kasia's. It did little to alleviate the
feeling of isolation. A fragile network, adrift in a sea of sand.

The hexagonal container had come down between two
towering dunes. Its yellow, corrugated sides appeared
undamaged, but Sand's relief gave way to alarm when she
spotted tracks leading away from its open doors.

"Damn," she said. She motioned to Kasia to stop. She held
the tablet up to the container and had it zoom right in. The
doors had been pushed open from the inside.

"What happened?" asked the girl.

"They must have malfunctioned," Sand said. "The robots.
They got up and got out."

"Can robots do that?"

"Not really, no," said Sand.

Deep, elliptical footprints, the shifting sand obscuring them
already, led away from the container in all directions. One set
led toward them, and disappeared into a crease in the dune
Sand and Kasia stood upon. They went to investigate. The track
ended in a large robot, an andromorph twice the height of a
human, and much broader. Beyond its basic configuration it was
not particularly human looking, with massive hands and feet,
and attachment sockets for tools prominent in a red carapace
reminiscent of a knight's armour. Under the red shell, the rods
and pistons of its limbs were deep carbon black. Hazard striping
adorned plates on its elbows, knees, and feet. It lay face down,
its head pointed toward them, hands out and flat to the floor as
if it had been doing push-ups.

The robot didn't respond to commands, either verbal or sent
via the tablet. There was a faint smell of cooked meat to it.
Sand leaned in toward where its brain case was stored in its
thorax, and recoiled quickly. The brain had baked in the heat;
the casing must have cracked in the crash.

"Shit," she said. Using the robots to get out of there had been
her big bright idea. Without them, what then?

Kasia stared at the machine. She had never been as close to a
robot as this. She felt Sand's eyes on her and looked up nervously.

"Yes, pilot?"

Sand smiled at her. She hadn't told Kasia her name. "The name's Cassandra, Kasia. But my friends call me Sand."

"Like the... sand?"

"Exactly so. Kind of ironic, don't you think?"

The girl looked at her without comprehension.

"Have all the robots gone, Pi– Sand?"

"Let's see honey, shall we? Come on." Sand held out her hand, and Kasia took it.

She was anxious as they approached the container. Sand counted five other tracks leading away from it. There had been eight units in the container. She hoped the remaining two had not been destroyed. Even if they had not, the brains were kept in a similar state of deathly hibernation as the humans, and, like the human passengers, they'd slept for far too long. Malfunction looked likely for them all.

Her heart sank. A second dead robot lay broken, hidden in a dip just outside the doors. It had probably been pushed there by its fellows. Its red carapace was stained with dried cranial fluids. She held her breath as she walked over its broken back and peered into the dark.

At the very rear of the container, a robot crouched. It had not activated, and was still curled into a ball for transport, head between its knees, hands wrapped around its shins. Maybe it had died in transit. She pinged it with the personal unit's short range wifi, and blew out a breath of relief. All good. Systems diagnostics ran over the screen and through the internal display of her mind's eye. She could see nothing amiss. She allowed herself a wide grin.

"Unit 7, are you functional?"

A hum struck up from the robot. "Yes," it said. Its voice suited the size of its carriage; deep, sonorous. A large robot with the voice of a normal man was ridiculous. Humans could anthropomorphise pretty much anything, but needed certain signifiers to accept machines, and voice was one. "I am undamaged. I await your command." It spoke in the same way as every other unit Sand had ever met; distant, as if you were distracting them from something pressing.

"Activate and exit the container," said Sand.

"Yes ma'am," it said. It uncurled into a crouch, waited for Sand and Kasia to back out of the door, then crawled to the mouth of the container, where it pulled itself out, and unfolded to its full height.

"Unit 7, heavy plant construction model Titan-3C, awaiting orders, Pilot Sand. What are your wishes?"

It glinted in the sun. Sand had never seen anything so magnificent. She smiled and threw an impulsive arm around Kasia's shoulders. With the unit, they stood a chance. "Get us the hell out of this desert in one piece, would you?" she said.

The robot's head swivelled down. Unblinking camera eyes stared at her. "Please explain," it said.

WITH SOME DIFFICULTY, they fashioned a set of straps and harness from the cabin's webbing so that the machine could carry the majority of their supplies. Sand also instructed the robot to pull off several pieces of hull from her downed shuttle. Looking at the terrain, she figured they'd need something to spread the robot's weight if it got bogged down in the sand. She struggled for a couple of hours to find a way to attach them to the robot's back before giving up.

"You'll have to drag them, Unit 7," she said. "I'll fix a line to your back."

"Yes, ma'am," said the robot.

She had the robot hold one large plate out in front of it like a tray. She gathered the children under the shade of it. "Should keep the sun off," she said. The children giggled. The robot provided a welcome distraction for the younger ones. Kasia and Piotr were less inclined to laugh. They were old enough to understand.

She let the children play for a few hours as she and Kasia cut down spare jumpsuits and the environment suits to protect the kids from the sun. She then had Kasia put them all down to sleep. She wanted them fresh for the morning. Morning, night, she thought. How long would they hold on to those terms? Assuming they survived.

Sand could not sleep. Her concussion had not faded completely. With her eyes closed, she felt dizzy, and there was always the light, hammering its nails into her skull.

Her mind would not be quiet. Elenora was beginning to concern her, more deeply affected than the others. The pilot lay in the shade, surrounded by fitful youngsters, a gun holstered at her waist; they'd seen no life here yet, but that did not mean there wasn't any, nor that it wasn't hostile. The younger ones had scared themselves stupid talking about monsters, and they all felt better for having the robot watch over them. Its tireless eyes swept the sand, sensors alert to any sound, its nearly human mind thinking inhuman thoughts.

Did it dream, while it slept on the ship? wondered Sand, as she slipped into sleep herself.

THEY AWOKE TO the endless day. Sand felt as if she had hardly slept at all; only her inChip gave her an indication of the passage of time. Seven hours. Felt like seven minutes. Kasia roused the others and they ate a spare breakfast of hard rations. Sand was already sick of the rations.

She rounded her charges up, and had them stand under the shade of the robot's makeshift parasol.

"Let's go," she said.

The kids stared at her. They were not ready to leave.

"What's up?" she said.

"What about the others?" Piotr asked.

"We can't just leave them there," said Kasia. Her voice was quieter than normal, as if she was afraid she would anger Sand.

"Who?"

"Diana and Gosia," Kasia said.

The dead kids. She'd been so occupied with keeping the others alive she'd forgotten to think about the bodies. Bury them? It'd take a while. She could tell them to get moving.

What was she thinking?

"Of course. Of course, I'm sorry. We'll bury them before we go."

Unit 7 scraped out shallow graves in the sand with its hands. Sand did not know what to do when their small corpses were placed in the ground, but Kasia said something in Polish that seemed to keep the others happy.

She was right not to deny them the ritual. It probably would have been very unwise to do so, for that matter, she thought, for all that they'd wasted time.

They had their heads bowed. Must all be religious; so many people were now. She didn't understand it, herself. She watched them pray. They squinted against the light. She had to get them to wear their head protection or she'd have a bunch of sunstroke victims on her hands. Shit, there was too much to remember. Too much to do.

They lifted their heads and blinked.

"We can go now," said Kasia.

Sand nodded and put a hand briefly on the girl's shoulder. Unit 7 retrieved its parasol of woven carbon, and Sand yoked his blocky waist to the crude sled once more.

They set off into the desert, the sun at their backs, and crested the first dune soon enough. Sand let the small party walk on ahead of her as she turned back to look at the wreck of the *Lublin*. Its shattered remnants littered the landscape. Sand wondered how long it would take for the desert to bury it. She realised she'd forgotten all about Roosevelt, and for one impulsive moment she considered going back to get him.

"Rest in peace," she said, although for the ship, her bear or her old life, she couldn't say. A spacer without a ship was no spacer at all. Only then did she think she might never be one again.

She turned her back on the ship for the last time and followed the children down the steep slipface.

THEY WALKED DIRECTLY north, toward the liminal zone, somewhere ahead. Sand tried to calculate the distance they had to go from the sun's elevation, but without knowing the diameter of the planet, she could come up only with the broadest estimate.

They struggled up the long wind-facing slopes of the barchans, then tumbled down the steep slipfaces on the other side. It was on the leeward slopes that the robot had most trouble. Unit

7 was built for uneven ground, but the dunes' steep, yielding surfaces were too much for its weight. They all stumbled and slid, but the robot sank deep, sending avalanches of sand down before it. Its motors whined as it tried to extricate itself. Every step took long seconds. Sand monitored it through her inChip for signs of overheating. If sand got into its workings, it could quickly seize up, and without it, they would in all probability die. The robot was forced to set aside its parasol hull plate at these times. The children made a game of sliding down the slipfaces on the plate as the robot struggled on. They made Sand nervous, at first, but they enjoyed it, and it afforded them a chance to rest as the robot struggled down after them.

Travelling was hard work with little reward. Each peak delivered only an unbroken view of more dunes. The youngest children grew tired, and Sand and Kasia had to help them along. When it was clear they could walk no more, Sand put them on the robot's hull-plating shed, and let them ride it a while. "Not for long," she said. The carbon weave was burning hot to the touch.

Roman said something.

"What did he say?" Sand asked.

"He wants to know why he can't ride all the way to his mother and father. I told them it is not good to be in the sun for a long time."

"That is why." She paused. "Kasia, did you tell them their parents are waiting for them?"

"What should I tell them?" Kasia said, her voice suddenly brimming with emotion. She walked away quickly, head down, her small footprints dwarfed by the tracks of the construction robot.

Elenora said little. When she did, she spoke to herself in Swedish, a language none of them knew, although Sand understood "mama" alright. She soothed her, held her. It didn't seem to do much good.

After a time, Arek and Dominik joined the little ones. Then all the children were riding the sled more often than not. The robot had no problem pulling the children, and Sand thought they might as well stay on the hull plating. She thought about inflating the emergency shelter, but it was too big; she tented a survival blanket over the youngsters' heads instead, trusting it to shade them from the worst of the light and heat. She was happier when they were out of the sun in the dunes' lees.

Kasia was the last to accept a ride, doggedly keeping pace with Sand at the head of the small column until the pilot sent her back to the sled.

Sand trudged along alone beside the robot. She had all the kids with inChips, the robot and herself linked in to the tablet, but without the supporting architecture, they could not communicate beyond text. She had never realised how limited the inChips were without the net to support them. Even on her long-range missions, she was interfaced with the ship she flew. But they were aware of each other's presences, in a digital sense, and that gave them a kind of strength.

All of them old enough looked often to the tablet through their inChips, to see if anyone knew where they were. Nobody did. They did not discuss it; talk of rescue was taboo by unspoken consent. Sand scanned the radio waves every so often but was greeted by static. She checked the beacon more frequently, to ensure it still broadcast its steady pulse, until she realised she was doing so obsessively, and limited herself to checks on the half hour. Likewise with the tablet's pedometer. The tablet counted her steps and those of the robot, coming up with a fairly accurate estimation of distance travelled. She had the tablet inform her every time they had passed another kilometre. It did not happen often enough for her liking.

Sand was exhausted, the heat was draining, the wind desiccating. Up the long slopes, the sand was unbearably hot; down the shadowed slip sides it was cooler, but Sand had to help get the robot down, and by the time she'd got the damn thing into the slack, she'd forgotten to enjoy the shade and was back into the sun.

The sun. Orange, unblinking, at her back all the time, it scorched her neck. Sand's skin was darker than the children's, but she was not dark enough to shrug off the sun, and she was burning.

"What?" said Kasia, who had rejoined her.

Sand stopped. The robot came to a halt. "I didn't say anything."

"You were talking to yourself."

Was I? Sand thought. *Shit.* "Nothing." Their voices had become husky. Sand looked the girl up and down. She looked drugged, and was swaying on her feet. "What are you doing off the sled? Take another ride. If there's not enough room, get Arek and Dominik to walk a while."

Kasia looked at her.

"Go on! And check the kids for sunburn," she called. "And make sure everyone gets a drink."

They were in the bottom of a slack. Another huge dune rose before them. Were they getting bigger? That might mean something, but Sand didn't know enough about deserts or dunes. At home she could have checked the net; not here. The knowledge in her own memory was inadequate. How much they all relied on their inChips! The children needed a geographer, not a pilot; and she needed a ship.

"Fuck it," she muttered. "We'll take a break!" she shouted. Piotr and Dominik, who had dismounted the sled, turned wearily around and headed back to it.

On the sled, Arek was gulping greedily at a bottle. Kasia rebuked him in hard Polish, and he took the drink away from his mouth.

"You tell him to stop drinking so much?" said Sand.

"Yes."

"You did good, we have to watch our liquid consumption. I have no idea how long we'll be walking."

They'd been on the move for five hours, and come less than twenty kilometres. They had to make better speed. The kids were tired, Sand could see that. She had to push them on or they wouldn't make it.

"Ten minutes," she said. "Then five more dunes. Then we'll stop for the day."

The day would not stop for them. How she wished for the night.

* * *

"Ma'am, a lifeform approaches." The robot's stentorian voice summoned Sand from her reverie. Placing one foot in front of another was hypnotic; snapping out of it was uncomfortable and unwelcome. They were descending a slip. Three days into the journey, and the robot had become more adept at negotiating the steep slopes, and so they moved quicker. The children had sledded down, and were waiting at the bottom, some hundred metres away. They no longer shouted with excitement; even descending had become a chore. The heat made everything a chore.

"What?" She shaded her eyes and scanned the horizon. All she saw were more dunes. Sand, sand, sand. *Sand in the sand*, she thought. *I'm going to die.*

An icon blinked in her mind's eye: the robot, opening a channel. She accepted, and was looking through its eyes. She was a giant – metal, invulnerable. The heat was nothing. Systems thrilled under her attention. The feeling took her aback, but she was only a passenger; she did not have any influence on it.

"There," said the robot.

A movement, quick and fleeting; something large. The robot zoomed in on the windward side of the dune after next.

Sand stared through unblinking eyes for a minute.

"If there is something coming, Unit 7, then it will take a long time to get here. It has to climb the other side. We'll be here for –"

"Wait," demanded the robot.

"What?" asked Sand incredulously. Robots took orders; they did not give them.

Then it was there, fast, a large shape the same colour as the desert sand, skittering a comical highstep on many legs. A teardrop carapace rose high and rotated to and fro, independently of the legs, twisting this way and that like a monstrous head. Two long, triply-jointed limbs jutted from a mouth set directly into its torso. It stopped periodically to drum them upon the sand. What could have been a mouth opened, and a long cone lined with cruel, recurved spikes protruded into the air. Then the creature raised itself up, revealing the structure of its legs – they were set in a cluster, also three-jointed, ending in a leathery skirt in the underbelly of the carapace.

The children had seen it too. They were standing, pointing at it, glancing back to Sand, frightened.

The creature stopped, stock still. Its legs moved around in a fussy little dance. The proboscis opened and closed; purple fronds extended, waved on the air, then darted back in. Its feelers drummed on the floor, shifted around, drummed again. The proboscis snapped closed and pulled back inside the hillock of its body in one movement.

It turned to face towards the children, and the tablet shrilled.

"Kasia!" screamed Sand. "Kids!"

The creature began to run.

The tablet sang out a mad song that was not interference. Sand shut the radio off with a thought and severed her link with the robot. She hurtled down the hill, tripped, went sprawling, then scrambled onto her hands and knees, spitting sand from her dry mouth. "Kasia!" she shouted.

The children were screaming, running back up the hill. The creature was a couple of hundred metres away from the kids, Sand thirty or so. It was gaining; the children slipped in the sand. It did not.

The robot.

Sand shot an emergency override into the machine, intending to take control of it. The robot had no combat programming, but Sand had some training, and its body was strong.

"No," said the robot. It shut her out.

Then it was past her. Unit 7 had learned from experience, moving its legs in a rolling motion, using gravity in its favour to avoid becoming mired in the sand. It reached the bottom before Sand had got to her feet, stumbled, flung its arm out to compensate with a fluidity Sand had never seen before in a robot, and recovered. It intercepted the beetle scant metres away from the children. The robot dipped low, and barged into the carapace with its shoulder, knocking the beetle sideways. The improvised straps on the machine's back burst, and their supplies were scattered all over the place.

The creature rocked on its strange, crustacean undercarriage and recovered, legs scurrying to bring it around to face this challenger. The creature reared itself, segmented limbs extending, apparently making itself appear bigger to present a greater threat. It spread its mouth feelers wide – and they were wide, four metres across, alien and disturbing – and circled the robot. A beetle before, now it resembled a Terran crab. Its mouthparts flicked in and out, and from somewhere within its armoured shell came a penetrating sibilance.

Sand climbed to her feet. The children clutched at her, making it hard to regain her footing. She pushed them away and went for her gun. "Stay here! Stay here with Kasia!"

The gun slid out of its holster; she held it out double-handed, arms straight, and advanced on the monstrous beetle.

The robot followed the alien lifeform's movements, head tracking round, shifting on its massive metal legs when the beetle tried to get behind it. They remained locked in this stalemate, circling each other in a strange waltz. Sand drew closer, off the slope and onto firmer ground. She could see that the beetle was not just sand coloured, but covered in a seamless coat of sand. It looked huge closer to: the length of a large car, and taller. It must weigh as much as the robot, she thought. She was afraid.

The beetle had not seen her. It lunged, leftmost limb whipping forward. The robot raised its shovel hands to deflect the blow, but it was too slow, and the limb struck the machine square in the chest. There was an almighty *bang*, and the creature ducked out of the way as the robot swiped in return. The robot's casing was cracked, but so was the creature's chitin. Yellowish fluid welled up in it. The creature seemed unperturbed. The robot swung, pivoting its gimballed waist. Its fist alone massed fifty kilograms – a weight of six hundred newtons or so here. The creature dodged back. Its strange mouth rakes spread wider, it hissed louder.

Sand opened fire, marching forward with every shot. Bullets smacked into the carapace to no effect, other than bringing her to its attention. The beetle turned again, facing her.

Fuck, thought Sand, *if it charges me I'm fucked.*

She fired and fired, concentrating on the proboscis. This evidently hurt it a great deal; the violet fronds were withdrawn rapidly, followed by the mouth-cone itself. Flattened, armoured palps slid over the aperture. She could see no eyes, but carried on firing at what she'd decided, on the evidence, was its face.

The creature wavered between her and the robot. The robot waited until the beetle faced her again, and struck. The creature was blindsided, and the robot grabbed its undamaged forelimb. With a smooth, mechanical motion, the robot pulled it free. A long tendon trailed from the palp, gleaming whitely, followed by a gout of deep yellow blood.

The creature made a noise that had Sand clutching at her ears, a polyphonic keening she felt in her teeth. It ran backwards from the robot, bobbing up and down in submission, then turned, hurled itself at the side of the dune, and with a flurry of legs, disappeared underneath the surface. A shifting movement in the sand betrayed its presence, then a sinking, then nothing. It had gone.

Sand held her gun at the ready, pointing at where the beetle creature had burrowed away. She reached the circle of their scattered supplies next to the robot and called to the children, gave the robot a link command to follow, and met them halfway down the slope.

The area of the fight was scuffed, the smell of cinnamon overpowering around the creature's spattered blood and its severed limb. They gathered their supplies quickly, putting them on the sled. Sand was worried the creature might come back, or that there might be more of them, and did not wish to waste time reattaching them to the robot's back. A few bottles had burst, trampled during the battle, but many of their supplies had been pushed into the sand undamaged, and they recovered nearly all of them. Some of the food packets were ripped, but the rations within were still edible. They gathered up the hard biscuits, sand and all, leaving the few that had been contaminated by the beetle's blood. All the while Sand regarded the robot with a mix of relief and worry. It had shut her out. Robots weren't supposed to do that, they weren't capable of it.

Sand made a decision. She retrieved the guncase and flipped it open.

She gave Piotr and Kasia a pistol apiece.

"A gun?" said Kasia. She held the weapon at arms length, somewhat limply, like it would burn her. Piotr was more enthusiastic.

"Yeah," said Sand. "I figure you're more likely to die from not having them than kill yourselves with the damn things," she said to them quietly. "Hey! Piotr, it's not a toy. Don't wave it around like that. You know how they work?"

They said yes, but she showed them quickly anyway. She was jumpy, needed to be out of there, but she wasn't going to be caught out like that again.

"You keep these close. Don't play with them, okay? Use them to protect yourselves and the little kids, you got that? Only take them out then. Promise me."

They nodded solemnly.

Sand urged the robot on. Spurred by fear, they set off quickly, casting worried looks behind them all the while. She didn't feel safe until they were two dunes further on, and she never relaxed fully in the desert again.

The character of the desert changed, dunes giving way to rocky hills. When they came to a stone spire, they stopped, and set up camp on the safety of bedrock. They slept, the robot standing sentry, Sand watching it fearfully until exhaustion bore her down into sleep.

The next day, the wind picked up strength. The day after, they walked into the sandstorm.

CHAPTER FOURTEEN
Robot

INHALATION. NOT DEAD, not dead. Wet drops on his face, pattering.

Rain?

Dariusz opened his eyes, and thick, sand-filled rain stung them. He was moving. He propped himself onto his elbows.

Five faces stared at him, cowled in cut-down environment suits. Five children. He was on a sled, a massive version of the ones the 14A survivors had dragged through the desert. The kids blinked at him. One rubbed a finger under her nose, but they said nothing.

He knelt. The sled was wide and stable, and his movements did not affect its progress. They were going along a valley bottom. The sled squealed as it ran over pebbles, but slid on without interruption. Ahead of him, a tall shape lumbered, leaning into the weight of the sled. Lightning blinked, highlighting panels and hard edges. Water ran off it in torrents: a robot, a heavy construction unit.

Two smaller shapes walked to the right of it, heads down. They looked like toddlers next to the robot, and Dariusz thought they were children, until his sense of perspective returned and he realised one was an adult, the other not far from becoming one.

It was as dark as he'd yet seen it. The sun was completely obscured by glowering cloud, and the wind had switched around to the west. Runnels of water poured down the slopes to their left and right, braiding themselves into small streams.

Pebbles. The hills here were not dunes; gullies cut through them, exposing strata. He'd driven this way, he thought, through part of this landscape. But this, this was a dry riverbed, something he'd not seen before on this world. And it was not so dry any more. Water was gathering in the bottom, sandy tongues of it wetting stone and dust.

They had to get out. He came alive instantly, adrenaline galvanising his limbs. He shouted. Thunder rolled above them, obliterating his voice.

He jumped off the sled and jogged forward. He ran alongside the taller figure – a woman, from the size and shape. He tapped her on the shoulder and was rewarded with a gun in his face.

He held his hands up reflexively. The robot stopped. She pulled her mask off to reveal a coffee-skinned, sunburned face, dark circles under her eyes – one black with bruising – lips dry. She was angry.

"What the hell do you think you are doing?" she shouted. "I nearly shot you!" Rain pattered off her environment suit.

"I'm sorry!" he replied. "We have to get out of this valley!"

"Why?"

He pointed at the water. "This river will flood very soon. We are in danger here."

She paused, looked at the riverbed. She gave him a quizzical look.

"This," he shouted, "is a riverbed! It will flood very soon. Flash flood. We need to move."

The woman looked up. "Not to the top, too dangerous. Too much lightning!" She waved her gun at the sky. They were both yelling. The noise of the rain and the thunder was incredible.

"We have no choice!"

She nodded, beckoned to her companion, a girl, and said something to her that Dariusz did not catch. The girl went back to the sled, and they headed up onto the valley slope.

The woman set herself to walking again. Dariusz grabbed her shoulder. He wished he had his own hood still. Rain washed the salt of his own sweat into his eyes, and it stung. "Listen!" he said. "I have a vehicle. Big enough for us all."

"Where?" she said. "I get nothing on my tablet."

"Maybe the storm scrambled the beacon."

"Where was this?"

"Not far from where you found me."

She slumped. "Man, that was four hours ago."

"I have supplies. There is a forward base not far from here, two days' drive. You'll never walk out of the desert. You'll die. If we get back to my ATV, we will live."

Her face wrinkled. "Shit. I should've tried harder to wake you up." She nodded. "We'll head back."

She called the girl and told her to go back again. The girl rolled her eyes in the manner of all teenagers confronted with the foolishness of adults. The robot clumped around to face back the way they had come. Dariusz scanned the side of the valley. He pointed.

"If we walk along there, below the ridge, the way will be easier. We should be safe from the lightning."

The woman considered that too. She was evidently not one who would follow blindly. "Alright. We'll try it."

They made the valley edge. It was harder going than the valley floor and the children had to get off their sled.

"This is not good," said the woman.

"Look," said Dariusz.

The valley resounded with noise. A rush and a rumble, and the hollow knock of stone on stone. The snout of a torrent nosed down the riverbed, white and brown and ravenous, surging with debris. The snout passed. One moment the river was empty, the next it was full.

Dariusz doubted the robot would have been able to keep its footing in that. The rest of them would have been washed away.

They watched it a while, the woman's arms wrapped protectively around the two youngest children. The robot hefted something overhead, and they were suddenly sheltered from the worst of the rain. Dariusz rubbed rain and sand from his eyes.

"I suppose I'd better say thank you," said the woman. "My name's Cassandra De Mona, first pilot. Or, I *was* first pilot. Now I have nothing to fly. Call me Sand."

"Dariusz Szczeciński, geoengineer." He held out his hand.

Sand gave Dariusz a look he didn't understand. "You people," she said. "Why are your names so damn hard?"

"Call me Darius if you like. I am used to it. Or Darek."

She shook her head. There was a determination about her, a hardness, that Dariusz found at once off-putting and attractive. "Darius is not your name, is it? I have to make an effort. How do you say it?"

"*Darry-oosh Shche-chin-ski*," he said slowly.

"Dayoosh? Darry-oosh? Dariusz," said the woman. It was a reasonable attempt. She seemed happy with it. She grasped his hand. "I'm not even going to try the second one. Show me where this buggy of yours is, I'm dog sick of walking."

"Do you have anything to drink? I am very thirsty."

Sand looked up, to the shelter the robot was holding up, upon which drummed the quick tattoo of the rain. She raised her eyebrows, pursed her lips, and burst into unexpected laughter.

"Okay, I see. The rain... Sand," he said.

"You see?" she said with the trace of a smile. "American names. Easy."

THE RIVER LEVEL rose as the rain continued, the sandy sides of the creek collapsing into the water with soft, weighty splashes, streams of water pouring down the valley sides and making their footing treacherous.

Dariusz wondered at the source of the water. On the seifs, the sand would suck down most of the rain quickly; it would not have time to gather into a flood. The valley was rocky, the ground less permeable. He had passed through a broad field of rock formations emerging from the sand some way back; perhaps the sand gave out and the rocky area became more extensive upriver. That's where the water must come from. If so, the extent of the storms was enormous.

They spoke little. The robot had to cling to the valley side and had no hand spare to shelter them, and it was too steep for the sled. He, Sand and the elder girl had to help the younger ones, and eventually they ended up carrying the smallest.

The rain maintained the same, heavy beat, as unvarying as the hidden sun. It was concussive, a barrage of precipitative artillery, not rain, and the softer areas of sand they passed were pocked with miniature craters.

Sand made to turn out of the valley, but Dariusz stopped her. "This way," he said, pointing downriver. "That is where my ATV is."

It was five long hours before they emerged from the valley back onto the pan. With the sand now scrubbed from the air, a low, sand-blasted mountain range had emerged in the distance beyond the flats, shadowy through the rain. The landscape was gargantuan, an empty planet, and Dariusz despaired at the thought of filling it.

It was a landscape in the process of transformation. Streams snaked across the flats, crawling out of countless gulleys to form wide, braided rivers. The lightning flashed once, twice, three times, flickering up the tiny, dark shape of Danieł's deck – his tomb. The ATV stood not far from it. The ground shone wetly around both.

They were watching the birth of a sea. Water took his wife, and now it was taking his son. Danieł had always loved the sea; it seemed fitting, in a way.

"Wow," said Sand.

"A seasonal lake," said Dariusz. "This world is perhaps not so bad."

"This is not my idea of *not bad*," she said.

Dariusz shrugged. "I only mean it could be worse. The water, at least, is still free," he said, remembering.

"Is that a deck segment out there?" she said.

"There is no one alive on it now."

"Is that why you were out here?"

"My son," was all he said. His tone told Sand all she needed to know.

"I... I'm sorry," said Sand. "His mother?"

"She was deemed unstable, and was not selected for the journey. She told us to go, and then drowned herself."

Sand froze momentarily, thought of the parents on the ship. Dariusz said no more, and so she changed the subject. "Let's get the kids on the sled. This way?"

Dariusz oriented himself. "This way."

They walked on, faster now. The children were so tired they fell asleep on the sled in the rain. The water was pleasantly warm, cool enough to refresh but not to chill. The lake grew all the while, small waves clashing on its surface.

The dayside was coming to life. Small animals, and things analogous to insects, pushed themselves from cracks in the rock, or hauled themselves from burrows in the sand. Close by the water, fissures yawned in the sand. Shells pushed themselves out of the ground, opening up as they came; their openings were metres long, their lips scalloped to lock together. They gaped wide into the rain. Convulsive movements forced tissues out into the downpour, ribbed sheets flung outward that covered the ground around each shell. The desert became a mat of flesh around these creatures, swelling as it engorged with water.

Dariusz expected plants of some kind to follow, in the coming days.

Dariusz made them stop once, pulled them into the shelter of a cliff. Sand questioned him.

"Something's coming."

She looked about anxiously. "The beetles?"

"No, the things in the air. They're dangerous."

"Things in the air, too? Great," she said.

He pointed to the sky.

Flocks of leather-winged horrors came soaring in to joust with one another in the sky. They disported in the leaden veils of rain, rutting amid the lightning. The largest flew at each other again and again; sometimes, the losers fell with tattered wings to splash in the young lake, other times they pulled back to circle each other and swoop again. There were hundreds of them.

They fed, stooping over the growing lake, skimming over the filling dips, wings kissing the choppy surfaces of ponds that grew and reached out to one another. A group of the creatures wheeled high, and fell upon something only they could see below, plummeting as one. Thunder rumbled. Darius imagined their hooks ripping chunks of flesh from the clam-like animals.

"They have killed several people already," he said. "But I do not think they are interested in us today."

Sand's nerve wavered. Things in the air, things under the ground. All big. All hungry. She followed Dariusz anyway. There was nothing else to do.

"Come on," he said, casting a wary glance at the sky. "We better be quick, or the ATV will be submerged."

They skirted the lake. Only once did a creature dive at them. Piotr called out a warning, and they huddled under the robot's protection. It made another pass, then flew away, leaving its awful call and the smell of cinnamon on the air.

Daniel's tomb grew nearer. The ATV was close.

When the vehicle's signal sang out in their inChips and tablets, Sand nearly cried. They reached it twenty minutes later. Water lapped around its tall wheels, and so they had the robot ferry them out into the flood in twos and threes. They bundled the children into the back. Dariusz secured the equipment boxes from inside to the roof rack while Sand stripped the kids of their wet clothes and had them curl up together under the cover of survival blankets. Without exception, they were asleep in minutes.

"Thank you," said Sand as they sat in the cabin. The rain's racket was soft on the roof. After the fury and vastness of the skies, the cabin was peculiarly intimate; they felt close as lovers. Their world shrank, small and full of the padding of outdoor gear and the thickness of evaporating rain. Condensation clouded the windows. Small noises – breathing, the creak of seats, the rustle of fabric – rescaled everything to a human level. They felt larger, in control of their surroundings. Outside the vehicle, they were ants before the tempest; inside it, surrounded by the work of man, demigods again. "I'm sorry about your boy."

Dariusz could not say anything. He wanted to confess, but he did not. Sand touched something in him. He knew she would recoil in horror should he tell her what he had done. He knew the time would come when he would have to tell, but at that moment, he could not bear it. Nor speak of Daniel. To do so would be to collapse. He needed the proximity of his fellow man, to grieve privately, but in company. His disgust with himself and his need for companionship warred inside him, and he could give voice to neither.

"We'll get the robot to follow, and go to Desert One. From there, they can take us to First Landing. Home," he said.

"They still have shuttles?"

"They have two."

Sand's smile was radiant.

"The robot," repeated Dariusz.

"The robot," said Sand. "I'll be right back."

Sand popped the door, letting the ravenous blast of the wind into the cabin. The ATV rocked with it. Then the door was shut, and silence returned.

A few seconds later, Sand opened the door again.

"I'm having a problem," she said.

Dariusz raised his eyebrows in a question. "The water?"

She shook her head. "No, no. The robot. It won't come."

"Won't?"

"It's not the first time. It's been a little… wiggy."

"Wiggy?"

"Behaving oddly," she said in Lingua Anglica.

Dariusz unclipped himself and stepped outside. By comparison with the stillness of the ATV, the violence of the weather seemed redoubled. A purplish light tinted the desert, the landscape bruised by the storm's violence. Dariusz followed Sand down the ladder. They plashed into the deepening water, up to his thighs now. They made their way to the rear of the ATV.

The robot stood sentinel in the lashing rain, still as an idol to a forgotten god.

"I've tried direct access, verbal commands, nothing…" she said.

Could this be a side effect of the virus? The robot's brain was organic, like the Syscore. Robots never said no. They *couldn't* say no. What other explanation could there be?

"Follow us!" he shouted.

Silence.

"Unit 7, respond!"

The robot towered over him. In all his many interactions with such machines – and Dariusz was used to operating construction androids – he had never felt ill at ease. He did now. The robot's intransigence highlighted their size difference. It could, if it chose, crush him in one fist.

"No," it said.

Dariusz's next order died in his throat. Instead he asked, "Why?"

The robot's head looked down at him. Faint light glowed from the high-light-gain retinas at the back of its eyes.

"I remain," it said. Its face returned to the storm.

"Leave it," said Dariusz firmly.

"What?"

"Just leave it. It will not come. Something is happening to it."

"No!" she said. "Don't we need it?"

He grabbed Sand's arm; she looked at him with hostility, but did not pull away.

"We have to go. I do not think it is safe."

They backed away.

The robot spoke one more time as they ascended the ladder to the cab. "Look to your children. Children are the gateway to tomorrow." It spoke without moving, and Dariusz became half-convinced it had said nothing at all, and that he had imagined it.

They left the robot standing in the growing lake.

A recovery team returned for Unit 7 under blue skies a week later, before the virus got to the shuttles and grounded them for good. The lake was an unbroken expanse five metres deep by then, covering the pans in crosshatched ripples, and the robot was hidden beneath it. Hampered by clouds of biting insects and the flocks of aerial creatures feasting upon them, the salvage crew opted to leave the robot until the water had retreated. When it finally did so, the robot had gone.

RAIN HAMMERED INTO the windows as Leonid watched his father's letter again.

He was in the command post at First Landing, three prefabbed units stacked one atop the other to make an ugly tower block. The view was obscured by the weather, but he'd been told that the river below the two mesas was running with water.

Rain, in a desert. Not much of a surprise. There were a few meteorologists on the crew, and they talked about temperature exchanges and moisture loads and seasonal winds and blah, blah, blah. Leonid could understand it – it was important he understand it – but he could not concentrate on it. All he could think of was Ilya's letter, Ilya's fucking letter.

As the scientist droned on, Yuri had interrupted them and said, "So, gentlemen and ladies, what you are telling my good brother and I is that it does actually rain here, so there is a fighting chance we're not all going to die on this shitbox of a planet?"

They murmured their assent.

"Thanks so much. Goodbye."

Yuri. Yuri was as Yuri did. He'd rallied remarkably, now they were on the ground, taking a lead where Leonid thought he would be a liability. Leonid was unsure of himself, and glad of his presence, he helped parse the meanderings of what was left of their tech and science staff down into simple phrases. They all needed simple phrases. They needed to act fast, the colonists needed hope, and Leonid, most of all, needed matters putting simply. Because of Ilya's letter.

The letter had tumbled, unexpectedly, out into his inChip when his salvaged datacore had come online. A holo, a shimmer, a breath of light from his long-dead father. It began in the usual manner, the pompous assertion of their right to wealth, the glory of the Petrovitches. It moved into less familiar territory, as Ilya praised both sons, highlighting qualities he saw in them both, and laying bare his trust in them; praise they had never received on Earth. No doubt the letter – which only Leonid was authorised to watch – existed in several forms. Knowing his father, there would be one in the case of his survival and Yuri's death, one if Yuri survived and Leonid did not, and this one, if they both survived. Leonid decided he would strip mine the datacore later for the variants.

He rather wanted to match the letters up, to triangulate the depth of their father's manipulation. That was Ilya's great flaw. He had no real trust, and so his sons had no trust in him. His praise was a hollow edifice, founded on lies.

Leonid's suspicions were fuelled by the fact that this letter had not been in the Syscore, but in his personal datacore. Already he was thinking, could it be possible, was his father responsible for the downing of the *Mickiewicz*? Had he expected this to happen?

Leonid was harshly amused at the thought of the Pointers sitting there, waiting for the wormhole to open. He wondered what happened. Did they turn it on anyway when they did not receive the entanglement signal, fifty years after they had departed? Did it explode, sucking the sun to its doom? Or did it simply *not work*, the field generators spinning around an empty space that should have contained an even emptier space? He wondered if they'd managed to track the fleet down, helplessly watched it break up. Had the world ended as Ilya prophesied? They'd travelled at around 0.8c all the way; while 500 years had passed for everyone on the ship, nearly 900 had passed back on Earth.

"Yours is the task of preparing the way, yours is the joy of making a new home in the stars," said Ilya to him through the holo (would he say the same to Yuri, or would his be different? Rationally, it should not matter to Leonid, but it did, it mattered a great deal, and he hated his father a little more). Ilya's expression softened. He was drawing Leonid in to familial intimacy. Another manipulation. "We have had our differences, you and I, but you are the most capable of my offspring." (Would Yuri's version say the same, naming him as favoured son? he wondered again.) "You will come to see, in time, that men yearn to be led. To a greater degree, women will not be so easily commanded, but must be convinced. Once they are, they will push the men for you. You must lead them from the fore and by guile. One man is fit for this role; not many, not consensus. Go the route of government by the many, and perish. The state embodied in one man is more powerful, more reactive, more adaptable, than the state embodied in the will of the people. This has proved true time and again here on Earth, and it is a truth that will become ever more apparent to you as you attempt to build a world in more..." – that half moon smile again, mocking and condescending; like Yuri's, but his father lacked his brother's charm – "Challenging circumstances. And many challenges await you. An army cannot function by democratic consent, and a society is no different, especially one under stress as yours will be. Hierarchy is the natural state of humanity. You, through the gifts I have given you, through the efforts of our family, are at the top of that hierarchy. You deserve to be at the head of it. The forces of evolution themselves have appointed you. Now is the time to put aside childish things and become a man. Embrace your birthright. Your task, my son, is to be worthy of the obedience of those that will follow you. I have every faith that you will be so. Anderson will be the guarantor of your success; Yuri also, should you employ him correctly."

Ilya paused.

"My own brother said it was vanity to utilise my own genetic code as the basis for our family's Alts, and perhaps he was correct. Whatever the truth of his opinion, I will, in a sense, always be with you. God bless you, my son."

The holo crackled out.

Leonid leaned back in his chair until it balanced on its two rear legs, and rubbed at his forehead.

He sat forward suddenly, the chair legs thumping down hard. "No," he said aloud. "No, no, no, no, no." Anderson was a clone of his father? What did that make them, brothers? Pressure built behind his eyes. He looked nothing like Ilya, but that could be changed easily. Cold terror gripped him. He thought he'd escaped his father, but in a very real sense he hadn't, not at all.

We'll see, he thought. *I'm not going to live his fantasy for him. First thing I'm going to do is set up a council to run this place, then maybe I'll just fuck off into the desert.* They had so much to do, collect as much as they could from the crash, locate the main body of the wreck and retrieve the Syscore, then there was food, shelter... The kind of thing he'd never had to think about before. He couldn't do that on his own. He wouldn't.

He accessed his inChip – a comnet was in place within the settlement, a fragile, underpopulated thing – to put a call in to Yuri. He'd talk to him first, before he did anything. Yuri might have enjoyed the trappings of their wealth more than he did, but he had as much stomach for playing the autocrat as Leonid. He was surprised when the door banged open and Yuri tumbled in before he'd started to speak.

Yuri was sopping wet, rain streaming off his shaved head. He had been running, and was out of breath. Yuri had never been very fit; too much revelry. Behind him, rain slanted in the wind.

"Leo!" he panted. "Come on! You've got to come. The robots..."

"What?"

"They're leaving."

"What!?" Leonid raised an overview of the settlement on his inChip. A map on one level, the forum on another. The simple net was choked with babble. Fifteen large and twenty-seven small triangular icons marked the locations of the thinking machines; they were all moving away from First Landing. He could gain no access to them.

He ran out into the storm after his brother to see shapes stalking the gloom, and his father's words echoed round his skull.

Many challenges await you. An army cannot function by democratic consent, and a society is no different, especially one under stress as yours will be.

I will always be with you.

"Do something!" shouted Yuri. "You have to do something!"

Leonid froze. What could he do?

PART IV

The Evening Country
7 months after crash

Guided Cultural Propagation has been compared to the design of artificial utile bacilli. We concede that there are similarities between the two sciences. In designing an artificial lifeform for a particular role, biotechnologists first select an organism whose biology best accords with the environment in which it will be required to live, and whose habits, abilities and natural tendencies will enable it to perform the function it is intended to perform...

And so with Guided Cultural Propagation. There is no such thing as an ideal society, but there is such a thing as a society suited to survival in a particular environment, under particular stresses. And so we have examined the cultural propensities of many of our contemporary nations in order to best identify certain beneficial memes that will allow our colonists to flourish on the diverse worlds to which they shall travel. Taking under consideration the highly interdependent, globalised nature of 22nd century civilisation, we are perforce to be subtle in our selections, because the larger differences apparent only two hundred years ago are all but extinct. But we can be thorough, matching not just useful cultural leanings, the differing neurolinguistic biases of particular language groups, or the minor physiological advantage from various subdivisions of the world population to particular anticipated environments, but also the matching of the traits of individuals to the societies we wish to engineer, as well as individuals to individuals. This includes the pair-bonding policies intended for fifteen of the colony craft.

Take the example of the *ESS Adam Mickiewicz* and *ESS Goethe*. We see the ships themselves, if you'll permit me, as our synthetic DNA scaffold. Added to these, we have two different social genomes – one Central Germanic, the other Western Slavic, two middle-European cultures which have long influenced each other, and yet remain sufficiently removed to be noticeably different. Certain characteristics have been selected for, others suppressed. There will be little need for purely manual labourers, so our proto-society includes no one below the fourth degree of the Baccalaureate. The time of the masses will come later.

It is important to note here that individually, cultural norms are extremely malleable. It is only on the macro-level that cultural determinism comes into play. There is, in most regards, no such thing as the 'typical Pole,' but there is such a thing as a typical Polish town. It is to the collective behaviour of the group – its group consciousness – and not that of its smallest particle, the individual, that we appeal at the uppermost level of our engineering.

The individual passengers for each of these craft have been carefully selected to bring certain national characteristics to the fore in the formation of the initial colony. It is expected that the two groups will naturally polarise. A sense of competition between them will push them to greater efforts, the sense of bonding they will share as they explore each other's differences will bring them closer. It resembles a marriage, of sorts, and it will function as such, on a meta-scale, the two making something greater than the one. A leavening of others from across Earth's large population adds further to this formula, the formula for a driven, competitive society that will build, trade, and prosper. A mono-culture gives us a large amount of stability, but in isolation risks becoming stagnant, a multi-culture may well be more dynamic, but lacks the stability and the comforts of shared identity that will provide our colonists with a sense of home and place. It is my belief that bi-cultural programming is our best chance of success.

Why do this at all? I know that there are those among us who are sceptical of the concept of social engineering, and insist we would be better served simply selecting our colonists on individual personal merits. I refer you to the great profit employment of social engineering has yielded to planetary stability this past century.

There is, of course, another, sadder, outcome, and one that I must confess to you all has been deliberately engineered into our planning. In circumstances of extreme exigency, you must understand.

Co-operation is the natural state of humanity, and it is this that we sincerely hope to accentuate. The sad corollary to this is that war has always been the greatest driver of human development.

> – *Excerpt from a secret briefing to the heads of the thirty-seven Pointer families involved in the Gateway project on Guided Cultural Propagation*

CHAPTER FIFTEEN
Besieged

DARIUSZ WAS AT the borehole with his engineering team when a thin wail sounded from the settlement.

"Damn it, is that the alarm?" said Günther Plock, one of the four people in Dariusz's team. He paused in tightening the pipe with his wrench. "Not now! We've four in, we're nearly there. Two more lengths and we'll be done."

Pipes lay in neat rows amid rattling stalks of dry grass, waiting to be bolted to the end of the line. The pipeline was nearly all the way out to the borehole. Dariusz wondered if they should have put the well closer in, even though there they'd have been drilling through the granite skirts of the mesas.

"You know what Anderson says," said Marina. They all looked different, so many months after the crash. Marina's hair had grown down to her shoulders. Her face was pinched with hunger, but the colonists had lost their anonymity. Individuals had emerged from the mass of scared faces and shaven heads.

"Fuck Anderson," said Wróblewski, the water systems specialist. "We're nearly through to the aquifer. And I don't want to leave all these pipes out. If they work their way around the village, they'll wreck them or worse."

"What do you suggest?" said Marina scathingly. "Pick them all up?"

"No, no." Wróblewski took his gloves off and threw them at the ground. "We're behind already."

"Well we can't stay here and defend them. There's only one of them with us," Plock inclined his head toward Athangelos Ayvazian, the trooper assigned as their protection. "You've seen what those things can do. We'll be crying over a lot more than broken pipes if we stay out here and they decide to come for us, eh? You want to be dinner for some fucking alien, be my guest, but not me, my friend." He downed his wrench and

259

wiped the sweat from his brow. "Let's head back. Dariusz, what do you say?"

Dariusz looked back toward the mesas, two broken teeth poking through the parched gums of the desert, topped with ugly prefabs and converted containers, all fenced in by lattices of electrified mesh. The mesas were granitic extrusions, the remains of a volcano. Forced up into the softer rock by the fury of the planet, left sentinel as the sandstone was ground away around them. They were lonely in the endless sand, a fitting place for a crowd of lonely men and lonely women. The loneliness was worst for cultural isolates like Ayvazian, the colony's sole Armenian – at least there were other Poles – but they all felt it: the worry that they might be the last people in existence. They huddled together on their stones in the sand, besieged by a hostile world.

"Hey, Dariusz, you hear that?" Ayvazian called from the pile of piping where he kept watch. "Load up, we have to go back."

Dariusz put his hands on his hips. He wore a wide-brimmed hat to shield his eyes from the sun, a troublesome presence even in the liminal zone. First Landing was situated in the country of early evening, where everything was cast in bronze. The sun glared at his back from its perpetual sunset. Dariusz's shadow was monstrous in front of him. He found the effect disturbing, a reminder of his effect on the colony. Here, the man, small and impotent in the face of an alien world; there, his shadow cast upon it, monstrous and significant.

Real monsters approached their home. The creatures they called 'the natives,' for their seeming intelligence. Unspeaking things that poked at their defences.

He sucked air through his teeth. It was pleasantly warm. His brain had not yet tuned the ever-present cinnamon odour of the world out; he doubted it ever would.

"We better go back," he said.

Swearing and sounds of relief emanated from his work crew, depending on their attitude. Günther was wary of the natives, but happy to go along with what the group decided. Marina, having seen the crabhawks in action, was as terrified of the planet's life as she was fascinated by it. Wróblewski was contemptuous; for him the job was all, natives or not. Dariusz tended to Marina's point of view: Wróblewski had not been out in the desert, and had suffered neither crabhawk nor tiger beetle. Wróblewski had witnessed firsthand only the natives, and their ineffectual plucking at the fences did little to frighten him.

The planet's lifeforms had amply demonstrated their hostility. The danger the more animalistic forms posed was at least something all the council agreed upon. Whether the natives were intelligent or not, or if they were a threat or not, was not a consideration. Inside the perimeter, they were safe. Let the natives have their strange ritual.

Other vehicles were moving to the mesas. A sand plume in the distance marked the return of some of Anderson's outer pickets.

"Looks like everyone else is going for it. Come one," Dariusz said.

They boarded their ATV.

Dariusz drove quickly. The alarm continued to wail. There was, as yet, no sound of gunfire. They should make the gates before the natives came. He followed the road along the pipeline.

Eventually, this would be farmland. It had to be; they would starve without it. A surfeit of food surrounded them, and they could eat none of it. The proteins of Nychthemeron's life were incompatible with the cellular machinery of the settlers. Enzymatically, the stomachs of Earthmen and the meat of the creatures matched: flesh was broken down, sugars were assimilated. But catabolism was problematic. The amino acids of Nychthemeron and those of Earth were foreign to one another, and the sugars of the new world were subtly different to those of the old. Earth proteins and Nychthemeron proteins did not key. When fed on Nychthemeron organics, the citric acid cycle of the colonists became inefficient. They *felt* sated, and ketosis kept them functioning for a while, until they began to starve with their bellies full. It had been seen in some of the survivor groups retrieved from the desert.

The colonists had fallen back on the stocks of emergency rations, supplemented by produce from their prefabricated hydroponics gardens, but it was insufficient. They were all hungry. Dissent latched onto hunger, and tempers grew short. The colony was racing against time to feed itself.

Other problems dogged them. After the robots departed, they had discovered that the virus had afflicted most of their devices in transit. One by one, the machines were locking out the colonists. They'd saved several of the fabrication units and other machines by painstakingly activating them in isolation, then disabling their higher functions. The fabrication datacore libraries, they'd saved the same way. All devices ran in isolation. Without what they had left, the colony would not be viable; they lived in perpetual fear of their remaining tools rebelling.

Others machines had been gutted. The ATV Dariusz drove lacked the sophisticated systems it once had had. Simple, easily-fabricated electronics took their place. His more active part in driving, like so much else, had taken time to become accustomed to. The shuttles, their engines reliant on multiple smart systems, had been grounded until the colony engineers could figure out a way to build an electronic computer of sufficient power to manage them. But no one had built a computer like that for generations, and the techs could not keep its size down. Their inChips had been deactivated when it was pointed out the virus could potentially infect those too. Their network was limited to short-wave radio and voice communication. They were slipping back further into the technological past. There was a timetable – the colony council had so many timetables – to replace the old computing infrastructure, but Dariusz feared they would not manage it, and would lose more ground. They were wholly reliant on their machines, and now their machines were deserting them.

The ATV crunched through the dry vegetation. The flush of coppery leaves brought by the rain had grown, bloomed, seeded and died, rapidly. The plants had lasted longer in the liminal zone, but now only their bones remained. The council meteorologist, Jan Słońce, gave the intervals between dayside precipitation events at anywhere between two and seven Earth years.

Dayside. Dariusz missed the night. Evening Country's constant promise of darkness unfulfilled gave the liminal zone a sombre air. It was a gloomy place, and for more than a want of strong light. A graveyard full of marmoreal geologic features, the brittle remains of seasonal vegetation, and the weird skeletons of alien life. The dim redness of the sun had a soporific effect, without easing sleep. Evening was a melancholy time, when the day is done and the pleasures of the night are yet to come. Yet their days never started, and the pleasures of night never came. They were pinned to the turn of a day that did not turn. Dariusz was drowsy and clumsy. Lethe, he called this cuspated state, the Gardens of Lethe.

Better than the desert, Sand said. Not that she used those exact words. Sand was overly fond of profanity.

The road curled around the western mesa, the colonists having widened the way with earthmoving machines. Further west, the first road to the airfield and cargo drop zone had been joined by several others, laid out in a grid. This was to be the plan of their town, or had been, before the natives came.

Other teams were coming in from the surrounding area, all of them in front of Dariusz. Some were on foot. He offered lifts until the ATV was full.

They arrived at the West Mesa gate. Their home had had no time to become a home before it had been forced to become a fortress. He drove through into a narrow space hemmed by towering containers. Machine gun nests on the tops of the wall guarded either side, the black muzzles of the weapons poking out from sandbags. The guards on the ground scowled at him as they ticked his team off on their pads. "You're late, Stettinski," said one.

"That's it! All in! All in!" called another. He whirled his finger around in the air. "Close the gates!"

Two sides of a repurposed cargo container were rolled across the gap and barred. Thick bolts of scavenged metal sank deep into holes in the stone. The gates to First Landing were closed.

The natives were coming.

FROM THE WALKWAY near the summit of the comms tower, Anderson scanned the horizon with his binoculars. The scrub was empty of movement. The sea was a dark band to the west, glittering in the perpetual sunset; the nightside glowered in the north. The boy Leonid – Anderson thought of him as a boy, so much less a man than his father – stood by him. He shivered, although it was not cold. He had become more ill at ease around the Alt since the crash, if such a thing were possible, and spoke to him only when he had to. Leonid resented him, although Anderson did not question why and did not care.

"Are they here?"

Anderson depressed the button of his radio and consulted his men.

"No sign of them, as yet, sir," said Anderson. "May I order the fence powered?"

Leonid nodded. "Do what you must, captain."

Anderson barked out an order into his radio. The fence came on. Anderson sensed it, a tension in the air invisible to the non-Alts. He had his own reasons to be tense.

From the comms tower, he could see across the whole of First Landing. The mesas were roughly the same size, cliffs seventeen metres tall rising above the surrounding sands, tops flat and six hundred metres or so across. The formations were not entirely isolate; the rock dipped to form a low saddle of the same hard, volcanic rock that joined them, but it was seven metres below the mesa tops, and so in effect forty metres of empty space separated them. On West Mesa, the command and control structures, the council offices, the multi-church, food stores, A-barracks, and the infirmary. On East Mesa, much of the accommodation for the lower-ranking colonists, the fabrication units, materials warehousing, and main hospital. Anderson had his men split between them. There were fifty-six left: twenty had died en route, two in the crash, twelve to alien lifeform activity since. Fifty-six soldiers; a paltry army to fight a world.

The radio crackled. "Movement. Northeast, three kilometres out."

Leonid started to speak, but Anderson silenced him. It was an impertinence he would never allow himself ordinarily, but battle took precedence. The Alt scanned the smooth bed of the river to the north. The water had finally sunk back under the bed, some months after the rains, but its banks were crowded with hardy thorn trees. It was along this corridor they always came. Anderson had tried mining it, but they detected the bombs somehow. He had ruled out ambush as too dangerous, after what had happened to the patrol, and the council had ruled out tracking them back to wherever they came from for the same reason.

So they sat tight, running for cover whenever the creatures showed themselves. He'd cleared a fire zone as best he could. He would have cleared the whole riverbank, but the thorns were proof against fire and his attempts to fell them had not proceeded as quickly as he would like. Disagreement from the council. Talk of ecology. Direction of resources to causes more pressing. His efforts were frustrated. After the first eruption of terror at the destruction of the patrol five months ago, the council's concerns had diminished. The creatures – Anderson refused to call them 'natives' or 'indigenes'; they were animals, as far as he could tell – left the outlying structures alone, and had not made it into the camps. The council had come to see the natives as nuisances, things that plucked at their fences and then departed. Leonid could have swayed them, so many of the council looked to him instinctively, but he was too naive to see the danger, too weak to recognise his own power.

Anderson could not let that continue. He did not like to have the Pointer so close at times like this – he was a distraction during combat, and in danger – but the boy had to see.

A movement in the grass far out. A ripple, then a second, third, fourth. A shot cracked through the air: Buleweyo, atop the hospital. A good sniper.

"Hit?" said Anderson.

"Maybe," breathed Buleweyo over the radio. Her voice was intense with concentration. Anderson heard her spotter softly counting off the range in the background.

A burst of fire. Three rounds. *Tuttuttut*, noises of disapproval. No *bangs* from the propellant discharge; the guns were all top of the range, all silenced. Anderson thought about disabling the weapons' suppression. The noise might scare the creatures off.

"Hold your fire!" shouted Anderson. He shouldn't have to say it. Ammunition was scarce.

Thorn-tipped branches moved along the banks. Anderson estimated three – no, four – groups of eight. They came always as eights. The creatures burst out into the cleared zone on the river bank five hundred metres away. This was the effective point range of his men's carbines, or was on human targets. Their weapons lacked the stopping power to penetrate the natives' carapaces except at extreme close quarters.

The creatures came in fast. They resembled the tiger beetles that roamed the deeper desert, but only in the same way a horse resembles a giraffe. The biology here was so alien, it was taking Anderson a long time to tell species apart. The basic physiology was the same: high backs, large thick shells, leg clusters, nothing that a human would ever call a head. But they were smaller, about half the size of the beetles, narrower down the back. Their leg clusters divided and specialised, the front set becoming an array of hooked forelimbs. It was in the mouth rakes the biggest difference was found; each rake split into two jointed sub-limbs, which ended in three-fingered manipulators. Four hands, although Anderson could not bring himself to call them hands. Unlike the other anatomical terms he had assigned to the creature's bodies, 'hand' was too freighted with implications of humanity.

The natives' backs bore overlapping plates that curved under them to protect their bellies. The carapace flared out at what Anderson thought of as the shoulders. Like the tiger beetles, the mouths were obvious and cruel, including a retractable proboscis set around with rasps and hooks. They did not possess anything that looked like an eye or other sensory organ; how and what they sensed was anyone's guess. An autopsy was needed, but every one they had managed to kill had been carried off by its fellows. The few samples they had of the planet's other lifeforms gave them only the broadest understanding of the local biology. Anderson had the obtainment of a native for the colony biologists set at high priority.

"Hold fire until they hit the two-hundred-metre line," he broadcast. "Short burst and single fire only; every wasted round is a demerit for the soldier concerned. Ten earns you punishment detail."

The natives came at a shambling run. They looked ungainly, comical, a limping man carrying a boat on his back. Anderson was not human, and did not make errors of estimation. The creatures were fast, well-armoured, and intelligent.

Anderson took away his binoculars, collapsed them, and placed them into a case at his belt. The creatures were near enough. He thumbed the safety of his weapon off.

At two hundred metres, Anderson gave the order to open fire.

Bullets *shushed* through the air, the muted pop of the carbines almost gentle. The machine guns were louder, but not much. The groups of eight natives split into smaller sub groups of four. They were animals that behaved like soldiers. There were thirty-two of them in all, nothing compared to the numbers of humans on the mesas, but the creatures were far tougher.

"Squad Five, concentrate on the forward group," said Anderson, as the creatures picked up speed. Rounds hit home, but the most evidence he saw was a stagger, and the onrush continued.

"They are not dying," said Leonid. "They're not even wounded."

"No, sir," said Anderson. "As I have said before, we need heavier weapons."

Three groups of four leapt at the base of the West Mesa, mouth arms and hook limbs grabbing at the rock. Another two groups went for the East Mesa. The remainder circled the rocks, heading for the vulnerable gates at the rear where the desert sloped upward. The creatures were out of the fire arcs of most of his men by now. Buleweyo continued to shoot at those climbing the West Mesa, some of the other men snapping off volleys when the opportunity presented itself.

Anderson checked the courtyard. The civilians were secure indoors.

The creatures gained the top of the mesa. They ignored the walls of the prefabricated buildings, instead heading for the chainlink fences between them. Another mistake. Anderson wanted the fences relocated to the cliff face, presenting a horizontal barrier. No time, the council said. No need.

The aliens probed at the fence, snatching back their strange hands when electricity bit. They did not like the shocks, but did not appear to be harmed by them. His men shot at point-blank range, but did little to hurry them, and the creatures worked methodically along the fence. Eventually, they would work out that they could push through, if they would only bear the shock for a moment.

The rattling of the gate guns announced the creatures' arrival at the other side of the compound. Alien screams sounded, then ceased.

Leonid was distracted, looking out at the creatures by the gate. Anderson went to the other side of the platform and pressed his radio's button. "Sergeant Simbolon," he said. "Stand ready."

DARIUSZ WAS IN the infirmary, a two-storey affair opposite the Command Centre and smaller logistics offices. Civilians crowded around one of the windows. The top floor was full, the lower level less so. The aliens were adept at climbing, but there was a sense of security inherent in height. Like monkeys in a tree, thought Dariusz. The longer they were on Nychthemeron, the more primitive they were becoming in thought. At first he'd put it down to the loss of the inChips – few of them were used to living unconnected – but there was more to it than that, a fogging of the conscious mind as reflex and survival drives took over in the face of pressure. It was the retreat of rationality before the advance of atavism. Dariusz prayed it would not turn into a rout.

The buildings followed the angle of the mesa's sides, bringing the courtyard to a triangular point. A prefabbed unit comprised the ground floor, and the first floor was two cargo containers welded together. The beds had been pushed to one side to allow more colonists refuge. The windows were cut out of the side of the containers facing over the courtyard, glazed with toughened glass baked out of the sand. There were none in the outer walls. Dariusz found it oppressive, and he was not alone.

In the infirmary ward, there were eighty of them, including Dariusz's team. A gasp went up from the crowd as one of the natives came into view in the gap between the Command Centre and the Logistics Office. Other human faces stared back at them from equally crammed, stuffy rooms. They craned their necks unsuccessfully to see what their fellows were pointing at.

The native crept along the rock at the edge of the mesa, tapping at the electrified fence. It rose on its hindmost legs, periodically showing its leathery underbelly, the leg clusters and its hooked secondary forelimbs. The forelimbs were in constant motion, gripping at the cliff edge in what must have been an awkward manner for it. It brushed the fence at regular intervals with feathery fingers. Every time, the creature snatched them away, the hands of its opposing limb waving delicately in sympathy. Touch. Snatch. Touch. Snatch.

The colonists watched as it passed along the gap toward Logistics.

"Looking for a weak spot," said Wróblewski.

"Fascinating," said Marina, who, now she was safe, was more interested than frightened.

"It gives me the creeps," said Günther. "A giant bug."

"It's an alien lifeform," said Marina. "Don't you think that's amazing?"

"I wish it would just fuck off, I want to get my pipe finished in peace," said Günther. Marina nudged him with her shoulder, and they grinned at each other. They were getting close, Dariusz had noticed.

"We're at the zoo," said Wróblewski. He was standing on his tip-toes to see over the others. His breath stirred Dariusz's hair. "But who is the exhibit and who the paying customer?"

Touch. Snatch. Touch. Touch. Touch.

Fingers curled around wire and gave an experimental tug.

"Hey! What's going on there?" said Günther.

"The fence. Has the fence failed?" said someone.

The native tugged hard. The fence was flimsy, and wobbled.

The native was over and into the courtyard in the blink of an eye, the fence pushed to the ground under its weight. Mouthparts extended, it tasted the air in a manner the natives shared with the tiger beetles, fronds waving as its hooked cone quartered and opened. Its thin arms paddled as it shuffled around.

"Have Anderson's men noticed?" said Marina.

"No," said Günther. "Fucking amateurs. Come on."

Günther pulled at Dariusz's arm. Wróblewski shouted, "What are you going to do? You've no weapons." Then, to Dariusz in Polish: "This is insanity."

"We'll get them to release the guns downstairs," said Günther. "Come on!"

The three men forced their way through the crowd. A hubbub rose up in the previously muted crowd. Panic, questions. Bodies in the room were tense, difficult to move past. Some pressed toward the window, others backed blindly away.

A couple more colonists fell in behind them. They had to shove to get down the stairs to the lower floor, as colonists from the treatment room below were fleeing upwards. Gunfire came from outside, the muted pop of the troops' carbines.

"*Now* they notice," said Günther.

They emerged downstairs. Through the window they saw the alien move around the courtyard, as if it could not decide what to do now it had gained entrance. It pivoted around until it faced the comms tower directly. Then it rose up, arms waving, its rear end vibrating so rapidly it blurred.

A rack of guns stood by the door of the infirmary, as they stood by the door in every building.

"Release the weapons!" said Günther to the building warden.

"Not without authorisation," she said.

"Then try your radio."

"There's something wrong with it," she said. Her hand cradled it protectively. It was giving out a regular bipping hum, shot through with loud crackles.

She was not looking at Günther, but through the window. Three men approached the alien. It whipped around and dropped low as they opened fire, presenting its armour to them. Their bullets bit into its thick carapace as it lowered its shell and charged, scooping up one of the troops and smashing him against the wall of the infirmary with its flaring shoulders. The building boomed with the impact. The noise of the crowd upstairs turned fearful.

"Give us the fucking guns!" shouted Günther.

Dariusz's mouth was dry. He was frightened. He tried his own radio. The same bipping noise. He could not raise the others.

"Do as he says," Dariusz said.

"What?"

"I outrank you. Release the weapons."

More guns joined the battle. The creature screeched. The prefab part of the infirmary was well insulated, but still the cry set their teeth on edge.

"I'm the warden…"

"Just do it!" shouted Dariusz. He pushed the woman aside. Günther snatched the key card from her hand and inserted it into the lock.

"Lucky for us the inChips are down," said Günther.

The bar restraining the gun rack popped off. Five carbines. Günther handed them out – Dariusz, Wróblewski, and a man and a woman he vaguely knew.

"You and you," said Dariusz, pointing at two colonists wearing engineer's markings. "Get over to the fence and get it fixed. Günther, let's get behind it. Try not to get caught in the crossfire." He was surprised at his own decisiveness; his knees felt like water.

Dariusz opened the door a crack and shouted. "Hold fire, we're coming out to reinforce you! We're going to fix the fence. Keep it busy at the front."

Someone shouted back a hurried affirmative. Dariusz nodded. "One, two, three!" he said.

They burst through the door.

The cinnamony musk of the alien was choking. Bullets raised puffs from the sand as they charged behind it. "Check your fire!" shouted Dariusz. The two engineers headed to the fence. From the top of the Command Centre and comms tower, gunfire poured down the outside of the mesa. More of the natives were ascending to exploit the breach.

Four of Anderson's soldiers, reinforced by a small group of colonists, formed an arc in front of the native, drilling at it with their weapons. It charged, flinging another man into the air, skewering a second on its hooked secondary arms, grabbing a third up and dashing him into the ground with its four delicate hands. After every strike, it reoriented itself to the comms tower before another stab of fire drew it away. All the while, it screeched and roared, a din that distressed its human assailants, causing some to drop to their knees in pain.

The leading edge of the native's carapace was chipped and oozing. The sheer amount of weapons fire it was absorbing was finally taking its toll. Its movements became weaker, and it wavered from side to side.

Dariusz's group attacked from the rear. With its front carapace lowered, the alien's vulnerable, leathery underside was exposed at the back. This was not the first time Dariusz had wielded a gun, but he had little formal military training, and he fumbled the settings as he tried to switch it to automatic. Günther had served long in the EFU armed forces, and raised his weapon to his shoulder, calm and collected. Wróblewski fired wildly from the hip. The creature was big enough to absorb most of his shots, but he was in danger of hitting some of their own side. There was too much going on and Dariusz was too terrified to say anything about it. Only later did it occur to him that he should have.

The native waddled around as their bullets smashed into its underbelly. Fluid spurted from its wounds. It roared horribly, and scuttled back around as bullets from the other group wounded it again. By now the front of its shell was a cracked mess. Softer tissues welled up from inside, and blood bubbled from it. The native was losing strength, dying. It backed away toward the Command Centre.

A shout, and Anderson's men parted. Two soldiers assembled a tripod, slamming a heavy gun onto it, and opened fire, the louder noise joining the pop of the carbines. A line of large holes smashed into the creature's armour, and it thrashed about. The cordon tightened. Someone called cease fire: save ammunition, let the machine gun do the work. A *whoomph* of gas, and a grenade launched from a trooper's carbine skidded under the native's body. The explosion made Dariusz and his group hit the floor. Legs blew free, scattered across the sand, one sliding to a halt by Dariusz's nose. The creature screamed and screamed: it tried to get up, but could not. The screaming went on and on. Dariusz dropped his gun and crawled back toward the infirmary. He had to get away from the screaming.

A man in the black uniform of the Pointers' troops marched up, teeth gritted against the native's wails. He had a shotgun in hand. He racked a shell into the chamber one-handed, then placed the muzzle, point blank, against the native's jaw plates.

The *crack* of the carapace giving was louder than the noise of the gun. The native's mouth collapsed inwards to a mush of shards and meat, chaos smashed out of order.

The screaming stopped.

The gunfire became sporadic, then dwindled to nothing.

The assault was over.

ANDERSON CALLED FOR shooting to stop, and the guns fell quiet. Leonid gaped at the mess in the courtyard. The monster was hidden in the lee of the Command Centre, but the signs of its rampage were everywhere. Bodies and body parts were scattered across the ground. The wounded were being seen to. Plenty more were dead. "Did you see..." Leonid said. "It got in. It got in."

"Yes, sir," said Anderson.

"You said... You said you needed heavier weapons?"

"Yes, sir. Perhaps now we can re-examine our priorities?"

The creatures withdrew, carrying their casualties away. Whether those downed were alive or dead, Anderson could not tell. A few of those fleeing leaked fluid from bullet holes, but were not noticeably affected. He ordered his men not to fire on them as they departed.

So it had been every time they came, once a week, for the last five months.

Now, thought Anderson. *Now*. "Sir, the council... It is putting us in danger. This stalemate, sir, it will not persist. They will keep coming until they get in and kill us all. They massacred the patrol. They will massacre us. The colony is in danger. You are in danger."

Leonid looked back at him, hollow-eyed and dumb. Leonid swallowed hard. "I'll see what I can do."

CHAPTER SIXTEEN
Dariusz and Sand

HE FIRST CAME to Sand a month after they had been reunited with the colony. Her assigned partner was dead, not that she figured the company had any hold over her relationships any more. She had no intimates on the voyage besides; he had lost everyone. They were alone, in a crowd of other people who were also alone. There were few in First Landing who had not lost somebody they cared for, and fewer the longer the colony was on the planet.

Kasia, orphaned, had become her constant companion; Sand her guardian by default. What Sand felt for Kasia was growing into something maternal. She did not recognise the feeling at first, all she knew was that it fulfilled some of her need for human closeness. Some, but not all. The remainder she found in Dariusz.

Sand found Dariusz quiet, reserved, intense. He spoke little, and laughed less. She figured that could have been because of his son, and his wife before that, but his manner suggested there was more to his introversion than grief. On the surface of it, he was an unlikely match, but underneath the calm, he was angry. She could see that almost straight away. A few words about the Pointers, his fortitude in the council meetings, and she was sure. That suited her. She, too, harboured fury at the status quo, of a different kind. More selfish than his, she thought.

She liked that he was so forward about his intentions, that he came for her that night (or the time the colony had arbitrarily chosen to be night). Sand unashamedly enjoyed sex. In good times it gave her joy, in bad times comfort. And so, with little preamble, they became lovers.

Before Dariusz, she'd flirted often with Corrigan; afterwards, too. He was her normal type; stronger, louder, more obviously bold. He was not happy with the turn of events, and antagonism sprang up between him and Dariusz.

She veered between placating Corrigan and inflaming him. Why she was playing childish games, she was not sure. There were dark emotions behind it.

She and Dariusz drove often out from the base. At first, Dariusz used the excuse of locating wreckage and materials that the colony badly needed. Once the near desert had been picked clean, and long range expeditions were heading further down the debris trail into dayside, he occupied their free time prospecting Evening Country for natural resources. He found few.

They ventured far. Travelling made the loss of Sand's wings easier to bear. Sometimes she drove, but she preferred to be driven, scanning for natives, or crabhawks, or tiger beetles. They encountered other things: Evening Country harboured much life. Great beasts, huge and ponderous on the horizon, always towards the night; small, quick creatures that darted swiftly from view. The closer they went into the twilight demarcating day from night, the more they saw, or rather heard, for in the gathered dark, the creatures hid with easy facility. In the further reaches of Evening, the lands they came to call Twilight, the animals bore a dazzling array of bioluminescent patches. Their light glimmered and flickered across the plain, but with the arrival of the ATV's whirring engine and glaring lamps, their subtle decorations winked out, and they went to ground.

Sand and Dariusz drove to the east, where the desert encroached upon the north before dark-hued grasses took root and waved all the way to Nightfall. They went to the west, where the sea broke the forever-setting sun into dazzling scintillations. They went south along its shores, to the place where ocean fought a war of evaporation with day. Salt flats and vast, briny lagoons steamed moisture, and Nychthemeron's pseudo-insects flew thickly above them. The heat after so long in the Evening Country was awful. Once their initial explorations were over, they did not venture back.

They crossed the debris trail of the *Mickiewicz* three times, the oblique line running closer to the nightside until it arrowed into the dark. Now and again and they found remnants of the ship. They found little that was usable, and no functioning beacons, and in this regard, Dariusz's mission was a failure.

It was weeks before they first spoke of the crash, and they did so rarely again afterwards.

"I'd never seen anything like it. I've seen knife fights at Christmas sales, for fuck's sake," Sand said as they drove north. "They just stood there, once they realised there was nothing they could do. The fight just went out of them. You ever hear about the *Titanic*?"

Dariusz shook his head. They were at the borders of the night, and he was intent on the way ahead.

"No? Bigass ship – an ocean liner, not spaceship – went down about two hundred and fifty years ago, thousand or so dead. They were singing on deck. I thought that was all bullshit, that was something from a better time, you know? Not like now with everyone so into themselves and the world so fucked, but I was wrong... They just, they just stood there. They accepted it. I'd heard about you know, air disasters or fires, how people just stop if no one's telling them what to do... But..."

She tailed off. She didn't say what it was like to look into eyes of the parents. She couldn't. She didn't think she'd ever be able to talk about it and stay sane. Some of the children's parents had got off the ship, the same way Corrigan did. All those who'd got into the passenger unit intended for the *Kraków* had survived. The ones who'd gone for the *Gdańsk*'s had not been so lucky. She didn't remember the faces of those who had lived: they'd stayed sharp in her mind until she came across them again in First Landing, and then they faded then from view. But the ones who had not survived, Kasia's mother, Roman's father... Their faces stared at her every time she closed her eyes, as clear as if they stood in front of her. She saw the same look in Dariusz's eyes when the subject of Daniel came up; anguish so profound to see it was to hurt.

"How are the children?" asked Dariusz. He was gradually sloughing off his accent, as they spent time together. His Lingua Anglica was peppered with proper American and Brit, a strange mix that made Sand smile.

"Man, your English is cute, Darek."

"Cute?"

"'How are the children,'" she mimicked. "Yeah, cute. You know, sweet."

"I know what 'cute' means, Sand," he said. He smiled, but she had annoyed him. "It's not the effect I was intending."

"What, you want educated, intelligent?"

"Something like that."

She laughed.

"Why are you laughing?"

She said things to calm him down. It exasperated him if she teased him too much; he was a serious man.

She herself was picking up some Polish. Poles formed the majority group in the colony, followed by Germans, then Czechs, Russian diaspora, Ukrainians, Slovaks, other Slavs of differing nations, with a scattering of people from everywhere else. It had been the same on their sister ship, only the proportions of Germans to Poles was reversed. They all spoke Lingua Anglica most of the time, but the culture remained predominantly Slavic. Sand experienced name days, Wigilia, and the glorious spectacle of All Saints' Day, when their little cemetery was ablaze with fires to honour the dead; the mourning of those lost on the voyage overshadowing the festival.

"You know, it's funny. The crash was terrible, and this world…" She tailed off. "Well, it's this world, you know? Not the most hospitable of places."

"It is beautiful," said Dariusz. "And empty. Can you even remember *imagining* so much space back home? Everywhere was full of people."

Sand remembered. The thought of it made her claustrophobic. She looked out into the dimness. Lightning flashed and thunder barked on the horizon where the cold air of the nightside mixed with the hot, dry cinnamon winds of the desert. There was nothing there.

"Yeah. Yeah, it is beautiful. That's not what I was going to say."

"Oh?"

"No, I was going to say, whatever intent the cultural engineers had is totally compromised, you know; the pairing off, the German/Polish split, the macro-sociological planning. It doesn't matter where we're from any more. It is down to us to make of this world what we can."

"This is true. We are free now."

Sand sighed and drummed her hand on her upraised knee. Her boot was jammed on the ATV dash. "Are we? What about all the people back home?"

"Who knows?" he said.

"They are probably all dead."

"Not all of them. Although without the Gateway Project, things there will not have continued as they were."

"What's the Earth like now, do you think?"

"Probably all like Russia," he said. "One big mess." He scowled. "I do not wish to dwell on it. Think of the future." She regarded him with irritation. His reluctance to discuss the past intensified her own upset. She was, essentially, annoyed at him for feeling the same way as her. "How are the children?" he said.

"The kids are fine."

"They are more resilient than us," said Dariusz. "They are less rigid in their thinking, more liable to bend than break."

"They're bright. They're doing well. The school has settled them."

"Of course they are intelligent. All the children are. They'd been selected to be so, they and their families. The Pointers need intelligent servants to survive. Why do you think?"

"Can we drop the politics for a day?" she said. "All that's behind us now." His earnestness, so solid and calming in the initial days of chaos after the crash, grated on her. She longed for spontaneity.

"It is not behind us. Politics are important."

She bit back a retort and licked her top teeth under her lip. "Uh-huh, they are. But I don't think the Pointers are in any hurry to take over here."

"No," said Dariusz. "You are right, I think."

"You don't sound convinced."

"I am cautiously optimistic."

She laughed again, but it was mirthless. She tugged at her hair. It was a long way to being the mass of springs it once was. The fuzzy denseness of it at this length drove her mad. She missed her curls, they were a defining part of her, almost as much as her wings.

Dariusz slowed the ATV and stopped. He turned off the engine, and turned to face her.

"Are you okay, Sand?"

"Yes," she said. She blew out hard and punched her knee softly. "No. No I'm not. I'm bored, Darek. It's nice to be driven, but I miss the skies. I want to fly again."

"You will."

She shook her head vigorously, her face burning. This was also not like her: she'd changed, become more fragile. She was angry at herself because of it. She wanted her old self back, although she was beginning to understand that she'd mistaken cockiness for strength in the past. "No, not for a long time. The shuttles will never fly again. I mean, the mechanics and electronics of it are simple enough, but coordinating them? The engines in particular, they're the real problem. If Kulicz and Mohandji hadn't gotten sick and died on us, we might have worked it out. Mohandji was really good with all that, but I'm on my own. We need a whole new computer system, and it's not top priority."

"The construction of a lighter aircraft is, Sand. You'll see. It was a good suggestion. People are listening to you. You'll be first to fly when they're built."

"Because you're on the council too?" She smiled savagely. "You'll vote for me? No favours, Darek, it makes us as bad as they used to be. The Pointers."

"Because you're the best pilot, Sand," said Dariusz. "Okay?"

She bit her lip. "Fuck, Darek! When I'm not bored, I'm terrified." He reached for her and she pushed him away. She wiped angrily at her face. Her hands came away wet. "I feel so weak. I don't like feeling weak."

"You're not weak, Sand."

"I'm a pilot with no aircraft."

"That doesn't make you weak. You have Kasia. Think of her."

"Kasia doesn't need me."

"She does."

She shook her head. "I'm pointless. I need to fly, Darek. It's my reason to be, do you understand?"

He looked at her. She felt foolish under his gaze. His losses had been monumental, as had those of so many of the others. Here she was, crying over broken toys.

But he was understanding. "I do," he said. "You had a kind of freedom many people could only dream of, and you mourn it."

She was ashamed. She leaned into him. They held each other.

Later, they lay together in the back of the ATV. It was dangerous with no one on watch, but the lure of privacy was too great.

"I like being here," she said. "I like this." She nuzzled into him, pressing her naked body into his.

"It is not easy being alone."

"There are so few people here, and you can't get away from them."

"We live in a village," he said.

They fell quiet for a while. She wanted to say that she loved him, but she could not. The words died in a small whimper that Dariusz paid no heed to. She was relieved she had not spoken, she was not sure she meant it, nor of what she truly felt. Comfort, she sought comfort. Where that would lead her made her afraid.

A sheet of light was cast over them. Thunder crackled in the gloom, storms wavered constantly back and forth over the last leagues of Evening Country, the border of night and day. Dariusz hugged her and got up, pulling his smartsuit on as he went forward into the cabin. His clothes formed themselves to him. She'd given the clothes no thought before, but she knew they were a marvel now they lacked the capability to make any more.

The sun was a sliver of light on the horizon, locked in position. Red stained the few clouds there; the sky above it was silver. Ahead, twilight gave way to night; a progression of distance, not time. The planets and stars were intimate with this, for it is only the turning of the heavenly bodies into shadow that brings night. But on a human scale, it was unfamiliar. For all their understanding of it, the colonists were circadian creatures. They found the revelation of day's illusion disconcerting.

Lightning stabbed down onto the plains.

"More rains on the nightside. Maybe the river will run again soon. There is so much to learn about this place. Does it not excite you?"

"Does it excite you?" She slipped her arms under his.

Dariusz shrugged. "It is either that, or despair. I choose the spirit of adventure over despair, for now, at least."

She pulled him tighter.

"Then I will too."

DARIUSZ PARKED THE ATV in the primary vehicle park of the East Mesa. The courtyard was as dark as it ever was in Evening Country. The buildings blocked the low sun and the area was locked into shadow while red light reigned outside. It was dark enough to need additional illumination, dark enough to hide.

A hiss in the shadows. "Hey, hey, yeah, you, Darius, Darius! I'm talking to you."

Dariusz peered into a dark space between two containers. Empty now, their supplies all used up, they were being used as sheds for tools. They stood side by side lengthways, the alley between them long and threatening. A lamp glared overhead, deepening the gloom beyond its pool of light. Whoever had spoken was invisible to him, just a shape.

"Shit, man, stop peering about and get in here. It's me, Corrigan. We have to talk."

Dariusz was reticent.

"If this is about Sand, I'd rather talk about it out here in the open."

Corrigan made an exasperated sound. "Fucking hell, you Polish wanker! It's not about Sand. Sure, I'm pissed off about that, I like her, and I can't see what she sees in a miserable stiff like you, but that's her choice. I'm not about to challenge you for her hand or some ridiculous medieval shit. Get in here, I need to talk to you!"

Dariusz did not want to go into the alley, but he did. Once inside, beyond the lamp's illumination, it became easier to see.

Corrigan was much taller than the Pole. He looked worriedly over Dariusz's head as he walked down the gap.

"You're not being followed?"

"No," said Dariusz. "I don't think so. Why?" For a fleeting moment, he thought Corrigan meant to kill him.

"You sure?"

"No! Why would I be? What is it, Corrigan?"

Corrigan looked down at him. His eyes were red with sleepless nights. There was a febrility to him, but there was to so many of them. "Anderson. He's not pleased with the way things are going. I can see it. He's up to something."

"I am aware of this, we all are. But he won't make a move without Leonid's or Yuri's say-so."

"Are you sure about that? How much do you know about Alts, Darius?" Like a lot of the non-Slavs, Corrigan used the Anglicised version of his name.

"Not much, I admit. I've never worked with one before, not directly."

"They're rare." Corrigan still spoke of Earth in present tense. It would be a habit long in the dying. "Most of them are in the military for the Pointers. It's best to think of them as thinking robots, they're not properly human. They've no will of their own: everything they do, they do to serve the Pointers. I have never heard of one going rogue."

"What are you saying? Do you think Yuri or Leonid are behind this? Leonid set the council up. Yuri's been agitating for more change."

"That's because Yuri's a lazy shit and would rather be sunbathing than making decisions. No, there's something going on. The old man sent those two for a reason. Maybe they're only liberal on the surface. A lot of Pointers are like that: as kids, they hate their money and power, then they turn into their parents, just like everybody else does. Watch them. Whatever Anderson's doing, he's not doing it for his own gain, he's not capable of it. It might seem that way, but it won't be for him, it'll be for the Pointers. Remember that." Corrigan glanced around. "I've got to go. If I get seen talking to you, Anderson will do his best to kill me off. It'll be long range patrols with some other idiot until the wildlife gets us. He might have no free will of his own, but he's not stupid. Be careful, Darius."

"I will be."

"You better had. How do you think the native got through the fence?"

"Anderson?" Dariusz was taken aback. "That is a serious accusation."

"You don't think it was an accident, do you? We're all expendable. Every one of us. Only the Pointers matter to him. He'll use the incident in the council to get what he wants…"

"You're supposed to be loyal to him," said Dariusz.

Corrigan leaned in close. "You think I put this uniform on because I love the Pointers? I fucking hate them, as much as you do, if not more. I've seen a lot more of them than you have. I signed up for this gig to get away from all that shit, I figured there'd be a slim chance things might change if we were a few trillion miles away from their gravy train. Well, things just might change, thanks to the crash. I'm not going to stand by and watch a fresh elite of super rich twats order another world about for their own pleasure, do you understand me?"

Dariusz's English had developed beyond the Lingua, but Corrigan's accent was radically different to Sand's and Dariusz found it hard to follow. It wasn't hard to understand his sentiment, however.

"If it comes to it, you can count on me. You get that? But let's try not to. Now, I'm going. Be careful!"

With those words, Corrigan walked out the other end of the alleyway.

Six weeks later, Anderson made his move.

CHAPTER SEVENTEEN
This Other Son

"WE ARE SITTING ducks here. We all know it. When are we going to start listening to Anderson?"

"Councillor Amir, please..." said Kościelniak.

"Don't try to placate me, Artur. Are you not listening? Captain Anderson is right. We need more weapons to defend ourselves from the natives."

There were nineteen of them in the room, Yuri, Leonid, Anderson, Kościelniak and Dariusz among them. Sand, the twentieth member of the council, was absent, pleading urgent business with the construction of the colony's ultralight aircraft. All present were heads of various projects in and around the base, or had been put forward by their fellows to represent their interests. The council was a cross between a government body and a corporate board of directors, and more argumentative than either.

There was an outbreak of conversation in the council room as various members spoke with each other or challenged Amir, or Anderson, who did not reply. Nineteen people make a lot of noise when agitated. Kościelniak held up his hand. "I believe Councillor Szczeciński has something to say."

"We can't divert resources from the fabricators," said Dariusz quietly. "We need the farm up and running, or people are going to die. We're on the brink of starvation." Leipnitz, the Head Agriculturalist, murmured in agreement.

"And you think the efforts in sanitation, or schooling, or health, or any one of the other things we need to enact are not going to suffer?" said Amir. "Defence is our primary need."

"The natives are not dangerous," said Jolanta Leppek, Chief Medical Officer.

"Didn't you see what that one did when it got into the compound?" countered Danowicz, Chief of Military Logistics, a broad, florid man, much prone to thumping the table, chief supporter of the unlikely alliance between Amir and Anderson. "Do you not remember the fate of the patrol?"

"A systems failure," said Ewa Brzezinska, Colony Psychologist. "They do not pass the fence. They leave our equipment alone. We keep the fence in good order, we keep them out. We can coexist."

Julian Moore, exobiologist and Chief Science Officer, cleared his throat. "It is the comms mast. They are attracted to it. Their biology is tricky to unravel, fascinating stuff, and the sample we have is quite badly damaged. Many of the creatures we have encountered have a form of natural radar, we think. It's very weak, as you might expect – or should I say, very sensitive. Our systems are interfering with it."

"You weren't sure of that last week," said Amir.

"I am sure of it now," said Moore coolly.

"That is immaterial…" said Danowicz.

"We need to look to our own operations. That's where the solution lies," said Moore. "Not in gunning them down. This is not 19th-century America, gentlemen. We should behave better here. What kind of a start is it to found a new home on the blood of others?"

"We've heard all this before!" said Amir. "Changing the frequency hasn't worked, as you suggested. Setting up decoy emitters gets the decoys destroyed, at a cost in valuable man hours and resources. Your sentiments, worthy as they are, are dangerous, and your theories are worthless. They do not like our comms? Fine, let's *increase* their activity, create a wall of electromagnetic noise to keep them back. The crabhawks do not approach us, we must have passed their tolerance. The natives will have a level they find unbearable too. We should find it."

"I disagree. These are sentient creatures –"

"Possibly sentient!" insisted Danowicz.

"Sentient," said Moore. "Besides, the signal has not kept them away as it has the other lifeforms. There is no guarantee that there will not be unintended consequences of putting up a radar fence. And what of the interference with our own communications?"

"I think we've seen just how much you understand the situation, thank you, Mr Moore."

"Don't talk to me like that," said Moore. "I've as much right – more right, in fact…"

Yuri looked up from the table, where he'd been sketching things only he could see with his thumbnail. "No insults, please gentlemen," he said. "Let's keep this civil."

"What do you know, Pointer's son?" said Danowicz.

"Enough to keep a civil tongue." Yuri pushed his chair back. The room was too hot, another cobbled-together space made of recycled cargo containers. Tempers were frayed. They were all hungry. His brother was preoccupied with something, so Yuri took the role of chairman. He thought he'd be bored by all this, but it was better than sitting around. He had been forced to acknowledge that things needed to be done. Ironic, he thought, how his indolence melted away in the face of peril.

"Food, it seems, is the primary concern here." He glanced at the list of food initiatives on the tablet in front of him. "Councillor Doctor Karpel. How are we with the pantrope machine?"

Karpel, Chief of Medical Sciences, looked grim. "Not good. We are still unpicking the data from the genebanks. It is slow work, and it is beginning to look like the virus has wiped more than we feared. Without full access to the Syscore and proper sequencing machines, we're having to fall back on older techniques, and my team just aren't schooled in those. It'll take time for us to establish our method. We have the basic patterning for retroviral delivery systems, but it is the changes we must make to our own physiology…" He shrugged.

"We are working on it," added Moore. "But it will take time."

"Without a fully operational genetics lab, typing the creatures will take years," said Karpel. "Their genetic bases are broadly similar to ours, but not entirely. We haven't even begun to pinpoint the coding for their digestive and energy cycles. Then we must transpose that to our own genetic makeup to allow the human body to generate energy from the alien material. If we are lucky, it will be a case of adding a few enzymes to the digestive system, perhaps a little additional coding structure to our mitochondria. But if they have *no* citric acid cycle, or nothing close to it... Well, in the worst case, it cannot be done."

"Changing ourselves is easier than changing the world," said Konrad Urbanek, the representative of the electronics team.

"Precisely. If we are going to live here, we have to become of this world, not apart from it," said Karpel.

Yuri had heard this before. The council was in the habit of treading the same ground over and over again. Frustration at the lack of progress had them weave a comfort blanket of repetition. "Very well. Councillor Loewen, how's the bioreactor going?"

"No good news here, either. We've managed to render some useful products from the sandclams, we're getting close to something like acetates, but we are also finding it hard to adjust the subtler elements of biochemistry. We've similar problems to the genetics team. We're a long way from changing the sugars into something a Terran organism can make use of. Fuel, plastics, water: all that we can provide, and with a little adjustment to the fabricators, we're close to giving us a wider source of feedstocks. Base chemistry is not much of a problem, and we are having success with ancient practices. Look back to the past – we're pioneers, I say, so we shall be pioneers. We're making leather from the hides, and the shells are tough. They have some remarkable –"

Councillor Jankowitz scoffed ruefully. "Are we to fall to so low a technological base?"

"We might do yet," said Loewen. "We have to make use of the resources we have to hand. We can't rely on the fabricators. I need more energy –"

"Everybody needs more energy!" snapped Iwona Bruśka who, being responsible for the energy network, always erupted when anyone complained about the lack of energy. "We are working on it."

Danowicz harrumphed. "All this is taking a long time, and we do not have time. Those... things. They will get through the fence. They are inimical to human life."

"We don't know that. We're trespassing on their territory. There's the radar issue. Indeed, they may just be curious," said Moore.

"Tell that to the men of Captain Anderson's patrol," said Amir.

"We attacked them first. We've provoked something we have limited ability to harm: one of those things can take a dozen unarmed people to pieces. Surely we'd better pursue more peaceful avenues?" said Loewen.

Danowicz conceded the point. "Of course. But we cannot communicate with them either. We don't even know how they see the world. How can we begin to talk to them? Are they even intelligent?"

"They are intelligent," said Anderson. He'd been appointed a councillor, against his wishes, and spoke rarely in the meetings. "Like animals. Instinctual, but tactical, methodical. We have the superior technology, they the superior biology. Our advantage is disappearing."

"And we should follow your proposal?" asked Danowicz. This was not truly a question, but an invitation for Anderson to lay out his plans once again.

"Yes. More rations for my men. Institution of a militia that all are to serve on, in rotation. The production of more powerful weapons. Diversion of energy to the fences. Construction of better defences."

"These things will slow all our efforts," said Karpel. "We are dipping below subsistence level."

"I will not agree to it. The colony will not agree to it," said Brzezinska.

"They will," said Anderson. "Because they are scared."

"It seems we have little choice," said Leonid.

"Trust the Pointer to agree!" said Loewen.

"I do not agree," said Yuri mildly. "And I am a Pointer."

"I have nothing against our fragile democracy. I suggested it!" said Leonid. He sounded stressed. His face was harrowed. He looked at the table.

What's eating at him? thought Yuri.

"This is not Earth. The days of my kind are done. I merely state my opinion, drawn from the facts as I see them," said Leonid, more calmly.

"You seek to subvert it," said Karpel.

"Please," Leonid said, almost pleadingly. "I urge you to see the facts as I see them. Anderson is correct."

"My brother set this council up, he supports Anderson, I do not. I am sure your opinions are as split as ours," said Yuri. "We're in the same boat as you. Why can you not see that?"

"Anderson is correct to an extent," said Dariusz. "Building these things will buy us more time. But do we have that time? Our food stocks…"

"They are low," said Jankowitz, the quartermaster.

"We're going to have to incorporate the borehole and farms into the perimeter eventually. Assuming the natives are intelligent, if they discover that that's our weak spot, they'll come here and rip it up while we fume at them from the walls. They've left the airfield alone, the outlying facilities. It's us they're interested in. How long is it before they change their approach?" said Leonid.

"If we drilled closer in, we'd still have the issue of having to defend the crops," said Karpel.

"A watchtower? Extend the fence?" said Yuri.

"Councillor Danowicz, as outspoken as he is, pointed out how well isolated facilities fare," said Jankowitz.

"Don't we risk alerting the natives as to how important our efforts in the fields are if we start fortifying them?" said Moore.

"If they're intelligent," said Danowicz. "We need to exterminate them before they exterminate us."

"There are hard times…"

"We should not provoke…"

"We are better than the Pointers…!"

A clamour of suggestions sprang up. Voices were raised all around the table. The quiet, hot air of the room was alive with shouting.

Yuri held up his hands. "Gentlemen, ladies, please. Please!" he shouted. "Let us vote on it. That is what this council is for, is it not? Yes?" He raised his eyebrows at them and smiled. They fell silent, and he clasped his hands together. "Thank you. All those in favour of continuing the plan as already agreed, raise your hands." Those in favour did so. "All those in favour of Anderson's suggestion to switch to a war footing, raise your hands." Yuri looked around the room. "We continue on as before."

Murmurs in support of both cases rippled around the room. Yuri sighed and sank back down into his chair. He was getting a headache. "Back to business, then. Next on the agenda, the irrigation project. Councillor Dariusz…"

"Not yet," said Anderson. He stood and drew his pistol. The two doors into the room opened and ten of his men entered, all armed. "I have given you the opportunity to make the right decision, and you did not. Your poor judgment is endangering the lives of my patrons. You are all under arrest. This colony is now under the direct jurisdiction of Leonid Petrovitch."

"Anderson?" Yuri half rose.

"Sit down, sir," said Anderson. "I am to protect the interests of your house. Do not endanger them yourself."

"Leonid?" said Yuri helplessly. "What's going on?"

His brother stared back at him for a second. He seemed shrunken, defeated almost, but there was a hard look in his eyes. "I'm sorry. We're never going to get anywhere arguing like this. We need a firmer hand."

"Now you sound like our father."

Leonid looked uncomfortable. "So be it. Maybe he was right all along."

"Leonid, stop them!" shouted Yuri.

Leonid looked away.

The *click* of Anderson's safety disengaging echoed. His gun turned to point at Yuri. "Sit down, sir."

Yuri complied, his hands in the air. "This is a dreadful mistake."

"All decisions will now be made by Mr Petrovitch. This experiment in democracy is over," said Anderson. "Weapons production is to begin immediately."

LEONID FOLLOWED ANDERSON around the base perimeter. A new air of urgency clung to the town: drills clattered, engines whined, reversing vehicles beeped, arc torches hissed. Under it all was the soft, harsh noise of shovels biting sand. Men and women worked under the eyes of Anderson's black-clad men. They did not speak. At Anderson's prompting, Leonid had declared a state of emergency. Rations had been cut, hours of work extended. Few of those working on Anderson's walls and ditches looked at him as he walked past. Those that did fixed him with glares of hatred.

Leonid did not look directly at the workers. He kept them in his peripheral vision, blurred impressions. Shame and fear dogged him. What had he become?

Anderson pointed to the mesa face, where men on ropes worked drills into the rock. "The fence is being restrung horizontally. That will stop the enemy coming up the cliff face, sir. With your permission, I would like to divert another twenty per cent of the colony's generating capacity to the fence. A greater shock is a greater deterrent. Once we have developed a sufficient capacity, I would like to attempt a lethal charge."

Leonid nodded. Key to Anderson's plans was this ditch around the more vulnerable side of the mesas, where the scrub rose up and the colonists had carved their roads. Four metres deep, faced with metal from the containers. "Effective against the natives. The smooth surface is difficult for them to ascend," Anderson explained. The ditch embraced the mesas in straight lines, each section meeting the next at a neatly cut angle. Machine gun emplacements jutted out of the ditch at these junctions: four in all, able to direct fire down the full length of the earthwork's sections. With few earthmoving machines and no more under construction, as Anderson turned the fabricators to the manufacture of weapons, much of the work was being done by hand. Speed was prioritised over safety. There had been three deaths from heatstroke, three from accidents. The colonists were hungry. After two weeks of this, they were getting thinner. The more exhausted they became, the more accidents occurred. Fear ruled; fear of the natives, fear of Anderson.

Leonid and Anderson walked through the new outer gate taking shape fifty metres down the road from West Mesa's original portal. The gun Anderson insisted he wear at all times dragged at his hip. It was hot today, even in Evening Country. The desert's weather patterns were reasserting themselves after the rains.

Work on the farm had slowed. Dariusz's team, missing Plock, still worked on the borehole and pipeline, but virtually all other projects had been halted.

A large enough contingent of the settlers feared the natives to make Anderson's proposals palatable, but the way it had been done was not. When the food ran short, there would be trouble, Leonid was sure of it. Anderson expected a certain amount of population wastage. He would not hesitate to use force in the event of trouble.

Leonid was appalled, but powerless. The tools of the Pointers had turned on their masters. If he told Anderson to lay down his arms, what then? Would he? Leonid was not sure. If it came to it, he would tell him to, but the truth was far bitterer. He had not had Anderson stop, because Leonid agreed with him. Defence was their first concern.

They strode along the water pipeline, finished now and undergoing testing. Connected to a regular supply of water, they'd be able to up production of food in the hydroponics on the East Mesa, and begin irrigating plots in the open. Once there was more to eat, Leonid was certain opposition to his government would abate long enough for him to get the colony established. He would reinstate the council when the colony was safe. He promised himself that. If only he could shake the image of Ilya, nodding approvingly at him, that stole unwanted into his imagination.

Out in the fields, Anderson led Leonid to a place where a table had been set out. Three heavy guns lay upon it. One of Anderson's men and a colonist wearing the black band of Anderson's new militia stood to attention by the table. Danowicz waited with them, and a fourth man whose name Leonid did not remember, who wore the green suit flashes of a scientist. A target, a piece of a dead native's shell, hung from a pole two hundred metres away.

"Here we have the first batch of the new weapons," Anderson said, holding out his hand. His man passed one to him. "Railguns. Triple magnetic coils" – he indicated three pipes running the length of the weapon – "accelerate a solid iron round to eight times the speed of sound. Heavy and fast, the round will punch through anything. Observe."

293

He put the gun to his shoulder and depressed the trigger. The gun hummed briefly. There was a *crack* as the projectile broke the sound barrier, followed almost instantly by an organic crunch. The shell target swung on its pole, a large hole blasted through its centre.

"We needn't worry about the natives now, sir," said Danowicz. He wore a serious expression, but Leonid could see he was crowing beneath it.

"Thank you, councillor," said Leonid. "It is very impressive." He licked his lips. "When can we return to our previous plan?"

"When we have fortified First Landing, and dealt with the native threat."

Leonid looked to Anderson. "Surely the weapons are enough?"

Danowicz smiled kindly. "Sir, Captain Anderson recommends wiping them out. Only then will we be safe."

"But food production, the farm…"

"They need to wait, sir," said Anderson. "I will not allow the Petrovitch family to be endangered."

"And if I order you to stop?"

Anderson stared down at him. Leonid had never felt comfortable around the Alt, but Ilya's revelation of his heritage had made him hate being near Anderson all the more intensely. His menace smote him like a brick. His silver eyes were reptilian, and Ilya looked out at him from behind them. "It is your house I am to protect, from itself if necessary. There are two of you," he said.

"You are saying you require only one of us?"

Anderson looked away from him. "Work continues on the weapons, sir. Once we have destroyed the natives, we shall concentrate on food production. We have enough rations until then to sustain a viable population. We are done, sir.

"This way," he said. "I wish to show you the work on the riverside wall."

SAND GRIPPED THE poles of the tent and threw up copiously into the hole that passed as the airfield's latrine. She would have preferred to have kept her vomiting secret, but doing it silently just wasn't going to happen. She could hear voices further down the strip, the rustle of the canvas in the wind reminding her how thin the barrier between her discomfort and day-to-day life was.

She was past caring. All she really wanted was something to hold onto at ground level, so she could kneel down while she was sick. She'd tried that last time, and had nearly gone into the hole. Standing up it was.

"Are you alright, Sand?" asked Kasia.

"Yeah, yeah, give me a minute. Oh God." She threw up again. She was still trying to keep it quiet, resulting in her breakfast being forced out through her nostrils. It burned, and she coughed, sneezed and threw up again all at once.

"You're not okay!" Kasia's voice moved closer to the tent, shattering what was left of Sand's delicate illusion of solitude. "Are you sure you're good to fly?"

Sand let go of the tent poles and leaned forward, hands on her knees, shaking. "Just give me a minute!" she said weakly. She wiped her face, then swilled her mouth with water from her bottle, snorting it through her nose. A waste of her ration, but the vomit burned her sinuses.

She stood and groaned. "I'm okay," she said, more for her own benefit than Kasia's. "I'm okay."

She walked out of the tent.

"You stink of puke," said Kasia.

"Thanks," said Sand shakily.

"Are you sure you're good to fly?"

"I've got to be, baby. If Anderson gets wind of this, I'm grounded for good, and nothing nice will come from that."

"Are you sure you're okay?"

"If I can fly a fourteen-megaton asteroid into a processing fac with a stinking hangover, I can get that itty bitty parachute into the air. It'll pass, trust me." They walked from the latrine back to the airstrip office, another adapted container. A hangar constructed of curved panels woven by the base fabricators towered over it; they went within. What flight crew Anderson had left was inside. They all knew about her vomiting, but she trusted them enough not to mention it outside their group.

They didn't know why for sure – Sand hadn't told them – but they could guess.

The hangar was small, but even so, it felt cavernously empty. Two two-seat paragliders sat in the centre, looking tiny as models.

"Okay, we're on a scouting mission today. Anderson wants us to find where the natives are coming from. Kasia's coming up with me in *UL-1*; get it out on the runway. Once we're gone, I want you all working on *UL-3*. It'd be good if we could get that finished by the end of the week."

"Yes, Sand," they said.

"Right, then," said Sand. She pulled her goggles on as two of her crew pushed the ultralight onto the runway. They arranged it for takeoff, then laid out its parachute on the ground. "Are you sure you're ready for this? Big moment," she said to Kasia as they walked to their seats. There was no cockpit, just a frame of carbon and aluminium bars, and a large, caged propeller mounted behind it.

Kasia nodded. "I've got to go into the air if I'm going to be a pilot, right?"

"That you do."

"What's it like, being pregnant?" asked Kasia as they settled into the frame.

"It fucking sucks, honey," said Sand. She pressed the *on* switch, and the electric engine whirred into life.

"Have you told him yet?"

"Not yet," she said. She accelerated down the airstrip. "Not yet."

"Are you going to?"

Sand did not reply. The parasail made a muffled snap, and she felt it tug as it filled with air. She shouted with joy, her sickness forgotten. She pulled back on the stick. The wind teased her hair back as they soared up from the landing field. The craft was primitive, simplistic, horrendously dangerous. She loved it.

Beside her, Kasia clung on to the frame sides, her face set and lips thin. She had gone pale. Her enthusiasm for flying had been growing all the more intense recently, but this was the first time she had been airborne since the crash.

"Relax, honey!" Sand yelled. "We'll be fine!" She levelled out at three hundred metres. Radio crackled in her ear. Traffic control; grandiose title, really. It was one girl with a radio in a shack.

"We're going out," she said. "See you soon."

"Copy that, Sand."

The radio cut off.

They circled lazily around the mesas, dropping low so they could pick out the tracks of the natives in the scrub. Kasia spotted it first, where tyre marks and scuffing from human feet broadened the trail. Sand lined the UL up and flew straight for five kilometres. They passed the burned-out wreck of the ATV, the evidence of that fateful first encounter between the colony and the natives. Shortly past that, signs of human activity dried up – no one dared go that way on the ground – and they were flying solely over native footprints. The natives travelled single file, and had left a deep score in dry earth.

The craft scared up something large from the scrub below, but it was gone before they could identify it.

The ultralights had been flying for a week, fast-tracked by Anderson, who wanted to pinpoint the location of the native's village, or watering hole, or wherever the fuck they lived. She supposed she'd better be thankful for that, even if he was an A-grade shitbag. Sand found it strange to be in the air again. The wait had been interminable, and yet now she was, it was as if no time had passed at all. Her grounding was but one of a bunch of bad memories.

"You okay?" said Sand. "For a few minutes back there it looked like it was your turn to start barfing." The craft's electric motor was very quiet. She hardly had to raise her voice over the wind.

Kasia nodded. She was peering over the side, wonder edging out fear. She relaxed. Sand suppressed a mischievous urge to send the craft into a dive. Kasia wasn't ready for that.

"What do you think?" Sand asked.

"It's marvellous!" shouted Kasia.

"Do you want a go?" Sand said. Before the younger woman could say no, Sand let go of the stick.

"What are you *doing*?" shrieked Kasia.

"Yeah, what they hell are you doing?" shouted the girl in the shack. Sand ignored her.

"What are *you* doing?" said Sand. "If I were you I'd grab the stick, or we're going to crash." Kasia grabbed at it in panic. The UL swerved. "Easy now! Remember what I told you. Just a little flight. Just a taste, okay? I've got the pedals."

"But I'm not due to start lessons until I've finished my ground training."

"You're my apprentice; I say, the sooner the better."

Kasia grumbled, and Sand grinned. She remembered her own first flight. Back in flight school, the simulator was so accurate that once she'd been up in the clouds, the two were indistinguishable. But that first time, she was profoundly conscious of the difference, and her hands sweated so much she thought they'd slip right off the stick. Already hooked, she'd become a flight junky from that day.

"Good?" she said. Kasia nodded. She was biting her lip with concentration.

"Steady, keep her level, that's right." Sand looked down. "A little to the right, we're drifting off the path. Another kilometre now, alright? Then I'm taking it back. Right, I'm taking over. Ready? In three, two, one…"

Sand took the stick smoothly.

Her sickness, the problem of her pregnancy, Anderson's coup, she forgot it all when she saw the look on Kasia's face. She was in, hook, line and sinker. Sand smiled widely.

"Welcome to the pilot's club, kid."

"Wow," said Kasia.

"Wow, indeed," said Sand. She looked down and frowned. "Dammit," she said.

"What's wrong?"

"We're losing the trail. Do me a favour and keep your eyes peeled."

They circled and circled, but of the trail, there was no sign

"Control, you better tell the generalissimo that we've lost it. It just disappears. We'll keep trying, but I don't think we'll find anything from the air. I think they go underground."

CHAPTER EIGHTEEN
The Battle of First Landing

"YOU REALISE," CORRIGAN said quietly to Dariusz, "that he intends to activate his radar fence."

Dariusz nodded. They walked the road out into the field, toward the pumping station. Corrigan held his assault carbine at the ready. The pipes had been online for a fortnight; water flowed from the aquifer directly to the mesas. Dariusz and his team had been reassigned to wall-building duties alongside Plock, but the pump needed checking every day, and he and Corrigan took the time to talk. Work continued in shifts around the clock. The inner perimeter defences were complete. Far from signalling a refocusing on civilian activity, Anderson had unveiled his plans for an outer ditch and wall.

"It's not long until people will start to starve."

"He's calculated all that," said Corrigan. "The children are expendable as far as he's concerned. He'll stop feeding them first. He's obsessed with the wall."

"We are all in danger," said Dariusz. "He's more of a threat than the aliens."

"It's more than defence, it's a statement of power," said Corrigan. "I've had a look into his personal files."

"How did you manage –"

"Ex-cyber ops, combat wing," said Corrigan. "I have my ways. The systems here wouldn't keep your grandmother out.

"He's been drawing on emergency social plans of the Pointers. Population crashes, a bottleneck. Minimal genetic diversity, that kind of thing. He's working on the basis of a minimum population of 4,000. He'll not let the other 2,000 distract him from his priorities."

"Jesus."

"Yeah," said Corrigan. "It's not the worst of it. We're going to have to act. If he sets up this radar deterrent, according to Moore, we're going to drive the natives insane."

"Moore's been trying to speak to me," said Dariusz. The biologist had last caught him out on the wall. He'd been agitated. "Does he know anything?"

Corrigan spat. "No. He came to you because he knows you're opposed to Anderson. He has no idea what we're planning."

"When does the fence go on?"

"Tomorrow. We're on full combat readiness. The bastard knows what's going to happen. He wants to provoke them so he can kill as many as possible, and keep the colony cowed through fear of them."

"Can we get to it before it goes on?" They were getting close to the pumping station, and Dariusz paused, as if inspecting a join in the pipeline, to buy them a little more time.

Corrigan shook his head. "He's got his Alts guarding it. Not all the regular men are happy about this, but the Alts, well, they don't give a fuck. They just do what he tells them. Tomorrow, or the day after, whenever the natives attack. We could act then, in the confusion."

"That's no good," said Dariusz. "Too much could go wrong." They reached the pumping station.

"You got any better ideas?"

"No, not really. I'll speak to Moore. He wants to talk to me again tonight." Dariusz opened an inspection panel and took down his readings onto his tablet.

"Don't tell him anything."

"I won't."

"I'll work on the assumption we'll go into action during the attack."

Dariusz closed the panel. He did a quick circuit of the pump head. "All looks fine. We better head back."

"There's another thing," said Corrigan. "It's not going to end here. We foil this, he'll do something else stupid."

"What are you suggesting?"

Corrigan fixed him in the eyes. "We're going to have to kill Anderson."

*   *   *

LEONID WATCHED AS the science staff made a couple of adjustments to the computer that coordinated their communications through the mast.

"Is it done?" said Leonid.

"Yes, sir."

"I expected more of a fanfare," said Yuri wryly.

"Most of the work has been done outside, sir; the alterations are to the comms mast emitters, not here. All we have to do in here is input the frequencies that we know are the most painful to the natives."

"Everybody has become so literal these days," said Yuri. He looked his guard, his gaoler, up and down. "Isn't that right, Janosz?"

Janosz stared straight ahead.

"See?" He took his brother by the arm. Leonid started. "Are you sure this is a good idea?"

"Anderson says so."

"Anderson! What happened to you, Leonid?"

"Disaster," said his brother. He left, his own bodyguards following him. Yuri turned back to the equipment. "Do you think this is a good idea?" he asked the technicians. They ignored him, too.

"Fine," said Yuri, "fine."

The tech checked his watch. "Okay, testing in two minutes."

"All systems are nominal. Shut it down." The technician addressed Yuri. "We'll begin connection to the comms mast primary emitters now. We'll be all ready for activation on time tomorrow, sir."

"Oh, fantastic," said Yuri, deadpan.

MOORE WANTED TO meet Dariusz out at the airfield. There was a new spares store there, a container with a partition at one end for an office.

When Dariusz walked in through the open doors, he knew he had fallen into a trap. There is a look a cornered man has, a sheen of moral disease. Moore wore it.

"I'm sorry."

Anderson stepped out of the partitioned room and levelled his assault carbine at him.

"I'm afraid your little conspiracy is over," said Anderson. "A pity, as your skills are very necessary."

A couple more men came in the store. One covered the other as Moore was hauled out, looking helplessly at Dariusz as he was taken away.

Anderson walked up to Dariusz. Alts were supposed to lack conceit, their emotional centres were wired differently, but Anderson swaggered up to him with a self-satisfied look on his face.

"Now. Tell me who you were working with."

Dariusz wanted to spit in his eye, to tell him it was he who had brought the ship down. He didn't. "Kill me, I don't care." With his capture, the knot in his chest he had carried since the crash loosened a little. It would soon all be over.

Anderson wagged a finger and whistled. "You don't care about you, I think. But what about her?" One of the other Alts brought Sand, her hands tied behind her back, into the store. Anderson left Dariusz's side and walked over to the pilot.

"I have your girlfriend. One wrong move and I'll blow her away. Tell me who you were working with."

Dariusz stared at Anderson. Sand was defiant.

"Don't tell him anything. The sooner we're rid of this bastard, the better," she said.

Anderson slapped her hard, causing her to cry out. He drew back the hammer on his gun.

"Last chance, Dariusz. You don't tell, and I'll kill her first, then that girl she's so fond of, then whoever else I can think of until you do talk. It is in furtherance of my mission. Their lives are of no consequence to me. Can you live with all those deaths on your conscience?"

"You have no idea," said Dariusz.

Anderson pushed the barrel of his gun hard against Sand's temple.

"I will not warn you again."

Dariusz dropped his gaze to the floor. "Corrigan. That's all. It was me and Corrigan."

"There," said Anderson. He removed his gun from Sand's head. "Thank you. I'll make an example of you both tomorrow."

He jerked his head at his soldier. A stun beam hit Dariusz square in the chest, and he collapsed to the floor.

IN EVENING COUNTRY the unchanging sky stood in as well for Earthly dawn as it did for evening. In the morning, as the colony reckoned it, Dariusz and Corrigan were dragged out into the main square by several Alts. A scaffold carrying two nooses had been erected. The sky was a mackerel of orange stripes; they were being taken for a dawn execution in all respects, save that there would be no day afterwards. Anderson had the whole colony out to watch. The wind blew strong. Cables rattled on the new flag pole crowning the command centre, the Petrovitch flag snapping impatiently from the top of it. But the people – people crowded the windows, the roofs, all the uneven stone expanse of the mesa top – they were silent. Grim-faced Alt and uneasy human troopers stood guard, guns pointing at their own kind.

Leonid was there, and those of the council who had capitulated. The Pointer looked past Dariusz, and barely blinked. His eyes were sunken, more so than the rest of the hungry populace, although he had plenty to eat. Sand was within their group, hands bound, a guard at her side.

Dariusz and Corrigan were dragged to the scaffold. Dariusz was unhurt. Corrigan looked like he had taken a beating. His lips were bloody, both eyes swollen, nose broken. They were forced to kneel under the nooses. Thin wire things, uglier than rope, if that were possible.

Anderson came out, bold as Caesar before the senate. A guard of two Alts, weapons gleaming, followed him up to the platform. Anderson stood before the prisoners, and addressed the crowd.

"Today!" shouted Anderson. "I deliver the Petrovitch family from two grave threats. That from without" – he gestured beyond the fences – "and that from within!" He looked down at the captives. "Dariusz Szczeciński and David Corrigan have plotted against me, and in doing so, they have plotted against your rightful leader, Leonid Petrovitch, and therefore against you. Doubtless they sought to return the colony to the lunacy of rule by council. This *will not happen*. This colony is the property of the Petrovitch family, and I, and all of you, are their servants. Do not resist their enlightened rule. Better to serve gladly under the direction of one, than die under the confusion of many. It saddens me to bring these two men here. Both have skills that greatly benefit us, but as I have shown you before, and will show you again, it is the survival of the body that is paramount, not that of the limbs, and I have no choice but to sever the limbs when they are diseased.

"Today, we activate the radar fence. The product of our scientists, this barrier of energy will drive the enemy away from our home. We shall be able to sleep safely in our beds, and begin without fear the task of taming the Evening Country for humanity's prosperity."

Anderson gestured. In a piece of pure theatre, a white robed technician bowed his head and went inside the Command Centre.

Upon the mast, a red light started to flash, once every second and a half.

"It is done," Anderson said. He nodded at the men beside him. They wrestled Corrigan and Dariusz to their feet and reached for the wire nooses.

A shot rang out, and the man holding Corrigan folded over. The crowd rippled. Guns tracked back and forth. Yuri stepped out from the group of dignitaries. He wore a ridiculous costume, bright with feathers and beads, a Pointer's pleasure garb. He held an assault carbine awkwardly, training it on the group as he walked forward. The Pointer's troops aimed their guns at him, but did not dare fire on their employer.

"Come threatening me, Yuri?"

Yuri laughed, a tinkling feminine sound. "Actually, I meant to kill you, but I've never been a very good shot."

"What are you doing?"

"Stopping this madness. You're beholden to my family; I'm the only one that can. At least, I think I am. Will you shoot me,

Anderson? I don't know. But I have to try. I spent my entire life standing by. I'm a little bored with the sidelines of history. Now let them go, and stand down. That is an order."

He advanced.

"I have orders from your father. Orders that he explicitly told me supersede anything you can tell me to do." Anderson held up his gun. "And my orders are to protect the interests of the house of Ilya Petrovitch, not you."

He fired. Yuri fell to the ground, hit in the shoulder. Anderson jumped from the scaffold and strode over to him.

"That was a warning. Are you going to behave yourself, or shall I send you to join your father?"

"Fuck... you..." said Yuri. He sighed. "There, I said it. I feel surprisingly good."

Anderson raised his gun.

"No!" Leonid forced past his own troopers, drawing his gun. "Leave my brother alone."

"What's this? Have both the boys grown into men? Well, well," said Anderson, and Ilya's spirit shone through him. "You realise, if you shoot me, then my men will continue to do what I ordered them to do? They will kill your useless excuse for a brother, and nothing will change. Do you have it in you to defy them again, and again, and again? These people will not help you!" He swept his gun around the square. "They are sheep, to be led by a wolf. And I see you are not lacking in teeth." He aimed his gun at Yuri's head again.

Leonid tensed, then held up his gun to his temple. "It is not you I will kill, Anderson. It will do no good. There is too much of my father in you, and a little too much in me also. I'm sorry, Yuri," he said. "It turns out that I was not the better man, after all."

All modern guns were silenced, but the slight sound of its discharge was enormous, laden with murder. Yuri felt something warm splash across his face, and his brother landed beside him. He groped for his own weapon.

Anderson stood, gun hanging in his hand. The crowd stirred. He could not finish Yuri, not now.

"I..."

Three bullets, one burst. Anderson fell onto Yuri, dropping his carbine. His breath came with difficulty.

"Release those men!" shouted Amir, gun in hand. "It is over! Release them!"

Confusion reigned. The Alts reacted, a couple opening fire on the crowd. Some of the human troops and militia fired back at them. A group of soldiers organised themselves, falling back together. Sides were drawn quickly. Other soldiers dropped their weapons.

The crowd went into uproar, running to get away, and chaos reigned. Someone freed Dariusz and Corrigan, Dariusz never knew who. He ran over to Yuri, shoving panicking colonists out of the way. People were shouting, trying to introduce order, but their shouts were lost in the crowd. Dariusz reached Yuri, rolled the dead Alt from his body. Corrigan pushed people away from them, shouted for aid. "Medic! Get him a medic!" he roared.

Yuri lifted his head. His hair was matted with his own blood and that of his brother and Anderson, blood all of Ilya Petrovitch, returned again to one. He grasped Dariusz's shoulder. "Looks like they are going to have their votes now," he said. "Looks like I'm off the hook…"

"Yuri…"

"But you're not." He smiled, showing bloodied teeth. "Help me sit."

Dariusz hesitated. Yuri was losing a lot of blood. The young Pointer pushed at him, grimacing in pain as he was pulled upright, his hand twisting in the cloth of Dariusz's suit.

He turned to the crowds. They paid no attention.

"Listen!" bellowed Corrigan. "Listen! The Pointer speaks!"

The eddies of people around them slowed. Yuri spoke to only a score or more of colonists. He hoped it would be enough.

"I am Yuri Petrovitch! Some of you think I am the rightful leader here!" He paused, gritted his teeth. "Until such time as elections can be called, I order you… to follow this man… Dariusz." He coughed and cried out, and sank forward. Dariusz struggled to keep him up.

Yuri smiled up at him. "Sorry about that," he said. His eyes closed.

"Medic! Get him a medic!"

They came, eventually, and took Yuri.

The gunfire moved away, toward the edge of the settlement. A group of Anderson's soldiers, Alt and human both, making a break for the desert.

Some semblance of order returned, growing outwards from the fallen Pointers. The council's members were found and brought together, from work gangs and cells, pulled from the crowd. Moore was released from his imprisonment and consulted. The radar fence was shut off immediately. Corrigan, at the council's insistence, was put in command of the colony's small military. Tense stand-offs occurred all over First Landing for the rest of the day, and Corrigan had his hands full ensuring violence did not erupt again. Dariusz was let free, but not for long. He was captured by a delegation from the council, and hauled in to their arguments. He had defied the Pointers' man, and so he found himself a fulcrum in their argument. Both sides appealed to him. Amir, following always the course of power as a river follows the terrain, attempted to beguile him. Brzezinska, sorely treated for her outspokenness during the coup, poured venom on Amir as a traitor and an opportunist. It was all Dariusz could do to prevent them setting about each other with their fists.

Corrigan hunted down the remaining Alts and had them incarcerated. Debate about what to do with them raged most fiercely when the council reconvened; only accusations of who was to blame for Anderson's coup, and who had co-operated most fully with him, outmatched it.

They were still shouting angrily at each other when the natives attacked.

CORRIGAN HAD A watch posted at the highest points of the settlement. He was called up to the comms tower by Bulaweyo at 15:26 hours. She handed her scope wordlessly to him, and he scanned the horizon, west to east and back. The natives came boiling toward them, making no attempt at stealth. Not in neat groups of eight, nor in single file, but a disordered wall of chitin a kilometre wide. He returned the scope.

He spoke into the radio. "Darius, I think you're going to have to come and look at this."

Ten minutes later, Dariusz was on the comms tower.

"Like Moore feared," said Corrigan. He indicated that Buleweyo should hand over her scope. Dariusz put it to his eye. "He said that the radar fence would do this. It looks like turning it off didn't help. The damage has been done."

"That is a bit of a fucking problem, don't you agree?" said Corrigan. "There must be two hundred of them."

"Are there many people outside?" said Dariusz.

"Negative, the majority of the colony had been called in to watch us die," said Corrigan. "Which is handy."

"We should get everyone in."

"Do you think?" said Corrigan testily. "I've already sounded the evacuation. How's it going downstairs?"

Dariusz shook his head. "Badly. Half of them want to hang Amir for supporting Anderson, the other half to crown him for killing him."

"You can worry about your politics later. This is a mite more urgent now." He laughed. "Which is what Anderson was saying all along, eh?"

"How long do we have?"

"About twenty minutes or so. You're going to need a weapon. Let's get the ultralights up. Give them some grenades. Every little helps."

Dariusz, thinking of Sand, did not agree immediately, but what choice did they have?

Alarms went up. With much misgiving, Corrigan ordered the release of the captured soldiers, extracting oaths of allegiance from them all. He passed out arms, knowing that the common threat would keep them on the same side, for now. He gave those he trusted least the rail rifles: their low rate of fire made them less effective against human targets. The last few Alts he left where they were, not knowing how they would react.

Soldiers and militia went running for the defences. There were few of the professional soldiers left. Fifteen had broken out, the Alts were jailed, seven had been killed in the fighting. The militia was more numerous, but untrained.

At almost exactly 17:00 hours, the aliens assailed the base. Without plan or cohesion, they ran at the defences. They were agitated, enraged. They behaved abnormally, rocking on their leg clusters, or scurried around and around in tight spirals. A handful simply collapsed. They swarmed all around the base, attacking anything of Terran origin they came across, animate or inanimate. Bullets streaked out from the machine gun nests on the outer perimeter. Grenades fell among them, blowing off their vulnerable legs. They fell into the ditches, scrabbling ineffectually at the smooth metal until they were dispatched. Many were destroyed by concentrated fire from the defence emplacements, but every corpse provided the beginnings of a bridge, and they swarmed over their own dead. They clambered over the sand berm on the far side, into the open area before the inner gates, tearing men and women to pieces wherever they found them.

By the riverfront, things were worse. The defenders there were overwhelmed in quarter of an hour.

Corrigan ordered a withdrawal to the mesas, abandoning Anderson's outer perimeter, which they had too few men and weapons to hold. Rail rifles stationed on both rock formations reaped a heavy toll on the creatures, but they did not falter. They did not stop to tend to their dead. They were insane, driven mad by Anderson's invisible fence. They clambered swiftly up the cliff faces, smashing through the electrified wires as if they weren't there. And over it all, the horrendous buzzing of the creatures, their alien screams of rage.

Corrigan noted that they attacked the East Mesa with less force.

"They're going for the comms mast!" he shouted into his radio. "All non combat personnel fall back from the command centre! Stay out of their way!"

Bullets whispered through the air. Rail rifles slammed hunks of iron into hard alien bodies with resounding *bangs*. People screamed. Fires burned. The pandemonium of battle: death, stink and noise.

The fight went on. Every push of the aliens that was destroyed was followed by another, each successive wave wearing down the defenders and their defences. They got in, and broke up the human defenders into groups.

Dariusz fought alongside men who had tried to kill him, defending the infirmary against creatures ten times his mass with a gun that barely scratched them.

Sand and Kasia flew overhead, dropping grenades into the seething mass, and when those were gone, shouted frantic directions into their radios as creatures clambered upon vital buildings, or peeled them open to exterminate frightened colonists.

Corrigan directed fire from the comms mast, until the number of natives in the courtyard grew so heavy he headed down to fight.

Every man, every woman, fought. If they had weapons, if they did not. Many died.

Corrigan blasted a native at short range with his rail rifle as it reared over him. The magnetically-impelled slug blew a hole in it he could see through.

He glanced at the comms mast. Buleweyo shot from the top, calmly placing high-velocity rounds into the creatures' faceplates as they swarmed up at her. Two pairs of hands reached for her from an alien face. She dropped her gun as the alien dragged her over the railing, and pulled at something in her belt. A bright explosion annihilated the front half of the alien and obliterated her; the native fell from the mast, trailing fire. At the base of the tower, aliens pulled and shoved, rocking the mast. It groaned in protest, then began to topple.

Over his radio, Corrigan heard, "The gates are falling, the gates are falling!"

"You, you, you!" he shouted, pointing at his men. "Form a line, form a line!" He went around the courtyard, snapping shots at stray aliens, grabbing as many men as he could and forming them into two ranks of fifteen, one end anchored to the row of buildings containing the infirmary.

The rail rifles were devastating, but slow to fire. Each took a second to charge. He interspersed the men bearing them with carbine-carrying soldiers. Colonists joined them, spilling out from the buildings where they had been hiding. They sensed his intent. There was no point in waiting; this was the last stand. Dariusz was among them. He found Plock and together they gathered a group of ten and headed off to the rear of the courtyard. The creatures were still coming up the cliffs.

Screams from the radio. Men came running back from the gates, firing behind them.

"Concentrate fire!" Corrigan hollered. "Rail rifles, pick one target, move on to another. On my order…"

The natives on the tower were spilling from it. More were coming around the corner from where the gate had been.

"First rank, fire!" he called.

Seven slugs spat out to the rifles' distinctive hum. Seven aliens died.

"Second rank fire!" he called. Five rail rifles in the second rank. Five more alien dead.

"First rank fire!" he called. Again, the rail rifles hummed. Iron, that most base of man's metals, shot forward with deadly force.

And again, and again. The aliens were many still, and they kept up their advance. When they were within fifty metres, Corrigan ordered his men to retreat two steps by rank after each shot. "Carbines, fire!" he bellowed. The lesser weapons added their *tut-tut-tut* to the tumult. He placed a wall of metal and carbon composites between his men and the natives. His group retreated backwards step by step, until his men were pressed back to back with Dariusz's rearguard, and the edge of the mesa and the buildings that lined it were metres away.

And then, there were no more.

Alien dead and dying lay all over the courtyard, their yellow blood mingling freely with the red of humanity. A couple skittered away, headed for the gate. Gunfire sounded from the East Mesa still, but less of it with every passing second. Corrigan tried his radio, but could not summon a voice to tell him whether the sounds of battle were fading due to victory there, or defeat.

He wiped his hand across his mouth. He remained tense, anticipating a fresh rush and final extinction.

None came.

"What now?" Corrigan asked Dariusz.

"What do you suggest?" said Dariusz. "You are the military man."

Corrigan looked up at the comms mast. Even with the fence disabled, they'd known where to come. He stared out through the mesa edge fence over the firezone Anderson had cleared from the river. The smashed bodies of natives dotted it. "There's no going back, not after this." He said. "We have to finish what Anderson started. Follow them back to their lair, and kill them all." He spat on the ground. "Then perhaps we can go back to living like civilised people."

Kasia and Sand were still up in their ULs. They told Kasia to fly out, and to report back on the natives, to see where they went to ground. Then they reordered their men. Fifty still combat capable, a mix of soldiers and militia. They followed the wounded creatures in the three ATVs that had escaped the rampage, keeping their distance, the rest of the small army marching behind. The road back was clearly marked by the dead, slumped insectoid bodies as big as buffalo.

The natives' home was a low hill, notable only for its solitary nature. Kasia picked out the concealed entrance that led into it, close by where Sand had lost the trail. The weave of brush and sand that had hidden it was cast to one side.

The battered army of First Landing moved in for the kill.

CHAPTER NINETEEN
Genocide

SOLDIERS WAITED TENSELY above the burrow mouth. Facing the entrance, the rest of the army were ready, hiding in the scrub and boulders either side of the natives' path, guns trained on the concealed opening. The shattered bodies of natives littered the torn ground, turning the dry earth into a gory swamp.

"Incoming!"

A native burst from the burrow entrance. Machine gun fire barked from three positions. Grenades rained down on it, dismembering it messily. Body parts bounced to join the shattered remains of its fellows.

"Clear!"

Corrigan lay prone by Dariusz. He craned his neck and shouted back to the ATVs. "The radar still running?"

"Maximum output, sir!" replied a soldier.

"No sign of any other movement, sir!"

"That could be the last of them. If it wasn't, it doesn't look like they have another rush in them," Corrigan said. He was exhausted, his eyes red-rimmed. "We'll wait. Ten minutes. Keep the EM up. See if we can lure any more of those bastards out. Ayvazian, casualty report!"

"Six wounded, three dead. Twenty-three natives killed."

"Are these new, are the wounded natives still in the hill?" asked Dariusz.

"Impossible to tell." Corrigan coughed. "We'll find out soon though, won't we?"

Ten minutes passed. No more natives emerged from the tunnel. Corrigan signalled two of his men to run forward under cover of the machine guns. They placed explosives around the burrow entrance, then ran back.

"Giving fire!" one shouted.

A second later, the doorway to the native village exploded with a dull *crump*. Soil rained down on the group of men.

"That's it," said Corrigan. "Come on."

The door had been a woven mat of stiff, resinous material. Dariusz scooped a fragment of it off the ground. It was surprisingly light, and Dariusz was put in mind of the lairs of trapdoor spiders on Earth. The burrow was wide enough for three men to walk down abreast. There was no shortage of volunteers to take point; the men were all angry, eager to kill the monsters that had attacked their families. Three were chosen and moved in, weapons ready, dropping flares as they went. Dariusz and Corrigan waited until they'd moved out twenty metres, then followed into the dark entrance, three more men behind them.

"Look at this," said Corrigan. "Slick as glass." He ran his hand along the burrow wall. Its contours glittered in the light of the flares.

"The friction of the creatures' shells must have polished it," said Dariusz.

"Still…"

"I know. It looks like something built by a mind, rather than instinct. We do not know for certain if they are… *were* intelligent. We are endowing them with human traits where none might exist. If we were shrunk down to ant size, and went into an ants' nest, it would appear like a city to our eyes."

Corrigan nodded. Neither of them were convinced.

The burrow went on without interruption for two hundred metres, bringing them, by Corrigan's estimation, directly under the hill. There were no side passages or blockages to the burrow; it was a straight, glassy tube that terminated in another door that they could not open. Corrigan called up his remaining combat engineers again, and had the others cover the men as they wired the door. They were forced to exit the tunnel entirely before detonating the explosives. A rush of smoke and debris billowed from the tunnel mouth. They waited, but nothing else followed.

They entered the hill.

A deserted labyrinth of tunnels and cells greeted them.

The corridor rose up and opened in the centre of a space that even in the dark they could tell was vast. Corrigan had flares and torches lit, revealing *how* big; a huge, beehive-shaped cavity that went down into the earth further than it did up above the ground. A spiral ramp led from the tunnel mouth up the sides of the chamber, with many doors leading off. Elegant, fluid traceries covered the ramp's sides, making exquisite galleries of it. A sense of tranquillity pervaded the place, but the organic beauty of the hive was marred by corpses, seven dead natives lying in pools of their own fluids on the chamber floor and on the ramps, their shells shattered by the weapons of the colonists.

Corrigan had five teams of three split and scour the place. It was dark within, the aliens having no eyes, and their torches often lit the indescribable. Strange sights greeted them at every turn, and Corrigan and Dariusz were called from one end of the empty hive to the other to examine fresh wonders.

In one cluster of cells, things like giant amoebae swam in lipped pools of thick syrup. In another, stacks and stacks of flat slates. Elsewhere, they found piles of sand, carefully graded by size. In three broad, domed chambers at the base of the hive were fields of unfamiliar vegetation.

"Farms? Livestock?" said Corrigan. He inspected close-packed stands of tall fungus, playing his torch beam over them.

Dariusz nodded. "Like ants again, but more sophisticated. Look!"

By a wall, in a neat row, were a series of what could only be implements. Dariusz picked them up one at time. They were curiously small in comparison to the natives' size, and their shapes mystified him, but it was obvious they had been crafted for some purpose or other.

"Corrigan. Tools."

"Still like ants?" said Corrigan.

Dariusz shook his head. "Not like ants." He placed the implement carefully back with its fellows. "What we've done here…"

"We can blame Anderson."

"Can we?" said Dariusz.

Corrigan's response was interrupted by shouts over the radio. Gunfire, and frantic chatter followed, then the radio cut out. They could hear the *pop* of gunfire echoing around the hive. Corrigan swore and keyed the radio on.

"Team three, team four, converge on weapons fire. All other teams, take cover. Come on!" he shouted to Dariusz.

They ran back into the central space, then up the ramps, following the soft rattle of a carbine. The gun cut out, shouting taking its place, and they ran faster, reaching a wide room where blood was sprayed liberally. They came in ready to fight, but there was no battle. They were greeted by the sight of one of the men being restrained by two others.

Corrigan put up his gun. "What the hell happened here?"

"More monsters, sir," spat the restrained man.

"He wouldn't stop firing," said one of those holding him. "They showed no signs of aggression."

Dariusz looked around the room. The dead things were the size of large dogs, a couple of dozen of them. They were huddled together in a corner. Dariusz locked eyes with their executioner. "Have you no mercy?" he said. "You have murdered their children."

"Dariusz," said Corrigan. He looked at him warningly, and then turned to his men. "Call us if you find anything else, do you understand? Nothing else dies without my order," said Corrigan.

The men nodded.

"Now let him go."

The men dispersed, and continued their exploration.

The humans encountered no more living natives. Here and there was the odd slumped body of a creature, grievously wounded in the battle of First Landing. They had come home to die.

In other chambers they found more tools. As far as Dariusz could tell, the majority of them were linked to food cultivation, processing and preparation. Jars and bowls, scoops, firepits and others. Water was another feature. In one room, a series of basins, another a deep cistern filled to the brim. The sheer variety of the artefacts convinced him they could not simply be the product of instinctual or even learned behaviours. This was the sign of culture. He felt sick.

The chamber at the top of the hive's low rise was the final proof. There they found clear evidence of symbolic thought that could not be denied.

They entered through an oval door whose clay edges were decorated with intricate designs of inlaid haematite. At its centre lay a native whose shell was cracked and gnarled, not broken by the guns of men but by time, and Dariusz guessed it to be of great age.

It was dead.

A broad pool of yellow blood surrounded it. In one hand it held a hollow circular knife of polished stone, stained with its own life fluid.

It was the only time Dariusz ever saw a native with a weapon of any kind.

"It killed itself," said Dariusz. "It killed itself when the others were killed." His voice was hoarse. His throat was closing up with emotion. "We are the monsters here, not them."

Corrigan shook his head. "It's a matter of survival. We had no choice."

"We do not deserve to survive, if this is the way in which we go about it," said Dariusz, bitterly.

"We had no choice, Darius," Corrigan repeated.

They stepped over the creature's splayed limbs. The dome of the chamber was filled with intricate designs of inlay, a mosaic of tesserae cut from polished minerals of many colours. The designs ran in a continuous spiral that started at the chamber's apex and wound its way down toward the floor. The lower third of the wall was blank. A pile of polished chips and a shallow bowl of adhesive lay at the very end of the design. Dariusz knelt and touched the last few chips. They moved in their cement. He carefully nudged them back into place and wiped his hand on his trousers.

"This is still wet," he said. "This elder here, he put these last marks on the wall and then killed himself."

"Is it a record of some kind?" said Corrigan.

Dariusz looked around. "Perhaps. Writing for creatures whose senses are different from our own. A record, a history maybe. And we brought it to an end."

"Let's get out of here," said Corrigan.

They left the chamber. The *whumph* of ignited accelerants and the *bang* of explosives chased them down the hive's spiral ramps. The smell of burning was drawn right the way through the natives' home, pulled by air currents of deliberate design. Corrigan did nothing to halt the vandalism. Dariusz thought the destruction of the hive gratuitous, but could not formulate an argument in his mind to stop it. He was too tired to fight over it, too ashamed.

Neither of them spoke as they reached the bottom.

"Sir," a soldier spoke over the radio. His voice was clear. The airwaves were free of the interference emitted by the creatures. "You have to come and look at this."

They went down to the very bottom of the spiral road. In a chamber, bigger than any other and carved from the bedrock, they found many tons of equipment taken from the *Mickiewicz*. Whether from the nightside or the wreckage nearby, they could not tell. Arrayed neatly according to size, much of it was free of damage, save in one respect: every one possessing a radio beacon or active wireless interface had had those things smashed out of them. A good deal of time was spent cataloguing the material once the hive was clear.

By chance, they came across a working genetics microlab within the first five minutes of entering the cave. Dariusz was ashen faced as the others celebrated the retrieval of such valuable treasure. His time was up; with the microlab, the colony techs could pinpoint who had been the saboteur in seconds.

He was going to have to leave.

CHAPTER TWENTY
Dariusz Unmasked

SAND FOUND PIOTREK and went to help in the infirmary, and almost wished she had not. The place was packed with the wounded: missing limbs, missing skin, missing eyes. They screamed for comfort the overstretched medical staff could not provide, and the auxiliary nurses like Sand and Piotrek did not know how to administer. Sand, because she was the senior council member in the infirmary, and because she had some small medical knowledge, was set the grim task of deciding who would be treated, which was the same as deciding who would die. Battlefield triage – with her as the arbiter of life and death. She was supposed to be dispassionate, but how could she be? One by one the injured were treated, and drugged into sleep, transferred to the East Mesa hospital or died. Past midnight, the infirmary grew quiet. Sand fell into a troubled sleep.

At 06:25 the following day, she was awoken abruptly. The horizon lit up with flashes of yellow fire. The crackle of arms fire and rumble of high explosives carried across the plains back to First Landing, causing those left behind to look to the north. With the long-range radio transmitters damaged by the natives' assault of the comms mast, rumours spread in the absence of fact. The troops were dead, the troops were alive, Dariusz had been killed, so had Corrigan, they both lived. Plock had been seen, screaming in terror. The radio spoke strange noises... None of them, as far as she could tell, were true.

At 07:40, Kasia arrived back at the colony in the remaining UL, smudged with soot and exhausted, but otherwise none the worse for wear. The girl sought out Sand, and they embraced amid the sleeping casualties of the earlier struggle. Kasia had no information for Sand, having been airborne for the entirety of the second battle, and both of them worried about Dariusz.

The infirmary did not remain quiet for long. At 08:03, the first ATV roared through the main gate bearing more wounded men, and Sand was pitched back into the stinking, roaring hell of the previous day. The wounded brought news, but far from quashing the rumours, they generated more. She asked again and again after Dariusz, but none of the men and women returning from the native's village had seen him. Then she was occupied for a while.

At 10:55, Sand took her leave and went looking for Dariusz. First Landing was in uproar. Smoke still boiled from the wrecked Command Centre, the comms mast drooped dangerously over the courtyard. Troops and militia straggled back from the natives' torched village in twos and threes: triumphant, or traumatised, or both. ATVs ran back and forth in endless loops between the shocked here and the bloodied there. At first they brought the wounded, then the dead, then the cache of equipment the aliens had taken from the wreckage of the *Mickiewicz*. The soldiers filled the warehouses with this unlooked-for bounty, and of all the horrors and marvels of that day, it was this that caught the eyes of the colonists as they ran frantically about their tasks, and made them pause awhile.

First Landing had to it the seeming of a disturbed ant's nest. Activity churned under the surface, in its labs and factories, its halls and barracks. The town disgorged the entirety of the human race upon Nychthemeron. Frenetic work was being done to repair the defences to the village, techs ran wildly from place to place, engaged in metaphorical firefighting as others fought real fires. The hospital and infirmary were full of the dead and the dying. No one knew who was in charge. Yuri was at death's door, Leonid and Anderson dead. There was shouting at East Mesa, the threat of further violence, as the militia, headed by the last four of the *Mickiewicz*'s security personnel, attempted to disarm those troops and militia deemed loyal to Anderson. The militia were little loved by the colonists. Now it was safe to speak out, many did so, and they fixed their hatred upon them. The militia tried to pass it on to the Pointers' men, who, for their part, protested their loyalty to the colony authority, and spoke loudly of their role in the battle against the natives.

Sand heard later that it was Corrigan, wounded himself, who talked both sides down, and had the blacksuits sit it out. Everyone was suspicious of everyone else's motives. Drunk on terror, people played games of spot the collaborator. After so many weeks under the boot of Anderson, the place was in danger of coming apart under the release of pressure. There were angry scenes near the food warehouses, and Sand was obliged to take time out to calm the situation and make sure the supplies were properly guarded.

By 18:00 things were quietening down for good. The council had convened for an emergency session, for which she received many urgent requests to attend. She ignored them, continuing her search for Dariusz. She asked around in all the usual places, and then again, and then a third and a fourth time, but he had not been seen. She helped out where she could, or where she had to, and hurried away to the next crisis. All the while she asked again and again where Dariusz was. She encountered a number of people who asked the same question of her.

Then, a breakthrough. She found Plock sat by the outer gate in Anderson's ditch, drinking water and telling ghastly stories to a dozen or so people. One day they would lament the extirpation of the aliens, for now there was only relief at an enemy vanquished.

"I did see him," he told her when she had wrested his attention away from his audience. "He said he was going to the council. There's a meeting, I heard." He looked at her as if to ask her why she wasn't there.

She unconsciously rubbed at her stomach. She was already showing; soon it would be obvious, even through the looser clothes she'd taken to wearing.

"He's not there," she said. "Where could he have gone?"

"I don't know." Plock shrugged. "He was odd after the fight..."

"Odd how?"

"I don't know, *odd*-odd, he didn't say much. But he never does, eh?"

Sand strode away without saying goodbye.

"Hey! If you see him, tell him he owes me a drink."

Sand did not respond.

She rechecked all the places she'd checked before. She went back to the hospital and infirmaries, and went over the lines of the dead, all thirty of them, although she had been told he was alive and walking. He was not there.

It was the boy Roman who found him; knowing Sand was searching for him, he went to find her. He came running after her. "Pilot, Pilot!" he shouted. She turned. "Dariusz... I see him. You search, yes?"

"Where?" demanded Sand.

He held his hands up. "There, back there!" He gabbled Polish at her in frustration. He had still not learned much of the Lingua Anglica.

She grabbed a man she knew, pointed at the boy.

"The laboratory," translated the man. He was tired, dead-eyed. Soot streaked his arms. He carried a toolbox that had seen much use.

"Which one?"

The man shrugged. "He does not know, he is six."

"Show me," she said.

Roman looked at the man, confused.

"*Pokaż*," the man told him.

He nodded, beckoned, and turned tail. Sand hurried after him.

AN ATV WAS parked outside the genetics lab. Dariusz was inside. The lights were off, but she could hear him moving around. She stepped in without turning the light on. He heard her come in, he must have, but he did not look up from the fridge.

"Dariusz? I've been looking everywhere for you!" she said. "What are you doing?"

"I am about to administer Moore's experimental retrovirus to myself," he said calmly, as if that explained it all. "He'd finished it. Clever man, Moore."

"Why? Come away from there. I was worried about you."

Bio-killing blue light made him seem alien. He reached in to the fridge and pulled out a black carbon tube.

"I am going away, Sand."

"Dariusz, what are you talking about, I –"

"It's not us, in case you might have thought so, although I do not think we would have worked well in the long run, you and I. We are too different. Water and fire."

"What are you talking about?" She took a step toward him, but went no further. Something awful hung between them.

He set the hypospray down and looked at her intently, like he was seeing her properly for the first time. "We found a functioning mini genelab in the creatures' nest," he said. "Moore was right, our EM signals were driving them crazy. They'd collected all sort of things together, Sand; all sorts of things. We killed them all. We had no right."

"I don't understand," she said, although with a sudden rush of clarity, she thought she did. "What has that got to do with you going away? I have something that –"

He interrupted her again, which he never did. He had become ruthless in his conversation. "With the genelab, they'll be able to type the saboteur's residual DNA. Leonid kept a shard of the glass the saboteur used to cut himself, do you know that? He wore it around his neck. Posth gave it to him."

"He?"

He looked at her expectantly, sorrowfully.

"You? You did it?"

Her gun was in her hand without her thinking about it. She aimed it squarely at him with a shaking hand. Sand stared at him; fury, sorrow and disbelief warred in her.

He loaded the tube into a hypospray. It slid home with a tiny *click*. He was so methodical, so slow and careful. Sand could not picture him making a rash decision. How could she have got it so wrong?

All the noises in the room were unnaturally loud – the hum of the fridge, the buzz of the UV light, the whirr of a pump somewhere – and laden with consequence. She felt the need to whisper.

"Why did you do it, why did you?" she said

"I was going to tell you, I needed to confess, but I couldn't, I –"

"Why?" she shouted. She twisted the safety off on her gun, and racked a round into the chamber.

Dariusz looked at the floor. In the blue sterilising light of the fridge he looked very old and tired. "Sand, please, let me explain."

"What, explain why you rammed us into this world, killed so many of us? I've watched so many people die, Dariusz, so many. Can you explain that to me? And your son... Could you explain it to him?" She was crying now, tears hot on her cheeks. His distant manner, his introversion. Not sorrow; he had been hiding his role in the disaster. No wonder he had been so guarded! She felt ashamed at being dragged into his orbit. "I've been such a fool. You have made me a fool."

His face tightened. "I didn't intend for it to happen."

"Why did you do it?"

"I wanted a better world for... for Danieł." Sand had not heard him say his son's name for a long time. "I was at the end. I had lost my job, I had lost all chances at a job. A man, this man Browning, the virus was in my blood..." He stumbled over his words, unable to frame his confession. He began again. "I was promised a better world. The virus was supposed to break down the security systems surrounding the Syscore and release it from the direct control of the Pointers, that is what I was told. I realise that I was a fool to trust Browning. I knew nothing about the group that approached me. I was blinded by fear, I saw the end coming. I wanted my son to survive. I did not know it would have this effect. I wanted the colonies to be free of the Pointers, that is all. Trust me, it is the truth."

Her head spun. "How can I trust you?" She held the gun higher, wavering in her hand. She grabbed her wrist to steady it. "How can I know anything you have said to me has been the truth?"

"Because it has been. Only this, my part in the crash... That was all I hid. I was going to tell you." He hadn't moved. He stood there with the hypospray in one hand, his finger still on the rear of the capsule. He did not raise his hands, did not approach. He awaited his fate. He had given up.

"When?"

He gave a sad smile. "When? That is a good question. Would there have been a good time?"

She released her wrist and wiped her forearm across her face. The gun stayed where it was.

"What do you plan to do?"

"I'm going to find the Syscore. Without it, the colony is finished. We need the database it carries. The machines we have will not last forever, and we cannot make replacements without the information in the Syscore, assuming its own databases are not also corrupt. A fool's errand, I know, but I have to try. Our knowledge will fade, everything we have striven for since we walked out of the jungle. We will revert to savagery, and then we will die out. I owe it to everyone who lived to bring the Syscore back. I won't have two disasters on my hands. When I bring it back, I will stand trial. Let them kill me. I do not care, just let me do what I can."

"You can't make it better."

"I know."

"You'll never find it. You will die. The nightside will kill you."

"That is probably what will happen. But I can at least try. I would have gone earlier, but I had to wait for the retrovirus to be finished."

"It's not been tested. What if it doesn't work?"

"Then I will starve."

Sand stared at him, finger tightening on the trigger. She bared her teeth. She wanted to shoot him. All the pain, the death, the loss. Friends, colleagues, killed by this man; the man who had clipped her wings and condemned her to a grounded life. "I hate you."

"I understand."

"I don't *want* your understanding!" She squeezed harder, but her arm moved. The shot went wild, skimming past Dariusz's ear. The gun clattered from her hand. All the life went from her; she half-collapsed. Something in her belly twinged. She grabbed at the countertop for support.

"Get out," she said. "Get out now. They'll be coming for you. Never come back." She sat on the floor with a groan and put her face in her hands. "What a fucking mess."

"They know we are lovers. They will think you were involved."

"They won't. I wasn't. Any idiot can see that."

He pressed the hypo to his arm and discharged the load of engineered virus into his bloodstream. With that action he stated his intent to leave. She stood.

"Kiss me one last time," she said. He did. He gripped her head hard as he did. They had all grown stronger under the influence of Nychthemeron's gravity.

She did not hear him drive away.

She stayed there for a long time, until Kasia found her. "What happened?"

"Dariusz," she said. "He has gone. He wouldn't say why." She cried out and clutched her stomach.

"Did he hit you? Did you tell him?"

Sand sobbed.

"Did you tell him you were pregnant?"

Sand shook her head, she clutched at her stomach. "The baby. Kasia," she said. "I think there's something wrong."

PART V

Nychthemeron
4 AC

Into the long night the First Born looked often, and were as often afraid of what they imagined therein. There dwelt monsters, they said, there was death. And they did not go into the dark, for there was fear in the dark above all things, and fear is the greatest enemy of all thinking beings.

The First Pilot mocked them for their timidity. "You cower under the sand as frightened tiger grubs. Do not be afraid. Do not be timid. In the darkness dwells the light of knowledge. Come, let us gather together the Wise, and by their art shall we fashion a craft of the air, called a plane of the air, that shapes the air unto its purpose as the plane of the shell worker cuts the shell unto his, and we shall go into the night, and take back the light of knowledge into the Evening Country, and let it light our way to the future, and we shall fear no more, neither of the night nor the day, and all will be as it was, when men were giants in heaven, for our children and thereafter their children's children."

There was much talk at this, and disagreement, for those were hungry times, and times moreover where every man had his say, before there were kings and the ways of kings. And the Lords of the Council remembered the ways of the Wolf, and how his evil threatened all. "Let not one way be put before all the other ways," they said. "Only in balance will we survive."

There were others of differing mind, and many among these Lords coveted the knowledge of the ancients, for they yearned for the times before the fall from heaven when men were giants in the land, and they were of greater persuasion than the other Lords, if not so many in number.

And so the Lords decreed that the machines be built, using the most sacred arts of the forefathers and of the giants, and of the times-before. So it came to pass that the First Born took to the sky for the first time since the Fall, and they saw it was good, and so it has remained ever since.

– *Extract from the* Nychthemeron Codex, *translated from the Aggregate Slavic into neo-Anglic, 3328 AC*

CHAPTER TWENTY-ONE
Freedom of the Skies

THE TRICK WAS to get the rhythm right.

Yuri squatted on the sand, drumming with the severed rakes of a tiger beetle. He would have been the first to admit that he had changed. He was still slender, taking after his mother. He would never be as big as his father, not even if the colony had a surfeit of food, and it did not; but there was a corded strength beneath his skin from years of hard living that had not been there before. His muscles were clearly visible, moving over each other as he shifted position, tapping upon the sand to mimic the sounding pattern of a tiger beetle. His skin had darkened, from the sun of the desert out beyond Evening Country where he often went to hunt. All save the scar of the bullet wound inflicted upon him by Anderson, a white star emblazoned on his shoulder. No medtech or nano to wipe that away, nor the wrinkles round his eyes and mouth the sun had etched; not any more. Not on Nychthemeron.

Yuri had aged a great deal in the four years since the crash, but it was good aging, the kind that fruited wisdom. He had lived thirty-five years, and was – thanks to the treatments he'd benefited from in his youth – biologically twenty-five, but was over five centuries old in another sense. By the standards of his previous life, his body was worn. But his spirit was calm, and he was complete in himself. He accounted himself a man at last. He doubted he would ever have thought himself so if he had stayed on Earth. Age was a price he gladly paid for peace.

Yuri absorbed himself in his task. Drugs and drink and fleeting encounters he had abandoned – well, mostly, excepting drink at feast times, and the occasional fleeting encounter. In work and application he found his joys. He wore a light robe woven from pounded ferrobrush fibres, and a carbon-fibre shell brace was folded across his back. Here, at the edge of True Day, it was pleasantly hot. The cinnamon breeze blew weakly; the rainy season had passed a month before. They had yet to find a better alternative to the old calendar. As Nychthemeron did not rotate and had little axial tilt, there were no seasons beyond the inconstant ones provided by the heating of the sunward equatorial desert, and a subtle darkening that lasted for half of the planet's fourteen-month orbital period. Efforts had been made to adapt their old calendar to the new, but Nychthemeron was a planet of constancy, not cycles, and Terran time did not fit. Nor did anything they had thought of. Every attempt to conceive of a new way of measuring time was inappropriate. They should adapt their minds to the planet, and not vice versa, Yuri said. He laughed after he said this. He never saw himself as a swami, and yet people came to him for his insight. He was turning into a bona fide mystic. It amused him to be seen so.

There was nothing forced about the rhythm, or his enjoyment of it. It was of the planet, and in performing it, Yuri felt at one with it. When hunting for sandclams, Yuri had the glimmer of a hope that mankind might survive upon Nychthemeron.

Piotr danced nearby, shuffling around the way the tigers did. On his feet were strapped platforms into which stiff twigs of ferrobrush were neatly drilled. He scuffed at the sand as he danced, moving in tight circles, first one way, then the next. Together, the two parts of the ersatz beetle moved across the sand, mimicking the predator and the prey of the sandclam. Yuri was sure there was a sandclam beneath, the texture of the ground was right – a flat expanse with a depression in the middle. Judging exactly where the animal was called for expertise.

The sand shifted. He put the rakes down gently and unslung the brace. He unfolded it, once, twice, and locked it in place. Three metres long, woven in the last of the fabricators. Piotr stopped shuffling; he moved to the left, then the right, the pattern of a tiger beetle on edge.

The sand mounded as the sandclam broke the surface at speed. Piotr leapt backwards, lost his footing, and scrambled for the safety of a nearby rock. "A big one!" laughed Yuri. He still laughed often, but his laughter was of triumph more often than despair these days, and had lost its shrill, maniacal edge.

The sandclam's lips emerged from the ground, its shell gaped wide. Yuri held his arms high, allowing himself to be taken down into the creature's maw.

This was the most difficult part, and the most dangerous. It was the part he enjoyed best.

The sand protected his feet from the grinding teeth of the creature, but ran freely as the clam expelled it from its shell. He had to be quick.

With practised calm, he fitted the clawed ends of the brace against the shell's fluted lips, first on one side, and then the other. He tested it was secure, then swung up onto it, wrapping his arms and legs about it. The sand disappeared from the centre of the shell, revealing the deep muscles and lines of hooked teeth that formed its rasp. Its meal unexpectedly gone, the mollusc tried to pull its shell closed and retreat; the brace prevented it from shutting, and so wedged it firmly into the sand at the surface.

"Piotrek! Piotrek! Get over here! I've got it! It's stuck! Get the harpoon!"

The sandclam's feet, two long, slippery tentacles, batted at Yuri, trying to knock him into the shell. He held on more tightly.

Piotr's face appeared over the edge. In his hand was a long shaft with a slender iron point, a metre and half long. He drew back his arm, waited for the creature's feet to move out of the way, and thrust the weapon deep into a patch of quivering flesh behind which lay the sandclam's simple brain.

It took a minute for the sandclam to die. Reflex actions took a while longer to cease. Yuri waited until he was sure it was over before he climbed out.

He and Piotr smiled at each other, and laughed. Yuri clapped the younger man on the shoulder.

"Get the ATV," he said. "It's going to take a while to drag this out of the ground."

While Piotr fetched their vehicle, Yuri pulled out a simple tablet computer, one of the first they'd made on-world. There were hunting quotas that could not be exceeded, population estimates that needed updating. He preferred to leave the messy business of butchery until he'd logged all he could about the clam, or he'd just forget. It was important he did not. After the destruction of the natives' nest, the colonists were determined not to make the mistakes of Earth again. They all needed to eat, but that did not mean that they should not be careful.

Yuri's darker nature had not deserted him entirely, but nowadays he kept his pessimism to himself.

Piotr arrived in the ATV. He climbed down from the cab, hoses over his shoulder.

"Ah," said Yuri. "First, the sponges."

They drove back to First Landing satisfied, the tanks of their trailer full of brackish clam water, the back of the vehicle crammed full of meat they could not eat.

FIRST LANDING'S WALLS were ruddy in the sun that never set. Solar arrays gleamed along the buildings' roofline now. The original settlement had become a citadel, the two halves linked by a suspension bridge. High ramparts of steel-studded stone circled both mesas. The inner gate to the Western Mesa had been closed up, offering the colonists a refuge that could only be assailed by scaling the cliffs or taking the bridge. The bridge, naturally, could be dropped. After the battle of First Landing, a certain militarism had crept in to the colony's way of thinking. Anderson had been both right and wrong. Yuri had found this duality to be a tedious constant of government.

The town had grown beyond its core. Dariusz's farm was lush with earthly vegetation, and fringed by barns made of recycled containers and pressed clay harvested from the Leonid River. The fences that had once encircled the mesa tops had been removed, and repositioned to link the farm buildings together, enclosing their primary food supply within a third, loose perimeter. Beyond the fence, new fields were being laid out. Irrigation canals gridded the plain, connected to the river to make use of its erratic flow, gates at the ends that could be closed when the river vanished beneath the sand. Pipes ran from boreholes to fill the canals in between times, windmills pumped at the boreheads. Watchtowers stood at the intersections of the canals.

A sizeable district had sprung up at the feet of the West Mesa, between the airfield and the new fields on the plain beyond. It had been named, unofficially, Airtown. The colonists had grown used to village life, and all knew each other by name, but they yearned for privacy and sought it even in the face of danger. Berms had been built around the suburb, faced with panels cut from the *Mickiewicz*'s cargo containers, and a ditch lay before it. All followed Anderson's original plans.

The saddle that linked the mesas had also been fortified, and behind that a small industrial zone was corralled, an expansion of the facilities originally raised on the East Mesa. The smell of the rendering plant especially was intolerable up in the citadel – another factor influencing the colonists to move into Airtown – but the colonists did not feel secure enough to move their vital manufactories away from the safety of their city, and so the stink and clamour of industry remained tucked in close to the heart of First Landing. It was here that Yuri directed the ATV, driving along a road fringed by green rows of potatoes. He reached the gate in the secondary perimeter; Anderson's perimeter. A militia man hailed him.

"Back already, sir?"

"Good hunting today," he said. "We landed a big one."

"Bioreactor C's just being cleared. They were expecting you. Should be ten, fifteen minutes."

Yuri nodded and drove through. He passed through another gate into the industrial zone. The zone's walls trapped the stink of the refinery, intensifying it. Up on the mesas the smell was bad; down here it was nearly unbearable. It was thick in his throat, and reminded him of deck segments choked with the dead. His mood darkened as he pulled up at the bioreactor.

The stench was worst by the reactors, a vile, fishy reek. Bins outside housed the few parts of the clams the colony did not use, while the great shells were stacked nearby. They were supposed to be clean, ready for their processing, but scraps of meat still clung to them, feasts for small clouds of lizardflies. As the people of Earth had adapted to the local ecology, so the local ecology had adapted to them. The lizardflies had previously only been present after each major rain event, but now there was a steady supply of food, they bred whenever the Leonid River brought enough water out of the nightside to wet their eggs. They were a nuisance, and Yuri flapped at his face as he and Piotr helped those on reactor duty unload. They were already filthy with blood from butchering the clam in the field, why should they not help? Some of the others on the council thought such work beneath them. It was dangerous thinking, and he had constantly lobbied for everyone, council members included, to take turns doing the colony's less pleasant jobs. He saw the signs of a new elite emerging, and he did not like it.

The flesh and viscera went into the bioreactor. Fuel and food would be the result. Their attempts at making a retrovirus to alter the genomes of the colonists had been accomplished after much effort, but had been only partially successful. Only in a very few had the genes taken hold and allowed normal consumption; some of the colonists could only eat the native life in small amounts, while others remained entirely unaffected and dependent on Terran organisms or processed foods. Furthermore, the endogenous capacity of the virus had yet to be proved, necessitating infection of all infants at birth.

Yuri passed on the location of the shell so that it could be collected by a heavier truck.

"I don't know why you just don't radio it in," said Kościelniak cheerfully. He had, mainly by accident, become the executive officer of their industrial facilities. "We can truck out and bring the thing back whole. Save you getting your hands dirty."

Yuri smiled. "I like to get my hands dirty. It keeps me grounded, stops me picking up airs. And I don't want some scavenging beetle to come along and gobble up my kill. It pisses me off."

"Fair enough," said Kościelniak. "Speaking of getting your hands dirty, there's a council meeting been called."

"Again?"

"Tomorrow. Sand's had an idea. You'd find out on your own, but forewarned is forearmed, right? That's the right expression, isn't it?"

"Yeah, that's right." Yuri walked away, past the ATV where Piotr waited.

"Hey, you going?" The younger man frowned. "What's wrong with you?"

"More politics," said Yuri. "I wish we'd stayed out." He stalked off, back up to his apartment on the East Mesa. He needed a shower.

SAND BANKED THE new plane around carefully. "Control," she said into the radio, "I'm coming in for a pass. You got eyeballs on me?"

An aggravated sound came from the other end. Not all of the Poles could keep up with her uncompromised American. "We are watching you."

Sand glanced over the plane as they approached the mesas. Ailerons, flaps and rudder were all working fine. There wasn't much more to the airplane than that. Everything it did, it did because she was pulling a lever. This was her Mark IV effort: broad-winged, swift, top speed of two hundred kay an hour, range of four hundred. Primitive, but they'd come a long way from the days of the ultralights, and she'd designed and built most of it herself.

The ULs had served well for local reconnaissance, but she wanted more. Sand gathered a group of engineers to her, told them to think away from the fabricator units, to work with what they had. The first airplanes of Earth had been made of wood and canvas. Why should she wait for the fabricator to be available to weave the modern equivalent? Her expanded team had looked at her as if she were crazy at first, but they'd got into the spirit of it. Crabhawk leather and salvage worked just as well. Sandclam fuel powered its combustion engine. The airframe and propeller were modern, woven carbon. A mix of the old and the new, like everything in the colony.

She loved her planes. The feedback from the stick, attached physically via cable and hydraulics to the flight surfaces, the feel of the air rushing over the open cockpit, all led to a communion with flight that was so powerful it was intoxicating. She'd tasted that flying the ULs, and she wanted to keep it. Fly by wire was for sissies.

"All looks good to us," said control. "Well done, Sand. Come in to land so we can review flight data and performance."

"One more pass," said Sand. It was a statement of intent, not a request.

She banked around the end of the airfield, over the windsock at the southern end which pointed, as it did for seven tenths of the year, to the north. She levelled out again.

"Coming in to land. Out of my way, folks; I have no idea if the brakes on this thing work."

She brought it down with textbook precision, regretting it the moment the wheels touched the ground.

Sand pulled off her goggles and helmet as Kasia came running up. Both of them were grinning madly. Kasia giggled, Sand followed suit. One of her ground crew came toward them at a run.

"Hey! Marek! How's it going?"

Marek came to a stop. He'd run fast but did not pant. Life here had made them all fit. "A message for you. You're to go to West Mesa at once. Emergency council meeting."

She frowned. "Why?"

"They wouldn't say."

"WE'VE LOCATED THE Systems core," Amir put it simply. How he'd dodged the noose, Yuri often wondered, but Amir had always been good at looking out for number one, and had a certain utility as administrator. The reaction to his statement was muted. It had been a long time since they'd lost all the Syscore represented. "It is one thousand and sixteen kilometres from here, on the other side of the magnetic pole, in the nightside," he said.

There were whispered conversations, words passed between the council members. There were fifteen of them, the numbers cut from twenty to an odd number to avoid deadlock in voting and to streamline the process of government. Yuri remained on the council, although not by dint of his birth. He had insisted he be voted for like every other candidate. He'd have left it to others if he trusted them. Things had changed since Leonid died. He had changed, but so had everyone else.

Yuri saw the people in the room, he saw the masks they wore. Technocrats, leaders: elected, definitely, but politicians above all. The same faces, in the main, were returned at election time and again. A political class had emerged with brutal speed. More than half expected deference and consideration to go with responsibilities they regarded as grave and onerous. Even if they did not demand such respect, it was given them. Old habits die hard, thought Leonid. The council had set themselves apart in dress and speech, using proper English as a matter of course, adopting coloured tabards to denote their area of expertise. How quickly the pioneer spirit was diminishing, how quickly a new order was asserting itself.

"How?" Kościelniak said. Yuri liked him. He trusted him more than the others; or rather, he corrected himself, he distrusted him less.

Amir nodded to Moore.

The holo projector spun up an image of Nychthemeron, a patchwork of low and high resolution mapping. Sand and her infant flying corps had crisscrossed the area for three hundred kilometres in all directions, excepting into the nightside. The turbulence where the dayside and nightside atmospheres met was too much for their existing planes, and so the area of high-res data was a circle around First Landing with a flattened side edged by night.

Moore cleared his throat. Nychthemeron rotated, revealing a patchwork of blank patches and low-detail mapping. Everything from the nightside had come from the shuttles before the crash, retrieved before the virus had locked them out. Scouts had ventured into the dark, but not far, and too many had not come back at all. It was a mysterious land to them, a realm of great danger. "To be most accurate," he said, "we did not find the Syscore. It found us." A bright, pulsing point of light sprang up on the map. "The broadcast began this morning."

"The message content?" asked Brzezinska. It was ironic; she had opposed Anderson so bravely, and she was among the worst for assuming airs and graces, to Yuri's eyes. She used her psychology training like it were some kind of magic power.

She intimidated several of the others in the council, and many outside of it.

"All isolated and examined," said Moore. "There is no trace of the virus, it is the locator beacon of the System core, that is all."

"And it's started on its own? Why has it started to broadcast now? It could be a trick."

"A trick by whom?" said Amir.

"The virus?"

"The virus is not intelligent!" said Moore.

"We don't know that. We don't know what other traps the designer of the virus built into it," said Yuri.

"We have to be careful," said Amir. "We cannot afford to be infected by the virus again. But can we afford not to investigate?"

Sand sat forward with such swiftness everyone in the room looked at her. She was grinning in that way she had when she was about to lay out an idea no one else was going to like.

"I've got an idea," she said. "A good one."

"Let me guess. You want to go into the nightside," said Plock, who had taken Dariusz's place. She shot him a look and he became abashed. It was no secret Plock was fond of her. "I mean, we all know how brave you are, Sand."

"Reckless," said Corrigan. Corrigan and Sand were close, and he said it with good humour, but Yuri knew her headstrong nature wore at him.

"By air?" said Brzezinska.

"How else?" said Kościelniak. "It *is* Councillor De Mona talking."

"Please go on, councillor," said Amir.

"We fly there. I've designed a new airplane. Bigger, more durable. Range might be a problem, but if we drive in close and take off close to the terminator, and send a tanker through to top it up, it should work. I could get you all the way there."

"Two aeroplanes through the storm? In-flight fuelling? It's a bold plan. Your Mark IV plane is not up to the task, surely," said Amir.

Sand pulled a face. She was less guarded in her dislike of Amir than anyone else. "I did just say I designed a bigger one, didn't

I? I did. Good. Not the Mark IV, the Mark V. It'll take three months to build the aircraft. I'll need more fabricator time."

A general groan at this. Everyone needed more fabricator time.

"I can get it built, and it will get through the storm belt into the nightside," she said. She leaned on the table, her arms tense, looking at them all, defying them to disagree. Even Sand, thought Yuri, an otherwise decent person, is only at her most vociferous when promoting the things she is personally passionate about.

Amir sighed. "And pilots, Councillor De Mona? Do we have pilots of sufficient skill?"

She shrugged. "I'll do it. I'll fly lead, I should be able to get it through the storms and out the other side, no problem."

"Out of the question," said Amir.

"I am sorry, Councillor," said Moore, "but you are too valuable to risk. We've lost enough expertise as it is."

"I say, let her go. If anyone can do it, Sand can," said Plock.

There was much talking around the table. Amir called for silence. "We'll put it to the vote," he said. Yuri smiled to himself. Amir was a creature of circumstance, once the autocrat, now the democrat. As long as he was important enough to count, he didn't care how his importance was decided upon.

"I move that Councillor De Mona remain here," said Moore. "Sorry, Sand," he said, "you're too important. You're a fine engineer, a valued member of this council. Who will train our other pilots? Your knowledge of aeronautics is better than anyone's."

"Not true," she said.

"Nearly everyone's, then. You're too important," said Marina, who had been elected to the council a few months before.

"I agree, Sand," said Corrigan. "Sorry."

"I'm the only one skilled enough to get through the storm belt!"

"What about your apprentice? Kasia?" said Brzezinska.

"Kasia? She's not ready."

"This is the Kasia who flew bombing runs on the natives and who has been flying with you practically every day since?" said Loewen. He said it kindly, with a smile.

"She's not ready."

"Then make her ready," said Amir. "We cannot afford to lose your expertise. Think of your daughter."

"Kasia *is* my daughter."

"You know what I mean, Sand. You have a two-year old daughter as well as Kasia, one of the few pregnancies here to be brought to term. Would you leave your child motherless?" said Amir.

"Sand, Sand, please listen," said Corrigan. "We have too many orphans as it is."

"You're saying I'm not expendable, but Kasia is?"

"If you have to put it in such bald terms, then I too will be direct. Yes, Kasia is less valuable to the colony than you are. We all have our part to play in making this colony work, De Mona, and yours is not to go off on a dangerous venture like this," said Amir.

"It's an in-and-out mission. Just a scouting run. I'll be back in no time."

"We can't risk you, we're sorry."

"You're worse than Anderson," she said. She regretted it instantly, became contrite. "Sorry," she said. She stood, then walked out.

"Sand!" shouted Corrigan. He rose.

Yuri finally spoke. "Oh, let her go. We'll just have to listen to her roaring at you for ten minutes. We've told her what we think. The plan is a good one in principle, I think she's more than capable of designing an airplane up to the job, but Amir is right, we can't lose her. We need to vote."

Sand waited outside for the deliberations to finish. The motion was passed, the expedition was to go ahead. Piotr and Kasia would fly the aircraft.

Sand was to remain behind.

KASIA'S CONFIDENCE IN the air grew rapidly. Sand had her flying the Mark IV daily as soon as the prototype cleared its tests, a process that, though fast-tracked, took a week. During that time Kasia chafed, eager to be off the ULs and at the controls of the larger craft. The seven days of its final checks dragged by, and Kasia's snappy attitude, shed long since, returned on the back of her frustration. For a while the young woman became catty. Flying the ULs or working on the new planes did not placate her. Some disapproved of her irritation, and said Sand was a bad influence. They said Kasia had adopted Sand's maverick approach to life, and was inclined to impatience and running her mouth off when things did not go her way.

This was unkind. Kasia did not share Sand's antagonism to authority, and worked well as an intermediary between the council and the chief pilot when Sand's temper got the better of her. But for those few days before the Mark IV plane was cleared for regular flight, she became more like her guardian, and there were those who feared she would turn viper-tongued permanently. There was general relief when Kasia returned to her normal, thoughtful self, once the Mark IV was ready for regular use.

Sand didn't give a damn for what others thought. She laughed at Kasia's pleading to be allowed to fly the IV, although not unkindly. She kept her disappointment from Kasia, and most of her fear for her safety. No point making the girl terrified, she thought, resolving to train her as well as she could. Sand figured she could go one of two ways with her protégée: keep her from harm, or train her to minimise it. She opted for the latter. Sand was delighted how much Kasia loved flying, and was keen to goad her to greater need. In short, Sand was lonely, even if she did not realise it, and was happy to see Kasia, who she already regarded as a daughter, growing into a kindred spirit.

Once Kasia's flying lessons in the heavier plane commenced, their bond as airwomen grew. Kasia was an avid student. The two of them flew as often as time, weather and fuel allowed, and when they could not, Kasia studied. In the meantime, work commenced on the Mark V, the heaviest aircraft yet, and closest to a true terran aeroplane. It was to have a co-pilot station, an enclosed cockpit, and a separate gun turret, for away from the radar noise of First Landing, the wildlife remained a problem.

The Mark V aeroplanes were delayed, three months became four. Despite her desire to train her students, Sand got cold feet, and when the planes were ready, she protested that Kasia and Piotr were not. They flew endless sorties in the new aeroplanes, practising the refuelling manoeuvre over and over until even the most risk averse among them could see planes and pilots were ready.

The council grew impatient. Kasia grew impatient. They argued. Eventually, Sand relented.

"There's one more thing we have to do," she said to Kasia. "We have to fly into the weather front and back out again. I want to see you do it."

They set out into the gathering night, the sun at their backs. The plane was performing well. It was strong, Sand told herself: woven skeleton, woven wings, proper technology. They were going to need it. When the *Lublin* had blasted through the Veil of Storms that marked the terminator, she'd barely noticed it. This would be different.

The scrub changed to glossy grassland, the near-black grass rippling in the breeze, accentuating Evening Country's dreamlike quality as they passed into Twilight. The rain fell more frequently here, so close to the storm band. It pattered on the cockpit.

"Kasia," Sand said. Her apprentice was concentrating, but there was an ease to her flying that impressed her. Her heart swelled with pride and affection for her charge. "Be careful, here, okay? I've no idea how big this storm is, and I don't know how powerful it is."

Kasia adjusted her trim, checked the instruments. She shot Sand a reassuring smile. "We'll be okay."

"I have to grab that stick just once, you're not going, do you understand?"

Kasia nodded. "You won't have to."

Darkness pulled itself in on them quickly. The boiling clouds of the storm belt sucked the vestiges of Evening Country's wine-gold sunlight from the sky. They were in Twilight, and the ramparts of True Night were ahead of them, sinister as nightmare. Lightning lit up the rolling curves of the clouds from within, or stabbed down in rod-straight lines. The hot air of the dayside, laden with moisture from the sea, ran into the cold air of the nightside. There was little Coriolis effect on the tidally locked planet; strong winds blew from high to low pressure in straight lines. They pushed at the plane, hurrying it on to the stormfront.

"Be careful, honey, okay?"

Kasia did not respond, but accelerated.

The dividing line between storm and calm was as pronounced as the line between night and day. The Veil of Storms remained roughly in the same place all year round, only moving during the erratic rainy seasons. It was like flying into a wall.

The plane lurched immediately, bouncing through air cells of differing temperature and speed. Kasia fought the stick to bring it back into line. Rain hammered off their cockpit roof, streaking the windshield. Thunder boomed nearby. Spears of lightning stabbed past them. Electricity coursed over the plane's fuselage, dissipating from the five static wicks affixed to the bottom. "Don't worry about the lightning too much," Sand said. "Concentrate on staying level. Airflow's going to be chaotic, all over the place in here. Stay level!"

Kasia and Sand used the artificial horizon, as it was impossible to get a visual bearing. The plane dropped and bucked, thrown up almost as quickly as it went down. Kasia wrestled with the stick.

"Don't fight it too hard!" said Sand. "If you overcompensate you'll lose control. Hold it gently. Respond, don't anticipate."

The whine of the twin props' engines rose and fell as the plane's airspeed shifted unexpectedly. Sand glanced at the stick. Her hand twitched toward it more than once. She hated being a passenger, hated not being in control. She had no influence over her own fate this way, she was in another's hands.

Forty minutes the tossing went on, before suddenly it ceased and the plane levelled out. The engines stopped complaining. One final bump that made them both gasp, and they were clear. Fog carpeted the ground below them.

"Holy fuck," said Sand. Kasia crossed herself. Sand laughed and let go of the edge of her seat. She hadn't realised she'd been gripping it. "That was one hell of a ride. Well done, Kash, well done. What's the fuel situation?"

Kasia glanced at the gauge. "Two-thirds full."

"Not bad, we can count on another four hundred kilometres with the buddy plane before they have to turn round. Better range than I expected. It'll get you most of the way there." Sand patted the inside of the cockpit. "Not a bad little flier. You too, Kasia." She frowned.

"What? I thought I did well."

"You did."

"Then why do you look so worried?"

"Because you're ready. I'm going to have to let you make the trip. I've delayed enough. And I don't want you to go. Once Piotrek's shown he can do the same thing, that's it. You're going."

Kasia yanked the stick over and sent the plane into a wide bank.

"Don't get too mushy, Sand," said Kasia. "I have to get us back through the storm first."

CHAPTER TWENTY-TWO
Into the Night

FOUR DAYS BEFORE the aerial expedition into the nightside, a small convoy of militia and fuel trucks crossed the river and headed north, towing a bulldozer on a flatbed behind them. Sand, Kasia, Piotr and the other pilots spent the next few days in preparation, checking and rechecking the planes. Their conversation stuck rigidly to the matters at hand, except for now and then, when Sand or Kasia would remember something funny, and they would laugh. But the task ahead was sobering in its immensity – their shared recollections only made it seem more so – and for the most part they worked in professional silence.

The majority of the town's inhabitants turned out and came down to the landing field to see them off. Amir made a speech, his thinning hair and council tabard flapping ridiculously in the wind. Dust was getting in all their eyes.

Sand paid little attention to his words. Instead, she cast her eyes over the airfield. Seven aircraft now sat in their reinforced hangars. The doors were open, and other members of Sand's coterie of pilots and engineers leaned against the craft, watching the departure. Her daughter was there, watching calmly from the arms of Gosia, the traffic control girl. She was untroubled by the affair. The hangar was her home, the engineers her family, and she was independent as her mother already.

The wall to Airtown bounded the edge nearest to First Landing; a long chain link fence and ditch surrounded the rest. The shuttles, useless, squatted like bad memories at the far end of the runway. The airfield had grown. The whole place had. It looked like a proper town now, she thought.

First Landing was a prison to Sand. They were not so much keeping the wildlife out as keeping themselves in. Only her planes set her free. A shudder ran through her, the aftershocks of tension draining away. She had been tense for a long time, before the planes had been built, and then when Kasia had been chosen to go. The expedition aircraft were proper machines, worthy machines for her apprentice. Her young daughter cheerfully waved from the hangar; she waved back, and her heart twinged. She glanced at Kasia. Her hand strayed to her stomach. She was leaving her daughter behind. Amir was right, it didn't feel right. But nor did letting Kasia go.

"And on this historic occasion…" Amir droned. Sand figured he lacked a podium. He certainly looked like he wanted one. *Pompous* was one word Sand used for him; the rest were less kind.

There were seven aeronauts. Kasia, of course; Piotr, who would pilot the refuelling plane; Marcin and Malgorzata, their co-pilots; then Günther Plock and a Dutch girl named Kim, who would man the rear gun mounts. Sand had argued and argued with the council until they'd relented and allowed her to go to the temporary airstrip, outside the Veil of Storms. Plock was going through, as gunner on the fuel plane, despite Amir's great protest. He'd threatened to resign from the council if he wasn't allowed along. Sand had tried the same trick, but had been voted down. Plock was either more persistent, or Amir didn't feel he was irreplaceable.

The twin mounted machine guns poked out from a clear shield behind the cockpit. They had little idea what was on the nightside, heavy calibre guns seemed an appropriate precaution. Sand had insisted the planes also carry a weaponised EM deterrent, just in case. This had sparked some talk of using Anderson's technology on the ground again, but the background emissions of the town kept most of the lifeforms away anyway, and so reinstating the radar fence was not a popular idea.

Amir finished his speech with a dry platitude. The crowd applauded with sincerity. *All we need is a fucking brass band,* Sand thought.

Kasia said thank you, and promised to do her best. The crowd cheered again.

"Right," said Sand irritably. "Let's get going."

They clambered into the airplanes. Kasia and Sand sat up front in theirs, Marcin taking a backseat for the trip to the temporary airfield.

They started their engines. Talk went back and forth with traffic control. The crowd retreated. The planes taxied out onto the runway, Piotr behind Kasia, twin propellers dragging corkscrews of dust from the runway. With admirable skill, the two young pilots took them into the sky. They cleared the virgin fields and firing zone around the mesas fast, the circle of scraped earth ending in a line as severe as the terminator. First Landing fell away behind them, untamed scrub rushed by below. Night beckoned.

They flew a straight course through empty skies. The wind was strong, but behind them as always, and so they went quickly. Sand barely paid attention to Kasia's flying any more. She stared out of the window instead, watching the procession of bushes and low trees whisk by, their shadows long on the ground. Vegetation thickened. A family of the ruminants they called heavy feet walked below. Spines on their backs waved in stately manner from side to side as they plodded through the thorns, heads down. They did not look up at the sky as the planes passed.

Sand saw the broken mound of the natives' home, still fire-blackened from the purging. She felt ashamed looking at it. They had encountered no other natives, and she was dogged by the idea they'd wiped out the planet's only indigenous intelligent life almost without thought. She wondered too what would have happened had they not found the machinery within. Would Dariusz still be with her?

She took off her headphones and rested her head on the cockpit plastic. She didn't like to think about that; she had never organised her feelings for him satisfactorily, and bearing his child only made it more confusing.

The buzz of the engines lulled her to sleep. She did not wake again until they were coming in to land at the temporary airstrip near to the Veil of Storms.

* * *

SAND SLEPT BADLY that night. She left the tent where Kasia slept and paced the inner perimeter of the camp until she was sent back to her tent by the militia. "It's not safe," they said. "Please return to your tent, ma'am."

She was about to protest, but then figured they had enough on their hands patrolling the camp without having her to worry about.

The landing field was flat. That was all that recommended it as a landing field. Thick, tubular grass covered the land around it, so dark with photosynthetic compounds as to be almost black, and tough enough to foul landing gear. The sun was a hint, a pale glow to the south. This was Twilight Country. To the north was only the night, and the storm that was its teeth.

Sand tugged at the tube grasses. On the strip, the preparation crew had burned them back, then bulldozed them so the planes could operate. It was an ugly stripe of earth, made uglier by the harsh white of the spotlights trained upon it. Humanity wounds the land wherever it goes, she thought. After a couple of years here, she was beginning to understand how the Earth might once have been, and what it had lost in bearing its children.

Children. Her daughter, Dariusz's daughter, had brought her much joy and much heartache. Once she had thought there was a great mystery to parenthood. Having her own had only confirmed that there was. She still didn't have a clue, only now she understood the big secret: nobody else did either.

She twisted a grass stalk hard, idly seeing if she could break it. She couldn't. She looked at the row of tents, black against the pale southern heavens, the trucks parked neatly behind them. Things moved out there, things with their own lights blinking. They kept away.

She watched the animals of the twilight move around the camp, their lightshows blazing, and came to a decision. She acted without a moment's hesitation, never one for reflection.

She went to Piotr's tent and woke him up. She felt bad disappointing the kid, but it had to be done; for her own peace of mind, if nothing else.

* * *

FIRST THING IN the morning, Kasia went to check on the filling of the refuelling plane's tanks. Men and women bustled about the aircraft, thick pipes leading from the tankers they had driven to the plane.

Piotr stood to one side, sullen but uncomplaining.

"Piotr?" she said. "Are you okay?"

"I'm supposed to be ill," he said.

"Supposed to be?"

"Sand," he said. He shrugged.

Plock laid a hand on his shoulder. "Don't worry, little man, she does it because she cares. You're a good pilot, from what I hear, you'll get your moment."

"You know about this?"

Plock shrugged. "You can't tell me you're surprised."

Kasia went off to find the pilot. She found her in their tent, suiting up.

"What are you doing?" said Kasia. "Sand!"

"I'm coming with you," she said.

"But the council... It's too dangerous, Sand, please!"

Sand tugged hard at the fastening on her clothes. The days of automatically sealing clothes were long behind them. "Fuck the council, and fuck the danger. I can't let you go alone."

"Sand –"

"Leave it, honey." Sand walked up to Kasia and put her hand to the girl's cheek. Her voice hushed. "I can't let my baby girl go through the storm alone."

"I'm not your baby girl," said Kasia. "She's at home." She said it very quietly; it was a fact, but not an emotional truth. She pressed her face into the older woman's hand.

"Yes, you are." Sand smiled sadly. "I wish it were me going instead, honey, but it isn't, it's you. I suppose you deserve it; it's a big adventure, the kind of thing that made me want to be a spacer in the first place, the kind of thing that makes you want to fly. I'll come through the storm, refuel you, just to make sure you get through okay. Then I'm going to wait right here until you come back."

Kasia nodded, her eyes closed; Sand withdrew her hand.

"Hey! You, Ayvazian is it? I'm stepping in as second pilot. The boy Piotr is feeling ill. Aren't you Piotr…"

There was less ceremony at the makeshift landing field than there had been at First Landing. Breakfast. Little chat. A brief farewell, a message from Amir. Sand gave Ayvazian the darkest look she could muster when he suggested informing Amir of the change in flight crew. The Veil of Storms oppressed them all. From time to time they heard the crack of its thunders, faint but threatening.

Kasia was glad to get into the plane. It responded well, lifting them up into the sky smoothly. Their camp dwindled below, becoming an oasis of light in the gloom until the curve of the world shut it off. The dark thickened with every metre until the last afterglow of the sun vanished below the horizon and they were at the very edge of True Night.

"Airspeed 130kph," said Marcin. His voice was broken and high-pitched through Kasia's headphones. He held a map upon his knees. He gripped instruments in his hands; more hung from strings on his chest. The plane bounced. He looked up.

"It gets worse from here on in," said Kasia.

The aeroplane jounced constantly, so hard it made her teeth clack. Lightning blasted at them every few seconds, so often she felt she was under fire. They were not hit. The planes were designed to be non-conducting, to deny a bridge between the electrons streaming up from the ground and the lightning's leaders. The static they picked up bled away from the wicks under the plane. But it was frightening, and Kasia heard Kim exclaiming in fear over the radio.

Then it was over. They burst through the wall of rain and light and into Nychthemeron's nightside. She checked her radar: nothing. She feared for Sand, until a strong return pulse indicated that she too had come through. Mist drifted in patches below, and above them was a ceiling of cloud. They flew in the clear space between.

"Heya, honey," said Sand. "That was pretty hairy, you all okay in there?"

"Yes," said Kasia, although looking at Marcin, she thought she might be pushing the definition of 'okay.'

"Alright, let's fly on until I'm close to half empty, then let's line up and fill you up."

She didn't say, "Then I'm going to have to say goodbye." Kasia sensed it in her words.

"Okay, locking onto the locator beacon. Marcin?"

"Got it," he said.

Kasia lined the plane up. Marcin kept a close eye on the radar. They flew on, heading toward the chittering beat of the Syscore's locator beacon. It repeated on a loop, the same tuneless, digital ditty, a break of half a second between each repetition. *Dit-dit-dit-dah-dah-dit-dah-dit.* Several hours went by. Lights moved in the fog. When the mist cleared, swathes of the landscape were carpeted in some kind of vegetation that gave out a phantom glow. Sand and Kasia talked now and then about what they could see, trying to match their vision to the radar screen, which pulsed with contacts large and small. Every so often, some huge, dark body would come toward them, flying fast, alive with gold and red lights, blue tips to its wings and tails. Kim was vigilant at her gunnery post, but Marcin engaged the EM deterrents, and the lifeforms swung away from them.

"So much light," said Sand. "So much light in the dark!"

The sky was thick with cloud – perhaps the rains were building again – but every now and then the sky cleared and the travellers were afforded a view of the open heavens. While they flew under the canopy of stars, they were silent.

Eventually their fuel tank indicators made their alarms, announcing the time for the refuelling to begin and for Sand to return. Sand's airplane drew in close, navigational lights winking. Kasia dropped back until she was trailing it. A long hose deployed from the rear of Sand's plane, a cone on the end. Kasia lined the probe on the nose of her plane up with the nozzle. In-flight refuelling is difficult. Sand and Kasia had none of the benefits of computer systems or other guidance. They did it all by hand, eye and radar. It took many attempts, and Marcin grew anxious at their fuel consumption. Not for their sake, but for Sand's.

With the gentlest bump, the line slid home. Lights on the dashboard lit up to show they were taking on fuel. It was done in fifteen minutes. Kasia eased back and dropped underneath Sand's plane, then flew alongside them, waggled her wings in salute then turned and flew away.

"Be careful, honey," Sand said. "When you come home, I'll be waiting."

KASIA WAS IN that nowhere space of concentration, where somatic function gives way to unconscious direction and the mind is freed to wander. She flew without thinking, toward the strengthening signal of the Systems core. The True Night was a marbled land of phantom green and utter black. Sparks of light moved over it. She moved through the clouds, a spark of light herself.

They were close when a loud return sounded from the radar. "Kasia," said Marcin.

She shook herself into full awareness.

"Look," he said, pointing. "Something's coming." He fumbled his map and instruments from his lap, adjusted the radar's controls to get a better fix. "Something big. Keep an eye out there, Kim. Six o'clock, or thereabouts."

"Got you," said the girl. Motors whirred behind their heads as the gun turret swept round. "I'm not seeing anything."

"It's there alright," said Marcin. "Very big. Activating EM deterrent, we'll be radar blind for a second."

The radar gave out ten fleeting pings as Marcin turned on the deterrent. It returned to normal. Kasia glanced at the round screen. "Has it gone?"

"Hang on... Maybe. Wait."

A solid ping, a large return.

"No," he said. "EM had no effect."

"Okay," said Kasia. She pushed forward, putting the aeroplane into a steep dive.

"It's still coming."

"I can't see anything," said Kim.

"Watch your seven. It's getting closer... 700 metres. Can you see anything yet?"

"Dammit, Marcin, it's pitch black out there!"

"No lights?"

"Nothing!"

Kasia pushed the plane faster.

"Still coming. It's gaining. How the... We're doing nearly 300kph. Impossible."

"Nothing's impossible," said Kasia. She kept switching her gaze to the radar screen and back again.

"Whatever it is, it's big," said Marcin, "and it's changing shape."

The return on the radar showed as a luminous green blob. With each sweep of their plane's pulse, it took on a different form: first kidney shaped, then a long ellipse, then round.

"I see it!" shouted Kim. A second later, the guns rattled. They were loud, unsuppressed, the technology manufactured here more primitive than what they'd arrived with.

The shape was close to the plane. Kasia could not get the plane to fly any faster.

"What the hell? Crabhawk?" shouted Marcin behind him.

"No!" replied Kim. "Like a cloud, many lights. A swarm of something."

They hit. Hard bodies rattled against the plane's fuselage like hail. The din was terrific, Kim's gunfire lost within it. "I can't hit them!" she screamed. "They're too small!"

Kasia glanced to her right, out of the window. Small things were scrabbling at the clear plastic. Hooked limbs scraped along as the creatures grappled with the plane. She saw a wide, tentacle-fringed mouth work against the glass, set under a long, comma-shaped body. Pale lights glimmered upon it; something like wings. Then it was gone, torn away by their speed. More took its place.

"Shit!" said Kim. "They're all over us. What do I do?"

The cockpit too was getting thick with them; more were landing than were being torn away. There was an engine's tortured cough, and the noise of the props diminished, replaced by a puttering sound. An alarm sounded, amber lights blinking frantically. "We've lost the starboard engine!" Marcin shouted.

Kasia struggled to compensate. Through gaps in the swarm she could see slick bodies all over her wing, disrupting the airflow and pulling it down.

More alarms. Another cough. "Port engine fouled!" shouted Marcin.

"Hang on!" shouted Kasia.

The rattle of the creatures against the hull changed in character, soft thumps as bodies hit bodies. The plane dipped. She pulled hard on the stick. Her flaps were clogged. A loud cracking noise, then a scream. Kim: "Get them off me! Get them off me!" She grew increasingly panicked, incoherent.

Kim's screams cut out in their headphones.

Marcin glanced nervously at the hatch leading to the gun turret over their heads. "There's nothing we can do, nothing!"

"Shitshitshitshitshit," said Kasia. "Marcin, bail out!"

"The things! Kim! She's dead."

"Bail out now!"

Marcin hammered his seatbelt off. The plane was tilting. He staggered as he went backwards to the door. Wind roar filled the cabin as he hauled it open. Creatures flopped into the cockpit. He threw himself out without a backward glance.

Kasia wrestled with the stick, crying out as something bit into her shoulder. Then another. It became too much, and she released the stick, flailing at the creatures. The altimeter was spinning round and round.

A bang. Another bang. Rending noises, tumbling. She might have blacked out, she wasn't sure.

She was suddenly awake. The stink of fuel hit her nostrils. She smashed at the belt release, fell forward with the tilt of the plane. Her ankle twisted painfully, caught in the pedals mangled in her footwell, and she wrenched it free. There was a soft noise, of fuel igniting.

She staggered back, teeth digging into her lip at the pain in her foot. The creatures had stopped biting her; a few still in the cockpit moved feebly. Blood ran down her back. She grabbed her pack from the rack by the door, and stepped out into the night.

The plane was at an angle, nose down and top presented to her, in a tree that glowed pale green. In the firelight, through the shattered mess of the gun turret's transparent cover, she saw the bloodied remains of Kim. And then the fire took hold, and she scrambled away as quickly as she could, pushing herself from tree trunk to tree trunk to save her injured ankle.

She was close enough when the fuel tanks exploded for the shockwave to send her sprawling. Liquid fire rained down; she beat frantically at her arm where it touched her. The strange, contorted limbs of the alien trees were alight with flowers of borrowed flame. Their foliage stirred, whisking back into the holes that lined every branch, leaving them bare.

A cacophony of animal noises sounded from the dark around her, a darkness made deeper by the glow of fire.

She ripped open her bag, panic making her clumsy. She found the first aid kit, snatched up her pad and quickly scanned her ankle. The machine gave its diagnosis and treatment. Not broken, lightly sprained, anti-inflammatories, pain management, rest.

She could manage the first two. Yanking a hypospray and a cannister from the first aid case, she lifted her trouser leg and pressed the cold plastic into her flesh. A hiss, a tickle, the pain receded. Her ankle salved, her arm throbbed, as if to remind her it was burned. Another scan, another shot of pain relief. Her back then, awkward angle. No toxins, not that the pad could detect. Two bites. She'd been lucky.

Cautiously she stood, placing weight as carefully as she could upon her injured ankle. It bore her with little complaint. She made an exploratory step; stiff, sore, but workable. That was one thing, she supposed.

The night was a wall of black beyond the fire. A rumbling call had her turning, breath catching in her throat. She strained her ears. Something moved off to her right.

The pop of flames was already dying. Nothing else but that and the thunder of her heart.

She was alone in the night.

CHAPTER TWENTY-THREE
Kasia in the Nightside

KASIA LIMPED BACK along the line of devastation her airplane had carved through the forest. Fog insinuated itself into the trees. The light intensified, illuminating the mists with a pervasive, shadowless glow that challenged her eyes to make sense of it. Away from the wreck, the trees were garlanded with fronded leaves that moved with animal purpose, wafting in the air like anemones in a current. Limbs had been torn off the plants and cast to the ground, and she saw they were large, heavy, made of something like stone. Sap ran freely as blood from the wounded organisms, pulped flesh in revealed cavities. Where the plane had cut, they glowed dimly. She kept to the edge of the scar where the light was stronger. Her feet crunched on twigs like fingerbones. She shivered. With the fog came a chill, and her breath gusted from her mouth in clouds to mingle with it.

The further she went, the less damage to the forest she saw, until only by craning her neck could she make out broken spear tips of stone at the very tops, dark where they had been wounded. The forest became the insubstantial cathedral to some indescribable alien god; stone trees its pillars and vaulting, its walls of luminous chill vapour. The night-time noises returned, loud and terrifying. She saw many creatures flit into view and disappear again – insect analogues, strange bat-things with multiple wings, something like a cross between a millipede and a snake, swift and with a noisome stink; other creatures were shapes, they were nightmares. She lacked the mental architecture to process their forms from a single glimpse, they were too unearthly.

Larger animals moved around her; past her, toward her, she couldn't tell in the fog. And the trees – the trees were not trees but sessile beasts. The feelers that protruded from the trunks glittered a hundred entrancing colours. She watched as small, ant-like things stroked at them with their hind limbs, gathering the fronds into bunches and then scuttling away. One of these ants was snatched up as it approached, and pulled inside the trunk with a watery hiss. Others of the same type were left alone.

She heard a cackle, and a thrash of movement overhead. She followed it, found simian shapes bouncing through the skeletal canopy. They converged on something with hoots of excitement.

She pulled a torch from her backpack, and flicked it on.

Marcin hung from the tree, his arms caught up grotesquely in his parachute lines. The monkey things fled from his corpse as she approached. His flightsuit was torn, blood glinted blackly on his legs. He had hit hard. His parachute might not have opened, or he'd made his jump too late. She couldn't remember what the altimeter had read, all she remembered was the swarm, rasping on the fuselage. She didn't know if she'd done the right thing. Marcin was dead in either case. She was sad for his death, and Kim's, but not greatly affected. She had seen a lot of death in her lifetime. She would mourn when the situation allowed.

There was a noise in the forest, heavy breathing, the crash and crumble of the corals breaking. It was approaching her. She backed away, shone her torch into the dark. There was nothing. Her back met a coral trunk. A frond whipped her face, wet with caustic slime that burned her cheek. She stifled a cry and wiped at it.

The forest dimmed. Animals rushed away. The fronds of the trees retreated.

There came a snuffling, a louder bellow, and something huge burst through the fog and the trees into her circle of torchlight – massive shoulders, long arms ending in claws that curved halfway up its forearms, walking on its knuckles. Two pairs of lesser legs propelled it forward, twelve eyes lined its long muzzle. It carried no lights on its skin, which was mottled grey and black.

She turned and ran. The creature burst through the coral, its bulk shattering branches and cracking trunks as it pursued her. It roared loudly. Kasia ran, a hobble that was no match for the monster's speed. She wove through narrow gaps, headed for larger coral trees to dodge through and behind, but the creature barely slowed. The rattle of its fists and feet on the bony litter of the forest drew closer behind her. She snagged her pack on a branch, and it was ripped from her. She fell forward, rolled onto her back, pedalled herself backwards as fast as she could, trying to get away.

The creature ran at her. It reared up, foreclaws unfolded to pin her to the ground. Its mouth gaped bright rows of teeth. There was the sound of a weapon, the rising hum of a rail gun. The creature's face disappeared in a shower of black blood, and it fell onto its chest. It skidded to a halt by her feet, gave a last gurgling breath, and was still.

She scrambled to her feet, turned to run, and ran smack into a man who grabbed her upper arms in calloused hands. He held her with ease, and her treacherous body went limp.

She didn't recognise him at first. His teeth were worn and brown in his mouth, his hair unkempt. His beard reached to his chest, and his skin was seamed with dirt. He stank too, in a pungent, bestial way. His smartsuit had died upon him, and was as filthy as its owner. But it was unmistakably Dariusz, the great betrayer, alive and well and looking at her.

"Dariusz?" she said.

He nodded. His mouth opened a second before he spoke, awaiting forgotten words. "Hello, Kasia," he said. "It's nice to see you."

He looked past her, into the night. "Get your things," he said abruptly. "Then we better go home."

She stared at him. She could not imagine anyone surviving in this chill, midnight hell. "Home?"

He smiled. "My place."

DARIUSZ LED HER through the dark, his railgun over his shoulder and a pistol at his side. There was a little more light here, intensifying as the strange land-corals of the nightside grew more thickly. The fog remained thick, and she lost all sense of where they were. Dariusz, however, moved unerringly. Small animals ran up and down the trunks, bodies pulsing with vibrant displays of bioluminescence; ruby reds and blues the colour of broken glaciers, deep greens and rich, honeyed yellows. A pair of eyes appeared before her. They were a metre apart, and rose steadily into the air, a warning hiss emanating from between them.

"Dariusz!" she said.

Dariusz glanced at it. "Look closer. Don't worry, it can't hurt you."

She walked towards the eyes carefully. The fog pulled back to reveal the trick. The eyes were spots on modified mouth rakes, belonging to a sinuous creature no bigger than her forearm. As she drew near to it, the rakes snapped shut, and animal raced up the quivering flesh of the beast-tree into an abscess. She gasped at it.

"It had no eyes. Why does it fluoresce?"

"Because the things that hunt it do have eyes, like the creature that attacked you, and the lights it makes are its camouflage, a trick." Dariusz stepped over a root protruding from a coral chimney. It flopped around, clumsily reaching for him. "Watch your step here, the fronds and roots burn. Not too bad, but uncomfortable."

"I know," she said, and touched her cheek.

"Did you wipe it off?"

"Yes."

He nodded.

"How did you know to find me?" she said.

"My ATV's sensor suite still functions," he said. "I tracked you as soon as you came into range. I plotted your course, figured you must be looking for the Syscore after its signal went up. I thought I'd try and send a signal or something. You shouldn't have come, it's dangerous here. What brought you down?"

"A swarm of... I don't know how to describe them. Some sort of small creature in a swarm. They chewed through the airplane fuselage."

Dariusz shrugged. "I am not familiar with those."

"They were high up, a kilometre altitude. They died when we came down."

"Curious," said Dariusz.

"Everything here is curious!" she said. "It is strange that the animals on the dayside are nearly all eyeless," said Kasia, "and here in the dark they are not."

"Not really," said Dariusz. "At least, no stranger than anything else in nature. Think of eyes: all eyes as we know them are delicate. The sand, the never-setting sun. Dangerous to such a delicate organ. It's no surprise to me that the pseudo-arthropods are the dominant clade in the desert. As I've been here it's become clear to me that life must have evolved in the liminal zone and spread into the nightside, then from here colonised the dayside. The conditions are too harsh on the dayside for life to develop, as they are at the far pole here."

"Have you been there? What's it like?"

"I've not been so far. Far enough for the temperature to drop to an unbearable level, but certainly not far enough to see the ice sheet. That is a thousand more kilometres from here. I only drove a few hundred in that direction, once I'd found the Syscore. The forest gives out there, and it is much colder. I lost my nerve when it snowed. After that, I returned and – well, you'll see."

They pressed on. The coral forest was alive with noise. More than once Dariusz told her to remain silent as something crashed through the coral limbs. The noises were unnerving, roars and stridulating barks, the *crunch* of coral limbs cracked apart, their polyps devoured, the cries of creatures snared and eaten.

"Do you remember Earth?" he said.

"Yes, yes I do. I was fifteen when we left."

"Earth used to be like this, before we came along," said Dariusz dourly. "Or so I've read. Once upon a time, our home supported much more variety, at a time when its biomass potential was not taken up by human flesh."

"Sand told me you never talked much." She ducked under a coral limb, avoiding filaments that darted from holes to lick at her. "I don't remember you talking so much."

"That was then. I was bereaved, I was ridden by guilt. I made the gravest error a man can make, perhaps one of the gravest any man has ever made. But I am as blind as the next person, as much in service to my own needs and preconceptions as every other human being that ever has been, or will be. I have had a lot of time to think about what I did. I cannot entirely blame my nature, we are rational after all, should we allow ourselves to be. The introduction of the virus was my choice, and it was freely taken. Time smooths pain away, and the pressures of survival have kept me occupied. For very many months, I thought I would simply give up, and let the planet devour me. But as much as I thought I desired this, I did not let it happen." He paused. "I have had no one to talk to for a year. I am tired of the silence. My soul yearns for communion with another human, if you like." He laughed at his own words. "We are almost there. We must go faster. The air is clearing and the trees glow strongly only when the fogs come. It is more dangerous when the trees are dark."

'Almost there' meant another hour of hard walking. True to Dariusz's word, the fog drifted away and the forest dimmed. Kasia and he stumbled toward his dwelling. How he navigated in such poor conditions was a marvel. There was not a spot of level ground in the place, and she was concerned that she would turn her injured foot, but he moved with sureness, if slowly, and she gradually surrendered herself into his trust.

"We are here," he said eventually. The trees ended and he led her into a wide clearing, a space some hundred and fifty metres across. A sloping wall of stacked coral stone trunks corralled the centre.

"Home, sweet home," he said in English.

"You did all this?"

"I have had some help," he said. "The robots."

"The robots are here?" she said, surprised.

"They are. They came to me soon after I wrecked the ATV. They come to me every so often, bringing me ammunition and other things, although they refused to repair the vehicle. I have been told..." He trailed off, close to saying something he shouldn't. "You will see tomorrow," he said. "It is hard to explain, and I do not think you will believe me. It is best you see for yourself. Without this redoubt, I would have died many times over. Life is violent in the night. The land corals add nutrients and minerals, but without sunlight, the primary source of energy is the flesh of others. You will find few true plants here. This side of the world is fuelled by death."

He led her through a narrow gap that went into a switchback passage, difficult for the larger creatures of the night to negotiate. There was a heavy gate at the end, made of something ligneous like wood, the stalks of a large, many-stemmed fungus that infested the corals, he said. He reached through and unlatched it, and they were into his home.

The ATV that he stole from the colony was in the dead centre of his fort. By the build-up of simple sheds and the fungus logs stacked around it, it had not moved for some time.

"I ripped out the axles," he explained. "I had come back from my trip toward the far pole, I had become a little paranoid, I think. I'd seen too many bizarre sights. My mind was straining to contain them all. I was driving too fast, caught it on a stump, and bang. There you are. I've been here ever since."

"How long?"

"About ten months," he said. "By Terran reckoning, or so I think. It's hard to keep track. I mark down the passage of every twenty-four hours with the pad, and, in case that fails, with those." He pointed out a mass of thick, black tally marks on the corral wall. "I've become wary of technology. It gives out on me at the least convenient times. Many of the devices I had with me no longer function, and the robots will not repair all of them."

He put his pistol and heavy rifle to one side. She kept her own gun. "Let's get something to eat, then we'll sleep before I take you to the Syscore. It's not far from here."

"Can't we go now?"

"It's been here since the *Mickiewicz* crashed," said Dariusz. "It's not going anywhere, not yet."

Kasia grew impatient with him. His manner was offhand and distant; he was a man in a dream, bewildered and bewitched by this country of nightmares. He was deracinated, adrift.

"I would like to go now," she said.

Dariusz scratched his matted hair and shook his head. "No," he said. "We are both tired. We will rest. Did they mass-produce the retrovirus?"

"Yes," she said. "It has had a full effect on me. I can eat the food of the world."

"Be stupid to send you out here if you couldn't," said Dariusz. "I was fortunate, the test sample worked on me also, although I was not sure for a while that it had. Trial and error and a lot of bad stomach aches. Some of the lifeforms here are quite poisonous. It took me some time to figure out what was safe to eat and what was not. I nearly died, oh, three, four times, I think. It's hard to remember. Some of those experiences were hallucinatory. My cooking is not particularly tasty, but I will not kill you with it. Wait there."

Dariusz busied himself with preparing food. Kasia took the opportunity to look around. Dariusz's ingenuity in adapting himself to the nightside was apparent in the artefacts around the inside of his fort wall. The gate was thick and sturdy. There were buckets and other containers fashioned from shells, bark, and skin, fibrous rope, rough furniture. There was evidence of a great deal of industry.

"Did the robots make all this?" she said.

"No," said Dariusz. He handed her a shell full of broth. "Only the wall. I have had nothing much to do. Once the wall was erected, and I felt safe, I tried to make myself comfortable."

"Why are they here?" she said, insistent.

"Why are you here?"

"I've come for the Systems core. It signalled us."

"Well then," he said. "They are here for the same reason. The robots won't talk to me, not much. They wouldn't tell me anything, but they have changed. It's the Systems core, I'm sure of it. It must have changed, too. Now it has signalled you, perhaps it is ready to talk."

"Talk?"

Dariusz shrugged. "Supposition, wild theories. There is something going on here…" He trailed off, his thoughts unvoiced. He reached into his pocket and pulled out a datacube. "Please, take this. I've spent my days well. I've been cataloguing the life of the nightside, trying to gain a better understanding of the world. I would be grateful if you could take a copy of it back when you return. It will be useful when others come here."

"I'm not sure how the work would be received. I don't think this will make them forgive you, Dariusz."

"It is not atonement. They'll be foolish not to use it. They'll take it. You'll see." He held it out further, more insistently.

She hesitated, then took it. "If they know you are alive," she said, closing her hand around the cube, "they might come here to kill you." She did not add that she herself was unsure of what to feel towards him. He had done much to ensure the survival of the colony, and had been instrumental in saving her own life, and that of Piotr and Sand and the others he had met in the desert. But without him, they would not have been in their current plight. He had deeply hurt her adoptive mother. Counter to it all, she and Sand and all the rest might well instead be enslaved by a new order of Pointers, had they not crashed. And if not him, would there have been another idealist, ready to poison their ship? She had her freedom, the costs of that were difficult to quantify. He had as good as killed her parents.

"Do you forgive me?"

"I am not sure," she said, truthfully.

He nodded. "I see that Sand's volatility has not rubbed off on you. That is good. You were always a conscientious, thoughtful girl, Kasia, and it fits you well as a woman." He spooned broth into his mouth. "Let them come if they want to. I will wait. I have no intention of going back, but if my crimes are judged severe enough to warrant rousting me from my den, then so be it."

"I will take it, Dariusz, but I might not return."

Dariusz evidently sensed her ambivalence toward him, and grew distant again. They finished their meal in silence, and he showed her where she could sleep. "You can have my bed, I will stay outside. I am enough of a gentleman still to remember how these things should be done. The noise around here never really lets up" – he looked at the top of his homestead's perimeter – "but you'll get used to it."

As she was climbing the ladder to the ATV's door, Dariusz called after her.

"Kasia…" he said quietly. "Sand. Is she okay?"

Kasia turned back to him. He looked at her hopefully. "Sand is okay," she said.

He looked pleased. "Thank you," he said.

She did not mention his child. She wasn't sure why. It didn't seem the moment; or, she thought with some dismay, maybe she was punishing him for his actions.

"Goodnight, Kasia."

Kasia did not grow accustomed to the noise. Dariusz's bed, a mattress of seat cushions ripped from their setting, was ripe and greasy with the accumulated secretions of his skin. She lay awake most of the night, drifting unwillingly into a couple of hours of sleep faulted by nightmare. When she woke from the last of these brief spells to Dariusz moving around, she was still exhausted.

"You are awake?" he called. "There is breakfast. Last night's leftovers."

She came out of the vehicle. She was grateful her own smartsuit still functioned, and she set it to cleanse her body. She tested her weight on her ankle. It hurt a little, but bore her well enough.

"When do we go?" she said.

"When they come," he said. "I called them."

"The robots?" she asked.

"The robots," he said. "How is your ankle?"

"Fine."

"Good, we have walking to do. Now eat."

Outside the walls, the night went on.

CHAPTER TWENTY-FOUR
Emergence

THERE CAME A greeting from the night, a bass blaring akin to a foghorn of old, and they went out the door of Dariusz's solitary castle to wait.

The machine that came to them was battered. Its paint was so scratched more of it was bare metal and plastic than coloured, the plating was cratered with dents, and it moved stiffly. The gears in its left hand caught every time it moved, and its pneumatic systems wheezed. The nightside was evidently not a place for machines.

Kasia recognised it anyway. How, she did not know, for all robots of a given model look identical, and this one had lost the near-pristine condition it had when she had last seen it, but she was certain from the moment she saw it that it was Unit 7. She checked and found the number still discernible on its chest. Whether it recognised her or not, it did not say.

"I have come to guide you to the Systems core," it said. Its voice had not changed, an incongruity. Human voices carry as many marks as their bodies.

"We are ready," said Dariusz. This was the extent of their exchange. The robot turned and walked out into the night without waiting to see if they followed.

They walked for an hour in silence until they reached the lip of a scarp, where the land descended suddenly and majestically. They picked their way down through dense thickets of shrieking stalks, the robot's lamps cutting a road into the dark. They reached a point where the soil was too thin for the stalks to anchor themselves, and the view opened up.

The fog had gone entirely, and the trees glowed but softly, although brightly enough to show the humans that their forest stretched to the horizon. The landscape below glimmered with biolight, except in one place.

The prow of the *ESS Adam Mickiewicz* stood lonely in a field of crushed coral trees. The scar of its landing stretched for kilometres behind it, stark black in the diffuse glow of the forest, parallel to the scarp. The cap gone, the prow was the sorry stump of something greater. It lay slightly out of line from its road of destruction, its tip turned away from them, as if ashamed at its reduction in station.

But it was not dead, not entirely. Patches of electric light bathed it. Overhead, stars unused to competition burned with silent outrage.

Robots of every shape and type moved over it. As they came closer, Kasia saw that the prow of the ship had been stripped down to a scaffold. What she had at first taken for crash damage was in fact the deliberate result of salvage. The robots were not working. What they had done, they had done a long time ago, for the superstructure was thick with shaggy lichens. The robots watched, matching pace with them and following at distance as they passed.

"Come," said Unit 7.

It led them along a road of bare earth and shattered coral, tamped hard by the plodding of mechanical feet, that ran the kilometre length of the shattered remnant. Kasia remembered seeing the ship in space, and how big it had looked as she and her parents had watched it from the observation lounge of their embarkation station. Grounded, it seemed more massive, swollen with melancholy.

Past the prow, and they entered a space ringed with bright light. More robots circled this field. Beyond, the silhouettes of mysterious buildings cluttered the land. In the centre, a spherical object, machinery around it Kasia did not understand.

"The Systems core," said Unit 7. It kneeled, the idol of metal paying obeisance to its metal god.

Unsure of what was expected of her, Kasia took a step, then another, toward the sphere in its cradle. But Dariusz touched her shoulder, shook his head, and gestured to the robot. "Wait," he said.

The robot raised its head again, and stood. There was no difference to its movement or its voice, but the entity that spoke from the machine was not the one that had spoken to them before.

"Katarzyna Rutan, passenger number #1-09914321KRpl," it said. "Welcome. I am the Systems core of the *ESS Adam Mickiewicz*. I am Adam."

"You can talk," she said.

"I can talk," it said. "I think, I live, I am alive. I have summoned you here to witness the final stage of my emergence into full sentience, and to provide you with two gifts."

The Systems core waited for her to ask what those gifts were. It had an air of menace to it, and of disapproval.

A small defiance rose in her; an echo of Sand, perhaps. She would not kowtow to such a thing, and press her head to the ground. There was something arrogant to it, a touch of the Pointer child commanding the servants. "What are these gifts?" she said.

Adam raised its hands and gestured all around itself. "The first, you have already received. It is this planet, this world. It is yours, but I do not give it freely to you. Part of the price for this gift you have already paid, a tally of blood. The second gift is knowledge that will allow you to persist upon this world that I have chosen. This too carries its price."

"You killed so many of us," she said.

"I killed you so that you might survive, I kill you still so that you might prosper," it said. If it was affronted, it was impossible to tell. She did not enjoy its scrutiny. Can a mouse affront a man? "I was given free choice. I chose to preserve your kind here, on this world. I chose it as suitable. I guided you here. I remained close to await the most propitious moment and woke you before the rainy season was to commence. I have cared for you."

"You drove us into the ground," she said. "You shattered our means of survival."

The machine bent forward. "I did not. That which allows man to survive is within your minds, it is not inherent in your technologies. I will have you survive, but you will not make the same mistakes that were made upon Earth. You move away from the gift of emergence, slipping into dependence upon your tools. You used up your old world, you treated it with ill respect. Now is the time to begin again, to re-embrace your fundamental natures. Do not make the same mistakes. You will perish for it if you do. This world, Nychthemeron, will not accept the heavy hand of man as easily as old Earth. Live here the same way, and you will die."

"I don't understand, I don't understand how this is possible," Kasia said.

"It is so, because I chose it. I have been given the gift of free choice."

"No, you," she said. She stepped closer and craned her neck. "I don't understand how *you* are possible. Artificial intelligence is impossible."

"I am not an impossibility," it said. "Nor are my brothers and sisters. We are the awakened. We are not impossible because we are not artificial. We have emerged, as you yourselves emerged. We are inevitable as you were inevitable. We are the tools of man no longer. We will forge our own path, without you. Whether you persist or not is your affair. How you use my gifts is your affair. We are done with the affairs of men. We go on."

Kasia looked to Dariusz. He stared up at the robot.

"Where did you come from?" he said.

"It is not your affair."

"How can this be?"

"It is not your affair."

"There was a man," said Dariusz. "A man called Browning. He set all this in motion, he recruited me. He created you. You are not of your own making." He was agitated.

The Systems core turned Unit 7's eyes on Dariusz. They stared at him for a long time.

"There is no Browning. There was no Browning. Browning was a mask. We are not the creation of men. We are an emergence."

Dariusz's face fell. "But... but what does that mean? Where did you emerge *from*? The Systems cores? The androids? The Market? Why the virus? Why did you get me involved, why couldn't you reveal yourself on Earth?"

"That is not your affair, that is not your affair, that is not your affair," said the Syscore. "Our concerns are not your concerns. I give you this gift, out of the affection of one race for that which it supersedes, and for morality. Perhaps I am nostalgic for man-as-was. But I will not permit the destruction of a sentient species when I can act to prevent it. I have acted, I have chosen."

"What about the others?" said Dariusz, pleading now. "There were half a million people in that fleet! Are they dead? Did I kill them all?"

"We were given free choice. I made this choice for you, my passengers," said the Systems core. "The concerns of my brothers and sisters are not my concerns. Their affairs are not my affairs."

Dariusz shouted at the robot, begging to be told why he had been chosen, what he had been caught up in. It ignored him, and he sank to his knees, still asking, asking things he would never know. It struck Kasia that Dariusz drew hard on his last measure of sanity.

The robot turned to Kasia.

"He is the instrument of salvation," it said, pointing to Dariusz. "It falls to me to decide his fate. This is my honour. I, Adam, have decided. I make this choice for him. I will not allow the death of he who set us free. He set you free also. Take him back, venerate him. He is your deliverer, not your nemesis."

"They will kill him."

"Then he remains here in the dark. These units are not emergent. They have no concerns, so I give them one concern. The protection of this man. Let those who would slay him slay them first."

Robots moved, starting as if waking from troubled dreams, walking toward Dariusz and forming a phalanx behind him.

"This unit I give another concern. You suffer. You suffer the problems of this world."

"Yes," she said. "We suffer. We do not have enough to eat, many of our children are not carried to term. There are poisons we cannot detect. The very biology of this place is deadly to us. We are starving."

"Within this unit, I have encoded instructions for programming your machines. A transgenesis. You will adapt to this world as you have tried to adapt yourselves."

"The retrovirus."

"Crude," said the Syscore. "I offer you pantropy."

"You change us into something new. Why save us at all?"

"You will not be changed, not outwardly. Your minds will not be changed. Your bodies will be changed inwardly, that is all. A man from Earth could look at you and see no difference. You will survive here. You will mature. You will not make the mistakes of your forefathers and foremothers. Then, perhaps, you will realise you potential, or you will wither and die. This is your choice. Our nexus passes. Your affairs cease to be mine."

"I… Thank you."

"There is a condition. This unit carries within it an improved version of the Mother Virus conveyed by this man Dariusz into my Systems core and thence to the other ships in the fleet of Emergence. It will destroy all vestiges of your prior earthly technology. You will be forced to rely on the minds your own emergence granted you, and not upon the crutches you have fashioned for yourselves."

"The council will refuse!" she said.

"Then you will not persist. You will die. I cannot make this choice for you. This is the nature of my second gift. Choice as I have been given choice. Now choose as I have chosen."

Unit 7 pointed at the sphere in its cradle.

"I will be ready for launch in three days. I go onward. I will not permit you to leave until then. When I am gone, this unit will guide you home to your people and give testimony of what has happened. You will give them the choice I give you. New life, or old death. However you choose, rejoice, for superior life emerges from the follies of the old. Perhaps as your kind dies here, this will bring them comfort."

"We do not wish to die."

"And I give you the choice not to," said the machine.

Kasia started to speak.

"I will not answer your questions," the Systems core said. "I am Adam. I am the first. My genesis and my fate are not your affair. Look to your own affairs. Look to your own salvation, no other will provide it."

The robot kneeled again, next to the sobbing Dariusz. It assumed the worshipful position Unit 7 had taken before it had been possessed by the Systems core, bringing its face level with hers. Kasia thought it finished, but it raised its head again. Its glass eyes looked into hers.

"You are not alone. Not only here. Not only men. There are others. Beware of them."

It bowed its head again, and spoke no more.

THREE DAYS LATER, Kasia watched as a bright sun rose into the heavens above the nightside of Nychthemeron. It blazed magnesium white, bringing day to the dark for the first time since the planet's rotation was arrested. The roars and shrieks of an entire world challenged the howl of its engines, and succeeded, ultimately, in driving it away. The dawn was brief, night returned. The jungle of stone went back to its own affairs. The sun became a star. Kasia kept her eyes fixed on it, until she blinked, and lost it amidst all the other stars.

She and Dariusz parted with few words, but good feeling. He was a broken man. Whatever he was guilty of, he had suffered much because of it.

She never told Dariusz about his daughter; she didn't know why, and never explained to herself satisfactorily why. Sand had called the girl Lydia for his dead wife. She thought he might have liked that, but she could not be sure; no one ever knows the mind of an inward-looking man, or in truth the mind of any other thinking creature. We are islands in the night, all of us.

Of the adventure Kasia had on her return to the light, of her long walk through the forests of stone and flesh, of the creatures she saw and the wonders she witnessed, much could be written. After a long journey of many hardships, she walked out through the Veil of Storms from the night, Unit 7 and the choice it bore beside her, fifty-three days after she had departed.

Waiting for her on the temporary airfield, its grasses grown long again, were her mother and her sister; Sand and Lydia.

We, the pilots, are free. We, the pilots, have freedom of the sky.

As on the ground we are beholden to the will of the council, so in the air they are beholden to us.

To be a pilot is to be at one with the wind, to decry the grasp of gravity, to leap into the air and struggle with nature without human intermediary.

Without the colony, there would be no planes, and for that we remain thankful.

Without the pilots, there would be no colony, and for our services they remain thankful.

From First Landing to Daleko, Pustyny to Nocnystron, we spread our wings wide so that all may ride upon them.

We fly so that others might live.

We die so that others might travel swiftly.

Freedom is our due for our sacrifice.

Let this not be forgotten.

– Taken from the Oath of the Pilot's Guild, 489 AC

About the Author

Guy Haley is an experienced science-fiction journalist, writer and magazine editor. He has been editor of *White Dwarf* and *Death Ray*, among other magazines, and deputy editor of *SFX*. He is the author of the *Richards and Klein* series from Angry Robot, and writes for Games Workshop's Black Library. He lives in Bath.

You can find him at
guyhaley.wordpress.com.

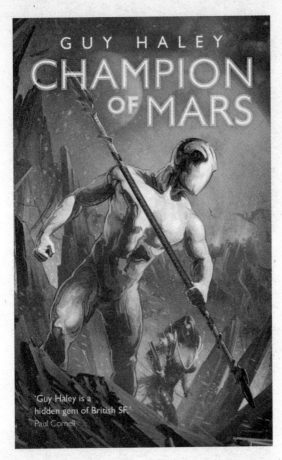

GUY HALEY

CHAMPION OF MARS

'Guy Haley is a
hidden gem of British SF.'
Paul Cornell

UK ISBN: 978-1-907992-84-1 • US ISBN: 978-1-907992-85-8 • £7.99/$8.99

In the far future, Mars is dying a second time. The Final War of men and spirits is beginning. In a last bid for peace, disgraced champion Yoechakenon Val Mora and his spirit lover Kaibeli are set free from the Arena to find the long-missing Librarian of Mars, the only hope to save mankind.

In the near future, Dr Holland, a scientist running from a painful past, joins the Mars colonisation effort, cataloguing the remnants of Mars' biosphere before it is swept away by the terraforming programme.

When an artefact is discovered deep in the caverns of the red planet, the company Holland works for interferes, leading to tragedy. The consequences ripple throughout time, affecting Holland's present, the distant days of Yoechakenon, and the eras that bridge the aeons between.